On The Dotted Line

Katie Stearns

Also By Katie Stearns

Trigger Warning

Contains strong language, depictions of domestic abuse and attempted sexual assault.

Chapter One

Dani

O h, this is bad. So, so bad.

This is exactly what it looks like when shit hits the fan. And I would know. I've had so much shit hit the fan in my life.

Really? *Really*, Universe? It's not enough that I lost my job two weeks ago and am already behind on my debt? No, let's just throw a fire in there, too. Cause at this point, why not?

This is no fire drill, ladies and gentlemen. We're not talking about a bit of smoke in the apartment building hallways or some singed carpeting. Oh no, this thing is a goddamn neighborhood bonfire. Except the thing that's burning is the neighborhood itself. Okay, not the *whole* neighborhood. But a big part of it.

My tiny apartment wasn't anything special, but it was my home. And I say *was* because I know by morning, there won't be anything left of it. Just ashes and soot and cinders. Ha, I should start calling myself Cinderella.

I shake that thought away.

Not appropriate, Dani.

But I can't help it if I'm one of those awkward people who laugh in serious situations. What else can I really do, anyway? Cry?

Well, yes. I could cry. No one would blame me for breaking down in hysterical sobs right now because this is just one more unappetizing topping on the shitty pizza that has been my life lately.

A dash of Wildly In Debt seasoning.

Ooh, how about a sprinkling of Unemployment Cheese?

And then the Chef of the Universe says, "Oh, I got it. This Dani Pizza would be just perfect with a handful of...FIRE." And then he cackles like one of those evil villains from cartoons and strikes the match.

Just the right amount of Apartment On Fire.

chef's kiss

A screaming siren has my head jerking toward the welcome sight of a fire truck. Its glaring headlights slice through the darkness of the night, and its strobing light bar mingles with the light of the fire on the pavement. I scramble back out of the way as firefighters hop out and begin hooking up a hose to the fire hydrant on the corner.

Silly firefighters.

It's way too late. The whole damn thing is on fire.

Even at midnight, my street is aglow with so much angry, dancing light that it might as well be daytime in front of me. Flames have engulfed the entire six-unit apartment building and are steadily turning every last wall and floorboard to smoldering ash. The windows have exploded with glass confetti shards. The cement steps are stained black from the smoke billowing out the front entrance. The roof is sagging and coughing smoke as the rafters disintegrate beneath it, the air thick and hot as the fire rages.

So yeah, there's no getting my apartment back. Not that it was anything special. It was kind of gross, actually. Peeling linoleum tile in my dishwasher-less kitchenette. Cracked walls due to a crumbling foundation. Smelly carpeting that I could never quite get clean, no matter how many times I vacuumed. A family of immortal cockroaches skittering around in the bathroom every time I entered. I'm sure the building wasn't up to code because the electricity was here and there. I won't miss any of those aspects of living in that puny studio apartment. But the whole having a roof over my head thing?

Yeah. Definitely going to miss that.

At least I managed to grab a few important things before I heeded the blaring fire alarm and dashed out to safety. My phone, wallet, a framed picture of my parents on their wedding day, and a small packet of important documents like my birth certificate. That packet also held the only thing I have left of my parents. Their wedding rings. At least I still have those.

The firefighters begin soaking the flaming building with water, but I feel like telling them to just save the water. There's no getting back the roof over my head. At this point, just let her burn.

A sullen police officer crosses in front of me to speak to my landlady, Sandy Johnson. I shiver. She's always given me the heeby-jeebies—something about her cold stare and demeanor that never waver, even when I'm nothing but delightful to her. Her face is set as she speaks with the police officer, her brown hair as disheveled as her worn, plaid pajama set. Why she's wearing winter pajamas in July is beyond me. I know this is Minnesota, but come on. She probably has the only apartment with air conditioning. Or she did, that is.

I glance behind her, at my neighbors, who all stand with gaunt and aggrieved expressions. No one is panicking or crying for a loved one stuck in the building, so I'm assuming everyone got out. The EMTs already checked everyone over for injuries and smoke inhalation. I wish I knew my neighbors, but I don't know a single one of their names.

In a neighborhood like this, you keep to yourself. It's better and safer to keep your head down and just live your own life. Because you never know who could be dangerous. I know that sounds harsh, but I literally don't go anywhere without mace, and I have—or had—three deadbolts on my door. I don't even flinch at the gunshots anymore. And I find myself critiquing the graffiti instead of criticizing it. The vandals around here like the color red way too much. I mean, mix it up, dudes. Where's the variety for the city walkers like me?

Oh, and there it goes...

The singed roof collapses with a *craaack*, and a heavy waft of smoke startles the small crowd of onlookers. The firefighters wave us off further, so I retreat to the sidewalk across the street with everyone else.

Well, damn. That's it. There goes the only home I've known since my parents died four years ago. It wasn't much, obviously. But it was mine. And now, it's burnt to a crisp, just like my heart.

The police officer approaches us then. "Folks, do you all have somewhere to go tonight?"

Oh. Right. Can't really stand out here all night watching a part of my life burn down. I dig my phone out of my purse and dial my best friend's number.

I won't lie; the idea of staying with Mel and her boyfriend, Max, doesn't thrill me. Not that I don't like Max, because I do. He's a good guy. But the dude likes to walk around naked almost all the time. I went over to hang out once, and he freaking opened the door with everything hanging out. His sausage and eggs, just, BAM right there. The man has no shame. Didn't even try to cover himself.

So yeah, I can't say the thought of living with Max's balls and penis in my face all the time sounds even remotely great. But I don't really have any other choices at twelve-thirty on a Monday night when my apartment is burning down. And hopefully, someone will hire me soon, and I won't have to stay with them long.

Mel picks up sounding groggy and confused.

"Edwin James, this is Melanie. How can—" She breaks off abruptly. "Fuck me, what the hell time is it?"

I chuckle softly. Mel works as a receptionist for one of those insurance companies. I don't know how she sits at a desk all day like that. I much prefer being on my feet. Or I did before I got laid off because Ben's little chain of restaurants went bankrupt.

"Mel, hey, it's me," I choke out, my voice a little raspy from the smoke.

"Dani? What's wrong?"

"Oh, no big deal. Just my apartment is on fire," I answer, and give an awkward laugh.

I watch the last remaining exterior wall of my apartment crash down with an angry hiss. The firefighters have contained the fire now and have managed to keep it from spreading to the neighboring building.

"What?!" shouts Mel, instantly alert. "Holy shit! Are you okay?"

"Yeah, I'm okay," I assure her. "But my apartment is *toast*."

"Really? You're fucking making jokes right now?" Mel sighs on the other end. "I'll be right there."

She hangs up without another word, and I feel a bit of relief that I'll be somewhere safe tonight. In the grand scheme of things, I feel lucky. I look over at my neighbors, most of them on their phones. I hope they'll be safe, too.

When Mel pulls up five minutes later, she bolts out of her beat-up Camry, still wearing her pajama shorts and tank top, and hugs me tightly. I hug her back just as tightly, feeling the first sign of tears sting in my tear ducts. When Mel pulls back, her green eyes are wide as she takes in what little is left of my apartment. By now, it's just a pile of charred rubble, with only a couple of recognizable pieces that hint at what this smoking structure used to be.

Seeing my best friend's stunned face makes my stomach twist. It really is bad, isn't it?

Orphaned, single, unemployed, indebted, and homeless.

You win, Chef Universe. You win.

I smell like Smoky the Bear.

I didn't notice it until I got into Mel's car. I glance at myself in the side mirror. I kind of look like Smoky the Bear. My long brown hair is piled on my head in a messy knot, and there's a light sheen of sweat mixed with smoke covering my face. I'm going to need a shower.

I'm a little too dazed to apologize for the burden I'm about to be on Mel. I know she would tell me to shut it anyway. But when we pull up to Mel and Max's apartment a couple of miles away, I already feel guilty for intruding.

They have a small one-bedroom apartment. They don't have room for me. Yeah, I can couch it with them until I figure something out, but I know living space will be tight, and I can't stay there longer than three days, per their lease agreement.

We found that out the hard way two years ago when things with Spencer turned into a nightmare, and I stayed with Mel and Max until I felt safe going back to my place. That was the plan anyway, but then

Mel's landlord found out and threatened that if he caught anyone else "squatting" in their apartment, he'd have both of them evicted.

At least this time, I won't have any luggage crowding the living room. There's one upside, right? Right? I chuckle to myself.

"What the hell are you laughing at?" Mel snaps incredulously.

"Nothing," I say, and get out of the car. I follow Mel inside the small entryway and up to the second floor, each step draining the energy out of my body like a magnet in this stifling stairwell.

Her building isn't much nicer than mine was. It's a three-story building with eighteen units and a nasty pool around the back that no one dares to use. We emerge from the sweaty stairwell to the second floor, which is covered in well-worn blue carpet. A canopy of warped and stained ceiling tile stretches above us to the end of the hall. Six doors, three on each side of the cramped hallway, greet my tired eyes.

"You can borrow whatever you need, okay?" Mel says as she leads me down to apartment 2B, the second door on the right.

Mel's sentence slaps me in the face. Because it hits me then.

I *have nothing.*

I didn't have much to begin with because I've been living as cheaply as possible to pay down my debt, but now I literally only have the smoky t-shirt and gym shorts I'm wearing and the contents of my purse.

Nothing of my own. My favorite purple sweatshirt is gone. The handful of resumes I had Mel print for me at work are incinerated. My cute little Craigslist coffeemaker sure ain't making coffee now. I don't even have a *toothbrush.*

Mel opens the door, but I can't move.

It was shock enough to lose my waitressing job out of the blue like that and struggle for weeks to find anything else. I've been feeling low-grade panicked every day that goes by without a call back from any of the restaurants I've applied for. And let me tell you, I've applied everywhere I can think of. My former coworkers are apparently snapping them up before I can even get my resume through the door.

Without any income, I'm behind on the debt I was saddled with when my parents died. And believe me, it's a shit ton of debt. Turns out, dying is super expensive. Especially if you don't have the right stupid papers signed. And not only did I lose my parents at the same time in the same car accident, I also was left to pay for a double funeral and all their medical bills while I recuperated from the accident myself.

And now, I don't have a place to live and can't afford to rent a new place, however run down and cheap, until I get another paycheck in my sad bank account. If I don't find a place to stay in three days, I'll be out on my ass.

How am I going to move forward? How am I going to get myself out of this?

"Dani?" she asks gently, coming closer.

I look up at my best friend, all five foot two of her, and feel my initial shock wear off. She sweeps her strawberry blonde hair out of her face and catches me in a hug as I let out my tears.

"It's okay, Dani. We'll figure this out, I promise," she says, stroking my back. "It's going to be okay."

"Mel, we b-both know your lease has stipulations about guests st-staying too long," I sob into her shoulder. "I'll be out in th-the street in three d-days."

"Fuck stipulations, okay?" She pulls back and holds me firmly by the arms. "We'll figure something out," she repeats, holding my tearful gaze. "You can live in my closet or something."

I give her a nod and a watery smile, appreciating the sentiment.

Mel has always been there for me. We've been friends since junior high. When her boyfriend dumped her the week before prom, I went as her date instead. When Spencer did the unthinkable, she was there to put me back together. My parents loved her spunk and no-nonsense attitude. After they died, she and I became even closer. We might as well be sisters at this point.

Mel squeezes my arms supportively and then ushers me into her little apartment.

It really is little. I'm not here very often because I generally prefer to not see Max's junk, so it's even smaller than I remembered. A little corner kitchen that's been painted white to make it feel bigger. There's no space for a dining room table, just the opposite corner where their shabby green couch is. There's a small desk next to it with a dated flat-screen monitor. Max plays one of those first-person shooter games on it. Through a doorway next to the fridge is their bedroom and adjoining bathroom. I can hear Max snoring from here.

Mel tells me to use whatever I want in the shower and grabs me a clean towel and some clothes for me to change into.

"Tomorrow, we can run to the store and get you your own shit, but for now, what's mine is yours, okay?" Mel says quietly, handing me the short stack of folded fabric. "I'll make up the couch while you're in the shower."

I smile at her with gratitude. "Thanks, Mel." It feels so good to have someone like her in my corner. Someone I can call when my life is burning down.

I waste no time hopping into Mel's shower and thoroughly scrubbing the smoke out of my hair and off my skin. Soon, the Smoky the Bear smell is replaced with cooling cucumber melon, and it's deeply appreciated. I dry off with the towel Mel gave me, and as I change into her spare sweatpants, I catch a glimpse of myself in the mirror over the steadily dripping sink.

My long brown hair is plastered to the front of my petite body, making me look like a mermaid or Eve from the Garden of Eden. I smile slightly at that phantasmic thought, but it quickly fades.

Being that I've been working like crazy up until two weeks ago, it's not unusual for me to look burnt out. I sort of have that perma-tired look going on, even being out of work lately. I can usually cover up my tired eyes with my spunky personality, at least before now.

Because I've never seen myself like this.

My hazel eyes look haunted beneath my full eyelashes and droopy lids. Dark shadows are pooled beneath them. Worry makes my usually full lips seem much thinner. Much sadder.

I look...defeated.

I glance over my slight frame and well-rounded lower half, so thankful that me and my creamy white skin made it out of that burning building completely unscathed.

I rub the towel through my long hair and then pull a thin, long-sleeved shirt over my damp head. Even though Mel is a good deal shorter than me, we still are close to the same size. I'm definitely glad about that right about now; otherwise, I'd be wearing one of Max's shirts. Because he *does* in fact own shirts despite his apparent need to live like a nudist.

I tip-toe out of the bathroom and skirt their bed on the way to the living room, both Mel and Max breathing slowly and deeply in their darkened bedroom.

I find the couch covered with a white sheet and a light blanket. Even if it isn't my own bed, it still beckons to me invitingly. I plop down and settle in, tucking a well-loved throw pillow under my left cheek.

But even though it's well after one in the morning and I'm exhausted, I can't get my mind to shut off. I can't get my shoulders to relax or my stomach to stop squirming.

I hate this feeling.

This...*homeless* feeling.

And I don't just mean physically. I haven't had a good sense of where I belong since my parents died. I thought I could feel some semblance of home with Spencer, but holy hell did that relationship derail me. It's taken me years to dig myself out of how weak he made me feel, but I still feel lost. Even in my crappy apartment, I didn't feel content or secure, and not just because of the gunshots. I don't know exactly what I'm looking for or if I'll ever find it, but all I know is I feel...*homesick*.

Max's loud snore shakes the wall, and I shift on the couch a little, trying to get comfortable.

Despite what Mel said earlier, I know I'm in deep trouble here. Even if I live in her closet and hide out from her landlord, I know that if I'm found out, they'll be evicted. I can't in good conscience let that happen to my best friend and her man.

I can't drag them down with me.

So, I need a plan. I need *help*.

I decide that I need to send out my Hail Mary. I need to call Lance. If there's anyone who can help me, it's him. He was a good friend of my parents, someone they trusted. When they died, he promised that he'd look out for me. He's basically my fairy Godfather. He won't let me starve in the streets. He'll find a way to help me; I know it. Even if it's just me sleeping on his couch instead of Mel's until I can find a job.

With that, I finally sink into sleep.

Chapter Two

Dani

The morning comes quickly, and I'm so tired I could cry. Well, I could cry for a lot of reasons, but crying isn't going to help me figure this out. Allowing myself to be swallowed up by grief and depression will only further my downward spiral. I need to keep it together.

Mel is making coffee in her little kitchen as I sit up and stretch my sore back. I forgot how lumpy her couch is. But it sure is better than the street or a park bench, right?

"Hey," she says to me over her shoulder as I stand up and come over to her. "Get any sleep?"

I shrug and fold my arms over my chest. Mel is wearing a long, emerald sleep shirt with "kiss this" scrolled in white script over her butt. I glance at my own backside, wondering if the grey sweatpants I'm wearing have anything written on the butt. I don't need anything drawing attention to my wide hips and full booty. They speak for themselves.

"I'll stop back here on my lunch break, and we can go get you the basic stuff you need, okay?"

I nod as my stomach sinks, mentally picturing the miniscule amount of money in my checking account. Hopefully, Walmart has some amazing clearance sale going on right now. "A sale so hot it'll burn your apartment down." Oh man, that's good. They should totally hire me to be their marketing person.

"I'm going to call Lance today," I tell her quietly, my eyes on the dated linoleum flooring beneath my feet. "Maybe he knows someone who's hiring or whatever."

"Who's Lance again?" she asks, squinting at me over her shoulder as the coffee maker percolates in front of her. The tempting scent of liquid life pervades the kitchen.

"He's my fairy Godfather," I answer with a small smile. "He was a friend of my parents. I've known him since I was a kid. We used to have lunch like once a month but he's been pretty busy the last couple months."

"He's the lawyer, right?" Mel pours us both coffee and hands me a mug that says "World's Best Boss" on it, from *The Office*. I take a much needed sip.

I nod. "One of the best in Minneapolis." He went to high school with my dad back in the day, and even though Lance went on to law school, he stayed in touch. He never forgot my dad, even when he moved up in the world. I know I can trust him to help me.

"Maybe he can loan you some money," Mel suggests, looking at me optimistically over the rim of her coffee mug. Hers says, "Bears. Beets. Battlestar Galactica."

"What? I don't want his money."

"I said *loan*, Dani. You'll pay him back."

I give her an unconvinced look. Aren't I already in enough debt? Lance would absolutely loan me money; I know he would. But I also know that he wouldn't let me pay it back. He wouldn't *need* me to pay it back. He's a single man in his fifties who doesn't like to throw money around if he doesn't have to. He's loaded, I'm sure of it.

Max appears to my right with a giant yawn. I quickly cut my eyes away from him and his well displayed wedding tackle. He steps over to Mel and gives her a quick kiss.

Something about it twists my stomach with longing. I don't even know what it's like to be loved by a good man. After Spencer, I haven't dared risk being hurt by anyone else. And I've been a wee bit busy. Working like crazy to keep myself out of poverty, you know.

"Morning, baby," he says warmly and then, almost like his tired morning brain just registered that someone else is standing there, he whips his shaggy brown-haired head toward me. "Dani, what's up?" he asks, surprised to see me here so early in the morning. He shows no shame whatsoever that he's standing there naked as the day he was born. He never does. If I didn't know him, I'd find it creepy or even rude. But I've known Max since they started dating, and he's only ever treated Mel with respect and love.

"Nothing good, Maxi-million," I answer and slurp a sip of my coffee, my eyes still averted.

Max glances at Mel and then back at me. Even in my periphery, I can see how confused and concerned he is. "It's not Spencer again, is it?"

My heart pounds at just the mention of his name. Thank God, he's never reappeared in my life. I don't know what I would do if he did. Probably pass out from fear. I subconsciously rub at the front of my neck, which suddenly feels tight.

"Fuck no," Mel answers for me, and swats his bare arm with her blonde eyebrows knit together. "Her apartment burned down last night."

"Shit, Dani," he says in shock, looking back to me with wide blue eyes. "I'm sorry. You can stay as long as—"

"No, I can't," I interrupt softly. "Not if you guys don't want to get evicted. I can't risk that...so I'll be here for a few days while I figure out where to go next."

They both look at me, and I can feel their concern. I can feel the gravity of my dire situation like a physical presence in the room. It's heavy. Like weights being pressed on my shoulders and squeezing my temples.

Homeless.

Lance is my only shot now.

I pace in a tight circle around Mel's teeny kitchen, my eyes on the worn, gray pattern of the linoleum with my phone pressed to my ear. The crooked white cabinets blur as I walk, my impatience and desperation colliding. Now that I'm calling Lance and waiting for him to pick up, I feel my anxiety rise in a wave through my body. My hands start to shake, and my breath grows shallow as the phone continues to ring.

No pressure. Just my fate in this man's hands. Not a big deal at all.

"Pick up, pick up, pick up," I mutter to myself as I pace, getting slightly dizzy. I feel the panic set in as my call goes to voicemail.

"You've reached Lance Bertram. Sorry I missed your call. Please leave your name and number, and I'll get back to you as soon as I can. Have a great day," says Lance's voicemail, and I curse under my breath. I wait for the beep nervously and take a deep breath when I hear it.

"Lance, hey, it's Dani," I begin, trying to hide the tremble in my voice. "I know we haven't talked in a while, but uh, I'm kind of in a pickle, and I don't know what to do, so I was hoping you had a minute to talk. Nothing serious. I'm fine. Everything's fine. Totally fine." I pause as my chest feels like it's going to explode. "No, it's not. I lied." The last of my composure evaporates, and I give in to the panic. "I'm not fine. I'm screwed, Lance. Royally screwed. Like put a damn crown on this problem and take a bow of respect. You know that kind of problem, right? Maybe? Sorry, I'm panicking here, so just please call me back."

I hang up, feeling feverish and shaky all over. I stop pacing and lean my hands on the counter to brace myself as I take deep breaths in through my nose and out through my mouth.

In and out.

In and out.

In and—

My phone vibrates and sings the song of its people, making my heart lurch. I glance down at my phone to see Lance's name on the screen. The desperation and panic ramp up again.

"Oh, thank God," I whisper, and accept the call. "Lance!" I exclaim hoarsely.

"Dani, I—"

"Did you get my message? My message about being royally screwed?"

"With a crown, yes, I got it," he replies with a pinch of humor. His smooth, familiar voice is so welcome right now. "What happened?"

"Oh, you know, just my life flipped upside down. No big deal," I say and laugh nervously. "No big deal at all that I'm about to become homeless, peddling the streets for spare change. I should learn an instrument. People will definitely give me more of their spare change if I play an instrument, right?"

Images of me perched on the corner of Emerson and Lowry begging for food and spare change flit through my mind. I add a trombone to the mix and shiver slightly. As I said, Hawthorne is not the safest part of Minneapolis by a long shot. Who knows what would happen to me? The homeless are treated with contempt here, especially by the police.

"Dani girl, tell me what happened."

"Sorry. Right. You're right." I clear my throat, bringing my mind back to the present. "Ben closed his restaurants. All of them. He's bankrupt— can you believe that? Bankrupt! So I've been out of a job for two weeks and behind on my debt, and then last night—" I suck in a deep breath, trying not to break down crying. "Last night, my apartment building burned down."

Lance curses under his breath. "Are you okay? Are you hurt?"

"No, no, I got out in time. I'm staying with Mel, but I can only be here for three days because of her lease agreement," I explain, tears welling in my eyes. "I don't have anywhere to go, Lance, and I need a job and—and I just really need a hand up." I sniff and put my forehead down on the cool, laminate countertop. "I just can't seem to catch a break."

Damn you, Chef Universe.

"I'm sorry, Dani. I really am."

I nod even though he can't see me. "Could I stay with you until I get back on my feet? I hate to ask...but I—"

"Dani, of course," he replies gently. "I have a guest room you can—" Lance stops abruptly, and after a moment of silence, I pull my phone away from my ear to look at the screen to make sure the call didn't drop.

Wouldn't surprise me. My phone isn't what I would call reliable. It's long past due for an upgrade. The only thing it does is text and make calls; I can't even use the internet on it. And I wouldn't anyway because it costs extra for that plan.

"Lance? Are you there?"

"I'm here," he says distractedly. "I was just..." he trails off thoughtfully. I imagine him sitting at an impressive oak desk in his office, juggling his job while also trying to keep me afloat. Maybe I should've waited until after office hours to call him.

"I'm sorry if this is a bad time..."

"Can you meet me for lunch today? I had a client cancel at the last minute, so my schedule is open from noon to one."

"Uh, yeah. Yeah, that'd be great," I answer gratefully. If there's anybody that can talk me down and figure this out, it's Lance.

"Good. Pick a place and text me the address, okay?"

"Sure. Thank you, Lance."

"Absolutely. Try not to panic. It's going to be okay."

"Pssh, me? Panicking? No. No, I'm totally good. Great, even!" I laugh like a maniac and then sigh. "Sorry. I'm a wreck. I'm crazy when I'm a wreck, you know that."

Lance chuckles under his breath. "I'll see you this afternoon, okay?"

"Okay. Yup. Sorry for the meltdown. See you this afternoon."

I hang up and weakly slide down the lower cabinets to the floor.

What would I do without Lance? He's saved me from the streets. I feel a wave of relief wash over me.

I have a place to go.

Lance won't let my situation get any worse. With any luck, I'll be back on my feet in no time.

It's just as swelteringly hot in here as it is outside.

I wait nervously at the little cafe around the corner from Mel's apartment for Lance to show up. It's really nothing more than an old office that was converted into a restaurant. Second Street Cafe is small, packed, and serves the most delicious smoothies I've ever had. Not that

I frequent this place often. I hardly ever eat out because even the cheap options aren't as cheap as just cooking at home. I only ordered black coffee because it was the cheapest option, which I'm regretting now because the extra caffeine is already making me feel even more zippy and anxious than I already am.

A smattering of little tables dot the space, headed off by the serving counter with plastic cases full of breakfast sandwiches and baked goods. Behind that, a handful of employees are running around like chickens with their heads cut off, swamped by the lunch rush. I feel a bit of sympathy for them, but I'm also utterly envious. Especially because I slightly harassed the barista about applying when I got here. I told her I'd scrub toilets, anything, but apparently, every position is full.

There isn't much room for style, but everything looks as clean and as orderly as it can be with so many people packed in here. I'm lucky I got the last table and thankful that I came early.

I just couldn't sit still any longer at Mel's. I texted her that I was going to have lunch with Lance, so she told me I could borrow whatever I needed to from her closet. She and I will go to Walmart after she gets off work tonight instead.

So I'm wearing a plain black t-shirt and a pair of jeans that I managed to squeeze into. I'm about four inches taller than Mel, so I had to roll up the too short pant legs into capris. Honestly, I've looked worse.

I sip my coffee and dart my eyes around the noisy place. Between the blender whirring here and there and every diner talking, it's a dull roar of noise. Honestly, I don't mind it. I think it would be much harder to talk about my pitiful life if it was quiet enough that other people could hear me. I guess I could've just suggested I meet him at his office, but it's too late now.

"There she is," Lance says from behind me, and I startle, even over the din of the blender.

I quickly get to my feet and launch myself at him. The Windsor knot of his royal blue tie indents my cheek as I squeeze his big body. He smells like peppermint chewing gum, and I breathe deeply like a creeper, letting that bit of familiarity comfort me. Lance pats my head, chuckling softly.

"I always forget how much of a hugger you are," he says quietly and releases me from his polite, though genuine, hug.

When I pull back, I swipe at my wet eyes and look up at him. Hugging him is almost as good as hugging my dad. God, I miss my dad. He was the best hugger. I know for a fact that I get my hugging skills from him. My philosophy is that if you're going to hug somebody, you commit to it and hug them like you might never get another chance. In the case of my parents, I unknowingly hugged them for the last time the day they died. I'm so glad they were good, tight, squeezing hugs.

"Thanks for coming."

"Of course." Lance gestures for me to sit down, and I do. He crams himself into the chair across from me, unable to sit back as far as he'd like with his long legs because of the close proximity of the people sitting at the table directly behind him.

I haven't seen Lance in a couple months, but I feel like even in that amount of time, he's aged a little, like he's been working overtime. His dark hair is thinning and graying around his temples, but his blue eyes still have that spark in them. He's tall and fit for a man close to sixty, but I know he runs three miles every morning before work. He's the kind of man who will likely work well into his retirement years. If he isn't working himself to the bone, he's bored stupid. I told him once that he just needs a girlfriend, but he only laughed at me and changed the subject.

"So," he says calmly, loudly enough for me to hear him over everything else going on around us, and folds his large hands on the table in front of me. His silver watch hits the tabletop with a gentle metallic *clunk* that I barely notice over the chortle of the woman behind me. "First things first, you can move in with me as soon as you need to. Everything will be set up for you, so whenever you need to be out of your friend's place, you're all set."

I sniff, my tears returning with a tingling sting. "Thank you," I whisper throatily.

"Second, you need a job."

"Yes." I take a deep breath, trying to keep the panic out of my voice as I continue but failing horribly. "I already harassed the barista about applying here, and she said there's no openings. Wouldn't even let me fill out an application! I'm doomed!" I exhale dramatically and fling my head and arms on the sticky table. Lance casually picks a tendril of my long, light brown hair out of my coffee.

"You're not doomed," he argues calmly. "But Ben Lafferty did have a handful of restaurants in Minneapolis. Now that he's closed everything down, I'm sure there's a surplus of people looking for the same work you are. So, have you considered doing something else besides waitressing?"

I lift my head to look at him but remain hunched over on the table. "I don't know how to do anything else."

His clean shaven face frowns slightly at me, his mouth dipping at the corners, as if chastising me for being hard on myself.

"Waitressing brings in a lot of money. I literally have been living on tips for the last four years."

Lance sighs and looks at me for a long moment, studying me with something akin to hesitation.

"What?"

"I've been thinking about what you said this morning. You said you need a hand up."

I nod solemnly, my eyes big. He smiles very slightly at me, like he's remembering the curious child I used to be and seeing it in me now.

"Do you have a job for me?" I ask hopefully. "Obviously, I prefer waitressing but I could clean houses maybe, or hell, I could be your personal assistant or personal shopper or—"

"No," he interrupts, because he knows I'll just keep listing things. My stomach drops in dread and disappointment. "Listen, Dani," Lance says, leaning forward with his elbows on the table. His crisp, navy suit coat moves with his broad shoulders like a well-fitted glove. "I know we could find you *something*. I could take you to a temp service or get you a job flipping burgers, but we *both* know that whatever you find isn't going to get you caught up on what you owe. Even a full time, well paying job wouldn't get you caught up."

My lip trembles at that piercing truth. I don't have any kind of qualifications or college education to get a respectable job like Lance.

Even before my parents died, I knew college would be too expensive, and I didn't have a clue what to study anyway. But Lance is right. Even if I *did*, there's no way I can ever hope to pay almost a quarter of a million dollars in debt.

"I've watched you work yourself to the bone these last four years trying to keep your head above water. But I..." He pauses and looks down at his hands. After a beat, he clears his throat and looks up at me with red, emotional eyes. "I don't want you to have to do that anymore."

My eyebrows puzzle in confusion. "Wait," I say quietly. Mel's words come back to me about him loaning me money. "I don't want your money, Lance, if that's what you're getting at."

One side of his mouth curves up. "Not *my* money."

I get the wild thought that he's suggesting some high profile bank heist where he and I are crawling through the duct system in all black clothing, planting detonating devices behind us as we haul out the loot we stole from the underground vault.

But no. Lance doesn't do things like that. He prosecutes people who do things like that.

"Uh...what? You're losing me here, Lancey."

He struggles for another moment and then sighs heavily like he's about to tell me something secret.

"I have a way to help you, but it's a little...unorthodox."

"Unorthodox? Pssh. I don't care. Unorthodox is my middle name." It really is. I mean, not *literally*. My middle name is Marie. But, I'm not afraid of unorthodox.

"I'm serious, Dani," he says, holding my gaze. I squint at him slightly, my mind going to extreme things I know he would never suggest because I can't think of anything rational.

"I'm not selling drugs."

Lance's head falls forward as he chuckles softly through his nose. "It's not selling drugs."

"Stripping? Cause I'm so not—"

"No."

"Then what?"

I hold his gaze curiously. I'm not used to seeing him anxious like this. He's usually very confident and even keel. Whatever he's about to tell me is going to be life changing...I can feel it.

He licks his lips, his eyes dipping to the wooden veneer tabletop. "You've been through the ringer, Dani, and if there's anyone who deserves a fresh start, it's you."

He's right, I have. Maybe Lance has a way to off Chef Universe. I imagine some powerful, evil chef slowly drowning in a huge vat of marinara sauce.

Oh boy, what's wrong with me?

But, come on, that jerk would deserve it.

"So, I think I have a way to help you." He pauses, his eyes returning to mine. "I have a client, a young man about your age, who—" Lance hesitates again, making me even more nervous. He clears his throat. "He's looking to get married."

My head juts back in surprise. "Married? What? You want me to get married? Like white gown and black tux married? *Married* married?"

"Yes."

That's by far the last thing I thought he was going to say. Drowning Chef Universe in marinara sauce would've caught me off guard less than freaking *marrying a stranger.*

I laugh heartily, squinting at him again. "You're kidding. I need a job, and you're trying to set me up on a blind date? Not even a blind date— a blind *marriage?*"

He sighs and rubs the back of his neck. "It wouldn't be a real marriage."

My mouth drops open. "Wait, what?" I can't be hearing him right. That or the blender and background noise must be messing with more than just my hearing.

"I mean, it would be a *legal* marriage. But, he only needs the marriage license in order to gain access to a trust fund set up for him by his father."

I laugh again, holding my stomach. I can't help it. It's just too crazy. I manage to stifle my laugh though when he narrows his eyes at me, his dark brows furrowing. I know that look. He's getting mad. I pipe down and listen closely as he continues, even though I can't believe a word of what he's saying.

"So, you agree to marry him. Not *really* marry him—just sign the marriage license so he can get a marriage certificate, and then my client can transfer those funds to his own accounts."

"But...how does that help my situation?"

"He would split the money with you."

I stare at him in disbelief. The lady behind me chortles again like she's in on this joke. Because this *must* be a joke, right?

"Just for signing something?"

"Well, there are some other stipulations, but yes."

I blink. This seems unbelievably crazy. I've never heard Lance say something so utterly crazy in all the time I've known him, which is basically from my early childhood. Despite this, I can't help but wonder...

"How much money is in the trust fund?"

He smiles gently at me, friendly little crinkles forming at the outside edges of his eyes. "Believe me, even with him splitting it with you, you would have way more than you would ever need, even after paying off everything you owe."

My eyebrows shoot up. More than I would ever need? That's...that's just an obscene amount of money.

"Are you serious? I could pay off everything?"

He nods, seeing the wonder in my eyes. "I could introduce you. In a weird way, I think you might hit it off with him."

I snort.

Hit it off with him—good one, Lance. I haven't had much luck in the men department. I definitely don't contain the smooth gene. You know? Attractive men make me break out into a sweat. Have you ever tried to flirt with someone while sweating profusely? Yeah. Doesn't work. So the idea of "hitting it off" with this money-hungry stranger is laughable at best.

"He must be a saint if you think we might hit it off," I mutter.

Besides, after what Spencer did, I'm not really psyched about letting another man into my life, crazy as it is. I'm not afraid of taking risks, but the risk of being harmed by a man again is too great, even for me.

"What's he like?"

He shrugs his bulky shoulders. "He's pretty serious, quiet, hard working. He wouldn't step on your toes, I know that for sure."

Hmm. No love involved then...which seems weird because it's a marriage. And I've only ever thought of marriage as being between two people who love each other. But maybe this is a good fit...because even with marrying a stranger, I could still keep my distance enough to not have a repeat situation like Spencer.

"So...I marry a stranger, and I pay off my debts..." I murmur to myself. If I wasn't backed into a corner, I would never consider this. I mean...this is pretty damn unorthodox alright. This sort of has that weird arranged marriage feeling. Kind of grosses me out.

"He's someone I've known for a long time. He's a good man," Lance adds warmly. "Think about it. I know it's sort of an out-there option, but it would really solve all your problems, Dani. Think of all the things you could do with that money. I mean, your future would be unlimited."

"Unlimited," I repeat dreamily.

No bills. No debt. No living paycheck to paycheck. No more living off of ramen noodles. *Unlimited.* I can't even fathom it.

But I remember what Lance said just a minute ago about how hard I've worked and how little headway I've made in paying what I owe. How little headway I'll *ever* make, even with a good job. Is this my chance to dig myself out of the hole I've been stuck in since my parents died?

Lance watches me think for a moment as my heart beats in my throat. When I told him I needed a hand up, I didn't mean like this... I didn't think he would have a way to literally free me from the shackles I've been living in for the last four years. This is like winning the lottery.

Except for the whole marrying a stranger part. Can I really do that? I blush slightly, thinking of how disappointed my parents would be that I'm even considering this. They were all about working hard for what you want and not taking the easy way out.

And yet...

"What do you think? Do you want to meet him and find out more about the details?"

I stare at him blankly for a moment, weighing my nonexistent options.

Just meet him, a quiet voice says from within. No harm in that, right? The worst thing that happens is I don't marry the guy, and I go back to job hunting.

"Yes," I blurt out desperately. "I'll meet the guy. What could go wrong, right?" I laugh nervously. "I mean he could murder me, but you said he's a good guy—"

"He is. Trust me. I'll set up a meeting."

My stomach gurgles anxiously. Well, what's there to lose, right? Like Lance said, it would solve all my problems. It's just so weird that it comes with marrying somebody I don't know. Yeah, people do that, but not *me*. I prefer to know someone before I marry them. Hell, I'd even like to *love* them first. But I'm desperate. And this could be the only chance I have to get out of debt for good.

I look down at my coffee, trying not to hyperventilate.

"Hey," Lance says, tapping my knuckle so I'll look at him. "Everything is going to be okay. I promise." He gives me a disarming smile, and I smile appreciatively in return.

I really, really hope so.

Chapter Three

Ronan

I push off the wall and glide smoothly through the cool water, surfacing halfway across my lap pool. I take a breath and power through the water to the opposite wall. I love the feel of the water cocooning my tall body as I swim laps. I love the mindlessness of the back and forth. The pool is the only place I can turn my mind off. I focus on each breath in and out, each kick, each stroke of my arms, and tune out the stress of my job. I tune out the internal countdown until my thirtieth birthday. I tune out the grief that this idiotic trust fund causes.

In the water, I don't think. I don't feel.

It's the closest thing to peace I can get.

My life is anything but peaceful. Admittedly, work dominates my life. I like it that way. If I have too much spare time, my mind wanders to things I don't like thinking about. Things that I can't change. Things I regret. Work is a well paying distraction. And damn, am I well paid. They don't call me the Son of Real Estate for nothing.

When my mind is blank and my body tired, I haul myself out of the pool and plop down in a lounge chair. I concentrate on the rapid rise and fall of my chest, willing my mind not to revert to the one thing that's been on my mind nonstop.

I don't want to get married.

I watched my parents until the day my father dropped dead from a heart attack, and what I saw disgusted me. I watched my father dote on my mother and treat her with nothing but respect and love. But I know she never loved him more than she loved herself. I saw the way she poured more of herself into her image, her fingers deep in his wallet. He fell for her beauty and charm. She fell for his money and connections. He was a good man, and she is a good actress. Their marriage was essentially a sham.

Despite observing my father loving such a terrible human being, I almost fell into the same trap once. I almost married a woman who cared more about my net worth than me, because that's what love does. It makes you a fool. And it breaks you.

So, there's no fucking way I want to go anywhere near the altar ever again, but the terms of the trust fund left for me by my father indicate that I have to be married by my thirtieth birthday. If not, my mother will gain access to it instead. And I would rather die than let her take anything that belongs to me. Especially something that's been gifted to me by my father.

And I know she wants it. Why wouldn't she? Besides herself, money has always been her true love. Even though she got a hefty insurance payout after my dad died, she still is after what he left me. Because she has always loved money and has always hated me.

For me, it has nothing to do with money. I have more than enough in the bank right now that I could retire tomorrow and never work another day again. I don't need the money in my trust fund. I need to keep my mother from taking what's mine. This is just another way for her to take more of my dad's money, even if it legally belongs to me. This is another way for her to hurt me.

Unfortunately, that means I have to get married. And even more unfortunately, there's no fiancée in sight.

It's getting down to the wire now, and I'm running out of time. But I don't want to just solicit some random woman to marry me. It has to be someone upstanding, who wouldn't use the money for embarrassing or inappropriate things. I have the Wells family reputation to uphold. I can't be tied to a reckless or untrustworthy woman.

I rub the back of my neck as my breathing rate returns to normal. I watch the way the overhead lights bounce and throw a glow over the cobalt, blue-tiled room.

The last six months have been a blur. I've been trying to find any kind of loophole possible in the paperwork for my trust fund, any possible way I could avoid getting married. But neither me nor my lawyer could find anything.

So when I had to admit defeat on that venture, I did try to find a woman I might get along with well enough to have in my life for the trust fund required two years. But I quickly ditched that as well. With how much I work, I don't have the time to be a decent husband, and I sure as hell would rather be left alone instead. It wouldn't be fair to anyone.

Now, I'm just hoping for a responsible woman who isn't a psychopath. I wish that narrowed it down, but it's surprisingly difficult to weed out the crazy candidates. And it damn sure isn't easy to gain my trust. It's been broken too many times.

My phone rings on the glass table next to me, startling me out of my thoughts. My lawyer's name lights up the screen. There has to be a good reason he's calling me after hours.

"Lance, hello." My deep voice reverberates through the space. One of my only happy places.

"Ronan," he answers me warmly. "Hope I'm not disturbing you."

"Not at all. What can I help you with?"

"I'm actually calling because I think I can help *you*."

My brows dip slightly. "I'm listening."

"I know a girl."

My whole body stiffens at those four words.

A *girl*?

My mind instantly demands every scrap of information Lance can give me about her. I have nine days until my birthday, so this girl could be the buzzer shot that I need.

I force myself to answer him calmly, even though hope is springing up inside of me. "Who is she?"

"Her name is Dani. I've known her since she was a kid. Her parents were good friends of mine."

One side of my mouth curves downward in a half grimace. Just because you've known someone your whole life doesn't mean you can trust them.

Hell, I can't even trust my family, and they're blood. Lance is probably the only person I trust completely at this point.

"And you trust her?"

"Yes."

Lance's lack of hesitation impresses me. I know he feels the same way about loyalty and trust that I do. If he says he trusts this woman, then I believe him. However, that doesn't mean I trust her. Trust is hard earned and easily broken. I've been through too much to change that now.

"I told her about your predicament, and she's interested in finding out more."

I lean forward in my lounger and blow out an anxious breath. Shit, he already told her about it.

"She's a good kid, Ronan. And she needs the money as much as you need her to marry you."

I reach for a white towel from the shelf next to me and stand up. I run the towel through my dark hair and then down my chest. My stomach sinks, wondering what kind of trouble Dani has gotten herself into that she would be considering marrying a stranger for money.

"What does she need the money for?"

Lance sighs uncomfortably. "It's not really my business to tell you her life story, but she lost her job and her apartment building just burned down."

"Shit," I mutter, feeling for this girl.

"She's in a bad spot, so the sooner you can meet with her, the better."

"I see." I take a deep breath, realizing that this could be my last shot. Obviously, I have to at least meet her. "I'll figure out a meeting for tomorrow."

"Excellent," Lance replies excitedly. "Send me the details, and I'll forward them to Dani."

"I'll do that. Thanks, Lance." I hang up and finish toweling off.

Dread and nerves fill me up as I tiredly mount the stairs leading to the main level of my house.

I hate not knowing what to expect. I like being in control of what happens. I like to have all the facts before I make a decision. But all I know about this woman is that she's a "good kid."

The whole marriage will be fake anyway, and I won't be seeing her often because of how much I work. But the idea of a stranger living in this house is making me consider calling the whole thing off. I value my privacy more than most, and I've definitely grown accustomed to living independent of anyone else.

I wander through the expansive kitchen, my bare feet slapping quietly on the white marble tile. I don't cook, but I know my private chef appreciates the layout and extra counter space that the light granite-covered island provides, as well as the top of the line appliances. It's open to the living room and dining room, making this floor suitable for entertaining guests. If I did that sort of thing.

The only reason I bought this house is because it had a lap pool. I couldn't care less about the extra bedrooms or the theatre room or even the neighborhood. Most people would buy a big house like this to fill with children, but I have no intention of doing that.

My only intention is carrying on the work my dad began with Wells, Inc. I wouldn't say that real estate is my passion by any means, but it makes me feel closer to my dad. It gives me a way to make him proud, even though he's gone. Really, that's the only thing that drives me. Making him proud.

That being said, I'm pretty pissed off about the way he set up this trust fund shit. I'm sure it was his way of making sure I find a nice woman to fall in love with, but that's just fucking nonsense. I don't have much left of my heart after Sadie ripped it out of my chest.

If anything, this trust fund is just another painful reminder that my dad is dead. And I could really do with less of those.

Upstairs, I rinse off in the shower and then settle myself in the office attached to my bedroom. I take a look at my schedule for tomorrow so I can try to find a time to fit Dani in. With some finagling, I plug her in at two o'clock and then text Lance.

I place the heels of my hands into my eye sockets and press, trying to knead away the tension. Little stars pop and sparkle behind my eyelids.

Fuck, I'm already nervous as hell. I don't get nervous. I get focused. But this mystery girl could either be the answer to my problem, or she could be an even bigger problem. A problem I could be legally bound to for the next two years.

Goddamn it, Dad. Why did you do this to me?

He knew damn well how in control of my life I like to be. Maybe this was his way of telling me he knew better.

Agreed to disagree on that one.

I made the mistake of going down this road before, and it nearly jeopardized my entire future. Is this just another opportunity to do the same?

I drop my hands and glance up at one of the picture frames I keep on my desk. The one of me and my dad back in high school, after I beat the record for 100-meter backstroke.

We're standing in the hallway outside of the locker rooms, his hand on my shoulder. Me in my navy and maroon Letterman's jacket with damp dark hair, him wearing the dark green suit he wore directly from the office that day.

He was so proud of me. And I love this picture so much because you can see the pride on his overjoyed face. He always made time to make my swim meets, even though he was busy with work stuff. My mother, on the other hand, never showed up once in my four years on the team. Even then, I knew I wasn't a priority to her. All that mattered was my older brother, Bodie, and my dad. I was always an afterthought.

I study his friendly face in the picture, my chest aching. He was a good man with a good heart. Talented. Honest. Driven. Warm. Loyal.

My eyes slide from my father's blonde hair and brown eyes to my young, grinning face next to him. Even at eighteen, I was already bigger and broader than him. A swimmer or not, I was taller than his slight frame by the time I turned sixteen. His body language was always light and happy, even in business, whereas mine has always been sharper, tenser. Bodie used to say I look mean. Severe. Even when I smiled.

He said it to get a rise out of me, I know that. That's what brothers do, after all. Anyway, even if Bodie *was* trying to piss me off, I know I give off a very "severe" vibe now. Ever since Dad died.

I wish he was still here.

Hell, I wish I had died instead. He's more missed than I would've been, that's for damn sure.

But he's *not* here. And it's up to me to uphold Wells, Inc. And the thing I care about the most is not letting him down.

Chapter Four

Dani

I'm going to throw up. I'm going to throw up right here, in public, all over this elevator. *Deep breaths.*

The man next to me looks at me nervously as I suck in a deep breath and blow it out slowly, willing my stomach juices to stay put.

"Everything alright?"

"Huh?" I whip my head toward my elevator neighbor. "Oh, I'm fine. I promise if I throw up, I'll do it over there in the corner."

A disgusted and scared look takes over his face, and he steps back.

"Good idea, buddy," I say and go back to my deep breaths.

It's no big deal. Just meeting some random guy that I might marry. Not weird at all. Totally normal afternoon, actually. People do this all the time. Probably.

The elevator comes to a halt, and the doors open. Mr. Disgusted gets out quickly, and a couple more people get on. I move over to the side and grip the metal handrail, trying to get myself together. If Lance knows him, he can't possibly be bad news. Lance doesn't associate with known felons or deviants or manipulators. Well, he does, but only because he's a lawyer. Not because he wants to. I'm in good hands here. This is going to solve all my problems.

No more debilitating debt, I remind myself. *Complete financial freedom.*

When the elevator stops again on my floor, I dart off before I can chicken out. I nervously smooth my plum-colored, seven dollar, Walmart clearance dress as I look around. The reception area is wide open and covered with dark gray carpeting. The lighting is bright and plentiful from the modern silver fixtures overhead, suggesting to me that they have nothing to hide here, including dirt or messiness of any kind. To the right is a line of cushy seats, some occupied by professional looking men and women, some vacant and welcoming. To the left is a wall of glass windows that would terrify me if I were afraid of heights. Because I'm not, I appreciate the view of downtown Minneapolis while I wait for the receptionist in front of me to end her phone call.

I should've asked what this guy does. The sign over the receptionist's desk just says *Wells, Inc.* and that tells me exactly nothing. Whatever he does, this office space reflects success and money.

Hmm. If this guy is apparently a high ranking executive, I'm assuming he's paid well. Why is he so desperate for access to his trust fund that he's willing to marry a stranger? Not that I can judge, obviously. But there's no way I would be even considering this if I wasn't in my shitty situation. Maybe this guy isn't as successful as he seems. Maybe he's hiding his bad financial decisions just like Ben did when he blindsided every employee with his bankruptcy. Or he just wants more money. Rich people always want more money.

I'm interested in finding out.

When the receptionist looks up at me, I'm met with a friendly face that is deeply welcome at this point. I glance down at the little slip of paper in my purse that has the information Lance provided me with via text last night.

Ronan Wells. Hennepin Avenue Offices in Minneapolis. Tenth floor. Two o'clock.

I almost blurted the whole thing out to Mel last night after we got home from Walmart with a handful of toiletries, underwear, and other clearance clothing items, but instead, I just told her that Lance for sure is going to let me stay with him and that he has a lead on a job.

It wasn't totally untruthful...but I still feel guilty. I never lie to Mel. Or really anyone. But I know how crazy this idea is, and I don't want to make my best friend worry about me even more than she already is. I'll tell her everything when it's absolutely necessary.

Besides, this isn't a for sure thing. I might go in there and find out it's not at all what Lance thought it was, or the dude might not think I'm the right woman for the job. I might find out he hates Harry Potter. That's definitely a dealbreaker for me. Why stress Mel out when there's such a slim chance that I'll end up doing it?

"Good afternoon, how may I help you?"

"Hi," I squeak out, and then clear my throat. "Hi, I'm Dani. I have an appointment—well, no, not an appointment. This isn't a doctor's office." I laugh a little too loud, which more than portrays my nerves. "I have a *meeting* with Ronan Wells."

"Right. I have you down for two o'clock," she says, glancing at her computer. She gestures to the line of comfy chairs nearby. "Have a seat and his assistant will be right out to bring you back."

"Oh, thank you. Thanks a lot." I shuffle over to a chair and plop down. This is crazy, right? It's not just me?

Man, I hope he isn't a jerk. I have no patience for jerks. I had to deal with the occasional jerk at Ben's On Main, and I just want to say, you can really tell a lot about a person by how they treat a waitress. I've been chewed out unnecessarily, cat-called, spilled on, and stiffed on tips more times than I like to think about. So, this guy better not be a jerk, because kindness is non-negotiable in my book. Even if he's rich.

I take a few more deep breaths, and then I hear my name. I jump to my feet and find a slender woman about my age standing there with a clipboard and a kind smile. She has blonde hair that's pulled back into a neat bun at the base of her neck, and she's wearing a tasteful white blouse and black pencil skirt with black heels.

I love how professional she looks. Being a waitress for so long, I always am just floored by people who wear things like that to work every day. It must be a dream to not wear jeans and greasy t-shirts at work.

"Hi, yes. That's me. I'm Dani," I say, coming forward. For some reason, I reach out to shake her hand.

"I'm Gina, Mr. Wells's assistant," she introduces with a genuine smile. "Come with me."

I follow her back through a hallway that opens up to a huge space filled with rows of desks and working people. Some are talking to each other or on the phone. Some are clicking away on their computer or scribbling notes. Again, no idea what this guy does for a living.

The space has high ceilings with all the pipes exposed, giving off the modern industrial vibe. Especially with the clean lines of the workspace dividers and white desks of each employee. Along the back is a wall of windows. From here, you can see the Basilica of St. Mary in the distance, which makes my heart skip a beat.

That's where my parents were married. I sniff, willing myself not to turn into a blubbering mess. For some reason, seeing the church feels like a good omen.

Gina takes me to the left, my emotions thankfully unnoticed, to the back corner where there are doors lined up, some of which are glass. Inside I can see meeting rooms. My nerves kick into overdrive. She brings me over to the last door on the left and knocks twice before opening it.

My eyes immediately fix themselves on the man sitting behind a massive desk in front of the floor length window.

My first impression is that he's...*intense.*

He has dark, perfectly-styled hair and dark eyebrows that hover low over deep, blue eyes. He has a chiseled jaw, high cheekbones, and extremely pronounced muscles that push at his tailored gray suit. There's nothing soft about him—his body or his expression.

But wow, is he all kinds of cute. As I mentioned before, I instantly break out into a sweat.

I hadn't given much thought to what this guy looked like, but I realize right now that I had expected someone more...nerdy? Maybe with glasses and pale skin that never sees the light of day because he plays video games as a hobby?

I definitely wasn't prepared for the solid mass of muscle in front of me. I wasn't expecting quads thicker than two of my own put together or the lean taper of his waist. His chest and shoulders look like they once belonged to an even bigger man and have been transplanted to stack above his abdomen. This is clearly a man who takes care of his body.

Drool.

Damn it, why didn't Lance tell me he was hot? I could've mentally prepared myself. I feel like that's something I should have been told about.

"Ronan, your two o'clock is here," Gina informs him, and then promptly leaves without a word.

I wipe my hands on my dress and tentatively take a step in. It's then that I sweep my eyes over the room, landing on the cognac-colored leather couch and packed bookshelves on the left to the handful of wooden file cabinets and a map on the wall of the Twin Cities area on the right. Then, I see that Lance is sitting in one of the chairs opposite Ronan, and I immediately feel a wave of relief rush through me. He must see it because he smiles at me. When he texted me the details for this meeting last night, he said he wasn't sure if he would be able to make it today. I'm so, so glad he's here.

"Dani," Lance says, and comes across the room to greet me. He gives me a quick hug that only mildly calms my nerves, and Mr. Hot Man stands and buttons his suit jacket. "This is Ronan Wells."

He crosses the room in a few strong, confident strides, his hand outstretched for me to shake. He's a man that exudes self-assuredness and professionalism. A man who knows exactly who he is and where he belongs in the world.

He's everything I'm not.

And it has me quaking in my shoes, which I borrowed from Mel and are not nearly as classy as this guy's shiny black dress shoes.

"Nice to meet you," comes his deep voice, which seems to vibrate through my chest. His tone is professional and even, not showing any nerves.

"You too, uh, Mr. Wells." I shake his enormous and warm hand, hoping he doesn't notice the clamminess of my palm.

"Ronan."

"Ronan, right. Of course. Love that name."

"Have a seat," he says, gesturing with a sculpted arm to the chairs in front of his desk.

I obey quickly, Lance following. Once we're all seated, I feel just slightly more at ease. Though I would feel better if Ronan offered me a friendly smile. Even a polite smile would be nice. Courteous, even. But no, his handsome face is quite set and serious. I almost want to reach across the desk and pinch his cheeks in my fingers to get him to loosen up, but I restrain myself. Pretty sure that would be unprofessional and an invasion of his personal space. Which, if I had to guess, he needs a lot of.

Also, I'm pretty sure if I touched this man anywhere other than his hand, I'd instantly forget how to form words.

"So," Ronan begins sternly, looking me in the eyes without wavering, "as Lance told you, in order to access the trust fund left to me by my father, I must be legally married by my 30th birthday."

I didn't know about the 30th birthday part, but I nod. "And he told you I'm royally screwed."

My phrasing raises his dark eyebrows just slightly in surprise, but he quickly rolls with it. "Briefly, yes. Ultimately, what I need from you is—"

"Wait, wait, wait. Hold up. What kind of introduction is that?" I interrupt, which seems to throw him completely. I'm guessing he's not used to being interrupted. "Start from the beginning. I don't know anything about you."

Ronan studies me for a moment, his blue eyes burning into mine as if he's trying to figure out how best to tell me "none of your business" without being rude.

I sweat some more, and my knee bounces slightly.

He clears his throat, his Adam's apple bobbing. "There's really not much to know."

I squint at him. That's the vaguest thing he could have possibly said, and he said it on purpose. Does he really expect me to even entertain this crazy idea without knowing literally anything about him?

"Don't be silly. Tell me about yourself. What do you do? What kind of business is this?"

"I do a little bit of everything, but real estate is my biggest venture."

I nod knowingly, though I know nothing. "So, you're a mogul."

"Something like that."

"I was a waitress before my boss went bankrupt. I used to live in an apartment over in Hawthorne, but it burned down two nights ago. I lost my parents to a car accident four years ago, and I miss them terribly.

Lance here has looked after me ever since." I give Lance an appreciative smile, to which he nods.

"I lost my father six years ago," Ronan admits quietly, almost without meaning to. My smile vanishes.

"Oh, I am so sorry to hear that."

He holds my gaze, studying me again, and I sense he's caught off guard by my sincerity. I want to ask him more about his father because it's something we, very unfortunately, have in common, but he doesn't give me the chance. He presses on back to what he must feel is familiar territory. Ronan is definitely not an over-sharer like me.

"As I was saying, I need you to enter into a legally binding marriage with me so that I can receive those funds set aside for me. Once that money is in my name, I will give you half."

"How much is half, exactly?" I almost hate to ask because Lance already said it would be more than enough to pay my debt and whatever. But the facts are important, right?

Ronan glances at Lance and shifts slightly in his leather desk chair, the first sign of nerves I've seen from him. For whatever reason, his nerves relax me a little. The guy is human after all, even if he looks like an Armani suit model. There's obviously more to him than just his enormously delicious body.

"Fifty million dollars."

The words take a long time to reach me from across his desk. I blankly stare at him and then Lance, and then back to Ronan again.

No, *that can't be right.*

A loud, unattractive laugh erupts out of me. Ronan furrows his eyebrows at me in confusion and possibly irritation. Lance shakes his head and covers his face with one hand.

"I'm sorry," I say, still guffawing. "It's just—I thought I heard you say fifty million dollars."

Lance and Ronan exchange a very similar serious look, and neither one corrects me. My stomach drops.

Fifty. Million. Dollars.

"Holy shit—" I whisper-shout, then slap my hand over my mouth. "Sorry. Sorry. But holy...*shiitake mushrooms* that's a lot of money. Who needs that much money?" I take a few deep breaths and fan my face with my hand to keep my brain from exploding. I feel myself quickly backtracking at that outrageous number. "*Fifty*—that's—that's way too much. All I would *really* need is enough to pay my debt for a month until I can find a new job."

Ronan's eyebrows lower even more over his incredulous blue eyes. He's clearly dumbfounded.

"You don't *want* the full amount?"

"Are you kidding me? In my twenty seven years of life, I've never had more than seven hundred dollars in my bank account. Fifty million dollars is—that's so much more money than I can even fathom. I don't need that much."

I *don't*, okay?

At the most, I'd love to have my debt completely paid and maybe a bit extra to use to find an apartment while I'm job searching. Because more than that? More than what I need? That seems...wrong. Undeserved. I don't like being handed things. My parents taught me to work hard for what you want in life. And if someone just dumped cash in my lap and I did nothing to earn it...that wouldn't feel good to me. That would feel like I cheated somehow.

I mean, yes, I'm in a bad situation here and would love someone to bail me out of it. But within *reason*, you know?

No?

Hmm. I guess I'm alone on this one.

Well, now I understand why Ronan is willing to marry a stranger to get access to his trust fund. That's a lot of money to leave unclaimed, even to someone who makes good money already.

Ronan considers what I said for a long moment, his mind working and calculating. I've never seen a man think about something so carefully.

It's kind of a turn on.

I blush all the way down to my toes at that thought and try to think about dead puppies and old grandmas instead of the beautiful tone of his forearms or the hard planes of his intense face.

He makes eye contact with Lance, and I see almost a shadow of a smile, but then it's gone, and he looks back at me.

"I would feel uncomfortable splitting it unevenly." He says it with finality. Confidence.

Something about it triggers me. Spencer used to speak to me like that. I wasn't supposed to argue with what he decided. It was my role to obey his decisions blindly, like a good little woman.

I fidget with the hem of my dress and try to match Ronan's confidence, intent on not backing down. "Then...I'll accept enough to pay my debt in full. Two hundred and forty thousand dollars." Saying that number out loud makes me want to throw up. Ronan doesn't seem swayed by that number in the slightest.

"Fifty," he insists firmly. I fold my arms across my chest stubbornly, desperate to feel like I'm in control of my own destiny for once.

"Five hundred thousand," I retort. He narrows his eyes at me, making my stomach squirm. I don't get the sense that Ronan is dangerous, but I can tell he's used to getting his way.

"Sixty."

My mouth drops open. "One million."

"Eighty."

"Stop that," I demand, though I'm suddenly enjoying the way he's looking at me. He's all business, and yet, there's a bit of playfulness to his expression that gives me a rush of affection for him. Maybe the stiff, cold exterior is just a front. Maybe he's a big old softy when he's not at work in business mode.

Maybe he's not Spencer.

"I'll stop when you agree to fifty."

I look over at Lance, who seems to be enjoying this, and remember what he said one more time. I've worked so freaking hard, and it's gotten me nowhere. This is my way out.

I throw up my hands in resignation, making a show of it. "Fine."

"Great." Ronan folds his big hands and rests them on the mahogany desktop. "So, you sign the marriage license. We get married and sign the marriage certificate. I get access to the trust fund. You get half."

"Right. Yeah. No big deal. All in a day's work."

"There are a few more conditions, however. The terms of my father's trust indicate that we be married and living together for a minimum of two years. If not, the funds will be seized."

Only two years? Fifty million dollars for a two year marriage to a stranger? Seems doable. Crazy? Yes. But doable. I don't have anywhere to go right now anyway.

"Even though this would be a fake marriage, for public purposes, I would need you to accompany me to events and charity functions."

"Oh, arm candy. I'm game," I comment with a smile. Ronan clears his throat again, apparently choosing to ignore what I said. Not much for laughter, this one.

"Also, we're under a bit of a time crunch. I turn thirty in nine days."

Nine days? Holy hell. That's quick. But honestly, the quicker the better for my situation, right? I'm about to be sent to collections any day now.

"Thankfully, there's no waiting period for a marriage license in Minnesota," Ronan continues as though he doesn't notice my eyes are as wide as saucers. "There is a mandatory 72-hour waiting period to be married by a Justice of the Peace or officiant. And, of course, there will be turnover time for running background checks and getting the appropriate documents notarized. That being said, if you need a couple of days to think this over, I can still make it work. This isn't the kind of decision you should take lightly."

I nod solemnly. He's right. I'm basically forfeiting the next two years of my life to a stranger. Then again, this money would solve all my problems. And after two years, I'll get to start over and do whatever the hell I want to without any debt weighing me down.

Wow, just imagining that kind of freedom eases me.

"So if you don't get married in nine days, what happens to the money?"

He sighs heavily, so audibly it almost sounds like a growl, and a dark and menacing look crosses his features that makes me shiver. "My mother would receive it."

"Oh." It's all I can think to say because of the way he ground his teeth together as he said those words. Clearly there's some bad blood there.

"All of these conditions will be spelled out into a contract that you and I will sign. That way, any breach in that contract will be prosecutable."

"So, it's like a prenup?"

"Essentially, yes."

I nod. I'm not sure why the idea of a contract makes me feel better about this whole idea. But then again, why wouldn't there be a contract in place for something like this? A verbal agreement sure as hell wouldn't do it. Not even an elaborate handshake would do it. Oh, I would *love* to see this stiff, serious man do some ridiculously elaborate handshake. I should put that in the contract.

"Once we're married, you would move into my house. Even though this would be a legal marriage, our relationship would be more like roommates. I'm typically not home much, so we would really only see each other in passing."

That's good. Not that I don't want to at least be friends with this guy, but as I said before, I'm not exactly looking to fall in love or catch feelings.

It quickly dawns on me that I've never lived with a guy before. I bet Ronan's a neat freak. I bet he has a whole separate closet just for all his suits and ties. I wonder if he has names for each one. This gray suit he's wearing right now looks like a Tyler. No doubt he has more clothes than me, though at this point, that's mostly because everything I had went up in flames.

"Even so, I intend to honor our marriage. Meaning, there will be no outside relationships. No mistresses or boy toys."

I stifle a chuckle. *Boy toys.*

"The less people involved, the better."

"No need to worry about me bringing home a boy toy," I assure him with a soft laugh. "I don't even know how to find a boy toy. Is there a hotline?"

Lance shakes his head. I think I'm embarrassing him.

"What questions do you have for me?" Ronan asks, thankfully ignoring my boy toy comments. He's ignoring a lot of my comments, I realize.

"What side of the bed do you want?" I ask jokingly because I'm awkward like that. He doesn't laugh. I wonder if he *ever* laughs? Or smiles?

"You would have your own master suite separate from mine."

"Oh. Good. Right." Damn, this guy can't take a joke. Somehow, I'm going to have to get him to relax a little and have fun. Though, to be fair, this is a pretty serious thing we're talking about. I inwardly kick myself for my uppity personality.

"So, tell me what you think. Is this something you're interested in moving forward with, or do you need some time to mull it over?"

I bite my lip nervously and glance at Lance. He gives me a reassuring smile.

I've worked myself to the bone to make ends meet while paying my debt. I've been feeling like a hamster trapped in a wheel, running and running and running but never getting anywhere. I haven't rested in *years*. Haven't enjoyed myself in *years*.

"Yes, I'm interested," I blurt out. "I'll do it."

Ronan looks surprised, which unnerves me. "You'll do it?"

"Yes. Feel free to call me wifey." I wink at him. "That is, if you want me to be your partner in crime. I don't know if you have any other, uh, candidates or whatever?"

His mouth does a weird kind of half-grimace. "I don't."

"Awesome." I take a cleansing breath. "Did you have any questions for me? Anything else you want to know? Ask me anything. I'm an open book." I smile expectantly at him. He continues to give me the same stern expression. The urge to pinch his cheeks resurfaces.

"Are you always this..." he pauses thoughtfully, apparently trying to find the right word; this should be good, "*lively*?"

I snort. "Pretty much."

"Hmm."

"Is that a problem?"

He pauses for much too long and then says, "No."

"Great." I clap my hands together. "Then wifey it is."

He studies me sternly. "Right." He nods to Lance. "Lance here will be our lawyer. He'll be present for the creation of our contract. I have a very full schedule tomorrow, but I could meet with you after the office closes to negotiate the terms of the contract."

"Sure, okay."

Ronan takes a business card from the holder near his desk phone and hands it to me. He's careful not to brush his thick fingers against mine. "This is my information. If you think of any other questions, don't hesitate to call."

"Thank you." I glance down at the card and then back up at his handsome face again. Strange that he doesn't have a girlfriend. Or anyone interested in him. Or even any other candidates. He seems like a pretty damn eligible bachelor to me, aside from the whole intense, serious aura thing. "I do have a question, actually."

He settles himself back into his chair a little more, as if preparing himself. "Sure."

"You're a very successful businessman with a lot going for you, who has a drop dead gorgeous body. Literally anything with ovaries would be dying for your attention." His blue eyes widen slightly. "So, why haven't you gotten married already? Have you just not met the right girl?"

My question makes his broad shoulders tense, creasing his gray suit coat. I guess it's a personal question, and I did tell him to his face that he's gorgeous. And I'm pretty sure I mentioned ovaries. But seriously. With those deep blue eyes and those muscles, I can't imagine it would be hard to find a woman.

"I'm married to my work," he replies sternly, his voice dropping even deeper. "I don't have the time, or frankly the interest, in being in a romantic relationship."

I nod. "Gotcha."

Hmm. I feel a little bad for him. Work is a pretty terrible spouse. Sounds lonely. Not that I can talk. I haven't been in a relationship for two years, but that's on purpose.

"To be clear, this is not in any way a situation in which we become romantically involved. This is a business deal." Ronan holds my gaze with laser eyes, making goosebumps raise on my skin.

"Right. I understand. But if feelings *were* to happen, then what?" I regret the question as soon as it exits my stupid mouth. Of course, there won't be any feelings. I don't know if this man even *has* any feelings.

He sighs and pins me with an almost taunting glare. "If you're worried about me falling in love with you, I assure you, you don't need to be."

I can't help but scowl at him. I know I'm not as good looking as he is. I have a pleasant enough face, I think, and maybe some extra junk in the trunk, but I'm definitely not a monster. Then again, maybe my personality is too much for him. It is for most guys.

He gives me a questioning look, as if to say "understood?" and I nod. Roommates it is, *buddy*.

"Great. So, I'll see you tomorrow and we can hash out all the details. Then, we can obtain the marriage license at City Hall and get the ball rolling." Ronan stands, towering over me, and offers his hand. I stand as well, feeling slightly tremulous, and shake his strong hand. Such a businessman.

"Thanks, Ronan," says Lance warmly as he rises out of his seat. "I'll get to work tonight drawing something up so we have a place to start." He shakes hands with Ronan too, but there's less professionalism between them, like they're old friends.

"That would be great."

"See you tomorrow." Lance turns and heads for the door of the office. I give Ronan a smile.

"It was nice meeting you," I say simply, but I do mean it. I feel his eyes on my back as I make my way to the door.

"Dani," he says, and I turn to find him standing tall in the middle of his office, making everything in the room seem smaller by comparison.

"Yeah?"

"You said your apartment burned down, so where are you staying? A hotel?"

"No, I'm staying with my friend, Mel, for another night, and then I'll be at Lance's place. Why?"

He thoughtfully frowns at me for a moment, like he's deciding something. "It won't be necessary for you to move in with Lance."

"What? Why?"

"We'll get you moved into my place tomorrow. No sense in moving twice."

I stare at him in surprise. Mostly because he's being thoughtful, but also because he's doing it before we've even sat down to write the contract, much less sign it. A warmth spreads through me. Lance is right; he's a good man.

"Well, honestly I don't have much," I say with a light chuckle. "I lost almost everything in the fire, so I barely have anything to pack."

He nods, a troubled look crossing his sharp features. "If you don't feel comfortable moving in with me before we get married, I respect that. But if you change your mind, you're welcome to move in whenever you like."

"Thank you," I say, smiling lightly. "I appreciate that."

He gives me a curt nod, which for him is probably the equivalent of a polite smile. "Have a good evening."

"You, too, Ronan. See you tomorrow." I smile at him again and then follow Lance out.

Once Lance and I are back out in the lobby, I throw my arms around his neck. "I'm *saved!*" I exclaim in relief and jubilation. He pats my shoulder, and I pull back to look at him. "Thank you. Seriously, Lance. If I had a position to promote you to, I would do it." I think for a second, tapping my chin. "Lance Bertram, *President of Saving Dani's Butt.* I like it. Has that ring to it."

Lance shakes his head, chuckling. "Just do me a favor."

"Sure, anything."

He holds my gaze for a moment, his fatherly face softening. "Be patient with Ronan."

I squint at him. "Because he's kind of a stiff fuddy duddy?"

He shrugs, going with it. "Yeah. He takes a while to open up, so just go easy on him."

I salute and jab the down button next to the elevator. "Yes, sir."

Chapter Five

Ronan

I hate every second of this.

Writing the terms of a contract like this is obviously not going to be an easy thing to do, especially between strangers. But I wasn't expecting her to throw out terms for secret handshakes and code names for charity dinners. And for the record, I will absolutely *not* allow her to call me Mogul One, and I will absolutely *not* call her Trophy Wife.

Looking back now, I guess I should've expected something less than serious from her. My first impression of her was that she was a little quirky. Quirky can be cute in the right situations. *This* is not one of those situations.

Maybe she's just nervous. People say weird things when they get nervous. Not me, but other people. And yet, the fact that Lance doesn't seem even slightly surprised at the ridiculous things popping out of Dani's mouth means only one thing. This is how she really is. All the time.

Thank fuck I won't be seeing much of her.

Not that I don't mind looking at her. Who would, really? She's a natural beauty. Stunning in an understated sort of way. When she walked into my office yesterday, I was momentarily mesmerized by her long, light brown hair bouncing over her petite frame and simple, purple dress. And the way her genuine hazel eyes met mine with humility and kindness…damn. But I don't think she has any clue how attractive she is, because if she did, she'd be using it to get all the weird, random things she wants.

Sadie did it all the time, though I didn't realize then how she used her body to get what she wanted from me. Now, I'm hyper aware when I see a woman flirting and being overly bubbly. I have a radar for it now. And Dani? She doesn't make a blip on that radar. Because of that, I know that if I wasn't in this situation and knew I'd never see her again, I would be pretty damn interested in familiarizing myself with the gentle swell of her hips. Not to mention the fullness of her bottom lip. Or the column of her neck.

But that can't happen. *Won't* happen.

This is a business arrangement. Strictly professional. Not personal, the way I prefer it.

So, I'm trying with everything I have to stay professional and not lose my shit. Because this is damn important and affects both of our lives for the next two years. My patience is wearing thin.

"Being someone who eats a lot of spinach and broccoli, I would love to have a mandatory out if I get something stuck in my teeth," she says casually.

"That's really not something we need to have in writing," I say, trying to keep the mental exhaustion from dominating my tone.

The office has closed, and all my employees, even my assistant Gina, have gone home. I almost thought to order dinner but didn't because it would've just stretched this out even more. Now I'm regretting it because on top of my growing irritation with my soon-to-be wife, I'm also starving.

"Alright. Whatever you say, Wellsley."

I fight hard to keep my expression neutral. I did not agree to that nickname. I *hate* nicknames and terms of endearment. I imagine this woman has a nickname for everything, inanimate object or otherwise.

I sigh and shift in my conference room chair. I suggested having our meeting in here instead of my office so we could spread out a bit more, but I'm missing the comfort of my own desk chair. Dani seems quite at her leisure, leaning back in her chair slightly with bright eyes. Today, she's wearing a plain white t-shirt and jeans with the hem rolled up. The quality of her clothing is low, and the style is purely casual, something I'm not used to. I don't know why I can't ignore that the simplicity of how she lives is soothing to me. Probably because she reminds me nothing of Sadie or anyone else I know. It feels almost like a breath of fresh air. A quirky, clean slate.

"Being that you'll be living in my home," I press on firmly, "I request that no visitors be allowed over. Except for family."

"I don't have any family," she informs me simply. "I can't have friends over? I mean, I don't have hoards of friends, but I do have a few."

"I would prefer it if you didn't. I'm a very private person." The idea of having strangers in my home makes me want to break out into a rash. I'll be having enough of an issue just with this crazy woman in my house. That change alone will be enough to constantly unnerve me while I'm home. I don't need other strangers snooping through my house.

"You? Mr. Serious Quiet Man? You don't say," she teases with a tempting smile. I'm not used to being teased, and I don't want to admit to myself that I like when she teases me. "Can I at least have my friend, Melanie, over if I give you a heads up first?"

I mull that over and decide that's fair, being that she doesn't have any family in her life. "Fine."

At the head of the table, Lance makes a note of that. He's been nothing but helpful, and I'll forever be grateful to him for introducing me to Dani and solving the problem I've been grappling with these last six months.

"Thank you," she says appreciatively. "I'll introduce you sometime; she's really great."

I look down at my own notes to avoid focusing on her eyes. They're so damn...*bright*. Despite her having lost her parents and being basically poor ever since, she seems unbelievably happy. Now, she's lost her job and her apartment just burned down. I can't figure it out. There's a *spark* in her. I should call her Sparky. Fuck, this ridiculous woman is getting to me. I need a drink.

We've already covered the living arrangements, financial guidelines (AKA, don't use the money for anything illegal), and public expectations and decorum.

Unfortunately, my brother is getting married in less than two weeks, so Dani will be attending with me. I haven't informed my mother about finding someone to fulfill my dad's terms. I'll have Lance inform her. I avoid her, if at all possible. I'm hoping I can skirt her during my brother's wedding, but I do look forward to rubbing this in her plastic face if I get the chance.

"What is your stance on impromptu dance parties?"

I look up at her serious expression. I swear she's trying to get under my skin. I can't decide if I like it or not.

"I would say I'm very firmly *against* impromptu dance parties."

She chuckles cutely and shakes her head in good-natured disbelief. "You're just no fun, are you?"

That stings slightly. But I know who I am. I know I'm not one of those guys who charms people or makes them feel validated if I speak to them, the way my dad did. I don't make jokes. I don't kid around. I'm all business.

And *this* is business.

I don't have room in my life for anything else. The times I've made room for something else, it came back to bite me in the ass, and my heart was hacked to pieces. Despite my father wanting me to settle down with a nice girl and get married because I love her, I know I can't do that. I don't *want* to do that. I'm better alone.

"If you're planning on randomly dancing around my house—"

"*Impromptu*, Wellsley. I don't plan it," she interrupts fearlessly. "And it's *our* house. Right?"

I narrow my eyes at her. I expect her expression to waver, but it doesn't, which makes me gain a bit more respect for her. "If you feel the urge to have an impromptu dance party, I would appreciate it if you limit it to your quarters."

I'm proud of myself for saying that instead of "no fucking dance parties," which is what I really want to say.

"Alright. But if you hear your jam come on, then you better join me."

I'm sure by now she should be able to guess that I don't dance. Or laugh. Or do anything she would call fun. She's teasing me again, apparently, and again, it both pleases me and irritates me.

"Right." I sigh heavily and look back at my notes. "The last thing I have on my list is the details of our day to day relationship. As I said, we will be roommates and nothing more."

"Not even friends?"

My jaw tics. I have no interest in being friends. This woman is a stranger. I have no intention of getting to know her or letting her get to know me. Not even as friends.

"I'm much too busy for that."

"Too busy for *friends*?" she blurts out in surprise. "That's a horrible work-life balance you've got there."

Tell me about it. But it's on purpose. Are there days I wish I wasn't so lost in my work? Sure. But those days pass. And because those days pass, I have a loaded bank account that I'm about to add to plentifully in eight days. As long as we can get through this godforsaken contract.

Dani gazes at me for a moment, and it's one of the few times I haven't seen a perky expression on her face. She's sad for me, I realize. I'm uncomfortable with how pathetic that makes me feel. But work is all I am now. It's easier that way. And when shit catches up to me, I swim until it goes away.

"You may not have a lot of time for friendships, but I promise I'll always be there if you need something, okay?" she vows with a sincerity I wasn't expecting. Her warm, hazel eyes hold mine, and something stutters in my chest, but I ignore it.

"Thanks," I mutter, almost to myself.

"Write that down, Lance," she instructs, her sweet smile returning. I can't help feeling like I won't mind seeing that smile every day.

Lance grins as he glances at me, then writes down Dani's friendship promise on the legal pad next to his laptop.

I don't know how I'll ever repay him for this. It's because of him that my mother won't be getting her greedy talons on what belongs to me, and just in the nick of time. Truthfully, he's more than just my lawyer. He goes way back with my family, especially my father. Lance was his best man and his best friend. Lance is one of the few people in my life who have never let me down.

"Let's add to that," he says thoughtfully, looking up at the both of us with seriousness in his eyes, "because you two will be living together for the next two years without *any* outside relationships. It's more than possible that one or both of you may develop feelings. It would be wise to not contractually limit yourselves to just being roommates or friends."

I feel my face harden into a glare at his ridiculous suggestion. "I disagree," I argue, shooting daggers at Lance from my eyes. "There should be nothing physical happening between us. Nothing romantic in any way."

A distant part of me squirms in disappointment, but I shake it off. Sex will only complicate things, even more than I feel like this woman is already complicating things.

"Yeesh, didn't realize I was that repulsive," Dani says under her breath, though she doesn't seem that wounded.

"You're not—" I pause and heave out a frustrated sigh, hating that Lance has walked us into this predicament. "It has nothing to do with that. It's just easier if we draw a line in the sand. That way, there's no confusion and no unnecessary complications."

She gazes at me for a moment, a mixture of exasperation and pain in her expression that I don't understand.

"Love is an unnecessary complication?" Her voice is soft, thoughtful, like she's never looked at love that way before. Kind of makes me feel like an asshole, but there's no getting around my answer.

"Yes."

I wait for Dani to concede, but she says nothing. Her eyes move absently to my teal tie, looking a little troubled.

Honestly, the only reason I'm doing this with her is because of her attitude about money. Bartering with me over fifty million dollars impressed the hell out of me. I knew she was the right girl for the job then.

That, and I respect how hard she's worked to manage her debt, even though there's no way she could ever hope to pay off almost a quarter of a million dollars worth of debt. Not before she met me, that is.

I hope I'm there when she sees her accounts paid off in full. It would give me a lot of joy to know how much I've helped her. It would make this awful fucking situation feel more worth it.

But does any of that information mean I like her? No. And I don't plan on liking her. Or falling in love with her. Or ending up with her when this contract expires.

"Let's be realistic here," Lance says calmly, tapping the end of his pen on the paper in front of him, "even if you go into this planning on being roommates or friends and nothing else, can you honestly say that there's zero chance you could come to like each other at some point?"

I clench my jaw at him. Why the fuck is he pushing this so much?

"I am absolutely on board with just being friends and roommates," Dani assures me, breaking out of her little trance. That's the first truly comforting thing she's said to me this far. It's a relief to know we're on the same page, that she isn't interested in more.

"I agree that it's less messy that way," Lance continues firmly. "But I think if you make a clause in this contract saying you two absolutely can't have feelings for each other, and then it ends up happening... Well, then we're looking at a breach of contract. The easiest way to avoid that is to not limit yourselves here."

I study Lance for a long moment, trying to determine his motive. He must be more of a romantic than I thought if he's trying to push me into Dani's arms. I see a mischievous glint in his blue eyes that sours my stomach.

But I know how to talk Dani out of this. I look across the table and arch one eyebrow at her, though I speak to Lance. "So, you're saying we should have a sex clause?"

Dani's face and neck break out in a deep, crimson blush, and she glances at Lance in a humiliated way. I inwardly smirk in satisfaction.

Lance narrows his eyes at me, unimpressed, and sighs. "Look, this is what contracts are for. Spelling out all the options in case a specific situation arises."

There's no arguing that, and Lance knows it. Damn him.

Dani nods, still recovering from her blush attack. "Then let's put a line in our contract that says a romantic relationship should be avoided, but isn't prohibited."

I glare at Lance again, but he only looks back at me pleasantly, like we're talking about the weather and not my love life. Which he knows for a fact is a painful subject for me.

"Fine," I cave, because it won't happen anyway. Not if I have anything to do with it.

"One more thing," Dani says. I inwardly curse. "I'd like to have dinner once a week. Just the two of us. No phones."

I lean back in my chair and study her, stymied. "*Why?*"

She gives me a bewildered look. "Is it so hard to imagine that I might actually be interested in your life? That I might like to get to know my husband?"

"That won't be necessary."

Her eyebrows angrily pull low over her hazel eyes. Damn it, why is that so adorable?

"I'm agreeing to sign over the next two years of my life to you and *only* you. The least you can do is give me one hour of your time once a week. That isn't asking too much." She folds her arms, pushing her breasts together in a way that makes my mouth instantly salivate.

I glower at her, but I know what she's doing is unintentional. I know what it looks like when it's intentional. Dani doesn't look at me with anything but fire, but not the sexy kind. Though I do find it sexy.

"Fine. But we will never, ever, refer to it as a date."

She opens her mouth to tease me but stops. I can tell she was about to tease me because she gets this evil little glint in her eye. I hate that I've already noticed it.

"Thank you," she says, though I can tell she's still holding back some weird comment.

"Anything else?"

She twists her mouth to the side, pretending to think. She's trying to make me sweat, trying to tease me some more. I stare her down for another silent moment, ignoring how my pulse races, and then she shakes her head.

"Great. So, Lance will finalize our contract, and we can sign it tomorrow when we obtain our marriage license from the County Deputy at City Hall. Please arrive no later than three o'clock."

"Perfect, that's only a handful of blocks from Lance's," she says brightly.

That's right; she doesn't own a car. I found that out from the background check this morning, as well as information about the car accident that killed her parents. I'm not sure she's aware that I know she was in the car when it happened.

She hasn't said anything more about moving into my house before we're legally married, but in a way that's good. I'll be soaking up the last of my bachelorhood anyway. That being said, it seems stupid to move more than you have to, even with so little belongings. But I'm not going to push her on it.

"So, how quickly will you receive the money once we get married?"

"It's an electronic transfer, so one business day." Lance just needs to be there to meet with my mother's lawyer, and once it's proved that all criteria are met, the funds will be transferred. And then, I will have won this idiotic fight with my mother over what rightfully belongs to me.

"Wow, that fast?"

I nod. "We'll get a bank account opened for you as well. I'd prefer if it was the same bank as mine."

She shrugs and nods. "And then, we'll be roomies!"

I try not to grimace. "Yes."

Even though the fight for this trust fund will be over, the nightmare with Dani is only just beginning.

Chapter Six

Dani

U sually, I'm pretty good at saying things like it is. I tell it to you straight. I'm not one to mince words or beat around the bush. But telling Mel about my little meeting with Lance and Ronan today? Well, I would love to beat around the biggest, bushiest bush I can find because saying it out loud to my best friend not only makes it real, but it also then becomes something she can comment on. And I know she is going to have more than a few comments about this.

Tonight, I leave for Lance's. He gave me a ride back to Mel's after our meeting and offered to wait for me while I grabbed my things so we could carpool to his place. I declined, only because I haven't told Mel. Part of me wishes I could hide this from her forever. Not because it isn't literally saving my ass from destitution, but because I'm agreeing to marry a stranger. For money. Which, as I've said, is crazy. And there's no way she isn't going to think it's crazy too.

In their little living room, I anxiously fold up my meager Walmart wardrobe, placing each item into a plastic grocery bag as I get ready to leave this tiny apartment.

Max is sitting in his desk chair behind me, headset on, playing his game sans shorts. Mel is leaning against the fridge, watching me carefully. I can feel her trying to figure out what I'm hiding from her. Because I wear my heart on my sleeve and can't hide shit to save my life. And she's known me for so long that even if I put on an award-winning broadway performance of normal Dani behavior, she would see straight through it. She knows there's something I'm not saying. It's making me so freaking nervous.

How do I even start this conversation?

Oh hey, I forgot to tell you! This guy Lance knows is going to take care of all my debt and give me a place to live and give me millions of dollars if I become his wife for two years! Isn't that awesome?

Is there any way I can explain this so it doesn't sound totally crazy? I can't think of a single one.

"What's going on?" she prompts, eyeing me as I straighten up.

"Huh? What do you—"

"Don't even fucking try, Danielle Marie Sanders," Mel threatens, pointing a sharp finger at me. "There's something you aren't saying. Now *spill it.*"

I gulp and place my bag on the couch in front of me with a plastic crinkle.

I guess this is it.

Just say it.

Just spit it out.

I can't.

"You *are* going to Lance's house, right?"

"Yes. I'm going to Lance's house," I answer, grateful for a question with such an easy answer.

"Then why are you acting so weird?"

"Me? Weird? Mel. Come on. You and I both know I'm one of the weirdest people you've ever—"

"Stop stalling." She comes closer, and I tense up. Mel may be a tiny thing, but she is absolutely a force to be reckoned with. It's one of the reasons I love her so much. I know without a doubt that if anyone hurt me, she'd have my back with ferocity.

I worry my lip, take a deep breath, and remind myself that Mel is my best friend. I need to just say it, get it out, listen to her freak out about it for a bit, and then console her that everything will be okay.

"You're right. I'm stalling. But what I have to tell you isn't...well, it's kind of crazy."

Mel's eyebrows furrow. "Crazy? What do you mean?"

I take her hand and pull her down with me onto the couch. I glance at Max, who's oblivious to anything but his computer screen, and steel myself to get the words out.

"Lance found a way to help me pay off my debt," I say tentatively. She squints at me skeptically.

"Okay..." She gestures with one hand for me to keep talking.

I swallow hard and look around the room, anywhere but at my best friend's face, as I gather my courage.

"He knows this guy who's really rich and—" I cut off abruptly as I break out into a sweat.

"Dani..." she growls in warning. My stomach churns with nausea as the words roll around in my suddenly dry mouth.

"And I'm going to marry him," I blurt out. I smack my hands to my face and wait for her reaction. I expect her to shout at me. Slap me up the back of my head. Stomp around the living room. *Something.* But everything is still; even Max's desk chair is perfectly still.

I take a slow breath and peek through my fingers to find Mel gaping at me, completely frozen in shock. My breathing picks back up.

"I know. Believe me, I *know.* This is just...certifiable. I know. But—"

"Dani, what the hell are you doing?" she interrupts, looking angry now. "Do you even know this guy?"

Her anger fogs my eyes with tears. I sniff and shake my head slowly, ashamedly. Mel's jaw drops open so far, I can see her shiny silver tongue ring. My tears do nothing to soften the verbal blow that comes.

"You're fucking marrying some guy for his *money*?" she screeches. She gets to her feet and stands in front of me. "What the ever living fuck? Dani, you can't do this!"

I cover my face again as a soft sob escapes me.

"What the hell is going on?" comes Max's confused voice, but Mel talks over him.

"I know you're in a bad place right now, but...fuck me, we'll figure something else out! This isn't like you—"

"Mel, please," I exclaim, finding my voice with difficulty. I drop my hands to look at her. "I know how insane this is; I get it. But this is like being offered a get-out-of-debt-free card. I can't just not take it."

She starts to pace in front of me, shaking her head, not having it.

Max has paused his game and turned his chair toward us, trying to figure out what we're talking about.

"God, I never pegged you for a gold digger, Dani," she mutters as she paces. "Goes to show how much you think you know someone."

"Mel," I gasp at her cruel words. "What else should I do? Just keep working myself to death? You've seen me do that for *four years*, Mel, and I haven't even made a dent in paying down what I owe."

She finally stops and faces me. "This is *wrong*, Dani. What would your parents think?"

The breath goes out of me at her question. I instantly hyperventilate as their faces flash through my mind, faces which usually look upon me with love and happiness, but now they're full of anger and disappointment.

"Jesus, breathe, Dani," Mel says and comes forward. She bends me over so my head is between my knees.

I struggle to calm myself, my body shaking with grief. She's right. There's no way my parents would've understood this. They taught me my work ethic. They taught me right from wrong. And Mel is saying exactly what my dad would've said. This is wrong. My parents dreamed that one day, I would find a man who loved me as much as they did, not a man who would just pay my way.

But things are different now. They aren't here. I'm on my own, and have been on my own for years without a hope of ever enjoying my life because of my debt. That can't possibly be what they want for me, right?

I lift my head slowly. "I—I don't think they would have wanted me to work myself to death and never enjoy my life," I say brokenly. Mel's harsh expression doesn't soften.

She shakes her head and puts her hands on her hips. Max looks at me sadly, though he continues to stay out of the conversation.

"If you're going to marry some stranger to pay off your debt, then..." She pauses and looks me in the eye, tears forming. "I don't want any part of it."

"What?"

"If I can't talk you out of this bad idea, then fine. Go. Ruin every idea you've ever had about love and marriage. But don't call me when you regret it because I know you will, Dani."

My heart shrivels up in my chest.

"Babe..." Max says softly, but she doesn't look away from me. She crosses her arms and nods toward the door behind her.

"Go on. I'm sure you'll be able to sleep at night with all that money to keep you warm."

I stare at her, tears pouring down my face. She points at the door, and this time, I see pain in her eyes, too.

Sobbing, I grab my plastic bags and purse. When I stand up, she moves out of the way to let me pass. I glance at Max's face, which looks beyond horrified at what's happening, and then I leave my former best friend's apartment.

I make it down the hallway, down the two flights of steps, and out onto the sidewalk before I completely fall apart. I drop to my knees and ugly cry into the cool night air. I cry so hard, the dog in the yard across the street barks at me.

She kicked me out. Literally ordered me out of her life. God, I knew there was a slim chance that she would take it well, but I didn't expect her to *disown* me. She's been there for me through so many tough times in my life, but now...now she's done. This is too much.

I left the office earlier feeling nervous to tell Mel, but I was also optimistic about marrying Ronan. His background check came back totally clear, and everything we agreed on for the contract was pretty straightforward.

But now, all I can hear is Mel's voice in my head.

You can't do this. This is wrong, Dani. What would your parents think?

She's right. She's so right. I can't do this. I can't just marry some guy for money. I know nothing about him. He could be just like Spencer. He could be a crooked businessman who does a spectacular job at keeping it from Lance. This could end up ruining my life instead of saving it.

Is sacrificing the safety of my friendship with Mel really worth fifty million dollars?

Can I live with myself if I do this?

Before I can think twice, I reach into my purse for my phone. I plugged in Ronan's information days ago and labeled him Mr. Serious Quiet Man. My thumb quivers over his phone number for a long moment before I press down and put the phone to my ear.

I have to tell him that I can't do this. Now is the only time I can back out. Tomorrow, we sign the contract. It has to be now. Then, I'll go to Lance's, and I'll go back to my plan of finding a job and working until I die.

I listen to it ringing, still on my knees, still reeling from Mel's brutality.

"Ronan Wells," comes his deep professional voice. I clear my throat and sniff.

"Hi, it's me. Dani," I say with a wobbly voice.

Silence fills the line, and my nerves emerge. His coldness hurts. I realize just how frigid our marriage would be. No laughter. No sweetness. No warmth. Just *this*. Silence. Indifference. That's not what my parents wanted for me. That's not what I wanted for me.

"What's wrong?" he finally says, which is the last thing I expected. "You're crying. What happened?" Even though his tone is level, I do hear a small measure of concern.

"I don't know anything about you, Ronan," I blurt out. "How can I be sure that this is the right thing? Because right now...it just feels wrong. It feels *wrong* to marry you for your money." It's a relief to say that out loud. "This isn't how this was supposed to go, you know? My life is just so..." I don't even know what word to say. Unpredictable? Tragic? Exhausting?

"Dani," he says, his voice softer than before, "I'm sure this isn't how you expected to get married, but it isn't wrong. We're two willing parties, signing a contract that we both are in agreement over. There's nothing wrong about that."

I sniff and look up toward the street, the assuredness of his logic soothing me slightly. Each streetlight casts an orange halo over the pavement. I mentally count each one, and it calms me a little more.

"That being said," he continues, "it's okay if you don't want to do this. I know that you're backed into a corner right now, but if you want, I can help you find a new job, or hell, I'll pay off your debt so that you can have a fresh start."

My body stills. He's...giving me an out?

"Why would you do that?"

The line is silent again for a moment as I hold my breath.

"Because I think you deserve it."

I wipe at my cheek with the back of my hand. The fact that he would do so much for me without getting anything in return is so stunningly selfless. I can't let him go through with his half of the deal without helping him, too. This is an agreement in which we help each other. We both need each other.

"I couldn't let you do that," I answer softly.

"You don't have to if you marry me."

I have two choices. Marry Ronan, pay off my debt, and learn to deal with my shame over marrying someone I don't love, or I don't marry Ronan, he pays off my debt, and I live the rest of my life feeling indebted to him with no way to pay him back, knowing that he was unable to access the money his deceased father left for him because of me.

Either way, I'll feel guilty. But the first choice comes with helping more than just me. And I *know* that's right.

"Okay."

"Are you sure?"

I take a deep breath and slowly get off my knees. I look behind me at Mel's apartment, feeling a deep, moving grief. I don't want to leave her behind, but she didn't give me a choice. There's nothing I can do about that now, not now that I'm going to really go through with this. Without her.

I look back to the street. Forward. I take a deep breath and let it out slowly.

"Yes."

Chapter Seven

Ronan

"Anything else you need before I take off?" Gina asks, peeking in through my office door.

"No, thank you. Have a good weekend, Gina."

"You too, Ronan."

The door closes, and I return my eyes to the marriage contract in front of me on my desk. I've looked through it at least twice, but I can't focus. I should be feeling relieved or happy that Dani and I got our marriage license earlier this afternoon, but all I can think about is how subdued and serious she was.

Obviously, I don't know her that well, but she wasn't her normal, lively self. It was so strange to see the color washed out of her expression. She was quiet and had this sadness in her eyes that unnerved me. I was worried she was going to back out, even after our chat last night, but she came with her copy of the contract already signed.

When I picked up last night, I assumed she had some other random requirement for our contract that she wanted to run by me, so I was completely caught off guard by her tears and insecurity over doing the right thing. I admire her sense of right and wrong, but this deal doesn't fall under the usual umbrella of morality or ethics. More people get married for money than she realizes. The only difference between what we're doing, is that we both know we don't love each other.

But I did mean it when I said I'd pay her debt if she backed out. She's been through enough. And I know it's something my dad would've done. He would've admired Dani's heart. He would've wanted to help her.

He also probably would call her and make sure she's okay, but that idea makes me nauseous. I don't know what she was upset about earlier, and it isn't my problem to solve. I have enough on my plate right now. I was supposed to be done looking over this contract an hour ago so I could start working on a proposal for a property in Chicago, but I'm not going to be able to focus on that any more than on this contract.

I sigh and look over at my phone.

What would I even say to her? I'm not good at this shit. And I don't want her to think I care about her as more than a name on a contract and a roommate in my house. I don't even know *how* to care about her as anything more than that. And I don't want to. I want this to be as uncomplicated as possible.

I move my eyes back to the contract, and I get through it with difficulty. I sign the last page and then stare at my scrawled name for a long moment. Because of my dad, I've always been proud to be a Wells. He was everything I wanted to be. And though I'm sure he stipulated this marriage clause in my trust fund because he hoped I would marry someone I loved, I know that I make him proud in my professional life.

Since his death, I haven't rested or taken a vacation. I've worked my ass off to make Wells, Inc. everything it can be. I've made a name for myself in Minneapolis, and now I've got my sights on Chicago. I know my dad would be proud of my work ethic and the way I treat my employees. I've done everything I can to be the successful man he raised me to be.

But this contract is a reminder that he also raised me to be a good man outside of work, too. He treated my mother with nothing but kindness and love, and impressed upon me the importance of finding an equal partner in life. That's what I thought I had with Sadie, but I was so fucking wrong.

Now, I'm about to have an equal partner in marriage, but it's strictly platonic. I want to believe he would be proud of me for that somehow, but there's no way for me to know that for sure.

My phone rings, startling me slightly. I reach for it and see a number not saved in my phone.

"Ronan Wells," I answer, gazing over at my bookshelf.

"Ronan, it's Judge Murphy."

I called last night to see if he could marry us on Monday, but he said he would get back to me. I was starting to think I wouldn't hear anything till next week, despite the rush I told him we were in.

"Hello, Judge."

"I wanted to let you know that I'm able to fit you in on Monday morning before 8 A.M."

Relief courses through me.

"Wonderful. We'll be there. Thank you so much, I really appreciate it."

"Of course. Come by at seven-thirty and we'll get you and your lovely bride hitched," he says with warmth.

"Thank you."

"Take care." He hangs up, and I lean back in my desk chair.

Everything is lined up now. This is really going to happen. I'm getting married on Monday.

Thankfully, because of our tight deadline, there isn't time to put together anything that will resemble a real wedding. After planning a wedding with Sadie years ago, I vowed I would never do it again. But there's no risk here for anyone getting hurt. I have every intention to lead my life the same way I have been, meaning that even with Dani living in my home and legally becoming my wife, I still am going to work as I always have and come home to be alone. We'll only be married on paper. No one's heart is on the line.

With that thought on my mind, I dial Dani's number.

"Hello?" comes her soft voice, sounding just as somber as she did this afternoon at City Hall.

"Dani, I just got off the phone with the Judge who'll be marrying us. He said he can get us in at seven-thirty Monday morning," I inform her evenly.

She gasps. "Monday? Like this Monday?"

"Yes."

She clears her throat. "Sorry. Of course—I forgot for a second how quickly this has to go," she explains in a bewildered manner.

"We'll need witnesses," I plow on, so I don't have to address that comment.

"Right. Uh...I'll ask Lance."

"I was going to ask Lance."

"Oh."

"What about your friend?" I struggle to remember her name. "What was her name? Melody?"

Dani sniffs in response. I wait for her to say something, annoyed that she's possibly offended at me not remembering her friend's name.

"Um, no I—I can't ask her because—" Her voice falters, and my stomach drops when I realize that she's crying.

Damn it. I scrub my hand across my five o'clock shadow. What the hell is wrong with her today? If she's really that unhappy, why didn't she take me up on backing out? Now we've both signed the contract, and it's too late.

"Dani, why are you crying?" I ask, trying to inject some sympathy into my tone.

She clears her throat. "Sorry. Sorry, I just got into it with Mel last night and she—she sort of disowned me because of all this," she exclaims with a wobbly voice. "So, no, I can't ask her because—because she isn't my friend anymore." She dissolves into quiet sobs again.

Is that what she's been so upset about? Her stupid friend? I guess that explains her distressed phone call last night and her behavior today. I try to dig deep and find something comforting to say, but I come up with nothing.

"I'll ask my assistant Gina," I say finally. I wasn't planning on involving her in this at all, but I know that at least she'll be professional about it.

"Really? Thank you," she murmurs appreciatively. Her sincerity makes my heart pound.

"Of course."

I hear her blow her nose and sniff again. My brain forms the words to end the conversation, but my mouth doesn't say them. Instead, I hear my dad's voice in my ear, telling me I should keep talking to the woman I'll be marrying in just a few days. I clear my throat and try to shake it away.

"There's no need to wear anything special. We're just going to be saying whatever the Judge wants us to say and then signing the marriage certificate." I imagine her showing up in some huge, gaudy wedding dress and shudder slightly. Even though it's a marriage ceremony, I don't want it to feel even slightly like that.

"Sounds romantic." Her sarcasm is welcome at this point if it means she isn't crying anymore.

Silence returns, and I fidget with my tie. I try to think of something else to say, something else informative, but the only thing I can think of is when she'll be moving in. And I don't want to push her on that.

"Listen, I just want to say thank you for what you said last night," she says gently. "You didn't have to give me an out like that, but you did. So...I just want you to know I appreciate it."

"Sure," I reply evenly, uncomfortable with her mentioning her gratitude. My professional response makes her chuckle.

"You know, you try really hard to come off like this untouchable, strictly professional man, but you know what? I think deep down, you're just a big softy."

"Incorrect," I argue stiffly, though I'm comforted by the return of her light, teasing self.

She giggles, finally dropping the doom and gloom. "There's nothing wrong with being a sweetheart, Wellsley."

I sigh and pinch the bridge of my nose. "Don't you dare start calling me sweetheart," I warn, because I know she'll take that and run.

She laughs again, and this time, it warms my insides. "Why not?"

"You know I'm not one for pet names," I growl back.

"That's about the only thing I know about you."

Good, I think to myself. I plan to keep it that way. Just because we'll be having dinner once a week doesn't mean I intend to subject myself to a game of twenty questions. The longer I can keep this girl at arm's length, the better. Even though I plan on going about my life the way I have been for the last several years doesn't mean Dani is going to go along with that. I have a feeling she isn't going to make herself scarce or keep to her room. Time will tell, I guess.

"So, since we're tying the knot on Monday, would it be okay if I move in on Sunday?"

That will leave me one full day left to myself in my house before this thing between us really happens. I'd like more time, but I don't have any other objection than that.

"If you want."

"Like I said, I don't have much. Literally two bags of stuff. I can get a taxi over or whatever."

"That would be fine."

"Okay," she says and takes an uncertain breath. "Well, I guess I'll see you on Sunday then."

"I'll message you my address. See you then." I hang up and realize my shoulders are sore from how tense I was while talking to her.

I blow out an anxious breath.

Here we go. No turning back now.

I stalk back and forth through the open foyer, glancing out the windows each time I turn.

Dani texted me that she was on her way twenty minutes ago. With each minute that passes, I get more anxious. I almost never have people in my house. I don't throw parties or host poker night with the guys. The only people allowed in are my housekeeper, private chef, and groundskeeper. Though, on occasion, my mother has been known to show up for a "chat." That's really just a front for her to either gossip or insult me to my face. Always a joy, that woman.

So, it's going to be quite the adjustment for me to have Dani in my house. I have a feeling she's going to make it difficult to maintain my previous level of privacy. But there's more than enough space in this house for me to keep my distance from her. And if that doesn't work, I can always stay later at the office so I'm literally only home to sleep.

A car pulls up the long drive and stops in front of the garage. My breathing grows shallow as Dani steps out with her two grocery bags worth of possessions.

My stomach clenches slightly. She really wasn't kidding. She has nothing. She's lost everything between her job, the fire, and her friend. The back of my neck tingles as I realize Lance and I are all she has now.

Until tomorrow, when she'll have a shit ton of money, too.

I roll my shoulders back, trying to ease the tension in them as she pays the driver and the car disappears back down the driveway. Dani stands stock still, looking up at the house with wide eyes as she takes in my home.

I was expecting her reaction. It's a beautiful house. I've always loved the look of greystone houses. The stateliness of them is something dignified and yet not overdone. This house has more space than I need, being a single man. Well, until today. Five bedrooms, not including the two master suites, with a theater room, gym, indoor and outdoor pool, an office, chef's kitchen, and open-floor plan.

It's definitely a step up from Lance's guest room and her apartment before it burnt down. I'm happy for her, in a way, that this arrangement is helping her so much.

Well, nothing left to do but get on with it.

I open the front door and step out onto the porch. The afternoon sun glints off the natural highlights in her long hair. She's wearing jean shorts that show off her toned legs and a pink tank top. The simplicity of her attire eases me, oddly enough.

"You just going to stand there all day?" I call to her.

Her head snaps over to where I'm standing, and then she smiles with bright eyes. Her little legs pump up the sidewalk towards me, her hand trailing through the ferns affectionately.

"Your house is beautiful," she says as she climbs the steps and stands in front of me.

"Thank you," I mutter awkwardly because my first thought in reply to that was *you're beautiful*, and what the hell is that about?

I mentally shake myself and gesture for her to go inside the open front door.

She gasps and walks past me into the house. Dani stands motionless as she takes in the open entry. To the right is a staircase that follows the wall and then crosses over the hall into the living space. I love standing on that catwalk actually. In the center of everything.

When I bought this home and was renovating it to my liking, the interior designer I hired did an amazing job. The whole house is done tastefully, in neutral tones, but with touches of navy and gold throughout. The floors are blonde oak, which only adds more contrast to the enormous navy and white rug she's standing on.

Dani takes it all in, turning slowly on the spot until she faces me, her hazel eyes wide. I close the door behind me and then beckon her to follow me under the catwalk to the living room. She walks slowly, not blinking.

"The living room is through here," I explain. "The kitchen, dining, and living areas are all open."

She takes in the white upper cabinets and navy blue lower cabinets, top of the line stainless steel appliances, and beautiful marble floors. The plush navy couches and stone fireplace. The twelve-foot dining table that I have literally never used.

"The kitchen is the size of my whole apartment," she squeaks out.

I glance around, figuring she's probably right. And while I would imagine she'd be excited to be moving into such an expansive house, she seems...uncomfortable. I don't know what to do with that, so I press on.

"The kitchen is always stocked, so feel free to help yourself. Carla should be in soon, and you can let her know what foods you prefer to eat."

"Carla?" Her sweet face turns away from the living room and toward me.

"She's my private chef."

Her eyebrows lift just slightly and then a loud guffaw pops out of her mouth. "Of course. Right. Naturally, you have a private chef."

I raise one eyebrow at her in a semi-threatening way. It doesn't work.

"Let me guess, you have a maid, too? A butler? Someone who trims your nose hairs?"

I stiffen, offended slightly by her nervous mocking, and then step closer to her. Her bewildered and amused expression changes immediately to apologetic and regretful.

I open my mouth to put her in her place, but she speaks first.

"I'm sorry. This is just all so crazy," she blurts desperately. "I mean this is—" she glances around wildly at my house. "This is just so far from what I'm used to."

I allow my body language to soften slightly. "I hope, in time, you *will* get used to it. Because yes, I do have a private chef and a housekeeper. I request that you make use of them, since they're paid well for their services."

She nods and clamps her mouth shut.

I point to the French doors. "Out there is the grounds. There's a pool and hot tub. Feel free to use them any time."

She nods again, and I take her downstairs.

"Another pool?" she questions as I show her the gym nearby.

"It's a lap pool," I explain.

"You're a swimmer, then?"

I shrug. "Swimming laps is something I do often, yes." I don't mention that it's the one thing that gets my mind to relax or the times I've sat at the bottom and thought about taking in a giant lungful of water to end it all.

Instead, I show her the theater room, which she looks excited about, and then I bring her back to the main level so we can head upstairs to where the bedrooms are.

"This is my room," I say, opening the door. I don't go in, and she thankfully takes the hint and just peeks in at my king-sized bed. "My office is through that door," I point to the right, "which is where you can usually find me in the evenings after I get home."

"So, you work all day at work, and then you come home and work some more?"

I nod and close the bedroom door.

"Married to your work, *indeed*," she mutters.

I cross the hall without commenting and open the door to her suite. "This is where you'll be."

Dani steps inside and I follow, planting myself by the dresser as she looks around. It's a big room with a king-sized bed like mine, two nightstands, a desk, two dressers, and a couch by the window. She opens the walk-in closet door and chuckles, then closes it.

"What?"

"I'll never fill that thing," she says with a smile. She puts down her bags on the bed and runs one hand across the soft, white comforter. I'd hazard a guess that everything in this room is far beyond anything she's had before. At least in terms of quality.

"If there's anything you'd like to change, let me know. Different bedding or paint colors. I want you to be comfortable here."

Dani looks at me for a moment, smiling softly. Her appreciation for these accommodations makes me feel strangely buoyed.

"The bathroom is there," I say, nodding toward the bathroom door on the left next to the window.

She goes to investigate, and I stay where I am. I hear her gasp and mutter something I can't make out from here. When she emerges from the bathroom, her hazel eyes are wide again. I put my hands in my pockets and rock slightly on my heels.

"Obviously, I will never enter this space unless you allow it. You will have your privacy here." I remove a key from my pocket. "You will have the only key, so you can lock your room when you aren't home, if you'd like."

"That's very thoughtful, but I can't imagine you would snoop through my underwear drawer," she says with a chuckle. She's right about that, though now that she mentioned her underwear, I find myself wondering what kind she wears.

I hand her the key, and she fidgets with it nervously. "Do you have any questions?"

Dani glances around her room, her small shoulders hunched in slightly. I sense that she's overwhelmed, but I don't know what to say to comfort her or put her at ease.

She shakes her head finally, looking back at me. She smiles, but it doesn't reach her eyes. I don't like it, but again, I don't know what to do about it. This is her home now. The only thing that can be done, really, is for her to get used to it.

I nod toward a manila folder on the dresser next to me. "Everything you need to know about how things run around here is in this folder. Wifi password, my social calendar, schedules for laundry and housekeeping duties. Laurie and Carla will help you if you have questions."

She nods, fidgeting with the key again.

I clear my throat awkwardly. "Well, I'll leave you to get settled. I'll be in my office."

Dani smiles more sincerely this time. "Thanks, Ronan."

I close her door behind me and then hide myself away in my office, attempting to ignore that even though she and I aren't in the same room, I can still sense her presence in this house. I'm guessing that isn't something I'll be getting rid of any time soon. I just hope she doesn't invade me like she's about to invade my life.

Chapter Eight

Dani

This house is bananas. Like *Lifestyles of the Rich and Famous* bananas. Every single aspect of this house is top of the line and, I think, way overboard. Who needs a voice activated oven? Or a Smart TV in every room? Or basically a miniature jacuzzi for a bathtub? I mean, I shouldn't complain, but holy batman, is it different than what I'm used to. Hell, this house is so far out of the realm of what I ever thought I would have that it feels like a dream.

I move my toes across the beautiful hardwood floor and then over to the plush gray rug that runs under the biggest bed I will ever sleep in. The walls are painted a light gray to match the rug, but the two dressers are painted a deep, dark blue. I spin slowly, taking in the trey ceilings and thick crown molding.

Everything is gorgeous and spotless and...

Sterile.

I sigh, feeling that strange sense of homesickness sweep over me again. I shake my head.

"This is your home now," I say aloud. It doesn't make it feel any truer. I take a deep breath and decide to try again.

"This is your home now, Dani."

I cover my face with my hands.

This room and this house just remind me of what I'm signing up to do. How *tomorrow* I'll be getting married. Married to a man very much like this house. Cold. Beautiful. Organized. Empty.

I turn then and dig through one of my bags on the bed, searching for the picture of my parents so that this room will feel warmer.

I gasp when I see their happy faces, slightly faded from time, smiling at me. My mom had those poofy eighties bangs, and my dad wore a white tux. They both look so happy and so in love.

Will there be some awkward-looking photo from my and Ronan's wedding? I can just see it. Ronan standing next to me, stiff as ever, without smiling, without touching me. And me, trying to put on my best smile but failing because who am I kidding?

The frame shakes in my hands.

"I'm sorry," I whisper, tears filling my eyes, and then lovingly place it on top of the nearest dresser. I step back and just stare at it for a long while, wishing I could reach through that picture and hug them. I would give anything for one of my dad's hugs right now. For some sense of familiarity...some semblance of peace. Of family. Of love.

I back up slowly and sit on the end of the huge bed, feeling my stomach churning with grief.

There have been so many times since I've lost them that I wished they were standing right here. The day I moved into my grungy little apartment. The day I met Spencer. The day Spencer left. The day I was let go. And pretty much every moment since my apartment burned down.

I hate that death steals so much and only gives us a morbid appreciation for life. What a freaking unfair trade.

But all there's left for the living to do is keep on living, right? I owe my parents that. And even if they wouldn't approve of the way I'm going about it, there's no going back now. Which means the only way to go is forward.

I wipe my wet cheeks and reach behind me for the rest of my stuff. I take my time putting each piece of clothing in its new place, but it still only takes me five minutes. The last thing to put away is my plum dress, which I hang in the walk-in closet. Forget walk-in. This damn thing is a sleep-in closet. This closet is bigger than the bathroom in my burnt down apartment. I could raise chickens in that closet, it's that roomy.

I chuckle to myself. Ronan would shit a brick if I snuck chickens into my closet.

I close the door and crumple the grocery bags in my hands. I wonder if he collects these. Does he even use plastic bags? I bet he has those fancy reusable ones. The vision of serious, professional Ronan pushing a grocery cart through the produce section has me chuckling some more. If I had to guess, he doesn't do the grocery shopping. His *private chef* probably does.

I shake my head slightly.

Ronan's life of luxury is far from the way I've lived all these years. Even when my parents were alive, we lived comfortably enough, but on far less than a businessman like Ronan. We lived in a small, two-bedroom house with a cramped little kitchen in the days before I left home. My youth was spent in close proximity to my parents, and I don't regret it. Especially now that they're gone. That cozy little house meant more to me than anything, and losing it after they died was tragic. So many memories in those walls that I can never relive. So much of my parents that I can never have back.

And now, instead of that homey comfort I grew up with, I'm living in someone else's emotionally empty house. Because there were no pictures of his family or anyone in the living room downstairs, or even in his bedroom. This house has nothing personal in it whatsoever. Just money and value oozing out of every piece of furniture and appliance.

What a shame.

How am I going to live here for two years in this frigid house with a frigid man?

I'm sure you'll be able to sleep at night with all that money to keep you warm.

I wrap my arms around myself as Mel's words echo through my head, and then I close my eyes. I feel overwhelmed and intimidated by this new, foreign place, and I don't know where to go to feel safe.

I don't have a safe place.

I sniff and try to keep the tears at bay. Maybe some fresh air will help.

I open the door and pass Ronan's closed bedroom door on my way down the hall to the staircase. I quickly descend and turn right under the catwalk, through the living spaces and to the French doors leading to the backyard.

Every step has my reality quaking.

This is my home now.

I burst out onto the back deck and glance around. The covered hot tub is to the right, beneath a beautiful wooden pergola with ivy growing on it. To the left is a huge, shiny black grill and some blue Adirondack chairs. Ahead of me and a little to the left is the pool with clean, aquamarine water surrounded by lush, tropical looking plants that I know for a fact have to be planted there every year because of the harsh Minnesota winters. There's a little fountain in the middle of the pool, splashing a pleasant sound to me from across the perfectly green lawn and crackless walkways.

I sprint over to the pool, chasing the serenity of that fountain. I stop at the edge, my toes hanging over a bit, my breathing ragged and my emotions about to explode out of me. I plop down and put my feet in the cool water. I watch the fountain for a long time, feeling slightly comforted but mostly frozen with too many conflicting emotions to move, even when my toes get pruney.

A shout from the deck catches my attention, mostly because it isn't Ronan's deep voice. A woman is standing on the deck in front of the French doors, waving at me.

"You must be Dani!" she calls to me with a big smile. She's wearing a white chef's coat, jeans, and hot pink tennis shoes. A folded black bandana holds her brown curls away from a face so friendly that I can see it clearly from across the yard.

I get up slowly, my butt a little sore from sitting on the concrete for so long.

"That's me!" I call back, moving toward her.

"I'm Carla, your private chef," she says when I get closer, and offers her hand to shake.

Oh, that's right. Ronan said she would be here soon. What he didn't tell me is how this middle aged woman radiates warmth like the sun itself.

That warmth is so needed right now. I shake her hand, and she squeezes mine extra tight, like she can tell I've been crying.

"I'm so excited to have someone else to cook for," Carla says. "Please tell me you like something other than steak. I could feed that man steak every night until the day he dies, and he wouldn't complain even once."

I chuckle, already feeling more at ease just from this short interaction than I have since before my apartment burned to the ground.

"Why does that not surprise me?" Of course, Ronan eats the same things all the time. Definitely a creature of habit.

Carla laughs softly. "And please, please tell me you eat dessert," she begs, actually clasping her hands together in front of her.

"Of course, I eat dessert. Who doesn't?"

Her friendly face points heavenward and she sighs heavily, like it hurts her soul to even think about it. "Ronan doesn't."

I gasp. "What a heathen!"

Carla laughs and pins me with an affectionate look. "I can tell already that I'm going to like you."

I beam at her, the first real smile I've felt on my face since I got here. "Me, too."

I loiter at the kitchen island while Carla makes dinner. Unlike Ronan, Carla is just as much of an open book as me. She's fascinating. She tells me about her travels to different cultures, in which she learned about the cuisines of the world and fell in love with food. She's dating a Harley Davidson mechanic named Paul. She goes with him to Sturgis every year. I could totally see her being a biker babe.

"How long have you worked for Ronan?"

"Years. Almost a decade now, I think."

"So you must know him pretty well, then?"

Carla pauses over the stove, her spoon halting. "Hmm. You know, you might think that, but I really can't say I know much more about him than you do."

"Really? He's that secretive?"

"I don't think he's *secretive*," she says thoughtfully. "I think he's just busy and likes to keep to himself. Especially after his dad died."

I nod as she turns around and begins skillfully chopping some herbs at the counter in front of me. The aroma of pesto is perfuming the kitchen and making my mouth water. God, when was the last time I had a home cooked meal like this? I'm calling it right now, I'll be twenty pounds heavier by the end of next week if this is the kind of meal I'll be eating every day.

"But I *will* say to watch out for his mother. I've only cooked for her a few times, but damn...she is not someone you want to cross."

It suddenly strikes me that Ronan has a whole family I know nothing about. The only thing I've gleaned is that he and his mother seem to be at odds with each other.

"Why? What do you mean?"

Carla looks at me for a moment, trying to find the right words. "You know, you just have to meet her to understand."

Great. So helpful. I study Carla as she continues to move around the immaculate kitchen. I wonder if she didn't explain about Ronan's mother out of loyalty to him. Or maybe she just isn't one to get in other people's business. Either way, I'm annoyed, but at the same time, I respect her.

As for my mother-in-law, I deeply hope I can have a good relationship with her. The idea of having a mother in my life again fills me with so much warmth. Even if this thing between me and Ronan isn't love, I'm still marrying into a family. A new family. And after losing Melanie, I could really get behind the idea of belonging to a new family.

Maybe this new step with Ronan is a brand new start full of new people and friendships and possibilities. Things are changing, but for the first time, I really have hope that things are changing for the better. I just need to keep one foot in front of the other.

Ronan comes down for dinner, eats the delicious pesto pasta and garlic bread that Carla made, and goes back upstairs without looking at me or speaking to me. I'm pretty sure he was sitting at the island next to me for all of five minutes. That man eats like...like it's a *job*. Not like it's comforting or enjoyable or tasty. Does he enjoy anything in his life? Ever? Is he actually a robot?

I feel bummed when Carla leaves. Back to feeling lonely in this huge, quiet house.

Damn is it quiet.

I'm used to hearing my neighbors through the adjoining wall and sirens and loud car mufflers and jaywalkers talking at all hours of the day and night. But here? This place is freaking silent. It just keeps reminding me that this house is just...lifeless. Even with a living and breathing man upstairs.

I go back up to my room and pace around for a minute, feeling anxious again and still unsure about how to live here. I look through the folder Ronan mentioned, mostly to have something to distract myself with. To my surprise, I see on Ronan's calendar that he has a wedding to go to next weekend. Hmm. I wonder who Bodie is. I guess I'll get to be Ronan's arm candy sooner rather than later.

It isn't until about ten o'clock that I hear a knock at my door. I'm standing here at the foot of this huge bed, determining how the hell I'm even supposed to climb into it. This bed is so big, I feel like I could do one of those fancy high dives off an Olympic diving board onto it. I have never slept in a king-sized bed. It seems like a waste for just little ol' me. I could fit like three more people and a hippo in there.

"Come in," I say to the door, surprised to see Ronan's huge build filling up the doorway when he opens it. He's still wearing his suit and has a tired look on his handsome face. "Hi," I say happily.

I twist my legs together as I realize I'm standing here in nothing but a pair of gym shorts and a tank top. Ronan's eyes unabashedly eat up every inch of me from my feet all the way up to my face. There's no mistaking the heat that builds up in his blue eyes.

Did he just—did he just check me out? My armpits prickle. I guess I'm not so repulsive after all.

"After we get married tomorrow, we're going directly to the bank to get the funds transferred," he tells me without pretense.

"Okay."

He hesitates then, his hands in his pockets, with a strange look on the sharp planes of his face. It's like he wants to say something, but he doesn't know how. Maybe he's not good at socializing outside of business. Maybe he's awkward and that's why he hasn't met a girl all this time. For some reason, I find that kind of cute.

"Lance wanted me to check on you, make sure you're ready for tomorrow," he says gruffly, like he's been inconvenienced.

My eyebrows raise slightly in surprise. There's no reason Lance would have Ronan check up on me. If Lance wanted to know if I was ready for tomorrow, he would've called me himself. My heart melts a little, because I'm pretty sure that Ronan really is a softy.

"That's so sweet of Lance to be concerned," I comment with a smirk, folding my arms casually.

Ronan avoids my eyes, which is proof enough to me that he just lied through his teeth. That's the sweetest lie anyone has ever told me.

"I guess I'm just nervous," I reply, still studying him. "I've never gotten married before," I add with a soft laugh.

He nods. Shifts on his feet. Looks at his shoes. He doesn't have to say that he's nervous, too because his body language is oozing with it. I'd bet anything that he is not one to get nervous very often. Anything in the work realm of his life, he probably feels confident and in control, but here, with me in his house...not so much.

I realize instantly that I'm not the only one struggling with this crazy agreement. I mean, yes, I'm more than certain I'm not his cup of tea. But even besides that, it dawns on me that I'm encroaching on his safe place. And will be for the next two years. This isn't easy on him either.

My nerves settle slightly with that thought. No one else is involved in this but us. The future is contractually in our hands.

"But I guess we're in this together, huh?" I say gently.

Ronan's blue eyes finally find mine, and a benign sort of look crosses them as he realizes that what I said was meant to comfort him. He nods, his mouth a little less of a grumpy straight line than before.

"Are you settling in okay?" he asks, his deep voice even lower, like he doesn't really want to ask but feels obligated to.

"Kind of," I answer softly, glancing around. My eyes land on the frame on the dresser. My stomach flips. "It's a lot to get used to. And I'm just...thinking about my parents."

He looks over at the frame, too. I wonder if it occurs to him like it occurs to me that it's the only picture of people in the whole house.

"They were good people," I tell him, my mournful gaze still on the two people I love the most. "But I don't think they would've agreed with this." I sniff, fighting back the tears welling in my eyes. "I guess I'm just struggling with that."

"Does it matter? They're dead."

My head whips toward him in shock. His expression is completely unapologetic, almost blank. My pulse skyrockets at his cold response. I shouldn't be surprised, but I am.

"Of *course*, it matters," I argue angrily. No one, and I mean *no one*, gets to lessen the importance of my parents in my life. Even my future husband. "I want to make them proud with everything I do. I owe them that after—" My voice cracks with emotion, and I can't finish that sentence out loud.

I owe them that after they died in the same car as me. After I lived and they died.

A chill shivers through me.

Survivor's guilt is totally real. And I fought that shit for a year with a therapist. I had to beat it into my brain that it wasn't my fault. That I didn't need to mourn the fact that I was alive. That I had every right to be happy again. To move on from what happened. To think of my parents with fondness and not guilt. The only way for me to dig myself out of the guilt hole was by realizing that my parents would've wanted me to live as well as I could. They would've wanted me to love with my whole heart and cherish every breath I took.

So, yes. It matters to me what they would've thought about this platonic marriage.

Ronan's throat bobs, tipping me off to his discomfort.

"I didn't mean to be an asshole," he says quietly. "Obviously it *matters*...I just meant that, well, they're *gone*." He sighs in frustration. "This isn't coming out right," he mutters and scrubs his thick fingers through his dark hair.

My anger cools slightly as he tries to collect his thoughts. Every time I see the unpolished side of Ronan, I'm comforted. It's always a relief to know that he's human.

"I understand wanting to make them proud. I make a *living* by trying to make my dad proud." He finally looks me in the eyes. "He set up this stupid trust fund stipulation because it was his way of letting me know how much he wanted me to settle down with someone. He wanted me to love someone the way he loved my mom. But I *don't*."

With his pause, I feel the unnerving silence of the house again. His blue eyes stay on mine, and I can feel the passion in the words he says next.

"That doesn't mean that marrying someone I don't love would make him less proud of me. I know that. By doing this, we're ensuring that our futures are set. It's...*responsible*. Why the hell wouldn't your parents be proud of you for taking care of yourself like this? Especially after all the shit you've been through?"

I think this is the most he's ever said to me at one time. I'm sort of...flabbergasted.

It takes me a long moment to consider what he's saying.

I'm taking care of myself.

Yes, if they were alive, they would absolutely talk me out of what we're about to do tomorrow morning. But what Ronan is saying is that they *aren't* here to talk me out of it. And because they aren't, I have to take care of myself alone. Without them.

I know that I can't handle one more unexpected shitty pizza topping from Chef Universe. I know that if I didn't go through with this, I would flounder for the rest of my life trying to pay off my debt and somehow also try to live my life, not just survive it.

Ronan and Lance think I've suffered enough. And for the first time, I realize they're right.

I've paid those awful dues.

I deserve to rest. Because I haven't rested in *years*. I deserve to breathe freely.

A hot tear slides down my cheek, and I swipe at it quickly. "You're right," I croak out, nodding once.

His big body relaxes slightly.

"Thank you," I say, meaning it and then clear my throat. "I really needed to hear that."

He nods in acknowledgement and puts a hand on the doorknob. A beat of silence passes in, which I see him retreat back into professional Ronan.

"Be ready to go by seven tomorrow morning," he instructs stiffly.

"I will."

He steps out into the hall. "Night," he mutters, and closes the door before I can reply.

I plop down on the edge of the bed and look at my parents again. I sigh heavily.

"I'm taking care of myself," I whisper to them. "Please be proud of me for that."

Just because I'm not marrying Ronan for love doesn't mean I don't have to mean the vows we'll be exchanging tomorrow. I can love him as a friend. I can support him as a friend. Through thick and thin. Richer or Poorer. This arrangement doesn't have to be a complete sham. I can choose to make it mean something.

I feel my body relax a bit as I realize that.

I'm taking care of myself.

I'm helping more than just myself.

I'm going to mean my vows.

Even if my parents wouldn't be okay with this, I can at least sleep tonight knowing that I'm doing this for good reasons. Honest reasons.

I can only hope that Ronan is the man Lance says he is because the last thing I could endure is another man overpowering me.

Chapter Nine

Ronan

My stomach squirms on the way to City Hall. I'm nervous as hell, and it's really pissing me off. Mostly because Dani seems in a much better mood today and not nearly as nervous as me. I glance over at her sitting in the passenger seat. She's looking out the window as the city whizzes by, humming to herself.

Fucking *humming*.

But at least she isn't wearing a goddamn wedding dress. Just that purple dress she was wearing the day I met her. The familiarity of it is definitely a welcome feeling.

My hands tighten on the steering wheel as I try to deepen my breathing.

"You okay over there?" Dani's sweet voice asks.

I clench my teeth without looking away from the road. "Fine."

"Uh huh. So, you're holding onto that steering wheel for dear life because you're totally fine?"

I relax my grip, but my hands instantly tense back up again. "I just want to get this over with," I mutter.

Dani doesn't know this, but I was engaged once. I planned out an entire wedding that never happened. I almost went the way my father did—falling hopelessly in love with a beautiful, charming woman who only wanted my money. I guess, if I really think about it, I should actually thank my brother for fucking my fiancée, instead of blaming him for breaking us up. I dodged a serious bullet. Doesn't change the fact that I still hate Bodie's guts. I always have, really, but the feeling is mutual.

I shake my head slightly. I have no intention of telling Dani about all of that. But it's definitely one of the reasons I'm such a nervous wreck right now. I have a bad taste in my mouth from what I went through. And even though this isn't a real marriage, or whatever, my mind is still being dragged back into the past to when I lost everything I cared about.

Fuck, I should've gone for a swim before we left. I was up early enough. But I slept like shit and was too tired. When Dani joined me at the kitchen island at quarter to seven, I was taken aback by how good of a mood she was in. Not that she seemed comfortable in my house, which didn't surprise me, but she smiled at me and made small talk with me. Or she tried to. I just drank my coffee in silence while she chatted on about the time a pigeon shit on her when she was walking to work.

I realize, in retrospect, that she could probably tell I was nervous and hadn't slept well, and she was trying to distract me or cheer me up. Hmm. That was kind of her.

I take another deep breath and try to remind myself of what she said last night. We're in this together. Not *together* together. Just...collaboratively. Professionally. There's no deception. No betrayal. No love. Just business and money.

I pull into the parking ramp near City Hall and stalk distractedly toward the entrance, Dani trailing along slightly behind me. She takes in the huge building constructed of rose granite and the beautiful green, patina, copper roof. I don't have a reason to be at City Hall very often, but when I do, I usually take my time to appreciate the clock tower and the building's many pointy spires.

But today, it's all a rusty blur as I rush inside. Even the rotunda, featuring the Father of Waters sculpture, doesn't faze me. Dani gasps and lags behind as she looks up at the ceiling two stories above us and then appreciates the marble-covered walls.

"Come on," I mutter over my shoulder, and she scurries to my side again.

I find Lance and Gina waiting for us at the information desk.

Lance shakes my hand heartily with a big smile on his slightly weathered face. I frown at him in return, mostly because he seems way too happy that I'm about to become a married man. I could tell myself that his smile is just because he knows that this is the day everything becomes final and the trust fund money will officially be snatched out of my mother's hands. But there's a twinkle in his blue eyes that reminds me of when he pushed for that stupid relationship clause. Like he knows something I don't. Like he thinks I could actually fall in love with this girl. Apparently, I need to have a private conversation with him about just how determined I am to ignore her.

It wasn't hard to ask Gina to be a witness, mostly because she didn't ask questions and just listened as I gave her the information she needed for our little ceremony today. It's one of the reasons she's such a good assistant. She only asks the important questions. The rest, she works out for herself.

I make quick introductions between Dani and Gina, and then Dani passes out hugs like candy. She beams at both of them with such brightness that it paralyzes me for a second.

Damn, I'm not used to that sort of warmth. My mother never breathed a warm word in my direction from the day I was born. I don't know what the hell I ever did to deserve it, but Bodie has always been her favorite. As I've gotten older, I muse that they just have more in common. They both care way too much about how beautiful they are and not damn near enough about people's feelings. Like mother, like son.

If there's any proof at all that love is blind, it's how my father blindly loved my mother. He didn't see her selfishness or vanity. All he saw was charm and laughter and beauty. He was incapable of seeing her flaws. And as much as I love my father, I always thought it was incredibly stupid.

Until I met Sadie.

Falling in love with her was...effortless. She was funny, and cool, and wasn't bored by what I did for a living. She made me feel important and valued and seen. Now I'm realizing I fell so hard for Sadie so quickly because she was everything my mother wasn't. Or so I thought until everything fell apart.

The receptionist directs us to wait outside the nearest doors for the judge to welcome us. Across from the closed oak double doors are a handful of chairs. Everyone sits but me. I pace because it's the closest thing I can get to the back and forth of swimming.

Gina knows me well enough to at least pretend not to notice my nerves, but Lance and Dani watch me like it's a sport as I stride back and forth. My footfalls echo slightly in the open corridor.

"For Pete's sake," Dani pipes up after several moments, "you have enough nervous energy to blow up the entire town! Just take a deep breath, man. We're getting married, not walking the plank."

Lance chuckles and tries to cover it with a cough. Gina continues to look elsewhere.

I pause and glare at Dani, who looks amused and exasperated, then resume my pacing.

Damn her and her calmness. Sitting there so still and chill. Like this isn't a big deal. I would give anything to just skip this part. Why do we even have to say all the vows and shit? Why can't we just fucking sign the document I need and get the hell out of here?

"Why aren't you nervous?" I vent at her but keep my voice down.

"Oh, I'm nervous, too," she says with a soft laugh. "Just apparently not as much as you."

I roll my eyes, still pacing.

"Ronan," she says softly, getting my attention. I stop, and she gives me a warm, comforting smile. "I know this is crazy. Believe me, I know. But everything is going to be okay. We're in the same boat, setting sail for the same destination, okay?"

We're in this together.

But I don't want us to be. I want to be left the hell alone. But that isn't an option. Not if I want this money. *My* money. So, it doesn't matter how I feel about it. This has to happen. With Dani.

I growl and fall back into pacing. Dani just shakes her head and mumbles something that sounds like "nervous, stubborn man." I'm pretty certain Lance "mhms" in agreement.

A few minutes later, the doors open, and Judge Murphy appears. I rush forward with my hand outstretched.

"Good morning, Judge," I greet tensely, shaking his hand. "Thank you again for getting us in on such short notice."

"Absolutely." Judge Murphy is a balding, portly man in his early seventies. He shakes my hand firmly and gives me an easy smile. "This must be your lovely bride?" he asks, referring to Dani, who is suddenly standing at my elbow with a bright smile.

"That's me," she answers and shakes his hand excitedly. "So nice to meet you."

Damn it, why is she so happy? Did she make up with her friend? Did moving into my house finally get her to understand how much better her life is about to become? I never thought I'd feel relieved that the bubbly, lively Dani is back. But at this moment in time, the relief is wearing off. Her lighthearted demeanor is just rubbing on my nerves and making me feel like a chump who can't get his shit together.

What happened to my professionalism?

But I know why I can't master myself right now. If this were a business meeting, I'd be in my element, but *this*? Getting married? This is something I never wanted to do. I still don't. But I don't have a choice.

Just suck it up, man.

"This is Lance Bertram and Gina Taylor, our witnesses," I introduce. They shake hands with the judge as well.

"Come on in, everyone," he says, gesturing into the room with one hand.

Dani takes my arm and pulls me gently. "Come on, *sweetheart*." Her touch is enough of a distraction to get my feet moving.

I catch Gina's eyes ping-ponging between me and Dani as we move forward, like she's trying to understand how I've had a secret fiancée all this time. But it doesn't matter. I just need her to sign that she witnessed me getting married.

We head to the front of the expansive, wood-paneled room. There are handfuls of benches that remind me of church pews and a huge, oak podium facing them. I can feel my breathing grow shallow as Lance and Gina follow, with Judge Murphy bringing up the rear once he closes the doors with a heavy thud.

The silence of the room just makes it easier to hear how fast my heart is beating. I swallow hard and try to focus on the judge as he comes to stand in front of me and Dani.

"Well, congratulations to the two of you," he says, smiling widely at us. Dani beams back.

"Thank you." She glances at me and hops on the balls of her feet slightly. "Big day."

"Big day, indeed," he agrees. "Now, you folks may sit," he gestures to Lance and Gina behind us, and they take a seat on the first row of benches. Judge Murphy turns his round, brown eyes to me. "Now, let's go over what will happen here today, just so everyone is on board."

Yes, a plan. I can get behind a step-by-step logistical plan. That's what I need to get myself to focus on the present and not on the past when I nearly married a heartless gold digger.

"So, I'll be starting with a few quick thoughts about what we're here to do today, and then we'll get to the vows. Have you written your own vows today or—"

"No," I interrupt, my deep voice echoing slightly in the large space. "Just the standard vows are fine." I don't give a shit *what* he wants me to say; I just want to get this over with.

Judge Murphy glances at Dani, who thankfully nods in agreement. It wouldn't surprise me at all if she had prepared some weird poem or a song or something.

"Great. Then once you two are officially married, you and your witnesses will sign the marriage license. We can go over details about that afterward."

I shift nervously on my feet, nausea rolling through me. What I wouldn't give to just press fast forward right now and get to the marriage license.

"Sounds great," says Dani.

"Ready to get started?"

Yes, for the love of God, let's start and get this over with.

"Yes. Let's do this," Dani replies, and I catch a hint of nerves in her voice. When I look down at her, she gives me a brave smile.

Judge Murphy clears his throat and clasps his hands around his belly. "I believe that marriage is a special calling," he begins evenly. "Not everyone can learn to compromise, communicate, and appreciate another person enough to commit their lives to them, and learn to do it all willingly. My advice to new couples is to never stop being a student of your spouse. The more you learn about each other, the better you'll be able to enjoy your relationship and grow with each other through the years."

Just the next two, I think to myself as I shift on my feet and dart my gaze anywhere and everywhere. Dani listens intently to the judge, taking in every word. I wish he'd stop talking already and get on with it.

"Marriage is all about mutual respect and mutual kindness. Those two things will get you through the hard times. Be open. Be mindful. Be committed. I have no doubt that if you fall back on these principles, your marriage will stand the test of time. And I deeply hope that for each of you." He takes a moment to smile sincerely at both of us, only getting a smile in return from Dani.

"Alright, enough of what I think," he says with a chuckle. "If you'd join hands, please."

Dani reaches out her little hands to me without hesitation. I grimace at them slightly, then bring my hands to hers. They're warm and soft and bring me even more into what we're doing here, which is exactly what I don't want.

"Ronan, please repeat after me."

I nod. My pulse quickens, making me even more nauseous.

The image of me and Sadie deciding how we wanted our vows to be worded floods unwelcome into my mind. We were sitting outside in the grass behind her house, arguing lightly over this word and that phrase. It seemed important that we agree on what we were promising each other. I wanted to make sure that I meant what I said on our wedding day, and I wanted to make sure our vows were a promise I would be able to keep for the rest of my life.

What a load of shit that all turned out to be.

Judge Murphy clears his throat, and I snap back to the present. My hands tense around Dani's.

"I, Ronan Michael Wells, in the presence of these witnesses, do take you, Danielle Marie Sanders, to be my lawfully wedded wife."

I swallow hard, my mouth feeling dry, and quickly repeat it without looking at Dani.

"To have and to hold from this day forward," continues the judge.

"To have and to—"

"Hold it," Dani blurts out. She lets go of one of my hands and puts one palm up to Judge Murphy. The whole room stops breathing. My heart pumps hard in my ears.

"We need a minute," she says, looking at me intently.

"What?" Shit, is she backing out?

"Oh—uh, is everything okay?" Judge Murphy asks with concern, clearly thrown off.

"Yes," Dani assures him kindly. "I just need a moment with my fiancé." She tugs on my hand with a strength that surprises me, and I follow her out of the room and into the hallway.

"What are you doing?" I hiss at her the second the doors close.

"Me? What are *you* doing? You're a hot mess in there!"

My jaw clenches. What the hell does she expect? I can't pretend I'm in love with her or even pretend I want to be here.

"Listen, I know that what we're doing isn't your typical marriage. There's no romantic love between us, and we barely know each other. Like, I get it. This is weird. Bonkers, even." She takes a breath, and her face softens. "But I don't take vows or oaths halfheartedly. And I don't want you to either."

My head jerks back. Is she serious? How can I wholeheartedly say these wedding vows if I don't love her? If I don't *ever* plan on loving her?

"My parents' marriage was so much more about friendship and companionship than it was about feeling madly in love with each other."

"...Okay?" My parents' marriage was a one-sided disaster, so I'm really not tracking with her.

"What I'm saying is, I have every intention of doing the things I'm about to vow to you. When I say I'll be by your side for better or worse, richer or poorer, I *mean* it," she tells me passionately. Her hazel eyes sparkle as she continues, leaving me mesmerized. "Even though we don't have any plans on being in a loving romantic relationship, I still promise to be your sidekick. Your cheerleader. Your confidant. I'm your girl, Ronan." She steps closer, and my knees shake just slightly at the earnestness in her expression as she looks up at me. I've never had a woman speak to me like this. "I promise to always treat you with respect and kindness, Ronan. To be on your side. To support you and your goals. And I don't promise you these things because of a contract or because some judge says I should. I promise because you're a human being, just like me, who deserves to be treated that way."

My heart beats wildly at her words. Not even Sadie, who was actively trying to convince me that she loved me, said things like this to me. Dani is a woman who believes in doing what's right...for the right reasons. She probably couldn't lie even if she tried.

I'm floored. How in the hell is this girl still single? By far, she is the most beautiful woman I've ever met, inside and out. She's fucking amazing.

Shit.

I...I think I like her.

"So, let's go back in there and get married based on *those* principles. Okay?"

I take a deep breath, willing my body to settle down. Get married on the principles of *friendship*. She wants this to be more than an aggrandized roommate agreement. Not because she has intentions of this becoming something romantic, but because she's incapable of saying words she doesn't mean.

I roll my shoulders back as I try to bring myself on board with what she's asking me to do. Not roommates. Friends. Friends who support and respect each other. Fuck, when have I had any friends who've done that? All the other trust fund babies I know couldn't care less about anyone but themselves.

And then, I realize with a pang that I belong in that category. Yes, I'm glad this money is going to help Dani, but she's only been a means to an end. She's only been a name on a contract to me. After Sadie, I haven't given a damn about anyone but myself. My dad would be ashamed of the man I've become outside of work.

Dani is promising to be a good friend to me and asking that I promise the same thing. Sadly, she's asking for something I haven't been willing to give anyone in years. But if I don't at least try, my mother will take the last thing my father left me.

"Okay."

She smiles, looking pleased and a little relieved, then turns to open the doors. Before I can stop myself, I reach out and grab her hand. My heart pumps in my ears when she looks at me.

"I'm sorry if—in there—I didn't mean to be disrespectful," I stammer out awkwardly. I owe her respect if she's dead set on showing it to me, for no other reason than that it's the right thing to do. My dad would've expected the same out of me.

She smiles and squeezes my hand. "I know." She nods toward the doors. "Let's go."

Feeling strengthened, we go back in. I think maybe I underestimated this girl. I realize now why Lance said he trusts her. She's a good person. And I don't have a lot of good people in my life. No wonder I didn't recognize it in her.

But can I really be for her what she wants to be for me? Can I support her dreams? Be in her corner? Am I even capable of showing this girl any kind of genuine love, even if it's an altruistic kind of love shared between friends? I'm not sure I remember how after all this time.

But it seems Dani can't marry me without it meaning something. I admire that. But I also know I'm getting in over my head.

When we're standing in front of Judge Murphy once more, he looks concerned and so do Lance and Gina.

"Is everything okay?"

"Yes," Dani says with a smile and takes my hands again. "From the top, Judge."

He looks at me, uncertainty wrinkling his bushy gray eyebrows, and I nod. He clears his throat. "Ronan, repeat after me. I, Ronan Michael Wells, in the presence of these witnesses, do take you, Danielle Marie Sanders, to be my lawfully wedded wife."

I look away from the judge and down at Dani. She smiles at me encouragingly. I take a deep breath.

Don't think about Sadie. Think about Dani. Think about being friends with Dani.

"I, Ronan Michael Wells, in the presence of these witnesses, do take you, Danielle Marie Sanders, to be my lawfully wedded wife," I repeat slowly, looking into Dani's hazel eyes. She nods slightly, as if to say, *you got this, kid.*

"To have and to hold from this day forward," prompts Judge Murphy.

"To have and to hold from this day forward."

"For better, for worse, for richer, for poorer, in sickness and in health."

I repeat the words, meaning them in the context of friendship, until he gets to the next line.

"To love and to cherish, till death do us part."

I hesitate for a moment, but I think about what Dani said in the hallway. Love and cherish her as a friend. As a human being. That's what I mean. And I know that as I repeat those words, Dani understands.

"Okay, now Dani. Repeat after me."

Dani says the same words to me but says them so meaningfully that I swear I hear Gina sniff behind us. Her voice holds so much sincerity that I'm actually ashamed that I ever believed Sadie when she said something I thought was genuine.

"Now, do you have rings to exchange?" the judge inquires, looking from me to Dani.

"No," I reply. We don't need them. We just need to sign the marriage license.

"Oh, my gosh, I forgot all about rings," Dani whispers, her eyes wide. Then, she gasps. "Wait! I have some!" One hand plunges into the depths of the purse hanging at her hip, and she brings out a yellow envelope.

"What? You—" I stop talking when she pulls out two silver rings from the bottom of the envelope.

She looks at them lovingly, her eyes filling with tears. "They were my parents' rings," she explains softly.

My heart skips a beat. We absolutely can't use those rings. That makes this so much more personal than I want it to be. I lean down toward her a little, wishing the judge wasn't standing right there.

"Dani, we're not using your parents' rings," I argue sternly.

She looks down at them and swallows hard before her eyes move back up to mine. "Can we just use them for now? We can get new ones later or whatever." Her tone is so gentle and hopeful that I would feel like an asshole if I said no, especially in front of the judge.

"Fine," I mutter.

Judge Murphy eyes the two of us questioningly, and then Dani nods at him. I'm sure he's never officiated a wedding ceremony like this one.

"Great," he exclaims and claps his hands once. "Ronan, please place the ring on Danielle's finger."

My stomach rolls as Dani hands me the small, silver ring. It's just a simple band without any frills or engraving. For some reason, that comforts me. I turn it over in my fingers once and then reach for Dani's left hand.

"Repeat after me, Ronan. With this ring, I vow to love and honor you from this moment forward. May it serve as a reminder of the lifelong commitment we made here today."

I slide the ring onto her finger and repeat him. As the words fall out of my mouth, I feel a strange tingling sensation in my chest and the hairs on the back of my neck stand up.

"Now, Dani, place the ring on Ronan's finger."

She smiles and takes my hand. She slips the plain, silver band onto my finger easily, and I'm surprised by how well it fits me. It's comfortable, like it was made for me.

Dani repeats after Judge Murphy, looking sweetly into my eyes as she does. My heart pounds a little harder.

"And now, by the authority vested in me by the state of Minnesota, it is my pleasure to pronounce you husband and wife. Ronan, you may kiss your bride."

My head whips toward the judge. Shit. I forgot about that part. How could I forget about that part? The panic must show on my face because he looks confused.

"What? Uh, no. No. We're not kissing."

"Sorry?"

Don't get me wrong. Dani is a beautiful girl with enticing lips. If I wasn't marrying her, I'd have no problem saying that yes, *hell* yes, I'd like to find out what it's like to kiss her. But kissing her now, like this, I can't do.

I look at Dani for help and find a deeply amused expression on her face. Damn her, she's enjoying this. But judging by the light pink blush on her cheeks, I don't think the kissing part of the ceremony crossed her mind either. She visibly stifles a giggle and looks back to Judge Murphy.

"He's extremely shy about PDA," she explains simply, "but don't worry." She steps in close to my side and holds onto my arm, which tingles slightly from her touch. "We'll kiss on it later, right, honey?"

I swallow hard. "Yes. Later."

The judge looks beyond bewildered, but seems to accept Dani's explanation. "Uh, in that case, I now pronounce you husband and wife. You may kiss...later."

Lance and Gina clap, which reminds me that they even exist, and when their echoing applause dies down, the judge comes a little closer and puts a hand on each of our shoulders.

"I truly wish you both a very happy life together. Best of luck to you."

"Thank you," says Dani, and hugs him.

The judge pats her back and looks at me in surprise, probably wondering how the hell a guy who can't kiss his wife at his own wedding ceremony ended up with a huggy sweetheart like Dani.

She pulls back and then goes to hug Lance and Gina. I take the marriage license out of my suit breast pocket.

"So, we sign this now?"

"Yes," says Judge Murphy, producing a pen from his pocket.

We gather around the podium nearby and each sign it. I feel incredibly good seeing everyone's signatures there. This is it. I did it.

I'm married.

I heave a long exhale of relief. I'm so fucking glad that's over.

The judge tells us he will file it immediately and that we'll be getting a marriage certificate in the mail. He gives me a copy of the signed marriage license, and then sends us on our way.

I feel about fifty pounds lighter as we head out to my car. And not only because it's done and over with. Dani is more than I expected. She doesn't mess with people and can't do anything half-assed. I'm impressed. And hell, I feel kind of fortunate to have her in my corner. I think I owe Lance big time.

Now, off to the bank to get my money. I mean, *our* money.

Chapter Ten

Dani

Oh, my gosh, he made that so much harder than it had to be. I mean, yeah, it's a weird situation, but honestly. Dude couldn't pull himself together without me spilling my emotions and intentions all over him. Yeesh.

But, I have to admit, it was more than a little hilarious when the judge told him to kiss me. Oh, the look on his face...just sheer *terror*. I wish I had a picture of it. I'd plaster that sucker on every surface of his bedroom on April Fool's Day. I was really close to just puckering up, but I couldn't do that to the guy. He had finally settled down his nerves. I didn't have the heart to plant a big, wet one on him. I'm sure it would've been a terrible kiss anyway—with it being forced like that. Besides, we're friends now. And I don't kiss friends.

To be honest though, I was really surprised to see him so nervous. I'm so used to him being all composed and professional. I've never seen him like that—just a ball of nerves. I can't help but wonder what that was all about, but he seems better now that we're on our way to the bank to transfer the trust fund money.

I guess I should be feeling pretty ecstatic about that. I'm about to become a freaking millionaire. But all I can think about is pushing my dad's ring onto Ronan's finger. All I can focus on is the fact that I just got married. I'm a married woman. I'm someone's *wife*. I look down at my mom's wedding band on my finger.

I know this whole situation would've been something my parents couldn't understand. But I hope that I've somehow made them proud today. Because I could have definitely just said the words and not meant them. I could've just straight up lied, but I chose to make my vows to

Ronan mean something. Not just to me but to him, too. Even if my parents wouldn't be proud of me, *I'm* proud of me.

Yeah, girl.

When we get to the bank, Lance and his mother's lawyer join us in the lobby, and then we're all ushered to the office of some fancy bank executive who probably makes way more money than he ought to. Without even any introductions, everybody gets down to business. Ronan produces the copy of the signed marriage license, I flash my ring finger at the banker like that's just as good, and I watch my new husband's handsome face as everything is verified and the funds are transferred.

He hasn't said a word to me or even looked at me since we entered this room, but when he sees the numbers change in his bank account, he puts his eyes on me and holds my gaze. A strange look crosses his features. Is that...is he about to *smile*? I've never seen his face do that. Ooh, I like it.

Then, he turns back to the banker—I glance at the plaque on his desk, Mark Miller—and tells him to put half of what was just transferred into my bank account. My fingers start tingling as I watch Mark do his thing. With just a few clicks and taps on the keyboard, there is suddenly fifty million dollars in my bank account. Just like that. Bam. *Millionaire.* Oof, I just got chills.

I look back at Ronan, tears in my eyes. I reach over and squeeze his beefy arm. I hope he knows how thankful I am. This is literally changing everything. And I know that the second I get back to the house, I'm going to pay off every single one of my outstanding bills. By this time tomorrow, I will be absolutely debt free. I'm relieved beyond words that I'll never be in the red ever again.

Ronan's mother's lawyer leaves the room without a word. Lance beams at me and does the same, apparently his work being done.

Mark gives me a box of checks to use until my debit card comes in the mail.

"Do you want any cash withdrawn?" he asks me, and I pause.

When was the last time I withdrew cash just for the hell of it?

"You'll probably need some to buy a dress for the wedding this weekend," Ronan suggests. "Not many shops take checks. A thousand should do."

My jaw drops. A *thousand*? For a *dress*?

Fancy Banker Mark just nods and produces a wad of cash out of nowhere with a little receipt, like it's nothing. I reach out and take it with shaky hands. I don't think I've ever held this much money in my hands. It feels...strange. Like power and freedom and guilt all at once.

Ronan thanks him and shakes his hand while I try to stop blubbering like a baby. He leads me out of the office and out to his car. Even with how crazy overwhelmed I am right now, I notice the pep in his step.

"I'll take you back to the house, but then I need to go in to work," he tells me as we drive away millions richer.

"Sure, thanks."

He takes a turn that heads down a familiar street. My heart thuds in my chest as we approach the cemetery where my parents were buried. I swallow hard and look down at my mom's ring again. The guilt resurfaces and punches me in the gut.

God, I have some nerve, don't I? Marrying a guy for money with *their* rings. My stomach sinks. Maybe I'll feel better if I talk to them.

"Actually, will you drop me off over there?" I point at the cemetery.

"Over there? Why?"

"I need to talk to my parents," I answer quietly. "I'll just take an Uber back to the house."

He pulls into the one lane road that runs along the first row of headstones and then parks. Then, he turns off the car. I look over at him. He's gazing out the windshield thoughtfully, his blue eyes hidden behind his sunglasses.

"You don't have to wait for me."

He sighs heavily. "My dad is buried here, too."

"What? Really?"

He nods. "It's been a while since I've visited him. Let's go." Ronan gets out of the car, and I follow. We enter through the gate and face the landscape of headstones. Some are richly adorned and look brand new. Some are cracked and weathered. The grass between is lush and well-kept, and the trees bordering them are mature and shady, casting lingering shadows across the quiet grounds.

"I'll meet you here when you're done," he says, and strides off in the direction of an elaborate headstone over in the corner.

I clear my throat and wind my way over to my parents. I didn't go overboard on their headstone. I couldn't. It's simple without any decorations or fancy script. But I made sure to at least get something appropriate. Something that would honor them.

I approach their names slowly, my emotions rising. There they are.

Lincoln Robert Sanders.

Marie Alice Sanders.

I sink down to my knees in front of them and smooth my plum dress over my thighs.

"Hey, guys," I begin with a trembling voice. "Sorry it's been so long. I've been crazy busy." I study their names and sniff. "I really miss you. It's been really hard without you here. So, please don't be mad at me for this...but...I—I did something." I swallow and press on painfully. "I know you wouldn't have approved of it. But there's sort of no going back now. I got married, so I can pay off my debt." I cover my face and cry for a moment because saying the words out loud to them just...hurts. "I'm sorry. I know this is not what you imagined for me. But I think everything will be okay. He's a good man."

I look over at Ronan. He's standing at his father's grave with his hands in his pockets, his brown head tilted down.

"He's already taken better care of me than anyone has before. He's nothing like Spencer, I swear." Yikes, Dani, don't talk about him. "Ronan is kind of sweet, and he values hard work just like you always taught me." I turn back to my parents. "I hope you know that I love you both, and I know how crazy this is...but I promise to use the money responsibly. Now that I have a lot, I promise I'll use it to help those who have a little. I know that would make you proud."

I twirl my mother's ring on my finger. "I love you. I hope you guys are living it up and not worrying about me. You don't need to anymore."

I stand up and take a step back. "See you around."

When I turn, I see Ronan standing at the gate waiting for me. His sunglasses are in his hand, giving me a clear view of the solemn look on his face. But there's also a look of curiosity and respect as he gazes at my parents' grave behind me.

I have the strange notion to invite him over to introduce him, but I tamp it down and join my new husband.

Ronan's blue eyes study my face for just a moment, and then he nods toward his car. I nod, too, and we drive home silently.

As he pulls to a stop outside the house, his pocket rings, and he takes out his phone.

"Hey, can I call you back? I'm in the middle of something. Thanks." He hangs up and puts his hand back on the steering wheel, looking out the windshield.

In the middle of something? I don't get out, just waiting, because I'm assuming he's about to say something.

He looks at my dad's ring for a moment. "What were your parents like, Dani?"

My eyebrows raise just slightly. That's the first personal question he's ever asked me. I clear my throat. "They were amazing," I reply softly. He continues to avoid eye contact. "They were hard working people who treated every person the same, no matter where they came from or what their social status was." I take a breath, and he waits for me to go on. "They loved each other and me very much. They were tough when they needed to be, but they were always very supportive of me, too. They wanted the best for me."

When I stop, he only nods. So, I continue on quietly.

"I think you would've liked my dad, actually. He was the quieter one of the family. My mom was much more outgoing. I definitely get my spunk from her." I smile to myself. "My dad would've shaken your hand and taken interest in your work. My mom would've commented on how handsome you are and said something awkward like how cute our babies would be." I chuckle, and when I look back to Ronan, he's looking at me, too, but there's a sadness in his eyes that I've never seen before.

"You would've liked my dad, too," he says softly. "He was good to people and did everything for everyone. He was always laughing and charming people. You would've really gotten along with him."

I smile at him gently. "You miss him?"

He nods and looks back out the windshield. "Every day."

I sniff. "Me, too."

I'm starting to understand why Lance thought Ronan and I would hit it off. We've had the same loss. And even though we've shared very little with each other so far, I feel encouraged that he's opening up to me about his dad. This moment makes me feel much more bonded to him. Though, I definitely got goosebumps when we said our vows. Damn, his blue eyes looking at me so meaningfully. I don't think I'll ever forget that.

"Thank you for letting me use my parents' rings today. It meant a lot to me. Made me feel like they were there with us."

Ronan gives me a soft look verging on affection.

"I want you to keep wearing it." My heart pounds as I say it. I feel very vulnerable, like suddenly I'm sitting here naked with all my lady bits showing.

He studies me for a moment, and I desperately want to know what he's thinking. *For Pete's sake, buddy, just say what you're thinking for once.* But instead of saying anything in reply, he looks back at the ring on his finger and nods.

"Anyway, thank you. I should let you get back to the office."

He makes no move to indicate that he's ready to leave, so I wait to see if he's going to say something else. After a long moment, he clears his throat.

"I would like to be there when you pay off your bills," he says finally, watching his big hand flexing on the steering wheel.

"Really?"

He nods. "Is that okay?"

I smile at him, even though he still isn't looking at me. "Yeah, sure."

"And—" he pauses nervously and sighs. "Thank you for getting my head on straight at City Hall."

I smile bigger. "Hey, what's a wifey for?"

He says nothing and then puts the car in reverse. That's my cue. "I'll wait up for you. Have a good rest of your day, Ronan." "You, too."

I thoroughly enjoy filling Carla in at dinner. Her enthusiasm makes me feel so good. I love that she's excited for us. Happy for us. *This* is what I miss about Melanie. I miss having a friend to share everything with, both the good and the bad. I wish I could call her and tell her how freeing it is to no longer have any financial limitations. I wish I could tell her that Ronan is a good man. A man I think I could have a good friendship with. A man I think I can actually trust. She would know how big of a deal that is for me.

But I can't call her. I won't lie; it really freaking hurts to be abandoned like that. I know this is a crazy situation, but I'm becoming less sure that what she did was warranted. I guess it doesn't matter now. It's a horribly painful thing to realize that Mel is a part of my old life. I don't want to leave her behind. It feels too much like the loss I feel over losing my parents.

There's no getting around the fact that everything is different now. This house is *my* house now. I have a freaking private chef. I could go buy literally anything I want. I don't have to look for a job or worry about money ever again.

This is absolutely a new life. A shiny, brand new life.

And even though it's been a crazy whirlwind of a week, when I pay off my bills tonight, I'll be starting completely over again. I can finally have the freedom to live my life and actually enjoy it. I'm about to have control over my life for the first time since my parents died. All because of Ronan. And Lance. I don't want to let go of Mel or the things I've learned about myself while I've struggled to get to this place. But I have to keep moving forward or else I'll forever be stuck in the past.

So I need to settle in here as best as I can. I need to pay off my debt. I need to find a way to help people with the money I've been given. I need to support Ronan, who became my friend and husband today.

This is how I move forward.

Ronan gets home about seven. I feel a zip of nerves when I hear the door open and he steps into the kitchen. I look up from my seat on the couch.

"There he is," I say, and feel a little stupid. Did I mention I still break out in a sweat whenever I see him? Cause I do. And probably even more so now that he's officially my husband. I'm *married* to that hunk. He's *my* hunk. Well, kind of. "How was your day?"

"Fine," he answers vaguely. His tall body hovers in the space between the kitchen and the couch somewhat uncomfortably. He glances at the TV over the fireplace. I'm watching *Chopped.*

"Ever watched it?" I ask, gesturing to the TV.

He shakes his head, seeming disinterested. He clears his throat and looks down at me snuggled up against the arm of the couch.

"If you want, you can come up to my office. We can pay your bills on my computer."

"Sure, yeah," I say brightly, and hop right up. It's been hard to wait for Ronan. I'm way excited. Totally an eager beaver about this.

I'm not sure why Ronan wants to be there when I pay my bills. I wouldn't expect him to care about my old life. Maybe he just wants to see what his money is doing for me. Maybe he thinks I need back up, and this is his way of supporting me. Such a mystery, that man.

I follow his tight butt up the stairs and down the hall, pausing on the threshold of his room. There's really nothing personal about his bedroom. No family photos or possessions with any meaning behind them. Just furniture. It looks like it could be anyone's room. It's that nondescript. Clearly, his room is only for sleeping.

I take a breath and move through his room to the office door, where I find Ronan bent over his huge wooden desk, peering at his computer monitor. I smile at the way his serious face is lit up by the screen.

His office looks more comfortable, oddly. The entire wall behind his desk is a built-in bookshelf packed with books. I love it. There's a framed picture of a swim team on a random shelf. His college diploma is on another. On his desk are a few more picture frames, but from here, I can only see the backs of them. Ronan looks up when he realizes I'm just standing there by the door, looking around. When my eyes land on his, I smile warmly at him. I feel like this is his place—his safe place—and I'm in it. It feels like an honor. A privilege.

He nods me forward, and I join him behind his desk. The pictures here are of him and who I assume is his father. I see Ronan at a few different ages. As just a small boy, grinning up at his dad and holding his hand. He couldn't be any older than seven or eight. Another of him as a teenager, handsome even then, though far less muscular, standing with his dad in a hallway. I almost choke on my own spit to see the smile on Ronan's face. Big and broad, full of perfectly straight teeth. He has a freaking beautiful smile. The last picture is of him, probably not long before his father died. It's a candid shot of them laughing, both of them looking handsome and happy in their suits and ties.

I notice there isn't a single picture of his mother or any other family he might have. Just further proof to me that he and his mother aren't on good terms.

"Here," Ronan says, snapping me out of this tiny peek into his personal life that I so desperately want to know more about. He pulls out the leather desk chair for me so I can sit.

"Oh—thanks." I take a seat and set myself to the task at hand—paying off every cent I owe.

Ronan watches silently over my shoulder as I plug in the banking information on each website. With each bill I pay, I feel more emotional. By the time I get to the last one, I feel like I'm about to burst. It's the hospital bill, which is the biggest one, and I pause before hitting the pay button.

This is it. This is everything. Everything I've been killing myself over since my parents died.

I take in a deep breath, and for the first time, I feel Ronan looking at me. I exhale and click. The payment is accepted, and I feel like I've been slapped in the face with emotions.

Relief. Joy. Gratitude. And then...sadness?

I cover my face with my hands as the tears overcome me. My chest hurts. *Just breathe, Dani.* Does this mean I have to move on now...without them? I only just realized how much this debt connected me to my parents. My debt is all I've been able to focus on all these years. So, now that it's paid, what do I do?

"Are you alright?" comes Ronan's quiet voice. There's a tenderness to it that I haven't heard before. It comforts me.

"I could use a hug," I admit with a soft laugh that I don't really mean. I feel him stiffen next to me, and then I really do laugh. I drop my hands and turn to look at him, smiling through the tears in my eyes. He's still bent over from looking over my shoulder, so the sharp features of his handsome face are closer to me than I expect. He looks nervous as hell that I'm about to throw my arms around him. "Oh, Wellsley," I murmur warmly. "Thank you. For everything."

And then something happens to him. I *see* it happen in his eyes as he looks back at me. It's like they...*open*, and that serious, distant man eases into the background. And in its place, I see the real Ronan. My heart is doing a drumroll in my ears as he lets me in for the first time. A warmth escapes him, and it's so much better than any hug I've ever received. My smile deepens as a peace comes over me that I've never known before.

Wow.

And then, I can't help it, I wrap my arms tightly around his broad shoulders. But as soon as I touch him, I feel that warmth disappear. Like a spell being broken, businessman Ronan snaps back into place, and the vulnerable Ronan evaporates. I release him quickly, realizing I've made him uncomfortable.

"Sorry," I mutter awkwardly and stand up to leave. "I'm a hugger," I explain, though that doesn't make me feel better. I clear my throat, heading for the door. "Thanks for letting me use your computer and stuff." I give a weird kind of wave and book it out through his bedroom and into the hallway, then I close myself in my room.

I blow out a long breath, feeling a little stupid, but then my smile returns, and I feel giddy and overjoyed and encouraged. Maybe it was just a second, but it was there—I felt it. There's something in him that he doesn't let anyone see, but I saw it. I feel so good. It gives me so much hope for the future. I know for sure that everything is going to be okay. There is nothing holding me back now. I'm a free woman.

I can *breathe* now.

Chapter Eleven

Dani

Ah, what a beautiful day. Day one of my new life. Day one of no debt.

I didn't know what this would feel like. I mean, I knew that I'd feel relieved. And I do, but it's much deeper than that. I feel like the tension in my shoulders that I've been holding all these years has finally relaxed. I can actually sleep *well* because there's no worries keeping me awake at night. Every bill is paid. Even my little dinky cell phone plan. Not one thing outstanding. I didn't think I would ever get to a point in my life where I wouldn't owe someone something.

I've been panicked since I lost my job, worrying because no one was calling me back. But now...I don't need a job. What a breath of fresh air that is.

I've never felt so...uninhibited. Except for the married part. But still. It's freeing.

And tomorrow is Ronan's birthday. Obviously, I can't not celebrate it because celebrations and fun are things I live for. So, I've set myself the task of making it the best birthday he's ever had. And now that I have some money, I can actually afford to make it amazing.

So, I buy balloons and a few party decorations as well as those noise maker things you blow into. I text Carla to ask if she can make some cupcakes tomorrow, and she joyously agrees. Even if Ronan doesn't like sweets. Heathen.

I call Gina and ask her to hand out notecards to his employees to write a quick birthday wish—in secret, of course—so that I can do a little surprise with them. And when she tells me that no one has planned anything for him at work, I obviously order a sheet cake with his face on it to be delivered tomorrow. Gina scanned in his photo from the directory for me. Did I mention how much I like Gina? She is so helpful.

Planning these fun things for him makes me so happy. My parents always made a big deal about birthdays. They always found a way to make things fun and special, even on a budget. But the nice thing about my situation is that suddenly there is no budget. And what better way to show my appreciation to Ronan than spending my new money on his big day?

Like I said, I'm pumped.

But when Ronan comes stomping into the house at three o'clock, I'm stunned to see him. Why is he home so early? He rips off his suit jacket and then grips the granite countertops. I can feel the tension radiating off him from all the way over here. For just a second, my mind flashes to Spencer and the way his anger felt around my neck, but I brush that off as I come closer.

Why is he so upset? My stomach drops. Oh, no. Did he find out about all the surprises I have for his birthday tomorrow? Is he mad?

"Ronan? What's wrong?"

He sighs almost violently and answers me through clenched teeth. "My mother will be here in fifteen minutes."

I inwardly gasp. *His mother.* I'm going to meet his mother. My new mother-in-law. I quickly look down at myself and assume that I'm underdressed.

"Oh, wow. Okay. I'm going to change quick," I blurt out both nervously and excitedly and bolt upstairs.

I really don't have anything very nice. Even though I just wore it yesterday, I throw the plum dress over my head. It's casual, but definitely better than jean shorts. I put on some mascara at lightning speed and look myself over in the mirror in my crazy lavish bathroom. I fluff my long hair with my fingers and shrug. It'll have to do.

When I get back downstairs, Ronan has poured himself a drink at the kitchen island. He downs the rest of it as I walk in.

"Here," he says gruffly, his eyebrows pulled low over his stormy eyes, and pours me a nip of whiskey.

"Oh, I'm good."

"Trust me, you're going to need it." He holds the glass out to me, and I take it nervously. I'm going to need it? I take the amber liquid down in one gulp and wince as it burns down my throat. I'm much more for rum than whiskey.

The doorbell rings, and Ronan's broad shoulders tense even more. With a deep sigh, he strides to the front door, and in walks the most beautiful, terrifying woman I've ever seen.

She's dressed smartly in a red pencil skirt and one of those blouses that has a decorative tie around the neck like a scarf. Her blonde hair is pulled back away from her pristine face and striking, *perfect* features. Even though she must be past middle-age, she looks decades younger. There isn't a wrinkle in sight, not even laugh or smile lines.

When her brown eyes land on me, she gives me a beautiful smile that also reads cold, which confuses me. She comes closer, walking confidently through the foyer toward me. Even though she's a thin woman, her presence dominates the open space. I get the feeling that this is not someone to be messed with.

"Ah, here she is. Your new *bride*," she says with that same cold smile.

Ronan follows tensely. I'm caught off-guard by the strange air of defeat about him. He usually has such a strong, stern aura.

"Yes, hi. So nice to meet you," I say brightly. "I'm Dani."

"Victoria Wells." She offers a hand with perfectly manicured, red fingernails that match her skirt and her lipstick. But instead of shaking her hand, I just hug her. Because even though this woman is a strange mixture of beauty and iciness, I'm desperate for a motherly presence in my life again.

But just like her son, she doesn't hug me back. My heart trips in my chest as I pull away.

Damn it, why do I have to be such a hugger?

"Sorry," I say with a smile and a nervous chuckle. "I'm just really excited to meet you."

She studies me with a calculating gaze for a moment, then glances at Ronan as a cruel laugh escapes her. He looks at me almost apologetically.

"How did you meet her, Ronan? Was she just the first woman to throw herself at you?" She laughs to herself and saunters into the living room like this is her own home, her heels clicking loudly on the marble tile.

I stare at Ronan in shock. Uh, did she really just say that? Right to his face? He doesn't look even slightly surprised or hurt by what she said. It's like he was expecting it. Almost immune to it. This can't be good.

"Where's your help?" comes Victoria's demanding voice from the kitchen. "Or do I have to serve my own tea?"

Ronan steels himself, and I follow him into the kitchen. Victoria is standing by the kitchen island impatiently and gives me a long, scrutinizing once over as I come closer. My nerves ramp up as Ronan silently puts on a tea kettle to boil.

I was not expecting this. I knew Ronan had some beef between him and his mom, but I wasn't expecting her to be so beautiful and yet so...frosty. And I thought *Ronan* was kind of frigid and serious. He has nothing on his mother.

"Tell me," she snaps at her son, studying me with a smile that doesn't reach her criticizing eyes. Yup, she's downright terrifying.

For a moment, I'm clueless about what she's asking him, but he seems to know exactly what she means.

"I met her through Lance Bertram," he replies with his back to us as he takes out three coffee mugs from a cabinet by the stove. His voice sounds distant. Hollow. It makes my heart hurt. What the hell happened between them to make him sound like that?

Victoria's eyes narrow on me at the mention of Lance's name.

"He was a good friend of my parents," I explain, even though she didn't ask me to.

She taps her fingernails on the countertop distractedly for a second and then huffs slightly. "And what do you do, dear?"

"I'm a waitress. Or, I was, before all this." I wave my hand vaguely.

Her perfectly arched eyebrows twitch and then raise in amusement. "A...*waitress*?" She glances at Ronan, who is still busying himself with making tea. She laughs cruelly again, and I feel the blood rush to my face. Ooh, she's definitely one of those people who yell at servers like they're not human beings. "And which establishment did you work for? The kind that requires you to serve food with your clothes *on* or *off?*"

My jaw drops, and my heart threatens to pop out of my chest and slap her in the face. Is she really asking me if I was a stripper? I hear Ronan exhale heavily and look over at him. His eyes are burning, but he says nothing. I'm starting to understand why he said I would need a drink. I gather myself and look back to my mother-in-law, intending to set her straight, especially since Ronan seems to have no intention of speaking up.

"I worked my ass off at Ben's On Main for four years trying to pay off my parents' medical bills after they died in a car accident," I explain fiercely, trying to keep my voice even.

Victoria's amused expression doesn't change. "Good for you."

I narrow my eyes slightly at her. I'm becoming suspicious that this woman doesn't have a heart. Unlike her son, who I'm almost positive has a caring and soft side, Victoria most definitely doesn't. Ronan pulls the hot kettle off the stove.

"Don't, Ronan. Let the waitress do it, since she has so much *experience*," she instructs smugly.

A rush of heat hits my neck and face. Oooh, no, she didn't. I clear my throat.

"I would be happy to, *Mom*," I say, which turns her face sour. Pleased with myself, I take the kettle from Ronan and pour the boiling water into each mug. Truthfully, I'm an extremely service-oriented person. I love helping people. But apparently, that's a trait to be looked down upon for, according to my lovely new mother-in-law.

Victoria watches me for a moment and then goes to take a seat on the edge of the couch. I try to catch Ronan's eye as he helps me bring the mugs and tea to the coffee table, but he's completely shutting down. He's dissociating. I feel my anger bubble up even closer to the surface.

I have an evil thought to "accidentally" spill my mother-in-law's hot water all over her lap, but I restrain myself. My parents taught me better than that. Even if Victoria isn't the warm and loving mother-in-law I was hoping for, it's still important for me to be respectful. For Ronan and for myself.

"So," she says, adding a tea bag to her hot water as I sit beside Ronan on the opposite couch, "I suppose congratulations are in order for the two of you. My lawyer informed me you were married yesterday by a Justice of the Peace."

Ronan just looks at her, his gaze stern and slightly defensive.

"Thank you," I say, mostly to fill the silence. I watch her take a sip of her tea. She eyes me over the rim, swallows, and places the mug on the coffee table.

"And here I thought you would never get even close to tying the knot again. Not after what happened with Sadie," she says with a smirk, as if she knows it will sow discomfort in her company.

Ronan's fist clenches next to me, and his entire body seems to clench along with it.

"Do you love this one, too, or is it just for the money this time?" she asks him directly, smiling evilly.

"Yes," he replies calmly. "Dani and I have an understanding."

Her eyebrows raise just slightly when I put my hand on Ronan's fist. He doesn't flinch or stiffen like he did last night when I hugged him, and I'm deeply grateful.

"An *understanding*? I see." Victoria glances at my hand and laughs, seeing it completely devoid of a giant diamond ring.

Did she just *laugh* at my mother's ring? How dare she—?

"So, tell me then, Dani," she says, smiling maliciously, "how do you feel about children?"

This time, Ronan goes completely rigid. I look at him to find pure hatred in his eyes, like he's trying to light his mother on fire with just his stare. I'm completely lost as to the reason for this. Is having children a sore subject for him? It doesn't matter, in our case, being that we aren't in love, and children were definitely not included in our contract.

Victoria grins with satisfaction. She sees the confusion on my face. "Some men aren't meant to be fathers, you know," she continues conversationally.

Ronan starts to shake. I hold his fist tighter, like that's the only thing I can do to keep him from exploding like a bomb.

"Well, not *good* fathers, anyway. I personally think Ronan would make a *miserable* father. Besides, he could never measure up to his own father, rest in peace." She forces a loving look that's meant to portray her devotion for her late husband and then immediately reverts to her sinister glare.

My body feels hot. I've never rage-sweated before, but I am right now. My ears are ringing as her words register in my brain.

Obviously, I don't know much about Ronan's family, but it's clear to me that he loved his father. If there's anything he doesn't deserve, it's to hear something so hurtful coming out of the mouth of his own mother—and purposely so.

I don't remember standing up, but suddenly, I'm on my feet. "Get out," I demand through clenched teeth.

Victoria laughs softly, like I'm just some silly little girl.

"I mean it," I assert, my voice shaking with anger. "*Get out.* You aren't welcome here if you're going to insult my husband to his face."

Ronan looks up at me in surprise. Victoria's amusement wanes when she realizes I'm serious.

"You can make whatever assumptions you want about me. You can insult me up and down all you want. But Ronan? No. I won't allow it. So, get out. And don't come back until you feel like apologizing."

She looks from me to Ronan, as if no one has ever spoken up against her before. It's clear that he certainly never has.

I point at the door and wait for her to move. She doesn't. Her face finally morphs into a disgusted, hateful expression. Suddenly, I realize just how deeply ugly she is. Her perfect outward appearance is completely worthless.

She stands up and seems much more threatening, even if she isn't much taller than me. "How *dare* you let this slut talk to me like that?" she seethes at her son.

"It takes one to know one," I bite back. I can feel the adrenaline pumping through my body as she gapes at me. An angry blush mars her pale skin.

"You've disgraced this family by marrying this woman. Do you hear me? You're a *disgrace!*"

"Get out!" I shout before she can say anything else.

"I've never been treated like this in my entire life!" she spouts indignantly as she stalks through the house to the front door.

"Well get used to it, lady!" I call after her. "And good riddance!" The door opens and then slams shut.

Silence falls as my chest begins to heave. That could not have gone worse. All of my hopes are completely crushed. I whirl around and book it outside as my emotions take over. I step down off the deck, my hands shaking, and begin to pace like a wild animal in front of the pool.

Here I was, looking forward to being part of a family again—having a mother figure in my life again—and Victoria showed up and broke my heart. Angry tears start to well up in my eyes.

It was so foolish of me to get my hopes up. Especially because Ronan gave me no reason to think that his mother would even be excited to meet me or get to know me. Maybe this is all my fault. Maybe I brought this on myself. All my loneliness and pain from doing this alone made me desperate to hope that I could belong somewhere. Losing my parents left such a void in my heart that I threw myself into the idea that I could be part of a family again.

Ronan appears on the deck a moment later. He says nothing. Just stands there and watches me self-destruct in front of him.

"That woman—" I choke out, pacing, "is the most—" I sob, "*awful* person I have ever met!" I wipe at my face, but it does no good. More tears fall. "What kind of mother speaks to her own son like that?" I lift my long hair off my neck, feeling warm. "The mother of the devil, probably."

Ronan continues to silently watch me pace. His calmness just eggs me on.

"And here I was thinking—" I shake my head and sniff. "Here I was thinking how amazing it'll be to have a mother again." I feel like chucking myself in the pool. Dunking my head in that fountain to wash away the words of that vile woman. "I'm such an idiot. I don't know what I was thinking." I pace a few more times, trying and failing to stem the steady flow of tears.

"I should've warned you. I'm sorry."

I stop and look at Ronan. He does look sorry. He has a weary, pained look on his face. My sympathy for him returns full force. How has he endured that woman all these years?

I sniff again and fold my arms. "What the hell is wrong with her? Has she always been like that?"

He nods, expressionless.

"Your dad must've been a freaking saint," I mutter, but he hears me. I take a few deep breaths, finally getting myself to calm down a little. "I'm sorry I lost it like that, but I just couldn't handle her saying one more completely unfounded, shitty thing about you."

Ronan looks down at the deck steps.

I hate that there's so much I don't know about him. I wish I knew how to make this better. I wish I knew what he was thinking and feeling. I wish he would just open his damn mouth and enlighten me. I'll give him credit for apologizing though. That's more than I ever got from my ex-boyfriend Spencer—and let me tell you, that asshole owes me one huge freaking apology.

I wipe at my eyes, finally mastering myself. "I meant what I said. She's not welcome here until she apologizes to you."

He looks up. "And to you." He swallows hard. "I shouldn't have let her—" He stops and shakes his head. "Over the years, I've just gotten used to letting her say whatever the hell she wants to say because it's easier than fighting with her about everything."

Damn it, Wellsley. I really want to hug him right now. Like bear hug his whole body. But I'm scared he'll freeze up like he did last night and pull back from me ever further. It's kind of unfortunate that I married a guy who doesn't like to be touched, when my go-to for any issue or emotional event is to hug it out.

"How can I make this better?" I ask pleadingly. "Please tell me how to fix this."

He sighs. "Dani, this has nothing to do with you and everything to do with my mother hating me." He digs his hands in his pockets and averts his eyes as his cheeks flush just slightly. "But thank you. Fuck, I think you're the most selfless person I've ever met."

I smile at him. "And I'm all yours, buddy."

Something happens to his mouth. It's not exactly a smile...more like just less of a straight face. I'll take it, honestly. At this point, I'm deficit in the warm and fuzzy department. Though I must say, this moment would be perfect for a secret handshake. And a drink.

"So can we drink the rest of that whiskey now, or...?"

He nods toward the house, and we go inside. All of this majorly messed with my plans to get everything together for Ronan's birthday tomorrow. But right now, I need to drink away this painful little meeting with his mother. I'll get to birthday plans later. Because if there's one thing I'm sure of, it's that Ronan deserves to have one hell of a 30th birthday.

Chapter Twelve

Ronan

I slept like shit.

My alarm is about to go off any minute, and while I typically would just get up and get on with it, I'm still lying here in bed, too tired to get up. After Dani and I finished that bottle of whiskey, I was pretty worthless for getting any more work done. I ended up downstairs in the gym, unable to sit still. Then, I swam laps until I could barely climb out of the pool.

Despite the exertion I put myself though, my mind would not let me rest. I tossed and turned all night, replaying bits and pieces of the conversation between my mother and Dani.

I should've defended her. Just the day before, I vowed that I would be in Dani's corner. And when that moment came, I did nothing. I did what I always do when my mother shows up. I pack myself away into the furthest corner of my mind so that I can keep myself from reacting to whatever bullshit she spews at me. So that I can keep myself from breaking again.

Because like I told Dani, this is nothing new. My mother has always put down everyone she meets, except my father and Bodie. Anyone else is a waste of space, of her time. I'm just a discarded wad of gum stuck on the bottom of her shoe.

I should've told Dani that. I should've explained what was coming. Instead, I said nothing like I always do, and she got caught in the crossfire. It broke me up to hear her say she had been hoping to have a mother in her life again. If I had warned her, she wouldn't have gotten hurt. If I had acted like a real man, I could've prevented it.

The alarm jolts my eyes open, and I slam my hand down on it to stop its harsh sound. I sigh and heave myself out of bed to get ready for work. I notice the bags under my eyes as I brush my teeth. I feel the fatigue of my muscles as I shower. I haven't taken a day off in literally years, but today, I consider it. But no, work is what I need to take my mind off of how shitty I feel about yesterday.

I grab a suit at random from my walk-in closet and fumble with each zipper and button. I don't even bother with a tie. Fuck, it's going to be a long day. I need coffee.

As I gather my things from my office, my phone dings in my pocket. I take it out and see a text message from my brother waiting for me.

I sigh and open it.

Bodie: *Happy Birthday, Asshole.*

I roll my eyes. How kind of him to even remember. Three dots wiggle below his text, and then another message appears.

Bodie: *Mom says you're a married man now. She sounds like a fucking firecracker. I hope she puts out for the big three-oh. When you're done with her, send her my way.*

Ronan: *Fuck you.*

His response is immediate.

Bodie: *Fuck you, too.*

I shove my phone back into my pocket. Goddamn Bodie. He'll never change. He's always been a selfish asshole intent on taking anything that means something to me. Even when we were kids, he was constantly taking my favorite toy or my new bike or asking out the girl he knew I liked. Then, there was Sadie. The bad blood between me and my brother runs deep and as far back as I can remember.

Hopefully once he marries Cara, he'll be too caught up in wedded bliss to mess with me and Dani. Though I doubt it.

In an even worse mood than before, I head back out of my office to the bedroom door. When I open it, I jump back in surprise at the enormous deluge of balloons pouring through the doorway into my room.

"What the fuck?"

Dani's door across the hall bangs open, and she leaps out with a huge smile on her face. "Happy birthday!" she shouts, and throws a balloon at me.

"Have you lost your mind? It's six in the morning."

"Oh, believe me, I know what time it is. You get up so early. It's ridiculous." She claps her hands and excitedly bounces up and down in her tank top and gym shorts. I don't know why, but the sight of her completely dressed down turns me the hell on. "Get ready, Wellsley," she says with bright eyes. "Today is going to be the best birthday you've ever had."

Shit.

I look at her warily. "What the hell have you planned?"

"Ah-ah-ah, you'll just have to wait and see. Can't spoil the surprise, now can we?"

"Dani..." I growl warningly. She should have been able to guess that I hate surprises. Apparently, I should've stipulated a strict no surprise clause in our contract.

She mimes zipping her lips closed, locking it with an imaginary key, and then chucking it over her shoulder.

I sigh heavily. Damn it, I should've known she would do something like this. I couldn't give two shits that it's my birthday today, but of course, she would. I look down and wade my feet through all the multi-colored balloons and out into the hallway.

"Have a good day, Wellsley!" Dani calls as I walk downstairs. She waves to me from the catwalk, full of excitement.

Damn it, she's so cute when she's excited. I stifle that thought and head out to the garage. There's a note on the driver's side window of my Rolls Royce. I hesitate, wondering if the thing will explode with confetti if I open it. I cautiously lift the flap and peer inside. To my relief, I see just an ordinary card. Nothing crazy whatsoever.

I open the car door and get in before taking it out to read it. Her handwriting matches her personality. Light-hearted. Fun. Cute.

Ronan,

Happy 30th Birthday!

I don't really know you well enough yet to know what to get you for your birthday, and honestly, you probably have everything you want anyway. So, just enjoy today and know how grateful I am that Lance introduced me to you. You're the best husband I've ever had!

Love, Wifey

I know she's making a joke there, about me being the best husband she's ever had. But for some reason, that sentence stays with me as I drive to work. It's the first time since my mother showed up yesterday that I've felt any semblance of calm. I still can't believe how passionately she defended me. I'm starting to understand just how deeply she meant what she said on our wedding day.

I don't want to admit it, but she's already starting to wear me down. I'm already hooked on her smile and ridiculous enthusiasm for life. She's shown me nothing but respect and consideration, and hasn't tried to push me too far or ask me to bare my soul to her about the toxic relationship I have with my family. She could've asked about Sadie. She could've asked why I physically shook next to her when my mom brought up having children and being a father. But she didn't. And I'm so fucking grateful she didn't.

I feel like Dani's inherent warmth has been making its way into my chest, curling around and softening the hardness of my heart. And it feels...good. My head is telling me not to lose my edge, to not get wrapped up in this girl. But my heart purrs every time I see her.

When I step off the elevator at work, my tired mind is still humming with thoughts about Dani. But when I get to Gina's desk, I'm immediately caught off guard by how she smiles at me. Typically, we just give each other a brief hello before we go over the day's schedule.

"Happy birthday," she says knowingly.

"Shit," I mutter. "What did she do?"

Gina's mouth squirms as she tries not to grin. She nods toward my office door, indicating I should find out for myself. My stomach clenches as I grasp the door handle and try to mentally prepare myself for whatever is on the other side.

I open the door and step in to see about a dozen gold balloons hovering behind my desk in front of the window. Each one has a little square of paper tied to the ribbon at the end. I come closer to investigate and quickly discover that each little paper has a written note on it.

My heart races as I reach for the first one, unsure of what to expect. It's from Greg, our IT guy, wishing me a happy birthday. The next one is from Susan in accounting. And then there's one from Tony, our maintenance guy. And ten more—every note full of well wishes and kindness.

Fuck. I'm really touched.

I have a good relationship with everyone who works for me. I make sure to always create a work environment that contains mutual respect and appreciation for hard work. It's my job to make sure they're happy. My dad taught me that. Treat your employees well and they'll do their best for you in return. I guess I just never stopped to wonder if my team cared about me.

When I've read them all, I step back. My thumb absently twists the wedding ring on my finger, something I'm already prone to doing even though I've only worn it for a couple of days. Dani didn't have to go to this much trouble for me. Just her little card would've been more than I was expecting for my birthday. This just speaks to how beautiful of a person she is. I make a mental note to do something nice for her on her birthday, and then I call Gina in so we can get to work.

She comes in with her tablet, smiling to herself. She pauses by the chair and looks at me pointedly. "I really like her," Gina says warmly.

I nod, not knowing what to say to that. "Did you help her with this?" I ask, gesturing to the balloons behind me with my pen.

"I did. Is that okay?" She eyes me questioningly.

"Sure."

"I thought there was a chance you'd be mad. I told her you might not like it."

I shrug.

"You know, being that we've *never* celebrated your birthday here before," Gina hints.

"What are you trying to get at?" I demand directly because I really don't know why we're talking about this. I'd like nothing more than to get to business and steer away from my personal life.

She smiles in an amused sort of way and then sits down. "I think she's good for you."

I narrow my eyes slightly. "Good for me?" Scaring the shit out of me at six in the morning is good for me?

Gina's expression softens. "I think she's just what you need. I'm really happy for you."

I sigh quietly. "Thank you." I clear my throat. "Alright. Let's get down to it," I say heavily, nodding toward her tablet. "What's in store for today?"

"Oh, you just wait," she mutters.

The balloons in my office were nice. That was a good surprise, I'll admit it. But the huge cake with my face on it? Not as much. The singing flower delivery guy that bellowed out *Happy Birthday* for the whole floor to hear holding a dozen red roses? Not. As. Much.

Good for me. Pfft.

Gina loved the singing delivery guy, by the way. I'm pretty sure she got the whole thing on video. She also told me to get home at a decent time, and I almost refused. The things Dani has planned have escalated in embarrassment all day. So, if I walk into my house to a surprise party filled with tons of people, or if she's hung streamers from every tree in the yard, or asked the neighbors to parade past the front door, I'll be leaving.

When I come in through the garage, I'm relieved that no one shouts surprise or serenades me. I glance around to see a few party decorations, but nothing overboard. I find Carla mixing a salad by the sink. She looks up and smiles at me.

"Happy birthday, boss," she whispers.

I narrow my eyes suspiciously. "Why are you whispering?"

She chuckles and nods toward the living room. I pocket my keys and warily investigate. At first, the living room looks totally empty. No Dani in sight. But then, I look down and see her curled into a little ball in the corner of the couch, asleep. This crazy woman is asleep with a cardboard party hat on her head and noise maker clutched in her hand.

"She said she was up late getting everything ready for your birthday today and got up early this morning," Carla explains softly from the kitchen. "Then, she went shopping for a dress for the wedding on Saturday. She passed out right there telling me all about it."

I sigh and lean a hand on the back of the couch. Fuck, I can't even try to be mad at her for the embarrassing things she did to celebrate my birthday at work today. Not when she literally exhausted herself to do it all. I fight the impulse to reach down and tuck her brown hair behind her ear.

"I think you found yourself a keeper, there," Carla says, coming closer to look at Dani, too. "She's a real sweetheart."

"Yeah," I say wistfully, and then I clap my hands in Dani's serene face and shout, "Up and at 'em!"

Carla smacks my arm.

Dani awakens with an almighty flinch and immediately puts the noise maker to her mouth. She blows, still bleary eyed, and then seems to realize the asshole way in which I woke her up.

"Wellsley!" she exclaims indignantly, and clutches her chest. "You scared me!"

"Serves you right for scaring the shit out of me with those balloons this morning."

Carla chuckles and goes back to the kitchen.

Dani gets off the couch, wobbling slightly. "I think what you mean to say is *thank you*."

"Thank you? I'll thank you for never doing it again."

I can see her trying to be mad at me, but she can tell I'm just giving her shit. It's adorable the way she scrunches up her nose like that.

"I'll never do it again if you wear a party hat while you eat dinner," she challenges. She puts her hands on her full hips and grins at me.

I shake my head. "No way in hell."

She giggles. My heart skips. "Then you better prepare yourself for an onslaught of balloons. I'm talking *all* the balloons, Wellsley. When you least expect it."

I stare her down, but she doesn't waver. I hate how much I like it. I hate how much she makes me feel.

"Just make him eat a cupcake," Carla calls from the kitchen. "They're so good!"

Dani smiles at Carla and then me. "They look really good, too. The most handsome cupcakes I've ever seen," she hints teasingly.

I raise one eyebrow at her, and she giggles again. She comes around the couch, grabs my arm, and leads me into the kitchen. On the counter next to the fridge is a plate full of cupcakes with white frosting, and each one has a picture of my face stuck into it.

"For fuck's sake," I mutter.

Dani laughs heartily. "I'm sorry. I couldn't resist."

I drag my hand down my face.

"Next year, I promise I won't go so overboard. I just really wanted to make it special," she says sweetly.

I look at her, hit with the realization that a year from now, she's still going to be here. And another year after that. That should scare the shit out of me, but it doesn't.

Why doesn't it?

"You have to admit, it's been a pretty special day," Carla pipes up as she opens the oven to check on the baked potatoes. "My man better step it up for me, that's what I think."

Dani smiles at her, and when she looks back at me, I understand that she's not like everybody else. No one has ever done something like this for me. My dad was the only person who made my birthday meaningful. To everyone else, it's just another day.

But to Dani, my new wife, who I've known for barely two weeks, this day is important. She did everything she could think of to celebrate me. I feel deeply humbled and incredibly lucky.

Her smile lessens as I think this, and I realize too late that I've let my feelings show on my face.

I clear my throat and step back. "What's for dinner?"

Dani's eyes light up. "Your favorite, of course."

I'm surprised that she knows what I like to eat. I'm guessing she's been hanging around Carla. It isn't a personal topic, but it's weird to realize the things Dani is learning about me. Though I'm sure in time, she'll learn plenty of things about me because she's Dani and has every intention of being a good friend and confidant. Even this early, I can tell that much.

"I'll throw the steaks on now, if you're ready," Carla says, looking to me for direction.

"Sure. I'll be back in a minute." I head through the kitchen and glance over my shoulder to see Dani jumping in to help Carla with dinner preparations.

I go upstairs to find the balloons from this morning are nowhere to be seen, and no more of them are waiting to surprise me in my bedroom or office.

I take off my suit coat and plop down on my bed. I'm exhausted, but damn, do I feel invigorated by talking to Dani. It hasn't even been a week of her living here, and I'm already liking the sound of her voice flitting through the floor from downstairs. I'm already noticing how much more alive this house is with her in it.

I'm already noticing the change in *me*. Because my heart softens a little more every time she smiles at me. There's something deeper than words between us, something even stronger than the vows we made. And surprisingly, I'm comforted by it. Her friendship comforts me.

I didn't want anything to change, vowed it, even, but maybe this kind of change is good. Maybe her presence in my life will be an asset, even with the surprises.

And maybe Gina is right. Somehow, Dani is good for me.

Chapter Thirteen

Ronan

It's Friday. Most people would be happy about that, but I'm much less so. Tonight is my first contractually required dinner with Dani, and tomorrow is my brother's wedding. I'm nervous for the former, and completely dreading the latter. If Dani hadn't already bought a dress, I'd suggest we just not go.

I know my mother and brother won't let me get away with marrying Dani privately, days before Bodie's wedding. Or even just marrying Dani at all. My mother forgets nothing. And she's pissed off about me getting the trust money, and of course, Dani kicking her out of my house. Our house. I'm fully expecting a scene of some kind will be made that will somehow make me look like an asshole. I intend to be there only as long as I need to.

As for dinner with Dani tonight, I'm assuming she's going to ask me a million questions that I won't want to answer. Maybe I can just ask all the questions so she does all the answering. I'll admit, she's growing on me, but the more she makes me feel, the more at risk I am for wanting more.

My former ideas of how I was going to live my life the exact same way after marrying Dani were tossed out the window when I agreed to be friends and companions. And after she stood up for me to my own mother, I can't help but feel an awed respect and even fondness for her. She's a good woman. And that's becoming harder and harder for me to ignore.

I make sure to get home right before six. Carla has dinner ready, and Dani is setting the dining room table when I walk in. She whips around when she hears me come in, a bright and beautiful smile on her face that frankly makes me feel really fucking good. She's wearing that purple dress again. Apparently, she only bought a dress for my brother's wedding and nothing else new. Not that there's anything wrong with her go-to purple dress. It certainly highlights her curves in a way that I'm both enjoying and cursing her for right now.

"There's my favorite husband," she says happily. My face heats up just slightly. I awkwardly nod at her.

"It's chicken parm tonight, boss," Carla informs me. "Dani insisted on family style." She brings a baking pan of chicken to the table. Dani grabs a small bowl of spaghetti and sets it down too.

"Make sure you grab some for yourself, Carla," she says with a smile.

"Oh, I've got a date of my own planned tonight," Carla replies. "But thank you, sweetie." She gives Dani a quick hug and then pats my arm as she makes her way out of the house.

"I wasn't sure what kind of wine you like," Dani says, holding two bottles of wine and reading the labels. "I don't know the first thing about wine." She chuckles. "Box wine is fancy for me."

I remove my suit jacket, feeling nervous and hating it. "Pick whichever you want."

She notices my disinterested tone, and her smile slips a little, making me feel like a jackass. I sit down at the head of the dining room table. Why do I even have this big of a table? When do I ever have that many people in my house?

"Alright, you know the rules. Gimme your phone," she says, holding out her little hand.

I sigh and remove it from my pocket. She removes hers from the pocket of her dress and places our phones on the far kitchen counter. Then she sits down, too and immediately begins serving me.

I feel weird watching her pile pasta and chicken on my plate, but it smells delicious. The sunlight through the huge windows next to the table is just beginning to fade, casting a glow onto Dani's sweet face. She's a beautiful girl. Understated yet unmistakable. And that sweet smile is quickly becoming my undoing.

"Carla let me cut the tomatoes," she says and then chuckles. "A horrible idea, actually. I almost sliced my finger off. Sometimes, my excitement to help gets me into trouble." She places food on her plate as well and then looks up at me with bright eyes. "Eat up, Wellsley."

I nod and do as she says. It's delicious, as always. Carla has never let me down with her cooking. Dani takes a bite and moans.

I stare at her, suddenly a different kind of hungry. I know I shouldn't let my mind go there, but I'd have to be dead to not react to that sensual sound. I can't stop myself from imagining her beneath me in my bed, moaning in pleasure as we move together as one. A flash of heat douses my upper body in sweat.

I mentally shake my head and try to think of something to talk about.

"So, tell me what you've been up to the last couple days," I request quietly, cutting into the cheesy chicken so I don't have to look at her while I ask. Since my birthday, I haven't seen much of her. When I get home at night, she's usually watching TV in the living room or hanging out in her room. I haven't engaged her in much conversation, which disappoints me just as much as it relieves me.

"Me? I've been doing some research, actually." She cuts her chicken into pieces and pops one in her mouth.

"Research?" I look up at her. "Shit, you didn't Google me did you?"

She laughs softly. "No, I didn't." She eyes me suspiciously, her full bottom lip quirking to the side slightly. "*Should* I?"

"I mean, you won't find anything bad if you do."

"Yeah? No naked pictures of you floating around the internet?"

"Fuck, I hope not."

She laughs again. The hearty sound of it eases the tension in my shoulders. This house feels so much more alive with her laughter lilting through it. Her presence here makes everything feel different.

She swirls her fork in her spaghetti, seemingly stalling. "I was researching foundations and charities." She hesitates, keeping her eyes on her plate. "I'm thinking about maybe starting one."

I pause my cutting. "You want to start a foundation?"

"Yeah. Or maybe a scholarship or something. I'm never going to use all this money. Might as well do something amazing with it, right?"

I watch her for a moment, impressed. She doesn't want to spend the money? I guess she wasn't lying when she said she didn't want the full amount. I like that she wasn't just putting on a show to get in my good graces.

"You'd be surprised how fast it can go after a shopping spree or two." Sadie used to drain bank accounts like nothing. Now, of course, I know why.

Dani looks at me incredulously and gives a humorless laugh. "A shopping spree? Let me tell you what would happen if I went on a shopping spree, Mr. Wells. I'd come home with a couple hundred dollars worth of Target brand clothing, and then feel so guilty about it that I'd probably just end up either returning it or donating it all."

I take a sip of wine and set down my glass on the wooden tabletop. The light from the window illuminates its contents, making the wine look like blood.

"I'm sure you could find more expensive things at Target. You could get yourself a new phone or—"

"Why would I do that when what I have works perfectly fine?"

I hold her gaze. I'm not used to that kind of attitude when it comes to possessions and money. I mean, I definitely don't splurge on every top of the line device, but I'm not opposed to upgrading if I need to. I wouldn't blame her for getting herself a new phone, at the very least, being that hers is probably a decade old.

"Anyway, starting a foundation seems super challenging." She pushes her spaghetti around with her fork some more. "I don't know if I have the brain for it."

I frown slightly and watch her take a bite. It doesn't sit right with me to hear her talk about herself like that. Though, to be honest, I have no idea how smart she is. And even if she doesn't have "the brain" for business, that doesn't mean she doesn't have other strengths or talents. Again, no idea what those might be.

Instead of saying any of that, what comes out of my mouth is, "Well, there are plenty of charities and foundations out there that you can donate to."

She nods, looking at her plate again. I'm about to retract my statement and try again for something more supportive or encouraging, but she goes on.

"Do you give to charity?"

"Of course," I reply simply. "It's tax deductible. I'd be stupid not to."

She gives me a thoughtful look, like that never crossed her mind. I'm sure it hasn't. With the debt she had, there's no way she was able to give to charity.

"You just have to be careful which ones you donate to because some charities are essentially scams designed to look like charity. Most of their donations get used for paying their employees or funding the catering at their events instead of going to the people who really need it."

Dani freezes, her fork hovering halfway to her mouth. "What? Really?"

I nod, giving her a pointed look.

Her eyebrows furrow in disappointment and she puts her fork down with a clatter. "That really sucks."

I put my fork down, too, hating to see how disheartened that made her. But it's important to look into that kind of thing. When you have a lot of money, it's vital you make sure you know where it's going. I'm glad she's talking to me about this first, before she decided to give five million dollars to a charity that couldn't care less about the disadvantaged or needy. I swallow and lean toward her just slightly.

"If you really want to help people, Dani, then help them directly. That's what I do. There are so many people out there who are struggling financially every day, just like you were. Helping homeless people get a job is much easier if you do it yourself instead of throwing money at a charity to do it for you."

She looks at me in awe. "That's what *you* do?"

I shrug. I've helped a handful of people over the years get off the streets by hooking them up with a job at either my company or a friend's. Every single one of them have flourished and made the most out of the opportunity I gave them. My dad believed in giving people chances, and I haven't forgotten the faith he had in strangers.

I guess he passed that on to me in more ways than I realized. Because I wouldn't have married Dani if I didn't have faith in her to be every bit the good woman she is.

She looks away, her eyes brighter again. "You're right. I should just get out there in the world and do it myself."

The conviction in her voice makes me want to smile. But I don't because it dawns on me that I've just inspired her to possibly put herself in danger. Not every gofundme page is legitimate. Not every homeless person is just down on their luck. Some of them are criminals who would easily overpower such a petite woman like Dani. My heart pounds at that thought. I clear my throat.

"You should start at the hospital," I suggest. "Ask for a meeting with whoever does the billing and pay the biggest one."

Her eyes snap to mine, and her mouth pops open. "Oh, my gosh, you're so right, Ronan. Why didn't I think of that?" Her full bottom lip trembles, and her eyes moisten. "I could help people like me—people who are drowning in debt." She covers her face for a moment, her slight shoulders shaking. My stomach drops at how quickly she got emotional. "Ooh, excuse me," she says with a watery smile and gets up to blow her nose. "Sorry." She sniffs and sits down again. "Reset." She takes a deep breath. "That is a freaking brilliant idea, Ronan, and I will absolutely do that." She picks up her fork, and I do the same, relieved that I've helped her and also kept her out of trouble.

"So, how are you?"

I shrug. "Fine."

Dani leans on her elbow and grins at me. "You know, you have *such* a way with words."

I smirk imperceptibly and cut another bite of chicken. "Carla said you got a dress for tomorrow. What color is it? I need to make sure I have something that coordinates."

"Aww, you want to coordinate with me?" she gushes cutely.

"As long as your dress isn't hot pink, yes."

She holds my gaze with a teasing smile and says nothing, just to make me sweat.

"It's navy blue," she finally answers.

"Thank God," I mutter and blow out a relieved breath that makes her giggle. Why does it feel so good to make her laugh?

"I picked a color I thought you would like."

"That was thoughtful of you," I say blandly, even though I'm caught off guard by just how truly thoughtful that was, and take down a mouthful of wine.

"Really trying to nail this wife thing."

"Mhm."

"So tell me about this wedding tomorrow. Is Bodie a friend or a family member?" she asks casually and sips her wine.

My appetite wanes instantly, and I wish the wine in my glass was whiskey instead. "Bodie's my brother."

Dani's hazel eyes widen. "Oh," she says in surprise. Out of the corner of my eye, I can see the wheels in her head turning. When I look over at her, there's a worried expression on her pretty face.

"So...that means your mother is going to be there, too then."

"Yes."

Dani nods and stirs her pasta with a sigh. "She hates me."

"Join the club," I mutter.

"What do we do? Just avoid her?"

Honestly, there's no way tomorrow isn't going to be a disaster. Despite my shitty relationship with my family, my mom is all about appearances. Meaning, she's going to expect me to take professional pictures with her and Bodie and Cara. Fucking kill me.

When I make no reply, Dani exhales in distress. "I'm really sorry. I feel like I made everything five times worse by sticking up for you the other day."

"You have nothing to be sorry for," I tell her sternly. "You didn't do anything wrong." It just makes me more angry at my mother to know that Dani feels like shit about what happened on Tuesday. I know for a fact that my mother doesn't feel bad at all about what she said to her or to me.

"Are you close to your brother? What's he like?"

"He's an asshole."

"Oh." She goes back to her food, seeming disappointed.

I study her for a moment, noticing all the little things about her that make her an attractive woman. Her trigger happy smile. Her bright hazel eyes. Her long brown hair. Her petite frame and perfect breasts. The slightly exaggerated curve of her hips. She's a beautiful woman. And I know the second my brother sees her, he'll turn into a predator. Even on his wedding day.

"Don't talk to him if I'm not with you," I warn her. She looks at me quickly.

"What? Why?"

I hesitate, uncertain how much I should say. "He'll try to touch you."

She gasps quietly, her eyes wide. "He'll...*touch* me?"

"Inappropriately," I clarify angrily. "Especially if he's been drinking, which I'm sure he will be. Just steer clear of him if you can."

She stares at me in shock for a moment. "Cheese and crackers, how did *you* turn out so well?"

"You think I turned out well?" My eyebrows lift with humor. "That's a good one."

"What do you mean?" she demands, pushing my wrist. "You're a good man."

I glance at her and then back to my food. Her assessment of me is uplifting. The only person in my family to ever think I was a good man is the same person who taught me how.

"Whatever good there is in me," I say in a low voice, averting my eyes, "I owe to my dad."

I can feel her smiling sympathetically at me. It feels almost like sunshine. "I wish I could have met him."

I nod.

"Well, I promise to be on my best behavior tomorrow. If anyone makes a scene, it will not be me. Scouts honor."

"You're not who I'm worried about," I mutter to my plate.

Chapter Fourteen

Dani

"**S**hit," I whisper, and reach for a Kleenex. This is the third time I've messed up my eyeliner. Damn, I had no idea I was so out of practice for doing glam makeup. Though, I guess it's been years since I even had a reason to get dolled up.

I won't lie, I want to look good for Ronan. I want to look appropriate for this wedding because I know that I'm a reflection of him now that we're married.

That being said, I also want to knock his socks off. What woman doesn't want her man to be totally gobsmacked by how gorgeous she looks? Obviously, he isn't *really* my man. But he also kind of is. So, I'm going for gobsmacked. Or, at least, I was before I messed up this freaking eyeliner so many times.

I sigh and take a deep breath, trying not to think about how good Melanie was at doing makeup. If she was here, she could easily make me look like a million bucks. Fifty million bucks, even. Ha, get it? Self-five.

Before I can try again, I hear a knock on my bedroom door. I freeze, staring at myself in the bathroom mirror. If that's Ronan, I do *not* want him to see me with one eye done up.

"Yeah?" I call nervously.

"It's Laurie."

I breathe a sigh of relief. "Come on in!" I peek out the bathroom door to see Laurie entering with a laundry basket on her hip.

Laurie is just as sweet as Carla. She's only made me feel welcome and wanted here. The first time I met her, she took out her phone and showed me dozens of pictures of her two grandbabies.

"Oh, dear," she says when she sees me. "Look at you."

"Ugh, I know," I groan. "I should've just gone to a salon or something." I duck back into the bathroom while she collects my minimal laundry from the hamper in the corner. Still weird to have someone else do my laundry, by the way. I give my eyeliner another shot, and this time, it comes out slightly better, but I'm still not content.

"If I were you," says Laurie as she comes in for the towels, "I wouldn't go overboard. You don't need much makeup, Dani. You're pretty without all that face paint."

I turn to look at her, deeply flattered. "Really? You think so?"

Laurie smiles, reinforcing the wrinkles around her kind, green eyes. "Yes. Putting gobs of makeup on a natural beauty like you just wouldn't be right."

I smile. "I just really want to make sure I look okay. I don't want Ronan to think I don't look formal enough or whatever."

She sighs thoughtfully and then smiles softly at me. "The nice thing about Ronan is he would still find you attractive even if you were wearing nothing but a paper sack."

I blush in surprise. "What? Really?" I laugh awkwardly. "No, that can't be right. He's way too good looking for a nobody like me." But then I remember the way he looked at me that one night when I was just in a pair of shorts and a tank top. That's the peak of nobody, right there...and he was definitely not repulsed.

Laurie adds my towel to her laundry basket. "He's a *man*, Dani. Trust me when I say he thinks you're a beautiful woman." She pats me on the arm as she walks by, and then I hear my bedroom door open and close.

I turn back to the mirror, still blushing. I shake my head, trying to fight the smile trying to break out on my face, but I can't help it. I grin like the devil himself. Ronan thinks I'm beautiful? Maybe just objectively beautiful. Yeah, that must've been what Laurie meant. Not like *he likes you* beautiful. Just, *yeah she's pretty* beautiful. That would make much more sense.

Not that it would matter if he liked me. Cause we aren't going down that road. Even if he was interested in me...I went into this marriage banking on the fact that I wouldn't be getting my heart broken. That I wouldn't get hurt. I need to remind myself of that. I need to remind myself that my heart isn't part of this deal.

I get back to doing my makeup, and I take Laurie's advice. I go for a step above what I normally wear for makeup and call it good. I french braid my long hair and then pin it into a bun at the base of my neck with a million bobby pins. Simple, but pretty.

When I slip on my new, floor-length, navy blue dress and step in front of the mirror to examine myself, I imagine my mother standing next to me.

What do you think, Dani? Do you feel beautiful?

I turn and admire the way the thick straps cross over my shoulder blades and leave my lower back completely open. I smile softly and turn back.

Yes.

I take a deep breath, and then I hear another knock on the door. "You ready to go?" comes Ronan's deep voice through the door, making my heart jump.

"I'll be right out."

Oooh, here we go.

I smooth my hands down over my hips and then grab my shoes and the little wristlet that matches my ensemble. I take a deep breath and open the door. When I step out, I spot Ronan down the hallway, standing on the catwalk. He's looking down into the living area with a gloomy expression on his face. He's wearing a navy blue suit and tie with a white dress shirt underneath. He looks handsome, as he always does.

My heart beats quicker as I move toward him. "Ready," I announce and hold my breath as he turns to look at me.

He freezes, his face completely blank as he takes in my attire. His eyes move from my feet, up my legs to my hips, along the curve of my breasts to my neck, and then his eyes stop on my face. He says nothing. Expresses nothing.

I glance down, suddenly worried that I look like a beast in a navy blue cloak. "Do I look okay?" I ask nervously and turn around so he can see the open back. Shit, what if this is too sexy? "Ronan?" I ask, when he says nothing.

His blue eyes find mine, and then I see it. It's that look—*gobsmacked.* I break into a sweat, of course, and smile shyly at him. My heart beats hard in my chest.

"Is it too much?"

"No." He clears his throat, trying not to stare. "No, it's fine."

I chuckle, though I'm deeply relieved. "Exactly what I was going for. *Fine,*" I tease.

He sighs quietly and licks his lips. "You look beautiful." His tone is even and professional, but I smile at the compliment, even if I had to fish for it.

"Thank you. You look devilishly handsome, as always." I gently tug on the end of his tie. "Though I was really hoping to see you in a bow tie."

"Next time," he says lightly, looking down at me with a warmth in his eyes I haven't seen since the night I paid all my debt. It staggers me for a moment. It makes me want to hug him again, but I resist.

"Shall we, Mogul One?"

He sighs, that warmth dissipating. "If you call me Mogul One in front of any wedding guests, I can't promise you a ride home," he threatens tensely.

I smack his beefy arm. He doesn't budge or flinch. I blush slightly. "Don't worry, Wellsley. I won't embarrass you."

"Thank you. Let's go."

I follow him down the long staircase and put my shoes on by the kitchen door to the garage. These heels aren't crazy high, but I'm used to cruising between tables in tennis shoes at Ben's. So, I know I need to be careful walking or dancing in them tonight. Though, if I had to guess, Ronan doesn't dance.

As I pull my seatbelt on, I try to picture him letting loose enough to dance and chuckle softly to myself. I just can't see it. I'm sure it would take about five shots to loosen this man up, maybe even six, given the way his shoulders are almost touching his ears as he drives.

Though to be fair, I'm nervous, too. I'm not even a little eager to see his mother again. And from what Ronan said, his brother isn't any nicer of a person. But I promised my husband to be on my best behavior, and I don't break my promises. If there's any trouble tonight, it will not be started by me. Even if I have to bite down on my tongue so hard that it bleeds.

Remember when I said Ronan's house is bananas? Well, it's nothing compared to this wedding venue. I'm sure this mansion has at least twelve bedrooms and five kitchens. It's huge. Impressive. Expensive. And everything is decked out in wedding things. White tulle. A shit ton of flowers. I'm pretty sure I saw someone releasing butterflies near the front door.

Ronan follows the line of cars in front of us anxiously, and when we get to the valet—yes, there's a freaking valet—we get out and head toward this ridiculously over-the-top wedding.

"So, just so we're on the same page here," I say, holding the skirt of my dress, "are we pretending we're in a loving marriage? Like, should I hold your hand or smile at you a lot or anything?"

He gives me the side-eye, and I stifle a giggle. He sighs. "I suppose." He reaches for my hand, and even though he holds it loosely, I feel my stomach vibrate. It smacks me again. I'm his *wife*.

We go inside and are directed into a huge ballroom that's set up with about a hundred chairs. At the top of the room is a little wooden arch covered in calla lilies. I'm almost too busy taking it all in to notice that Ronan chooses a seat toward the back.

People file in here and there, and all the while, Ronan can barely sit still. He keeps shifting, turning, crossing one leg over the other, and then uncrossing it. It could not be any clearer that he would rather be anywhere else on Earth than at this wedding.

"For the record," I say, trying to distract him, "I liked our wedding much better."

He looks at me curiously. "Really?"

"Seriously. This is all way too much." I gesture at the grand ballroom around us. "The only thing I would change about our wedding is who attended. But I can't bring my parents back from the dead. So..."

I feel a change in his gaze. Less curious and more sympathetic. I look at him to confirm it and smile at him softly. I take this moment to try to comfort him. Comfort my friend and husband.

"We're going to get through this night, I promise. If shit hits the fan, we'll just leave, okay?" I tell him in a low voice.

He gives me an appreciative gaze and then nods.

I say nothing else, sensing that he's maybe calmed down a bit by the way he's fidgeting less. More people find their seats around us, the volume in the room gradually building until the officiant walks up the aisle and takes his place.

Bodie follows after that. He looks nothing like what I expected. I assumed, for some reason, he would be this big, built guy like Ronan with dark hair and similar, sharp facial features. But Bodie is slender and lean, though muscular, with almost white blonde hair and brown eyes. He has a boyish-looking face and holds his head in a jaunty kind of way, like at any moment, he's about to crack a joke at someone's expense. He doesn't look nervous. In fact, he seems thrilled to have so much attention.

An usher escorts who I'm assuming is the bride's mother to the front row, and then he heads to the back of the room. Victoria is next, and I feel Ronan tense next to me as she passes us. I squeeze his hand and am relieved when he holds my hand a little tighter. Then, a string quartet begins to play as the bridesmaids and groomsmen make their way up and stand in a line. The men are wearing black tuxes, and the women are wearing floor-length, dusty rose-colored gowns. Every single one of them are beautiful, stunning people. Like out of a magazine. I've never seen so many attractive people in one place before.

I'm hit with the strange thought that Ronan isn't up there. That's his brother. And Ronan isn't even a groomsman or an usher. He's literally here as a guest, not like he's family. That makes me sad for him, but I don't think Ronan is sad at all. If I had to guess, I'd say he's pretty damn relieved he's not up there right now.

The officiant raises his arms to indicate that everyone should stand for the entrance of the bride. Because we're near the back, our view of Cara is mostly unobstructed. All I can say about her is that she looks expensive. Her makeup is dramatic, and her honey-colored hair is done up in some complicated-looking knot. She has a bejeweled tiara on her head that matches all the rhinestones on her fitted, sexy wedding dress.

I glance back to look at Bodie's reaction. He looks pleased by how his fiancée is adorned, but his eyes aren't locked on hers or tearing up at how beautiful she is or how much he loves her. He just looks...entertained.

The ceremony is shorter than I expect. It really isn't that much longer than my and Ronan's wedding. When they exchange their vows, I can't help but look over at Ronan with a small smile. It feels good to know that he meant what he said that day because Bodie and Cara seem so much more like they're just saying the words. I like that our vows mean more to us than some huge wedding event. Cause that's how this feels to me—an event. A production. A show.

After they're officially married, everyone is ushered into the rest of the mansion for cocktail hour while the ballroom is converted for dinner. Ronan and I find a quieter corner and keep to ourselves.

"This place is so crazy," I comment, taking in what seems to be a library or den. I reach over to the bookshelf next to me and pull a book halfway out, then push it back. "Oh, man, I bet one of these opens a secret passageway or something," I say with a chuckle. I try a few more and then give up.

Such a shame. Why have a huge freaking mansion with a library if you aren't going to put in a secret passageway? What kind of fool designed this place?

I turn back to Ronan, who is gripping his glass of whiskey like a lifeline. "Have you met Cara? Is she nice?" I ask him curiously.

"I haven't met her," he replies gruffly, his eyes scanning the room around us. I think he must be paranoid that his mother is going to sneak up on him.

I sip my wine and shift on my feet. These heels are already killing me. I should've just worn sneakers. You can't even really see my feet that much...I probably could've gotten away with it.

"Listen, we're not staying after dinner," he says anxiously.

"But I was going to liquor you up and get you on the dance floor," I whine teasingly.

He takes a mouthful of whiskey in reply, still keeping his watchful blue eyes on the doorways. I sigh, a little disappointed that my delightful sense of humor isn't disarming him in the slightest.

I step in front of him, but he still doesn't look at me. I take a nervous breath and grasp his chin, angling his handsome face down toward mine, so he has to look at me.

His blue eyes finally look down into mine, my thumb and finger still holding his chin. My pulse races. This is the closest I've ever been to him.

"Take a deep breath, Ronan. It's going to be fine," I tell him calmly.

He swallows and doesn't look much comforted by what I said. I release his chin but continue to hold his anxious gaze.

"Deep breath," I repeat. "Go."

A mildly annoyed look furrows his dark eyebrows, but then he takes in a slow breath and lets' it out.

"There you go," I encourage him. He seems only slightly less tense but gives me a small, appreciative glance before he looks up and stiffens.

I whirl around and see his mother making her way toward us. She's just as beautiful as I remember, but she's on another level for this event in a dark purple gown that I'm sure cost thousands of dollars. The front of her curled, blonde hair is pinned back, showcasing her perfect makeup.

I step back slightly, as if shielding Ronan from her, which is kind of a joke because I'm a small woman. But I'm confused by Victoria's expression. I expected her to have that cruel look in her eyes or even anger, but instead, she looks thrilled to see us.

"Oh, there you are," she says cheerfully.

I step back a little more, so that my back is almost against Ronan's expansive chest. I feel his hand grip my hip, and for a moment, my brain fritzes out at his touch.

"We're doing pictures out in the courtyard," she says, still smiling like the last conversation I had with her never existed.

"I'm not leaving Ronan's side," I say as menacingly as I can.

Victoria's eyes move from me to Ronan and then back. A remorseful look comes over her flawless face.

"I would love it if you were in our family photos as well," she says. "You *are* family now, after all."

I stare at her like she's crazy because she really must be. Just days ago, she was accusing me of shaking it for dollar bills and intentionally trying to humiliate her son. And suddenly, we're *family*? All hunky-dory?

She must know what I'm thinking because she takes a step closer, a gentle expression taking over. Ronan grips my hip tighter.

"I owe you an apology for the other day, Dani." She glances at Ronan and back to me. "I should've been more welcoming to you. I'm just—" She pauses, and I'm dumbstruck to see tears spring into her eyes. "I'm just hurt that I wasn't there when you two were married. I didn't even get to meet you before you married my little boy." She sniffs. Ronan's hand is shaking on my hip. "But that's really no excuse for how I acted. Please forgive me."

I hesitate. I don't know whether to believe her. She *seems* sorry. I know I'm starved for family, but I'm not *that* much of an idiot. I don't think she said those horrible things to me out of hurt that she wasn't involved in our wedding. I smell a manipulator. I swallow and put my hand supportively on Ronan's.

"I forgive you. But I can't speak for my husband. You owe him an apology, too."

Victoria looks over my head to Ronan's face. I don't have to see his face to know he's clammed up.

"I'm sorry, Ronan."

He must give her some kind of response because she nods with a small smile and then wipes at her eyes.

"Okay. Now that we have that settled, let's go. The photographer is waiting." She spins on her heel then and strides confidently out of the room.

I turn around and finally get a look at Ronan's face. He's pissed. Red-faced, glaring mad.

"She didn't mean a fucking word she said," he spits quietly.

I want to hug him so much. It's all I know to do, but I don't have any confidence that it would help.

"Let's just go and get this over with," I murmur and surprise myself by taking his hand and leading him out of the room.

We find our way out back to the courtyard where the wedding party and I'm assuming some family members are gathered. Surrounding the fountain in the center are a multitude of fragrant white roses and ivy growing up the stone walls, string lights have been hung across the space, making it feel intimate and magical.

I know I told Ronan everything would be fine, but as we move toward this group of beautiful, confident, successful people, I feel myself wanting to shrink back. These aren't my people. I don't belong here. This is a world I've never seen or even been close to seeing, and suddenly, here I am, thrust into it.

These people exude confidence and success and money.

I'm just a waitress.

I hold Ronan's hand tighter and do what I was just telling him—take a deep breath.

Bodie spots us, and his face lights up, but it isn't necessarily lit up with happiness. I mean, he smiles happily enough, but his brown eyes are saying something else. Something...mischievous. He saunters over to us.

"Well, look who it is. I wasn't sure you were going to show." They shake hands, each gripping like they're trying to crush the other's hand. Bodie looks at me heatedly and whistles. I blush in surprise and remember what Ronan said about him—that he would try to touch me. "This must be your new wife."

"This is Dani."

"Bodie," he greets with a toothy smile. "I'm the hot brother." He winks at me like a douchebag.

"Nice to meet you," I say, trying to smile like I mean it, and offer him my hand to shake.

Bodie glances at Ronan with a taunting sort of smirk. "Really?" he asks me. "No hug? We're family now." He moves forward to hug me, and Ronan instantly snaps me to his side by my hand. Bodie laughs. "Why so possessive, baby bro? You actually like her, or are you still pissed about Sadie?"

Ronan's face reddens, and he tightens his grasp on my hand. Within seconds, I'm already starting to lose circulation in my fingers, but I don't let go. Ronan has yet to explain to me who Sadie is, but it's becoming pretty clear to me that she's his ex, and it ended badly.

"She's here, you know."

"What? Ronan snaps. "Why the fuck would Sadie be here?"

"Uh, because I invited her? We're..." Bodie pauses and smirks, *"friends."*

Ronan glares at his brother in pure hatred. Bodie just smirks back at him, unaffected. Pleased, even.

"So, what's the deal with you two?" He gestures between us. "Is it the real deal here, or are you just fucking like Mom said?" he asks conversationally, like that's a perfectly appropriate question to ask.

My face heats up, and I inch closer to Ronan, my hand now completely numb inside of his. "That's—that's none of your business."

Bodie chuckles at me. "Well, actually it *is*, sweetheart. You see, I like to keep things in the family."

Before I can even have a reaction to what Bodie said, Ronan snaps and lunges at him. My heart pounds to see Ronan so physically aggressive. But instead of laying a hand on his brother, Bodie just steps back, laughing.

"Easy, easy, down, boy. I was just kidding."

Ronan is breathing like he's just run a marathon. "Stay the fuck away from her."

Bodie smirks and gives me a long, slow once-over that makes my skin crawl. Then he grins at Ronan and walks back to his beautiful wedding party.

I turn to Ronan, who is about to blow. I swallow down my own disgust at Bodie and tentatively rub his biceps in some effort to calm him. "Listen, I'm not really one to judge people on first impressions," I say, "but I reeeally don't like your brother." Unsurprisingly, my attempt at lightening the mood falls flat.

"We shouldn't have come," he says through gritted teeth, his eyes darting around to the faces behind me. "We should just go."

"Hey, don't give your brother the satisfaction of pissing you off," I say. "I may be an only child and have no experience of this, but I'm pretty sure he's just trying to get on your nerves."

"Yeah, well, it's fucking working." He runs one hand roughly through his dark hair.

I glance over my shoulder at all the beautiful people. Maybe we *should* just leave. I don't think there's much chance Ronan will enjoy himself tonight. But the part of me that's starved for family can't help but feel like we need to be here. That Ronan has a *right* to be here.

"Okay, let's start with the groom's family," the photographer calls over the assembled hoard.

Ronan sighs angrily, and I put my hand in his. I wish I knew what to say to make this better. I hate seeing him so upset. And there's no way in hell he's going to be smiling in these pictures anyway.

I lead him over to his brother, new wife, and his mother. He stands stiffly next to Cara while the photographer directs everyone where to stand or how to pose.

I can feel the eyes of everyone else on me, probably because some of them don't know who I am. I'm assuming some are his aunts and uncles, some are cousins or friends. All of them seem to be studying me, scrutinizing everything about me. It's like they can see past my expensive dress. Like they know I'm just some poor, orphan girl.

My ankles shake slightly, and I lean into Ronan for support, which draws his attention to me. I look up at him and force myself to think of how he told me I looked beautiful.

He gives me a questioning look, as if he's asking me if I'm okay, and I take a nervous, deep breath. He smoothes his thumb over the back of my hand, which is the first affectionate touch he's ever given me. It makes my heart lurch in my chest. I smile softly at him in thanks, and then we do the pictures.

This photographer is no joke. She wants every angle and every facial expression to be perfect and exactly what Cara wants. It takes so much longer than I was expecting it to. But thankfully, Ronan stays next to me until it's over. I would love to see these photos actually. Ronan and I don't have any pictures together. And I can only imagine the "smile" on his face looks much more like a pained grimace.

When we're finally dismissed, it's clear that Bodie loves the attention. He loves being photographed. I'm pretty sure he thinks he can make it as a model by the way he eyes the camera. I chuckle to myself as Ronan and I go back inside.

"Why are you laughing?" he asks me, confused.

"Your brother is a diva." I give a very unladylike snort.

He rolls his eyes. "Tell me about it. For his senior photo session, he had over four hundred pictures taken, and he had a mental crisis trying to narrow it down."

I snort again as we make our way back to the ballroom. "Of course, he did. I can totally see that."

The ballroom has been transformed in the time it took for pictures to be taken. The chairs are gone and have been replaced by a smattering of round tables that are lavishly decorated. Huge, tall flower centerpieces rise up from each table and are adorned with glittering crystals. The tables are set for twelve, each place setting complete with way more forks and spoons than I know what to do with. I'll have to ask Ronan.

"Do you still have your yearbooks from back then? I'd love to see some pictures of you in your prime," I tease. "Cause clearly, you've only gone downhill since then."

He gives me a stern look just on the verge of amusement. "If I remember right, you're the one who said anything with ovaries would be dying for my attention."

My cheeks flush slightly. "I did, didn't I?" I mutter to myself.

A tiny little smirk appears at the corner of his mouth, which for him is like a grin of satisfaction. Though if I'm honest, I like that he can dish it.

We find our table and sit down as the other guests do the same. Ronan looks bored and irritated at the same time. I know he just wants this night to be over. I wish I could get him to relax and try to enjoy himself. Maybe with another drink, he'll loosen up. And hopefully, his family will be too preoccupied with wedding guests that Ronan and I can actually have a good time.

As the wedding party takes their places at the head table, I take a cleansing breath. This has only been a small glimpse into Ronan's personal life, but I intend on committing it all to memory. Even if I don't plan on getting emotionally attached to Ronan, I know that I won't get through the next two years without caring about him deeply. And even if he doesn't ever open up to me, I have every intention of being the best friend I can be to him.

And tonight? That means doing my damnedest to get this stoic man to have a little fun.

Chapter Fifteen

Dani

"Can we stay for cake?" I beg Ronan as our last dishes are cleared away. Dinner was freaking delicious. I've never eaten so well in my entire life. I've also never eaten duck breast, and it's my new favorite thing. Freaking drool.

Ronan sighs. "It's just cake. It's not that exciting."

I giggle at him affectionately. "Oh, that's right. You don't eat dessert."

He sips his third whiskey of the night.

"If I had known that I wouldn't have married you," I tease. He raises one eyebrow at me. I down the last of my champagne, feeling a bit buzzed. "It's just a good thing you're a handsome male specimen or else I'd be out, mister."

He studies me suspiciously. "How much have you had to drink?"

I shrug. "I'm a lightweight. Doesn't take much for me to get lit."

He shakes his head, but I'm sure I catch a glimpse of his delicious mouth curving up on one side.

Bodie and Cara take the floor then for their first dance. I think they seem pretty uninterested in each other for being at their own wedding reception, but what do I know? Ronan and I didn't even have a wedding reception.

After that, the dance floor is opened up for other people to dance, and I'm surprised that so many people are already out there cutting a rug.

I look back to Ronan, who is putting his suit jacket back on like he's getting ready to leave.

"I'll let you off the hook about cake if you dance with me." I wiggle my eyebrows at him.

"No."

"Come on! Just one slow dance. *One.* I promise. And then we can get out of here." I hold his gaze as flirtatiously as possible. It's impossible to tell if it's working. Like I said, I don't contain the smooth gene that makes men crazy for me.

"Fine. One. And then we're leaving."

"Yes! Thank you. You're the best husband ever." I get up, wobbling just slightly because of my heels, and he stands up, too.

A slow song comes on as I take his hand and pull him toward the dance floor. His face is set, like he doesn't know how to enjoy a damn thing ever, but I don't care.

When we step onto the floor, I waste no time in moving closer to his big build and putting my hands on his broad shoulders. He stands there stiffly and almost robotically places his hands on my hips. I blush slightly at the way his warm hands span so much real estate on my body.

He and I sway back and forth, again pretty stiffly, but I am thoroughly enjoying touching and being touched by him, even if it's minimal and formal. For a second, I imagine that we're really married—like lovingly married—and I feel a bit of peace flow through me. It's actually kind of nice to have someone, I realize.

Maybe it's the champagne, but I can't help myself from moving closer. I look up at him, but his eyes are landing on anything and everything over my head, seeming completely oblivious that I'm only inches from him.

And—damn you, champagne—I sneak one hand along his shoulder to the base of his neck, where I gently stroke the short hairs with my fingertips.

His breath catches in his throat, but he doesn't pull away. Instead, he bows his head next to mine and lets go of me with one hand so he can bring the hand that's still on his shoulder and tuck it into his chest, where he holds it tightly. His other hand moves from my hip to the small of my back, his skin feeling electric on mine.

My heart is pounding. He's really dancing with me. Like we're a thing. A *real* thing. I smile like a fool and take a deep breath. When I move forward just a little more and rest my forehead in the crook of his neck, he doesn't stiffen like I expect. Just the opposite. I feel his body relax into mine. Then, he continues to sway with me to some sappy love song that suddenly seems very far away.

There is no Bodie. No Victoria. No mysterious ex-girlfriend. No strangers staring at me. Just us. Me and my husband.

This feels like...a piece of my puzzle fitting into place. It feels like something I've been missing for a long time. My heart warms in my chest as I breathe in the spicy scent of Ronan's cologne, suddenly so enticing and magnetic.

Rein it in, girl.

But the little warning slips out of my brain as soon as it enters. This feels too good. It feels too perfect to question at this moment. Later, I can kick myself for allowing it to happen, but right now...I just want to be *here*. With Ronan holding me like I'm more than just a name on a document.

When the music changes to something up-tempo, Ronan seems to flinch back to reality. He slowly pulls away from me. I smile at him, feeling more fuzzy in the head from being so close to him than from the champagne.

"That was way the hell better than cake," I say.

He scrubs his hand down his face, but I catch it—a hint of a smile. "So, we danced. Now, we can go."

"Right. Yes. Let me just use the bathroom."

He nods and heads in the direction of our table. I watch him stride away, still smiling, and then book it to the bathroom.

But I don't have to pee. I need a minute to sort out what just happened and what it means.

The bathroom is just as stunning as the rest of the venue and even has a couch. I approach one of the sinks and look at myself in the mirror. Wow. Look at that. I haven't seen that kind of happiness on my face in a really long time.

I don't think I imagined how amazing that was. It's not because I've been drinking or because we're at a wedding or anything romantic like that. It felt good because it *was* good. And I allowed myself to feel it...with him.

For the first time, I think that maybe...maybe it's time I allow myself to open up my heart again. Maybe this thing with Ronan could heal me from my past hurt. Maybe I can trust him not to hurt me. Maybe there's something more there than friendship.

Because despite both of our resolutions to be strictly platonic, there was nothing platonic about that dance. It was...intimate. More intimate than I've felt in years. And I can't keep myself from feeling like I want more of it.

The door opens, and another woman comes in, but instead of disappearing into a stall, she approaches me confidently.

"I just have to say, I *love* your dress," she compliments, drawing my attention to her.

She's one of those beautiful people, but not one of the wedding party beautiful people. She has medium-length, dark brown hair that is perfectly curled and flowing over her tan shoulders and black, glittery dress. Her impossibly long eyelashes wink at me as she smiles.

"Oh, thank you! Yours is beautiful, too," I reply happily.

She smiles at me even more warmly. "You're Ronan Wells's wife, aren't you?"

"Yeah, that's me. Do you know him?"

She comes around to the sink next to me and unnecessarily attempts to fix her hair. "I do, actually. You must really be something special to have caught his eye."

I'm really pleased to hear her say that. She's the first person here besides Ronan to not treat me like I don't belong here. I smile at her. "I'm Dani, by the way."

She turns away from the mirror and smiles at me, too. "I'm Sadie."

My stomach drops. *Sadie?* Like *the* Sadie I've been hearing about? It must be—Bodie said she was here.

Before I can say anything else to Ronan's apparent ex-girlfriend, there's a crash out in the ballroom that causes several people to scream and the music to abruptly stop. Sadie and I both rush out to see what's going on.

I gasp when I realize a fight has broken out near where Ronan and I were sitting before. When I don't see Ronan in the surrounding crowd, I get a sinking feeling in my chest.

"It was nice meeting you," I say to Sadie and quickly make my way through all the people to where the tussle is taking place. I can hear shouting and chairs breaking as I get closer. My heart beats hard in my throat.

When I get to the front, my fears are confirmed. Ronan and Bodie are at each other's necks.

"Come on, Rone! You can do better than that!" Bodie taunts through the blood leaking from his nose and into his mouth, staining his teeth.

"Boys!" Victoria pleads from the side, crying off her perfect makeup as she and Cara clutch each other in despair.

Ronan's suit is marked with red, his dark hair a mess, and his face twisted with such hatred and anger that I feel temporarily paralyzed by how much it reminds me of Spencer. Ronan lunges at Bodie once more, throwing a punch directly at his brother's cocky face. It connects, but so does Bodie's fist with Ronan's mouth. They both stumble back, breathless. Ronan wipes his bloody lip with the back of his hand and starts forward for more, but the groomsmen finally intervene and get between them. Bodie is ushered outside to the courtyard while Ronan stalks in the opposite direction.

I reach down and remove my shoes so I can run after him without eating the ground, then I go back through the mansion and spot him through the front window. He's outside by the valet. I race out to him.

"Ronan!" I call out to him as my feet pad on the concrete. He doesn't respond.

The valet pulls up with his Rolls Royce and gets out. Ronan moves to grab the keys from him. My jaw drops. He can't be serious. There's no way he should be driving. Not when he's this upset and could have a concussion.

"Ronan," I say again, following him around the car. "You shouldn't be driving like this. You're too upset."

Nothing.

"Ronan, no. Give me the keys," I try again, louder.

He opens the car door to get in.

"Ronan, *stop!*" I shout, and he finally looks at me. His eyes are wild, his hands shaking. "I already lost my parents in a car accident. I won't lose you, too." It comes out of my mouth before I even realize I thought it.

His crazed eyes soften slightly.

I hold out my hand. He gives up the keys and gets in the passenger seat without a word. I nervously slide into the driver's seat, overwhelmed by what I just saw inside. Our intimate dance is completely gone from my mind.

I've never seen Ronan lose it like that. He totally lost all sense of composure. I study him at each stop light we reach, trying to assess his injuries. As far as I can tell, he's only got a bleeding lip and a bit of a bruise forming on his cheekbone. I think Bodie got it worse.

Thankfully, I know the way home and it isn't terribly far because I'm afraid that Ronan is going to explode any second by the way he's trembling next to me. I want to ask him what happened, but I don't know if he'll answer me. And part of me is scared to know.

When I pull into the garage, he gets out of the car before I can even put it in park and disappears into the house.

I turn off the car and take a deep breath. I don't know what Ronan is like when he's mad. *Truly* mad. Does he throw things? Does he drink too much? Does he try to do something constructive like compulsively clean or go for a swim? Will he take out his anger on me?

I shake my head slightly. I can't stay out here all night. I'm going to go inside and try to figure out if I can be of any help. I vowed to be there for him, and that's what I need to do right now.

When I step into the empty kitchen, everything is quiet. Like dead silent. For some reason, that worries me more than if I heard him trashing his bedroom.

I drop my purse and shoes by the door and anxiously make my way upstairs and down the hall. I slowly approach his open bedroom door and peek inside. It's empty. I glance through the office doorway. Also empty. I look to the left where the door to his bathroom is and steel myself.

When I peer inside, I find him sitting on the edge of the clawfoot tub, slumped over a bit, head down. He's removed his suit jacket and, by the looks of it, ripped off his tie. His white shirt is open at the collar and missing a few buttons.

I swallow hard. I don't know what to do. I want to make sure he's not too badly hurt. But I also know that he might just need space right now. I'm also scared. Ultimately, I decide that investigating his injuries is the most important. That's the only for sure thing I can do for him.

I knock lightly on the doorframe. "Ronan?" I ask softly. He doesn't move or reply. I take a step toward him and pause.

He seems calmer than in the car, but I'm still afraid of his anger. I've been on the receiving end of an angry man before, and something like that never leaves you. I want to believe Ronan would never physically hurt me, but I honestly can't rule it out when he's in this kind of state. I just don't know what he's capable of.

I take another step. "How badly are you hurt?" He says nothing. I come closer and see that his lip is still bleeding down his chin onto his shirt. His hands on his thighs are shaking, bruised, and bloody.

I hesitate, not sure how he'll react if I touch him, but I can't clean up his injuries without touching him. So, I reach for a towel and wet it under the sink, then step up to him.

"Let me help you get cleaned up," I say gently, my heart pounding. Again, he doesn't respond. I crouch down and lift his heavy right hand into mine, then begin to gently wipe away the blood. He does nothing to stop me. He's just sitting there, breathing ragged breaths.

Once his hands are cleaned, I rinse the towel and then gather what courage I have to lift his chin. I finally see his eyes, and they're completely glossed over and checked out. It scares the shit out of me. It's like looking into the eyes of a ghost.

"Ronan," I say quietly, but he doesn't respond. Tears fill my eyes as I wash the blood from his battered face. I examine his lip and judge that he won't need stitches. He'll definitely need some ice though.

When I'm finished, I put the towel on the counter and move to stand in front of him. I'm pretty sure that if he was going to snap, he would have done it by now. But that doesn't mean I'm not trembling slightly when I lift my hand and run my fingers over his uninjured cheek.

He slowly blinks, which is the first reaction I've gotten out of him since I shouted at him to give me his keys. I do it again, and his eyes close. I look down into the face of my new husband and feel so much grief for him.

"Are you okay?" I ask him softly.

He swallows hard but doesn't answer me or open his eyes. My mind flicks back to the only time he's ever been relaxed in my presence—to when we were dancing. The thing that started it all was running my fingers through the hair at the back of his neck. Maybe if I do it again, it might comfort him.

I take a deep breath and gently thread my fingers through his dark hair, starting at his temple. His breath slows and deepens, so I lift my hand and repeat the motion. A soft moan of relief drops from his bruised mouth, and then he wearily leans forward and buries his face into the space between my shoulder and neck.

"Fuck, that feels good," he whispers, slightly muffled.

I'm so stunned that for a second I freeze, my heart hammering in my chest. But then, I quickly wrap one arm around his huge shoulders and continue to stroke my fingers through his hair. I feel his thick arms move around my middle, and he stays there, just breathing deeply. I hold him tightly, so freaking relieved that I can be of some help to him.

The wall between us, the one he's been so adamant about keeping in place, crumbles instantly. The professional Ronan is obliterated as he seeks my comfort. It feels like a wave crashing over me, leaving me breathless and surprised. But this wave is comforting and warm and...soothing. With just that one action, the line has been crossed, and I know nothing will ever be the same between us.

"What happened?" I ask quietly. I don't expect him to reply really, but his words come quickly and calmly, and they punch me right in the gut.

"He said he was going to fuck you just like he fucked my ex-fiancée."

The breath catches in my throat.

I'm stunned. I'm...*angry*. Who the hell does Bodie think he is? And the realization comes quickly why Ronan lost it like that. He was defending me. Defending *us*. My outrage eases as I focus on that thought.

I close my eyes and hold him tighter for a moment, my fingers still rhythmically smoothing through his hair. Comforting him like this feels so natural to me, and I know he needs more of it, but he also needs to know that my intentions do not match Bodie's. I will not be another Sadie to him.

I slowly pull back, my hands moving to the sides of his bruised face so that he'll look at me. He seems calmer, less checked out.

"I need you to know, Ronan—" I pause, my voice catching as I feel myself getting emotional with how fervently I need him to know this, "even though he said that he's going to fuck me, I would never—" I sniff and look deep into his blue eyes as my own begin to tear up. "I would *never* do that." My lower lip trembles. "Contract or not. I would never do that. I'm not a cheater. And I care about you. I made a vow, and I intend to keep it."

Ronan studies my emotional face, and I see his blue eyes clear. He reaches up with his thumb and wipes away a tear from my cheek.

"I believe you," he murmurs, his deep voice reverberating through me.

"Good." I stroke his cheeks with my thumbs and look down at his swollen lip. "I should get you some ice for this," I say and look back to his eyes. But he isn't looking at my eyes anymore. He's looking at my lips. I swallow hard, a strange tingling zipping through me.

I won't lie; part of me wants to kiss the wounds on his mouth. There's a maternal inclination to kiss his ouchies like my mother kissed mine when I was a child. But there's also a much stronger impulse to kiss his swollen lips like a wife would. But I don't know what he's thinking. I don't know for sure that he's even in his right mind.

"Please tell me what you need," I plead quietly. "I'm your wife, and it's my job to take care of you. But I don't know you well enough yet to know how to do that. You have to tell me."

Ronan slowly turns his head away from me, like he isn't good at asking for help, and I gently turn his face back to mine. He looks at me with so much vulnerability that I feel my knees weaken.

"Just come close to me again," he whispers.

I smile tearfully and instantly gather him up again. His arms wrap around me tightly, and I match my breath with his for a moment, a little fast and broken. Then, I slow my breathing down and smile softly when he does the same. I can't believe how good it feels to be needed by him. It feels so good to know that I can calm him down.

"Will you stay with me tonight?" he asks quietly from where his face is buried in the hair behind my ear.

"Stay with you?" I question, not sure what he means.

"Sleep in my bed with me," he clarifies. "You're the only thing holding me together right now," he whispers in a tortured voice.

I rub his broad back. "Of course." I pull away slightly. "Just let me change, okay?"

Ronan nods and seems to very regretfully release me. "Dani," he says when I reach the door. I turn to face him. "Thank you."

I smile at him, my stomach churning at how genuinely grateful he is, and then head to my room. I make quick work of washing off my makeup and taking down the bun at the base of my neck, leaving my braid down the center of my back. I instantly feel more relaxed as soon as I don some pajama shorts and a tank top.

When I close my door and step across the hall to Ronan's room, a wave of nerves hits me. I'm about to get into bed with my husband for the first time. We're about to share a bed.

The overhead light is off, the lamp next to the bed throwing a soft glow on Ronan, who is sitting on the edge of his bed, elbows on his knees, head in his hands.

Shirtless.

My mouth goes dry as I feel my body heat up at the sight of all that skin. He really is a specimen. I know that sounds all kinds of thirsty, but it's the truth. All the swimming he does has really carved out beautiful dips across his abdomen, as well as sculpted his shoulders and arms.

But that doesn't matter right now. This man is close to his breaking point, and ogling him is definitely not on the list of what he needs from me right now. Though it will be difficult for me to keep my hands to myself while I'm lying next to him all night. Especially now that I've hugged him and he's not only accepted it but asked for more.

I clear my throat, and he lifts his head wearily. I grin at him. "And you said we wouldn't have to worry about choosing sides of the bed."

His eyes soften at the edges, like only part of his face is smiling at me, but I'll take it. He turns and wearily climbs into bed. I make my way around to the other side, feeling nervous and strangely excited. I turn down the covers and get in. Even though we're both in the same bed, there's a lot of space between us.

Ronan is lying on his back, looking up at the trey ceiling with a distant expression on his face.

"Just so we're clear," he says in a low voice, still without looking at me, "we're not having sex."

My face blushes so deeply that I actually feel like my eyebrows are sweating. I swallow hard and fight back the urge to make some awkward comment.

"I know."

He nods at the ceiling and flips off the lamp beside his bed. When he rolls over toward me and doesn't close his eyes, I scoot over a little closer and put my hand on his. I smile softly at the ring on his finger and run my thumb over it.

"Thank you for defending us tonight."

Ronan's eyes find mine in the darkness. "I owed you one."

I chuckle softly. "My parents never kept score like that. That's not what marriage is about."

"Bullshit. All relationships keep score," he says bitterly.

I'm obviously not an expert, but I got a good idea of what a marriage should be like from my parents. They absolutely had arguments and got on each other's nerves sometimes, but they always made up and always tried to do better. Even though they worked a lot, they still had date nights and made each other laugh. They were friends, and they were lovers, too.

I sigh softly, feeling so deeply bummed for him that he's apparently never had anyone in his life treat him well or fairly.

"I don't keep score, Wellsley. Get used to it." Even in the dark, I can tell he's deeply thrown off by what I said.

"Why not?"

I gently work my fingers into his. For some reason, my fingers through his make the moment feel cozier and warmer. I've never felt intimacy being stoked from something as small as that. Proof that the wall between us really is down. I didn't expect it to feel so comforting.

"Because keeping score isn't loving. If I do something nice for you, I don't do it so that you'll do something nice for me. I don't give so that I can get."

He's quiet for a moment, apparently mulling that over. Eventually, he sighs.

"I've never met anyone like you, Dani."

I smile. "I'll take that as a compliment."

"Good. It is."

I look at our hands for a moment, feeling happy and weirdly content next to him in bed. I'm overwhelmed by how much I want to know about him. I wish I could snap my fingers and just be in his brain so I could absorb everything that makes him who he is.

Ronan gently tugs on my hand then, pulling me closer. My heart races as he comes closer, too. I fight back the urge to smooth my hand over his bare chest. He gazes at me, and I can feel him hesitating. I move my thumb over the back of his hand, which seems to convince him it's okay for him to come even closer yet.

"Come here," I murmur and bring him in close to my little body, so his ear is resting over my heart. "Just close your eyes and listen to my heartbeat."

His long, muscular limbs intertwine and curl around my body. I only have to stroke my hands through his hair a few times for him to start melting into me. I can't believe I'm holding this huge man and comforting him. Something about it comforts me too. I've finally broken down that physical barrier. This professional man has let me in. I know there's no going back, and right now, I'm fairly certain that I don't want to.

I take a deep breath and let it out contentedly. He does, too. And then, his breathing slows and deepens and steadies into something rhythmic. I lift my head slightly to look at his face and find that he's fallen asleep on me. He fell asleep to the sound of my heartbeat.

Wow.

Is this real? Am I actually asleep, too, and this is just a dream? Dream or not, it feels amazing. I didn't know what to expect when we got home, but I sure as hell didn't expect the night to end like this.

And if tomorrow, he doubles down on us being friends and never lets me this close to him again, at least I'll always have the memory of what it feels like to be needed by him. With one last contented sigh, I close my eyes and let the feeling of Ronan's body against mine ease me into sleep.

Chapter Sixteen

Ronan

I can't stop thinking about it. It's been days, but all I can focus on is the shitshow that was Saturday night. My mother left several angry voicemails on my phone over the weekend, claiming I ruined the whole wedding, just like she knew I would. There's no point in telling her what Bodie said that made me fucking lose control. It won't matter to her that her angel child is an asshole who wants to fuck my wife.

It felt good to come to blows with Bodie. The last time we got into a fight like that was when I found out about Sadie, which was years ago now. Just shows you how much people change. I guess I wish it hadn't been in public like that. I wish Dani hadn't been there to see it.

There was terror in her eyes when she stopped me from driving home. I put that look on her face. And I don't want to ever do that again.

And later...fuck. She comforted me in such a sweet, pure, selfless way. Even though I was an absolute wreck and I know she was scared of me, she offered herself to me—put herself in the middle of my shitty, fragile emotional state. And she did it without expecting anything from me in return. She did it without keeping score.

That's why I can't stop thinking about her. Meeting after meeting passes with my mind continually distracted. Waking up on Sunday morning with her tucked into my arms was unlike anything I've ever experienced. Dani just...*fits*. I can't ignore that no matter how hard I try.

My cell phone rings and jolts me out of my thoughts. I pick it up and see a number that I don't have saved in my phone.

"Ronan Wells," I answer professionally, just in case it's a client.

"Ronan, hi," comes a woman's voice. For a moment I'm confused by how warmly she greets me, but then her voice triggers something familiar in the back of my mind.

Shit.

I feel my blood pressure spike instantly.

"What do you want, Sadie?"

She laughs softly. "Well, I was just calling to see how you are. After Saturday, I mean. That was some fight you had with Bodie."

I clench my teeth. "I'm fine."

"Mhm," she replies sarcastically. "You forget how well I know you, Ronan."

"Well you seem to have forgotten that I don't want anything to do with you," I fire back ruthlessly.

Sadie clears her throat. "I know. I'm just worried about you."

"Save it. Don't call me again." I hang up and put my head in my hands.

Fuck, I did not need that. It's been a long time since I've had any interaction with her, and I had been hoping to keep it that way. *Worried about me?* What the fuck? I drop my hands and shake my head. Working any more today is worthless, I realize, so I grab my keys and head home.

When I step into the kitchen, Dani is nowhere to be seen. My shoulders sink slightly in disappointment, but then I push down that feeling and go upstairs. As I'm about to enter my room, I pause and go over to Dani's closed door. As I get closer, I hear music playing at a loud enough volume that I'm almost positive she's taking part in one of her impromptu dance parties.

I back away into my room and close the door.

I'll be honest. I don't know what I want with Dani. I have an almost overwhelming need to be close to her, but I'm also scared as shit to need her like that. I lost my head when I fell for Sadie, and I can't let myself do that with Dani. But fuck, do I want to wake up next to her again. Slow dance with her again. There's a part of me that wants to romance the hell out of her. Convince her to love me. Convince myself that I can love her like she deserves to be loved.

But I'm a coward. And I'm not as good of a person as she is.

I shed my clothes and put on swim trunks, intending to swim until my mind is blank. But when I get down to the pool and begin my laps, my mind doesn't clear. Sure, the confusion and inner turmoil tones down, but Dani doesn't go away. She stays firmly at the forefront of my thoughts.

I see her in that stunning navy blue dress she wore to the wedding. I see her standing in her room in her pajamas. I hear her sweet laughter. I see her sleeping beside me, peaceful and adorable. She's everything good. Everything light. Everything genuine and real.

Fuck.

I pull myself out of the pool and collapse on my back on the tile. I wait until my breathing slows down before I sit up. I didn't want this to happen. I just wanted to be roommates. I didn't think there was anything else to tempt me about her, aside from her smile and bright eyes. But I've never known someone with such a beautiful heart. And that's something I just can't seem to ignore.

In a short amount of time, Dani's managed to wiggle herself into my heart in a way no one else has. Her sweet, quirky personality is disarming me more every day. Is there any use in fighting it?

I go back upstairs to rinse off and change. When I sit down in my office, my eyes fall on the pictures I have on my desk of me and my father. I sigh heavily and pick up the most recent one. This was taken only a few months before his heart attack. I study his kind face and infectious smile, then I compare it to my own. That carefree, happy man died the day my dad did. The day I found out about Sadie was just the nail in the coffin. I've been a miserable cuss ever since.

It's moments like this, I wish I could talk to him. He would have the perfect advice for me about Dani; I just know it. He always knew what to say.

So, I do the next best thing to talking to my dad. I call Lance.

"Ronan," he says warmly when he picks up. "To what do I owe the honor?"

"I, uh, just wanted to talk about something," I say nervously. Shit, maybe this was a bad idea. I've never been good at talking about my emotions.

"Sure, let's hear it."

I hesitate. I get up from my desk and start to pace in front of it. "Well, I—" I clear my throat. "I was just—" I stop again and sigh in frustration.

"What is it, Ronan? Get it out," Lance encourages me, sounding a little concerned. Outside of marrying Dani, he's never witnessed me like this. I'm always professional. Composed. All business. At least, I was before Dani came along.

I run my hand through my damp hair, still pacing. "I've just been thinking a lot about Dani."

"Is everything okay?"

"Yeah, it's fine. She's—" I sigh again. "Fuck, Lance," I spit out and feel myself cave. "She's...*amazing*. Why didn't you tell me she's so amazing?"

Lance is quiet for a moment, probably caught off guard, and then he chuckles.

"I told you she was the right woman for the job."

I shake my head and go over to the window. George is down below, weeding the flowerbeds in the front yard.

"So, what do I do?"

"What do you mean?"

I clamp my mouth shut but instantly feel like a pot of water that's about to boil over.

"Damn it, you're going to make me say it, aren't you?"

Lance laughs again. "If you can't say it to me, you aren't going to be able to say it to her."

I growl and go back to pacing. I take a few breaths and then resign myself.

"I really like her."

"Attaboy," he says proudly. "Now, do you think she likes you?"

Fuck, I feel like I'm a teenager again. "How should I know?"

Lance chuckles some more. "You could ask her, for starters."

"Hell no."

"Then what do you propose here, Ronan?"

I sigh. "I don't know. I was hoping for some pointers or something. You've known her a hell of a lot longer than I have."

"She said it herself, Ronan. She's an open book. She doesn't have secrets. What you see is what you get."

I definitely agree with that. Despite her quirkiness, I love that she's so open. "Right. Yes."

"I can't say the same thing about you, though. You're a hard man to get to know. So, if you like Dani, then I suggest you let her get to know you. I know you're a busy man, but just spending more time with her is a good place to start."

I pause my pacing and rest my forearm on the doorframe of the office door above my head, realizing he's right. She deserves a man who has time for her, who is approachable and available.

"I know you've had some hurt in your past, but I know Dani. She will always be good to you."

"Even if things go south? What if we start something, and it doesn't work?" I question quietly, revealing more of my fear than I intend. The last thing I want is to be stuck in this agreement with an ex for two years.

"That would complicate things," Lance says calmly. "But that doesn't mean that Dani will stop being the amazing woman she is. She will always treat you with respect and kindness, even if there's hurt between you."

But can I? If shit goes down, will I be able to still honor the vows I made her? Maybe I shouldn't do this. Maybe I should just try to ignore these stupid feelings.

"Ronan?" Lance asks, as if he isn't sure I'm still there.

"Yeah."

"You haven't been happy in a long time. So, if she makes you happy, don't try to keep yourself from her." He pauses thoughtfully. "I know your dad would've loved her."

At the mention of my father, I close my eyes and lean my head on my arm.

"I know he would've."

My dad would've thought Dani was funny and cute. He would've recognized the goodness in her. If he were here, he would tell me to go for it and not to screw this up.

"Good."

"Thank you, Lance." I drop my arm and step back to my desk.

"And I want to remind you that she doesn't need the whole world to feel like you care about her. She's low-key. Easy-going. She likes the simple things in life. So, if you decide to go after her, just remember that."

"Right. I will." I take a deep breath. "Thank you."

"Of course. Keep me posted."

I hang up, feeling slightly better about what I need to do.

Be around her more. Let her get to know me. Reach out to her in simple ways.

It sounds easy, but it's been a fucking long time since I felt like this. And I know she isn't anything like Sadie, but that relationship has really left a mark on me. There isn't even a small part of me that misses her or wants her back. I just wish I could get back what I gave her. I was all in. Ready to commit for life. But to her, I was just a bank account.

At least with Dani, I know she wouldn't just want me for my money. She already has it. She would have no reason to string me along. My stomach burns at that thought. It seems so wrong to even think Dani would do something like that. If there's anything I've figured out about her, it's that she has a strong moral compass. She would never manipulate me like Sadie did.

Even with that knowledge, I'm still terrified.

What the hell am I even thinking? What redeeming qualities do I have? Why would she be interested in someone like *me*? I'm just a broken man with a lot of money, who doesn't know how to be anything but a businessman. Even if I open up to her, who says she would even like the guy beneath all the shitty things that have happened to me? Besides, she went into this wanting to be friends and nothing else. Just because she comforted me after the wedding doesn't mean that's changed.

I shake my head. No. It's too much to risk. Love is an unnecessary complication, and that's all. Feelings have only ever led to something bad. It's best if I just tamp them down.

The front door opens, and Carla walks into the kitchen. I'm lying on my back on the couch, still feeling like a moody teenager but unable to do anything about it. All I can think about is my little chat with Lance and what the hell I'm going to do with the advice he gave me.

"Hey, Carla," I greet grumpily.

"Hey, boss," she says. "Uh...where are you?"

I wave my arm, so she can see it over the back of the couch from where she stands in the kitchen.

"What are you doing?" she asks, chuckling.

"Nothing. I'm just tired." It's half-true. Well, no, it's not. I'm not tired. I'm just...stuck.

And I hate that I've gotten myself into this situation when I was out to avoid it from the start. But apparently, I underestimated Dani. And apparently, Lance knew exactly what he was doing when he suggested we add a relationship clause to the contract. I didn't think I would ever consider making use of that clause.

Carla starts cooking, and I stay as I am, just staring at the ceiling. I imagine Dani dancing around up there, being her usual adorable self. A few minutes later, I hear her door open, and she hops down the staircase.

"Ooh, smells amazing," she says cheerfully as she enters the room. My heart beats a little faster at the sound of her voice.

"Thanks, girl."

"It really does," I agree, peering over the back of the couch where I can see Dani from the shoulders up. At the sound of my voice, she whirls around so quickly that she loses her balance. I shoot up to a sitting position as she wipes out on the kitchen floor and lands flat on her ass.

"Dani!" Carla says in alarm.

"Wellsley!" she exclaims, breathless. I get up, trying not to laugh, and go over to help her up. "I didn't even know you were home."

"You alright?"

"I think you just shaved a couple years off my life," she says with an exasperated giggle. I hold onto her hand just a beat longer than necessary after I pull her to her feet. "Wait, why *are* you home?" Her face blanches.

"Shit, is your mother coming over again? I mean, I know she apologized, but—"

"No, no. Don't worry," I assure her. "I was just getting cooped up at work."

She gets a funny look on her face, like she knows I'm full of shit.

"Do you want to start with the carrots?" Carla asks, thankfully prohibiting Dani from asking questions.

"Ooh, I'd love to." Dani steps around the kitchen island. "It's so good to see you, Carla," she says and hugs Carla like they're old friends.

"Aww, you, too, girl."

My eyes narrow slightly. I feel a pang of jealousy in my stomach realizing that Dani didn't greet me with a hug. I almost open my mouth to ask where *my* hug is, but I resist. I come over to sit at the island as Dani takes a small handful of washed carrots from Carla. She glances at me nervously as she grabs a knife.

"Oh, you're going to watch me? I've never chopped vegetables with an audience," she says with a smile. I feel a warmth spread through my chest at the sight of it.

"Don't let me stop you. I can't judge since I don't cook."

I can tell she thinks it's strange that I'm just hanging around. Especially since I gave her a bullshit answer as to why I'm home. But I can't get myself to leave this room. Despite how I want to keep my feelings under wraps, I can hear Lance in my head, telling me to spend more time with her.

I watch Dani chop carrots for a few minutes, trying not to make her feel like I'm as laser-focused on her as I really am. Her light brown hair is tied up in some kind of knot on the top of her head, but there are a few wisps trailing down onto her shoulders. She's wearing a pink shirt I've seen her wear before and a pair of black gym shorts. She's casual perfection, and I don't know why that does it for me. Something about it makes me just want to wrap her up in my arms. I swallow hard and try to think of something to talk about. I wrack my brain and come up completely empty. Damn it.

Dani's head snaps up suddenly, pausing her cutting, with a look of so much excitement that it nearly jumps off her face and lands on mine.

"Oh my gosh!" she exclaims. "So I finally logged into your Google Play account, and I saw you have all the Harry Potter movies!"

"Oh," I say, caught off guard. "Yeah, I—"

"I'm so excited that you're a Potterhead like me!"

The thing is, I'm not. Part of me wants to go along with her just because she's so adorably excited, but I can't in good conscience lie to Dani. Even about something as small as Harry Potter.

"Well, I haven't actually—" I pause and rub the back of my neck, hating the dread that fills me to admit this to her. "I haven't actually seen them."

The excitement vanishes off of her face, and her mouth pops open. "What? You haven't? Then, why are they on there?"

"I've been meaning to watch them, but I don't usually spend my spare time watching movies. So, I just haven't gotten around to it," I explain, feeling shitty that I've disappointed her.

She shakes her head and chops a few more times, then stops again.

"Oof, I think you just broke my heart in two." She fakes a sniffle.

Carla giggles behind her at the stove. "You're such a muggle, boss."

"Get Lance on the phone," Dani says to me dramatically. "Tell him to draw up the divorce papers."

One side of my mouth curves up. "Really? You're threatening to divorce me over Harry Potter?"

She looks up at me seriously. "Always."

My eyebrows raise in amusement.

"Gah! You don't get the reference!"

I shake my head and force down a chuckle, feeling more fond of her by the minute.

"You'll see," she says, pointing her knife at me, "one day when you watch it, you'll totally get why the lack of Harry Potter in your life is a divorceable offense."

I watch her finish the rest of her chopping, my mind working and my heart racing. I take a deep breath and then force a sigh.

"Well, I can't have you divorcing me, now can I?"

Dani looks up at me curiously. I lick my lips.

"Let's watch the first one after dinner."

She gasps so loud, I'm surprised she doesn't choke. "Really?" I swear there are hearts in her eyes right now, and it makes me feel so fucking good. "But don't you have work to do?"

Yes, I have work to do. But fuck it. I'm addicted to making this woman happy.

I twist my wedding ring absently. "It can wait until tomorrow."

The smile that comes over Dani's face has me feeling like a lovesick puppy.

"Oh, my gosh, Wellsley, I am so freaking excited!"

And I realize right there that I would do anything to get that exhilarated reaction out of her.

Fuck, I think I'm a goner.

Throughout dinner, Dani tells me endless reasons why I'm going to love Harry Potter. If anybody else went on and on about a movie series I hadn't seen, I would be beyond annoyed. But not with Dani. I could listen to her talk about something she likes for hours. Her enthusiasm is contagious. By the time we're finished eating, I'm certain that I'm going to love those movies just as much as she does.

When we're finished eating, Dani excitedly leads me downstairs to the theater room. I get to work setting up the movie, while Dani wonders aloud which Hogwarts House I belong in.

"I bet you're a Hufflepuff because you're so hardworking and loyal and—wait!"

I stop what I'm doing to look at her. She's standing in front of the plush leather couch with her arms outstretched toward me.

"We need to build a fort," she says seriously and starts pulling cushions off the couch.

"What?" A fort was by far the last thing I thought she was going to say.

"Believe me, Wellsley, the only way to watch Harry Potter for the first time is inside of a fort made of blankets and couch cushions." I watch her constructing for a moment, bewildered but also amused.

I queue up the movie and then open the cabinet on the back wall to bring out blankets.

"Oh! Perfect!" she exclaims, her eyes bright with enthusiasm.

"I've never made a fort," I say absently, taking in the way she drapes a blanket over her little fortress. She instantly straightens up and stares at me.

"What? You've never made a fort?" Her exasperation is so fucking adorable. "Were you just *born* an adult? Just popped out with a tie and briefcase, ready to get to work?"

I shrug.

Truthfully, my childhood was probably pretty different than hers. My mother was obsessed with everything being neat and orderly and valued the possessions in our house more than me, so any time I made a mess or got into something, she would absolutely lose her shit. My brother and I were expected to look and act our best at every moment. I wasn't really allowed to be a kid.

"Ohhhh, man. You're about to learn, buddy." I inwardly cringe at that term. "I'm about to teach you all the things. When we're done, you're going to be an expert at building forts just like me."

I pay attention as she directs where to put each blanket and cushion, amused at how seriously she's taking it.

"My mom and I used to make forts on movie nights," she tells me. "She worked a lot, so they didn't happen that often, but I still remember the first time I watched Harry Potter. I was snuggled inside of this crazy, outrageous fort that we made out of every blanket and couch cushion we had. It's probably one of my favorite childhood memories."

I pause, a warm feeling spreading through my chest. She's recreating a favorite childhood memory...with *me*.

"That sounds amazing," I comment.

"Oh, it was," she agrees with a big smile. "The best." She gives our fort one more once over and then turns back to me, excitement on every feature of her sweet face. "I think we're ready! Let's do this!"

I hit play, and she squeals. I watch her kneel down and crawl on her hands and knees into the opening of the fort, her round ass disappearing inside. She pokes her head out and waves me in with her finger.

Something clenches in the pit of my stomach. I drop down and try to fold my tall frame into this little haven she made for us. Frankly, there's barely enough room for the both of us.

"Sorry," she says sheepishly as she and I struggle to get comfortable in such a small space. "I guess the last time I did one of these, I was a lot smaller." She laughs softly, though there's some nervousness to it.

It's cramped, but there's something cozy and secure about it. I feel like there's nothing else going on outside our fort and that I've been welcomed into a part of Dani's world that seldom few have experienced.

"It's fine," I assure her.

Even in the low lighting, I can see her smile at me. We back ourselves up to the foot of the couch and stretch our legs out, hers much shorter than mine.

She squeezes my arm with excitement as the title appears on the screen.

"Oh, my gosh, this is the best night of my life," she whispers through a gorgeous grin.

And I realize...this is the best night of my life, too. Dani and a fort and Harry Potter is all I really need.

Chapter Seventeen

Dani

What am I hearing right now?

I snuggle a little closer to the warm thing next to me, trying to get back to the dream I was having about dancing to some electronic pop song in Ronan's bedroom. The darkness and warmth has me slipping off to sleep once more, but then I hear it again—

My sleepy brain languidly flips through the folders in my mind labeled "sounds", and I finally recognize it.

A distant, electronic ringtone.

Something warm stirs against me, and I open my eyes.

Oh. I'm not in my bed, y'all. And that ain't my phone ringing. It's Ronan's.

The darkness of the theater room prevents me from seeing a damn thing, but I sure as hell know that the warm thing I'm wrapped up so cozily with is *Ronan.*

My heartbeat instantly races, and I lift my head off his broad chest as I remember what happened last night.

We watched the entirety of *Harry Potter and the Sorcerer's Stone* in the cozy little fort of awesomeness that I made, and then he just casually threw it out there that we should watch the next one. Well, who am I to turn the man down? So, we watched that one, too. I think we were about halfway through the third movie when I fell asleep. Apparently, he did, too.

Which sucks because *Prisoner of Azkaban* is my favorite one.

My eyes adjust enough to see that the blanket that had been the roof of our fort is now covering our entangled bodies. I feel a rush of affection for him. He could have absolutely woken me up so we could go to bed upstairs, but he didn't. Such a freaking softy.

I hear the ringtone again, and a low groan erupts out of him. He turns his head toward me and opens his tired eyes to look at me.

I smile at him in the darkness, and just as he's about to smile back, he realizes what woke him up.

"Shit," he says groggily and sits up. "That's my phone."

He reaches over me, groping around to find it. When he does, he brings it close to his tired face, which I find unbelievably cute. The light illuminates his panicked expression. Am I evil for thinking his panicked expression is also unbelievably cute?

"Fuck, it's almost ten."

With the darkness of this windowless room, I would never have been able to guess it was so late in the morning. He jumps to his feet as his phone rings again.

"Gina, shit, I'm on my way," he says into the phone as he stumbles over to the lightswitch by the door. "No I'm fine, I just—I overslept."

I giggle and stand up, clutching the blanket and squinting slightly in the harsh, overhead light. I wonder if Ronan has ever overslept for anything in his entire life. I'm not sure, but I *think* he likes sleeping next to me. I bite my lip, thinking that I like sleeping next to him, too. And even though I feel a little bit bad that he's late for work, I also selfishly loved waking up next to him again.

Ronan hangs up on Gina and hovers by the doorway, literally one foot out.

"Uh—sorry," he blurts out awkwardly. "I have to go."

"I know." I beam at him, and he blushes slightly. That man just *blushed.*

"Last night was—" He clears his throat. "Yeah."

"Yeah," I agree.

He bobs his head and continues to hesitate, which just warms my heart and makes me feel all gooey inside. I give him a nod toward the door to let him know he should go. He gives me an appreciative look and then disappears.

I grin to myself as I take in the state of the fort we built. It turned into a little nest of blankets and cushions in the night. I love it. I put the cushions back and fold the blankets, feeling butterflies as I relive his warmth and hesitancy to leave. I don't want to jinx it, but I think...I think he might like me.

Like...*like me* like me.

Ever since the wedding, when he let me in just enough to see what he's really like deep down, I can see him struggling whenever he's around me. Like he doesn't know how to keep being distant and professional with me. He knows a door has been opened that can't be closed. And the thing is, that door isn't locked. Last night proves that.

The possibility of him seeing me as more than a friendly roommate in it for the next two years is frankly pretty surprising to me. I mean, yeah, he's a secret softy, but he's also guarded. Also, he's a major hunk, and I'm...just a person. I guess I can thank my personality for once because my quirks don't seem to be driving him away. If anything, it seems to be the opposite.

The trouble is, I don't know much about him. If you asked me what it is that I like about Ronan, it would sound much more like giving a potential employer a character reference. Hardworking. Loyal. Honest. Sincere. It's all vague. Broad.

I want to know the little things. What's his favorite color? How does he like his coffee? What's his favorite movie? I want to know the important things. How did his relationship with his mother become so strained? Why would Bodie say something so awful at the wedding? What's his favorite childhood memory? What's on his bucket list?

I know that if I'm patient enough with him, he'll open up to me in time. And something in my gut says it will be worth it. That's really all I'm going with here. My gut.

Despite what my gut has to say about it, my head wants to pull back on my reins and give out a "whoaaa girl!" Because when I married this dude, I did it without intending to get my poor little heart involved. Yeah, I meant what I vowed, but I meant it as a friend. So, I should keep being his friend. Even if I can see through his seriousness now and I like what is showing through.

His sweetness. His hesitation in showing me too much. His vulnerability when he's broken.

Those are the things my heart wants to lean into.

Those are the things my head says I need to be careful with.

Because I've been seduced into loving a man who knew how to show me just enough to keep me hoping. And in the end, my heart was strangled and bruised forever. I don't want that to happen again.

Despite that warning voice in my head, a soft smile sneaks across my face as I get the room into some kind of order and then go upstairs to the kitchen. I search around for the travel mugs and make some coffee. I pour it in black because I can't imagine him loading his coffee with tons of sugar and cream, being that he doesn't like sweets. He thunders down the stairs a few moments later, still adjusting his tie as he appears. I love how flustered he looks, just because it's so unlike how he tries to present himself to everyone.

I hold out the travel mug and shake it slightly. "Black?"

"Thank you," he says, sounding truly appreciative, and takes it from me.

"Have a good day, Wellsley." I realize that, besides his birthday, this is the first time I've actually been present when he's left for work. I kind of like it. I give him a smile as he lingers at the door to the garage.

"I'll be home for dinner at six," he promises, and I smile bigger. That's right. It's Friday.

"Can't wait," I say and then blush.

His mouth softens into a very small smile, and even with the stress he feels because of being so late for work, I know he doesn't regret sleeping in with me. I don't regret it either, I realize.

I watch out the front window as he drives away. Despite what Melanie said, maybe this could be something good. Part of me desperately hopes it is.

About two hours after Ronan left for work, he texted me that Gina has been giving him shit left and right about sleeping in. I've been chuckling to myself about it ever since and feeling even more sure that he's taken a liking to me. It's the first time he's ever texted me. I can feel him reaching out to me, and instead of immediately feeling scared, it makes me...happy.

Oh, wow, am I happy? Like *really* happy? Because of Mr. Serious Quiet Man?

Take *that*, Chef Universe.

I chuckle to myself.

Carla usually has some kind of lunch prepped in containers, so I dig around looking for something that looks tasty. What am I saying? Everything she makes is tasty. I'm pretty sure I've already gained five pounds living here.

I decide on the container labeled *Chicken Caesar Wrap* and am just struggling to get the lid off of it when the doorbell rings. I pause, puzzled. I have no idea who could be here. Carla and Laurie just come in. Does a house this far back from the street get solicitors?

Oh, no. What if it's my dear mother-in-law?

I nervously head to the door, hoping that it isn't Victoria. Instead, I open the door to find Bodie standing there. Which, as I look at him in astonishment and dread, is just as bad as Victoria.

My stomach drops.

He gives me a charming, dazzlingly white smile. "Hey, Sis."

I plant myself in the doorway, still holding onto the door.

"Bodie," I say in surprise, "what are you doing here?"

He shrugs and puts one hand in the pocket of his khakis. He's wearing a salmon-colored polo with the collar popped like a preppy douchebag. I genuinely didn't think people really popped their collars. I thought it was just a silly movie thing.

"I was hoping we could talk."

He says it casually enough, but my brain quickly recalls when Ronan said he would inappropriately touch me. I didn't want to believe him when Ronan told me that, but after he said he was going to fuck me at his own wedding...well, I definitely believe Ronan now. I clear my throat nervously.

"Now isn't a good time," I reply vaguely. I've never been good in these situations. Especially after Spencer, my brain is basically useless when it comes to fending off a pushy man. His brown eyes study me for a moment, seeing through my little lie.

"Sorry to show up uninvited, but I had no other way to contact you."

I swallow hard, feeling myself inch backward into the house. Maybe I can just slip inside and slam the door in his perfect face.

"I just wanted to apologize for Saturday night," he says quickly, noticing my retreat.

I still, not expecting that. Could it be that preppy boy isn't a total asshat?

"I'm always razzing my baby bro, but that was out of line. I was a little drunk, and I guess I just pushed him a little too far."

I nod, holding his seemingly sincere gaze. "Yeah, I'd say telling him you're going to fuck me is pushing him too far."

"Right. Believe me, it won't happen again."

I don't believe him, for the record, because the thing to do now would be to spin on his heel and get the hell out of here. But he doesn't. He has more to say, and I don't really want to hear it. Before I can end the conversation though, he continues.

"The truth is," he says with a sigh, "I'm a little worried for you. I mean, you haven't pushed him too far yet, have you?"

I blink. "What?"

Bodie steps closer, his white-blond hair rustling slightly in the summer breeze. He has the air about him that he's about to level with me, tell me something secret and important. I hate that he's piqued my interest.

"Listen, you seem like a nice girl. I got a good first impression when we met at the wedding. So, I feel like you should be warned about Ronan's anger issues."

"Anger issues?" I'll admit, he lost his cool on Saturday, but it was for a legitimate reason. He's never lashed out like that, even with his mother. So, saying he has anger issues is a bit of a reach, I think.

A slightly incredulous look comes over his features that so much resemble his mother's.

"What, you think Saturday was an isolated incident?"

My mouth goes dry. I hadn't considered that, and now Bodie has me realizing just how much there is left to know about Ronan. All I have is Lance's good word. I feel a creeping sense of fear sink into my stomach that has much less to do with Ronan and much more to do with Spencer.

"It's only a matter of time before you accidentally set him off and he turns on you."

I gasp. "I don't believe you. Ronan would never hurt me." But my shaking voice betrays my words.

Bodie smiles sadly at me. "But he *would* Dani," he says gently. "He's done it before."

No, no, no, no.

My stomach launches itself at my throat, releasing a wave of nausea and fear. My brain quickly tries to refute what Bodie is saying, because I don't want it to be true.

"But if—if Ronan had a history of violence, it would've shown up on the background check."

I regret saying that out loud because it reveals the exact nature of my relationship with Ronan. Though, at this point, why the hell wouldn't he have guessed that? Ronan and I were married so suddenly and right before he would lose control over his trust fund. I'm sure Bodie has put it all together and so has Victoria. Not that it matters. Like Ronan said, we're two consenting adults. But I never would have consented if I had even an inkling of what Bodie is claiming.

Bodie slowly shakes his head, oozing sympathy and concern. "It wouldn't have because Sadie never went to the police. She came to me instead."

My heart pounds. I feel my knees start to shake.

Shit, shit, shit, shit.

"But you slept with Sadie," I point out desperately, "so why should I trust anything you're saying?"

He nods solemnly. "You're right. I did. And it was wrong because she was technically still with Ronan," he agrees, catching me off guard. "But what Ronan won't tell you is that she was scared of him and came to me for help. He was beating her up, Dani. And yes, she and I made love. But it was once, and then I helped her to break it off with Ronan so that I knew she would be safe."

This is insane. I feel like I just got punched in the gut with a hand grenade. I clutch the door for support as his words roll over me like a tsunami, throwing into question everything I thought I knew.

Did I really marry an abuser?

God, Mel was right. I can almost hear her shouting at me, "What did you expect when you married a fucking stranger?"

"I know this is a lot," Bodie says understandingly from what feels like faraway. "But I think you really should know what you've gotten yourself into. I'm just trying to look out for you, Sis."

My mouth is so dry that I can't respond.

"Here, this is my card," he says, putting his business card in my clammy hand. "If he ever does hurt you or even makes you feel unsafe or scared, just call me. No matter what he says, you're not alone." With that, he gives me a sympathetic smile and strides down the porch steps to his car.

I go inside and close the door, feeling disoriented and dumb. I have a deep sense of loyalty to Ronan, but I also have a history of being in an abusive relationship. And even though Ronan has treated me with nothing but respect, Bodie's words still hit me hard. I can't put myself through something like that again. I refuse to *ever* be with a man that has hurt a woman the way that Spencer hurt me. Even for fifty million dollars.

I wander upstairs, and for the first time, I lock myself inside my room. Then, I go into the bathroom, and I lock myself in there, too. I get into the empty tub and sit, my arms wrapped around my knees, completely devastated by what Bodie said.

There's no way Ronan could be capable of hurting me. Even in his anger on Saturday night, his eyes softened when I shouted at him to give me the keys. Even in his anger, he backed down. But maybe the reason why he's been so distant with me is because he doesn't want me to find out about Sadie. I haven't asked him what happened with her. He hasn't offered to explain.

Suddenly, comforting him on Saturday night feels tainted. And last night. And this morning. I hate it. What am I going to do? Do I really have to confront him about this? Do I have to ask him to his face if he hit Sadie? And if I do, will he tell the truth?

"Shit, shit, shit," I mutter.

I do the only thing I know to do. I unlock the bathroom door and get my phone. I dial Lance. Thankfully, he picks up.

"Dani girl, how are you?" he answers cheerfully.

"Tell me why Ronan and Sadie broke up," I demand, trying not to hyperventilate.

"What?" he says, deeply caught off guard.

"Bodie said he was beating her. I need to know why they broke up," I explain tearfully. "I need to know the truth."

There's stunned silence on the other end of the line for a moment. I wait, feeling like everything could change depending on what Lance says.

"Dani, I don't know those details."

I close my eyes and plop on my bed, so my knees don't give out.

"But let me tell you what I *do* know," he continues seriously. I hang on his words, trying to steady my breathing, trying to decide what the hell I'm going to do if Ronan did what Bodie said he did. "I know that Ronan is a good man, who lives to make his father proud, even though he's been dead for years. He treats everyone with respect, even to the point of biting his tongue when his mother is cruel to his face. Ronan is a man of honesty and integrity, who tries to do the right thing." He pauses, and I hold my breath. All of those things sound like the Ronan I've come to know. "Let me tell you what I know about Bodie. He thinks it's fun to get a rise out of his brother. He isn't afraid of stepping on people to get what he wants. He doesn't see anything wrong with cutting corners or lying or manipulating a situation in his favor."

I sniff, feeling a small amount of relief ease my fears.

"Now, if I were a betting man and I had to guess who would be more likely to beat their wife, I wouldn't bet it was Ronan."

I nod, even though he can't see me.

"I would trust Ronan with my life, Dani. Bodie? Not so much."

"But you're closer to Ronan, right? You don't know Bodie as well?"

Lance sighs. "I've known them both for decades, since they were boys. Yes, I'm closer to Ronan, but that's on purpose. Bodie has always been unkind and unfair. I don't let those kinds of people close to me."

I take a deep breath and let it out slowly. "Right. Thank you."

Lance's insight soothes me. Being an outside observer all of Ronan's and Bodie's lives helps me think that Lance is right. Bodie is trying to manipulate me to hurt his brother.

"Are you okay?"

"Yes. I'll be okay. That just scared the hell out of me to think Ronan could ever—" My voice breaks.

"Of course, Dani. And if anything ever happens, I'll be the first in the line to make sure he regrets ever hurting you."

"Thank you." I sniff. "I'll let you go."

"Okay. Take care."

"Bye." I hang up and take in another deep breath. I take a moment to do what Lance just did. I make a list in my mind of the things I know about Ronan and a list of things I know about Bodie. I obviously trust Ronan more, and it feels mutinous to even consider that Bodie could be telling the truth. I come to the same conclusion as Lance, and that's nice, but because of my past, I can't fight the fear I feel.

I have to know for sure. I have to ask him.

Chapter Eighteen

Dani

Carla can tell something is up.

She's been letting me help her make dinner almost every night, so she knows my uppity personality pretty well by now. I'm usually chatty and asking her questions about herself or about what we're cooking. But tonight, I'm almost silent. I can't muster anything funny or even normal. I can feel her watching me in a worrisome way, but she doesn't ask what's wrong or why I'm so solemn.

When Ronan comes in from the garage, I can barely get myself to smile at him. I instantly search his chiseled face, trying to see the truth somehow written in his eyes or his timidly smiling mouth. I know that, just like Carla, he notices my somber demeanor immediately but doesn't question me. But he will, though.

How am I even going to get the words out? I've been in a state of perpetual turmoil all afternoon. If there's anything I've figured out so far in my life, it's that the truth can hurt like hell and in more ways than one.

I help Carla bring dinner to the table, and then she gives me a tighter hug than usual. The kind of hug my parents used to give me. I inwardly thank Carla for it because I really need it. Even though Carla doesn't seem like the mothering type, I realize that sometimes, she does remind me of my mother. She's a deeper, sweeter kind of friend, like my mother was to me as I got older.

I watch her leave and feel my nerves kick in hard. I sit down with Ronan at the huge dining room table, feeling him eyeing me curiously, and serve him salad.

It's a cloudy day with dark grey clouds, so this end of the house feels darker than normal. It's fitting, really, because I sure as hell don't feel like sunshine right now. I feel like I could crawl into a cave and stay there forever, actually, but no one ever really means it when they say something like that. What they really mean is they just want to hide. And goddamn, do I want to hide from this right now.

I can tell he's waiting for me to say something as we dig in. I usually do. He knows by now that I'm more of a conversationalist than he is. I chew a bite of lettuce and swallow it down with difficulty. My stomach churns painfully. I'm too nervous and upset to eat.

I hate this. If Bodie hadn't shown up today, I would be flirtatiously teasing Ronan about Gina giving him shit for coming in late. Maybe we would be exchanging cute glances or making plans to finish the third Harry Potter movie.

But instead, I'm staring at my plate like it might sprout hands and sweating through my shirt.

He clears his throat, but I don't look up. Another moment of tense silence passes, and then, "Dani, is everything okay?" His voice is gentle, concerned, sweet. It makes me feel even worse.

There's no context for what I'm about to say, and I can only expect him to get upset. I stare at my plate, my nerves rising so much that my knees start bouncing under the table. I take in a shaky breath and close my eyes.

"Have you ever hit a woman?"

The room is so still that I wouldn't be surprised if Ronan had evaporated into thin air.

My breathing picks up as I open my eyes to look at him. The amount of shock on his face is immeasurable as he stares at me. My stomach churns even more. I may actually puke.

Once the shock wears off slightly, he seems to realize I'm completely serious and expecting an answer. He licks his lips.

"No," he says, his voice deeper than I've ever heard it. Before I can even process his answer and whether or not he's telling the truth, he swallows hard and puts down his fork. "Has—" he pauses, his dark brows furrowing, "has a man ever hit you?"

I wasn't expecting that question. I was expecting him to ask me where the hell my question came from. I was expecting him to be angry at me for asking something like that. Now I have to be vulnerable and tell my own truth.

I look back down at my plate, my hands trembling in my lap, and slowly nod.

Out of my periphery, I can see Ronan's chest rise and fall quickly. He wipes his hand down his mouth and then pushes his chair back. I look up as he stalks toward the French doors and out onto the back deck.

I take a few moments to try to calm myself so that I don't start crying, and then I wobble over to the French doors that lead outside. I stay in the doorway as I take him in, standing with his back to me, both hands gripping the nape of his neck, his head tilted down. Everything about his body is tense.

Before I can open my mouth to say anything, he drops his hands and faces me. His eyes are burning, but they're also wet. My heart hitches in my chest.

"Tell me everything," he demands in a low voice.

I hesitate, knowing that it will only upset him.

"Please," he adds sternly.

I take a deep breath. I had every intention of exploring *his* past tonight, not mine. But maybe if I go first, he'll feel like he can tell me what happened with Sadie. Why she slept with Bodie. Why he hasn't talked about her at all. Why Bodie would make up something so horrible about him.

It's been a long time since I've purposely thought about Spencer. I try not to wonder what he's doing or where he is in the world. I try not to think about what he did. I try not to come down on myself for staying with him long enough for him to hurt me.

"I met him a couple years after my parents died," I start quietly, tears already forming in my eyes. "He was cute. Fun. He—he had this light in his eyes that I felt like I sort of recognized somehow."

It was like finding someone who reminded me of myself before my parents died. I hate to think that now.

"He was sweet at first. It's always good at the beginning, you know?" I shake my head slightly. "But when I met his family, I started to notice how...how *heartless* he was about his mother and his sister. I tried to brush off his attitude toward them as just how his relationship is with them and not something bigger—not something that could spread to his relationship with me."

Ronan's eyes are glued to me as I speak, like every word is directly deposited into his memory bank. For some reason, it strengthens me. He really cares about what I've been through.

"I think I didn't want to see it. I needed a place to belong after my parents were gone. So, I didn't want to admit he was sexist or considered himself above me. But his sweetness started to change. He was...more demanding and less understanding. He became more assertive about what he expected out of me and what I should expect from him, and those two expectations were not equal." I take a deep breath, looking away from Ronan for a moment. "We started fighting all the time, and he was always trying to say that his word was final, even if he was wrong. Even if I said I wasn't done talking about it. Like he was trying to exercise his power over me."

My breath becomes ragged as I come to the next piece. It's never easy to talk about what it's like to be hurt by someone who's supposed to love you. Ronan steps closer, seeming to sense what's coming next.

I look up at him. "One night, he wanted to have sex. I wasn't over an argument we had earlier in the day and said no." My lip trembles angrily as the memory flows through me. "He said I owed him. That I don't get to say no when we're in a relationship."

Ronan's eyebrows quiver over his blue eyes, shining like fire.

"He didn't believe rape can exist in a relationship...and I—I couldn't believe it. He was standing there literally threatening to rape me. I called him out on it. I told him he's a rapist if that's really what he thinks, and I would absolutely not stand for that." I take in a shaky breath, tears brimming in my eyes. "And then, that light I used to see in his eyes went out, and he struck me." A tear drips down my cheek. "He hit me so hard I was actually confused—I didn't understand what was happening until he was pulling me to my feet by my hair and throwing me against the wall."

Ronan's tears fall over an angry and indignant face.

"He lifted me off the floor by my neck, and I watched the anger and hatred in his eyes as I blacked out...thinking that this is it. I'm dying, and I'm dying looking into the eyes of a man I thought I loved and thought loved me. But at least—" I sob softly, my tears finally getting the better of me, "at least I would get to see my parents again."

I cry for a moment, hurting to remember what it felt like to let go of my life. To accept that it was all over. That brief moment of hope I felt at the idea of being with my parents.

"But I came to, and he was gone. I think he thought he had killed me and got scared."

I don't know what more to say. I feel weary from speaking, from reliving these moments that I've pushed down as far as I could.

"Did you report him?" Ronan's deep, emotional voice rattles me more than the distant rumble of thunder coming from outside.

I slowly shake my head, knowing it's not the answer he wants to hear.

"Why the fuck not?" he spits. His anger makes my heart pound.

I swallow. "It doesn't matter now. It was years ago."

"Of course, it matters."

I stare at him, my heart beating even harder. His passionate and immediate defense of me buoys me slightly because I'm realizing that my gut was right. Ronan is a good man. He's the man I know. Sweet. Loyal. Supportive. He's in my corner. I want him to be.

He comes closer and then closer still, until he's only inches from me. With tears still in his eyes, he lifts his trembling hands and holds my face tenderly but firmly.

"I swear on my father's grave," he whispers, new tears forming, "I will *never* lay a hand on you in anger."

Bodie's words disappear from my mind. He can go to hell. Because I know, I *know* that Ronan is being sincere. Ronan is a man I can trust. He's my friend, and he will never hurt me.

I reach up and wipe a tear from his unashamedly emotional face. "I believe you," I whisper back.

He releases my face and wraps his arms around me, holding me tight to his broad chest. I cling to him, too, feeling like I can finally breathe again. He buries his face in my hair, seeming to need just as much comfort as I do, like what I've told him has wounded him, too. Something about my feelings for him solidifies in me, and it comforts me more than it scares me. Because I'm safe here. He will always protect me.

"Where did this even come from? Because I got in a fight with Bodie at the wedding?" he asks quietly, stroking my back with one of his large hands.

I stiffen slightly and slowly pull back. I wince at him.

"You're going to be mad if I tell you."

He raises one eyebrow at me. "Dani..."

I swallow and decide to spit it out because there's no way he's going to let it go.

"Bodie was here."

His eyebrows shoot up. "What? Bodie?"

"I know, I know."

He puts his face in his hands for a moment, and then he huffs inside. I follow him and see him grab his phone from the far counter where it's sitting next to mine.

"What are you doing?" I ask as he violently types.

"I'm telling him to stay the fuck away from you."

I hesitate to explain, but I feel like I should. "He said he was trying to warn me about your anger issues and the real reason you and Sadie broke up. He said you were hurting her."

Ronan pauses and puts down his phone. Shit, he's so mad. Because he *didn't* hurt Sadie. Bodie just made that up to get between us. And I fell right into his little trap.

"I'm so sorry, Ronan," I murmur. "I swear, I will *never* listen to a word he says ever again."

His eyes bore into mine for a moment, and then his hands tear through his hair.

"Good."

I swallow hard at the finality of his tone. I feel deeply guilty for destroying our dinner. I've really ruined this whole night. I glance over my shoulder at our plates on the table and know that there's no salvaging it. There's no way I can sit there and try to talk about anything else or nothing at all. I turn back to Ronan.

"I know it hasn't been an hour, but let's just call it early. I'm really not hungry and...and I think I've dumped enough on you tonight." Nothing like accusations and domestic abuse stories to kill the mood, right?

Ronan looks a little surprised, but he nods slowly.

"If that's what you want."

I give him a tight smile and move closer to grab my phone. I feel like he almost stops me from leaving the kitchen to go upstairs, but he doesn't.

In my room, I collapse onto my bed in a heap. That was a disaster. I should've never listened to Bodie. I should've just slammed the door in his face. I should've trusted my gut. I should've trusted Ronan. From now on, I promise that I will never doubt him again. That's the only way I can fix this going forward. That's the only way we can ever move on from it.

Despite learning my lesson, I feel a toxic, acidic sort of squirming in my stomach all evening. Ronan keeps to himself, and so do I. But when I go to bed, I lie there unable to sleep even though I'm emotionally exhausted and need this day to be over. I realize my guilt is still weighing on me. And recalling the worst moment of my life has destabilized me.

At midnight, I find myself standing outside of Ronan's bedroom door. I open it slowly and peek in to find the room dark. Ronan's large body is tucked into the covers, and everything is quiet. I take a deep breath and slip inside. I creep as quickly as I can across the room without making a sound. Before I can think twice, I lift the covers and get into bed next to my husband.

"Dani?" comes his soft, slightly confused voice.

"Please don't ask me to leave," I murmur back, hunkering down with my back to him. "I just feel like this is where I need to be right now." Alone in my room, in that huge king-sized bed, just made me feel so isolated from him, especially compared to last night and how we fell asleep together in our little fort.

The mattress behind me sinks slightly as he shifts his weight. "I'll never ask you to leave," he whispers, and I feel his warm hand find my side.

I close my eyes at his touch, feeling like I might cry. I cover his big hand with mine and then pull his beefy arm around me. His chest presses soothingly against my back as he wraps himself around me. My own little Ronan cocoon.

"Thank you," I whisper and feel myself relax for the first time since Bodie showed his face. The warning voice in my head quiets as my heart speaks louder.

He isn't Spencer. I'm safe.

My fear is slowly being swallowed by Ronan's edgy affection. Despite not knowing everything about Ronan, I feel like this is where I belong. This is where I want to be. With that knowledge, I give in to sleep.

Chapter Nineteen

Ronan

It takes me a long time to fall asleep, even with Dani snuggled in close to me. Her sweet scent is comforting, but I'm shaken deeply to know how she was abused at the hands of her psycho ex-boyfriend. She has seen so much fucking darkness and *evil* in her life, and yet she lives with such warmth and brightness. More than ever, I want to be the man she deserves. She needs to know with every interaction she has with me that I respect her and care about her—that I will only ever touch her with gentleness. That she's always safe with me.

Bodie texted back earlier, claiming he was just trying to look out for his new sister in law. But I know better. He's trying to tear her away from me, just like he did Sadie. It's what he does. He takes what he wants without caring about anybody else, just like my mother. No matter what happens, I can't let Bodie near her again. Especially now that I know about her past.

I nuzzle my face a little more into her soft hair and close my eyes tightly. To see her so upset tonight nearly killed me. But the fact that she shared it with me so fearlessly has me rethinking my hesitancy to open up to her. I know she trusts me now. She wouldn't have told me about the worst moment of her life if she didn't. And for her to get into my bed tonight because *this* is where she needed to be... Fuck. This is where I need to be, too. With her.

I almost knocked on her door about five different times before I went to bed. I didn't know if I should. I wasn't sure what she needed. But now I know that next time, if there ever *is* a next time, I won't hesitate to make myself available to her and let her know I'm here for her. I *am* her husband, after all. The only family she has. And right now, I'm damn proud to be.

I don't remember falling asleep, but the next thing I know, it's morning, and Dani is carefully trying to move out from under my arm. I groan my disapproval and pull her back into my bare chest, only semi-conscious.

She giggles softly. "I have to pee," she explains.

"Hmm?" I open my eyes and instantly release her. "Oh, mmmsorry," I mutter groggily.

She gets out of bed, and my tired eyes follow her until she disappears into my bathroom, the door closing quietly behind her.

I sigh and roll onto my back. I rub my eyes with the heels of my hands for a moment, trying to wake up. When I drop my hands, my thoughts from last night come back to the forefront of my mind.

I hate that she cut our dinner short last night. It isn't like her to pull away like that. Not that I know her incredibly well. I scratch my chin. I wish I could just go back and rewrite the whole evening. I feel like I should've handled everything better than I did. And more than anything, I never want to feel her pull away again.

The door opens, and Dani comes out, smiling almost sheepishly at me. She hovers at the foot of my bed as she takes in my shirtless chest. Fuck, does it please me to watch her eyes cloud with desire. When she realizes she's staring, she immediately turns red and glances away. So goddamn cute.

"Morning," I say, my voice slightly husky.

"Morning," she squeaks back. She avoids my eyes, smiling awkwardly. "Um, thanks for letting me sleep in your bed."

I sit up a little more, studying her. "You don't have to thank me for that. You're always welcome."

You're always welcome? Really? By far, not the smoothest thing I've ever said.

She swallows and nods, glances at my bare chest and then away again with a small smile.

"You're welcome in mine, too, just for the record. You know, if you ever want to mix it up a little." She laughs nervously. Her words comfort my slightly bruised ego. She smiles at me and then takes a step back, like she's going to leave.

"Hey, I want to apologize about last night," I say before she can get far. "I wanted to knock on your door, I just didn't know if—"

"Oh, no, no, Ronan. Please don't apologize," she insists, looking at me full in the face now. "I shouldn't have—I shouldn't have just word vomited all of that on you."

"I asked you to. You can always talk to me, Dani, even if it's difficult."

Her eyes start to mist. "Thank you. The same goes for you, okay?"

I nod, holding her gaze. We really are friends, aren't we? Although, the way she was checking me out says we're more than that. I'd be lying if I said I hadn't checked her out, too. And I'd definitely be lying if I said I don't love falling asleep holding her close to me. It's been a long fucking time since I've done that, but it feels different with Dani. It feels *right*.

My phone rings on the nightstand next to my bed, startling me slightly. Gina's name is flashing on the caller ID.

"Is it work?" Dani asks curiously.

"Yeah. It's Gina."

She gives me an understanding smile and steps back. "Go ahead. And say hi for me."

I hesitate, then do as she says even though I'd really like nothing better than to grab my wife and bring her back to bed. I bet if I tempted her with Harry Potter, she would gladly get back in here with me.

"Gina," I say, my eyes still on Dani as she retreats toward the door. Her long, light brown hair is a little messy, which only makes her sexier in my eyes. Messy hair, cotton shorts, and a tank top is all it takes to get me thinking about things that reside firmly in the relationship clause of our contract.

"Ronan, good morning," she replies professionally.

"What do you need?"

Dani points at herself and waves from the doorway, reminding me to say hi to Gina.

"Um, Dani says hi," I add awkwardly. Dani grins adorably and gives me a thumbs up.

"Oh, uh, that's nice. Tell her I say hi, too," Gina says brightly, though a little caught off-guard.

"Gina says hi," I tell Dani, and she beams. Damn it, she's so cute. I clear my throat. "What can I do for you, Gina?" My eyes stay on the place where Dani disappeared into the hallway.

"Well, Julie called to let me know that Roy Stanton is selling."

The breath catches in my throat. I've had my eye on Roy Stanton's property for years. He lives in Chicago and has a high rise right in downtown worth millions of dollars. It's the kind of thing that could kick start the extension of Wells, Inc. into Chicago.

"Selling? You mean—"

"Yes. He's interested in meeting up, so I booked you a flight out this afternoon."

"Thank you. Email me the details. I'll be there."

"Consider it done."

I hang up, a tangle of emotions. I'm fucking pumped that I have a shot at this deal, but I realize that it means I'll be in Chicago for a couple days...away from Dani.

I get up and pace for a moment in front of my bed. My stomach clenches uncomfortably at the thought of not seeing her for two days, especially after what she told me last night. I run my hands through my hair.

It's *only* two days. It's not like I'll be gone for a week.

But I can't get myself to shake how disappointed I am. I'm realizing that I'd prefer to not skip a single day of seeing Dani, even if it's only for pleasantries. Despite how ridiculous that makes me feel, I realize that maybe—*maybe*—Dani feels the same way. I don't think she would have gotten in my bed last night if she didn't feel something for me.

I gather myself and then go knock on her door. She answers with her toothbrush still in hand and looks surprised to see me. Her eyes glance heatedly at my bare chest.

"Uh, hey," I begin smoothly.

"Hi."

I clear my throat and hate that I'm avoiding eye contact. "I have to go to Chicago for a couple days," I tell her, glancing at her sweet face to gauge her reaction.

"Oh," she says and puts her toothbrush back into her mouth. She brushes for a second and then takes it back out. "You mean for work?"

"Yeah, for work. I'm going to look at a property that's just coming on the market, and it's a pretty big opportunity."

She nods. "Wow, that's really cool. I'm happy for you." She brushes again and then gives me a slightly embarrassed look as she points at her cheeks. "I have to spit," she says, her voice muffled.

I smile slightly. "Right. Go ahead."

She chuckles and heads back to the bathroom. I wait by the door as she rinses and spits. She returns with a shy smile.

"Sorry," she says with a laugh.

I clear my throat and fight down the sudden urge to bring her in close to me. When I hugged her last night, it was the most amazing feeling. Being close to her is everything.

"Listen, I don't know if you have anything going on or whatever, but I was wondering if you wanted to come along."

Her smile slides off her face in surprise. "What? Come along?"

"Yeah," I say over the loud beating of my heart. "Have you ever been to Chicago?"

Dani smiles and shakes her head. "Pssh, are you kidding? I never been anywhere."

Hmm. I hadn't thought about that. She's worked so hard since her parents died that I'm sure she hasn't traveled anywhere or probably done much of anything fun. This thought encourages me.

"Then, you definitely should come to Chicago with me. Obviously, I'll be working for some of it, but maybe we could do something fun there, too. Enjoy the city a little," I tell her, feeling optimistic at the way she's beaming at me right now.

"Oh, my gosh," she murmurs and presses her hands together in front of her. "I would freaking love that."

I feel a smile warming my lips. Her happiness makes me feel so fucking good.

"Great. I'll have Gina get you a seat next to me on the plane."

She gasps. "Oh, my gosh!" she exclaims. "We're flying?! I've never flown before!" She lets out a little squeal and then bounds forward to hug me. "Thank you, Ronan. I'm so, so excited."

The feel of her warm hands on my bare back makes my heart race. I hug her back, but then she quickly steps away.

"Sorry," she says, her cheeks flaming. "You're half-naked," she whispers to herself and fans her face while avoiding my eyes.

I smile and force back a chuckle. I can barely contain my affection for Dani. All I want to do right now is bring her back into my arms. Very suddenly, I feel like that's where she belongs.

"You didn't have any objections last night," I tease her with a smirk.

She tucks her light brown hair behind her ear as she blushes even more. She looks like an adorable lobster. She laughs nervously.

"Well, who *would*, honestly?" she mutters.

I gaze at her warmly and wonder if this little trip to Chicago could be a game changer for us. Is this my opportunity to romance the hell out of her? Show her that I care about her? How the hell do I do that and also clinch this deal?

Chapter Twenty

Dani

Ohmygoshohmygoshohmygosh!

I may actually pee my pants from excitement. I just boarded a plane. I just stowed my carry on bag in the overhead compartment and sat my cheeks down in first class next to my handsome husband, who sweetly offered me the window seat. There's the tray table in front of me that the flight attendant will ask me to stow in its upright and locked position. There's the little safety pamphlet in the seat pocket. There's the window shade, which I will absolutely *not* be using. I fully intend on glueing myself to that little window, so I can watch the world become tiny and faraway. I can't freaking wait.

Ronan, of course, is all business, as usual. He has his work laptop out and is probably typing up some kind of proposal or something for the big wig he's meeting with today. Even though there's more room in first class than in coach, he still looks too big for that seat. His long legs still look crammed in between his seat and the row in front of him. Like a little hermit crab too big for his shell.

I don't know what he has planned for us in Chicago, and I know I shouldn't get my hopes up because he's going there for business. But I can't help how hopeful I feel. He didn't have to invite me along. Frankly, I was flabbergasted that he knocked on my door and asked me to come with him. I'm becoming more and more sure that he likes me. I'm growing on him just like he's growing on me.

Oh, and did I mention how difficult it is to form full sentences when Ronan doesn't have a shirt on? I'm genuinely surprised I didn't spontaneously combust just from looking at him this morning. Man, if

I could choose a way to go out, that would be it. Looking at Ronan and then POOF. Pure fire.

When the passengers are all on board, the captain's voice comes on the intercom and says some things that I can't make out over all the talking people. My stomach twists when the plane lurches backward and begins to taxi to the runway.

The flight attendants go over the safety instructions, which I pay very close attention to, and then it seems like there's nothing left to do but take off.

Ronan puts away his laptop, and we each buckle our seatbelts. He looks at me then, as if remembering that I'm there, and gives me a benign look, like he's happy I'm there with him. I grin like a crazy person and try not to bounce in my seat with excitement.

The plane moves forward then and picks up speed. My heart races as I watch out the window, the runway and other planes whizzing by faster and faster. When the pilot has reached the appropriate speed, whatever that is, the plane tips back as it lifts into the air. My stomach swoops, and I instinctively clutch Ronan's hand and do everything I can from squealing like a pig.

The plane climbs higher and higher, and I stare out the window as the world below moves away from us and the clouds come closer. I love it. I love it so freaking much. I take in every bit of it I can, as if I'll never fly on a plane again, and when the landscape below is swallowed up by clouds and vapor, I finally look over at Ronan.

He's watching me with focused, happy eyes. I'm still holding his hand.

"Thank you," I say, brimming with happiness.

One corner of his mouth curves up, like he's trying not to smile too much.

"You're welcome, Dani."

The hotel is bananas, of course. Because why would Ronan stay in a hostel? It's a highrise in downtown Chicago that is nothing short of magnificent. I feel like royalty when we saunter up to the counter and Ronan checks us in. The woman working refers to us as Mr. and Mrs. Wells, and I try not to show how giddy it makes me. I've never heard myself referred to as Mrs. Wells before. I think I could get used to that.

The room is stupid nice. Plush everything. Couches. Huge TV. Balcony and seating. A kitchenette that's bigger than the kitchen in my old crummy apartment. I'm so overwhelmed by the granite and luxurious textiles that it takes me a moment to realize that this hotel room has one bed. Guess that means I'll be sleeping next to my hunky husband again tonight.

Well, *darn.*

My gaze lands on him, casually standing next to the kitchenette. He's just looking at me as I take everything in. I smile at him.

There are obviously still a lot of things I want to know about him, including his relationship with Sadie, but even so, last night's conversation, however painful for me, makes me feel closer to him. And I didn't think he would ever willingly let me closer. And I didn't think I would feel the need to get closer. But here we are. In Chicago. On our first little trip together.

"My meeting is at three," he says, his deep voice reaching out to me from across the room and shaking up my insides. "I'm sorry I can't hang out here for a bit longer."

"Oh, that's okay, Ronan. I know you're here for business. I get it."

He doesn't seem eased by what I said, but he nods.

"I'm not sure how long I'll be, but I made reservations for dinner at six."

"Oh, great." And I mean it. Dinner. Out. Non-contractually. *Swoon.*

He nods again and then licks his lips nervously. "I want you to enjoy yourself, but I won't pretend that I like the idea of you wandering around downtown alone."

My eyebrows raise slightly. "Even in the middle of the day?"

He shrugs.

He's so sweet when he's being protective. Maybe that's how he shows he cares.

"Oh, Wellsley, you don't have to worry about me. Remember the janky neighborhood I used to live in? I'll be fine."

Again, my words are ineffectual. He frowns and then sighs.

"Just text me and let me know where you're going, okay? I might not respond, but I'd still just like to know you're safe."

A smile splits my face. "Not even going to *try* to hide that sweet side of yours anymore, are you?"

His mouth twists to one side, but his blue eyes are smiling at me. I step closer to him, my eyes staying on his.

"For the record, I'd rather you not hide it," I say quietly as I stand in front of him.

"I know." His eyes slide down one of my arms, and then I see his hand reach for mine. His thumb smoothes over the back of my hand, making it tingle. "I'll be back to pick you up for dinner. I'll let you know if I'm running late."

I nod, trying not to blush at the way his touch, however sweet, makes me weak in the knees.

"Good luck with your meeting. Go knock him dead. You've got this."

Ronan gives me a small smile. "Thanks. I'll see you later." He releases my hand and then turns to go. I watch his broad shouldered body stride to the door, his grey suit effortlessly moving smoothly over each muscle in his back, then he pauses with a warm look in my direction before he's gone.

The afternoon wears on slowly. I do decide to get out of the hotel room and walk around, but anywhere I go, I just think about Ronan and how he's worried for my safety. I wander back to the hotel room after only being out for about an hour and whittle away the rest of the time before dinner by watching TV and sitting on the balcony, listening to the city.

It's here that I wonder what restaurant he chose for dinner. Is my old stand-by plum dress nice enough? I decide to go back out and buy a nicer dress, just in case. And when I say nice, I mean like a fifty-dollar dress. I have no intention of ever spending as much money as I spent on that navy dress ever again. So, I find an A-line dress at a boutique around the corner that I like very much. It's royal blue with white lace accents. Super cute and not too formal. I take my spoils back to the hotel and get ready for what I'm calling my *date* with Ronan. Even if it isn't, that's what I'm dressing for. A date. After being so vulnerable with him last night, the idea of a date with Ronan doesn't scare me. On the contrary, I'm damn excited.

He texts me at five-thirty saying he's on his way. And when the door opens ten minutes later, I can tell from the relaxed look on his face that he nailed his meeting. Pride bubbles up inside me for my amazingly successful husband. It's clear to me that I definitely married up. All I have to offer him is my zany personality, which historically has not been enough to keep a guy around. Well, except for Spencer. And we know how that ended.

I shake that thought from my head and smooth my hands down the skirt of my dress.

"Hey, Wellsley," I greet warmly as he closes the door and turns to face me.

His blue eyes take me in quickly, and I can't mistake the look of surprise that comes over his face. I, of course, break into a nervous sweat.

"I wasn't sure where you picked for dinner, but I figured it was probably somewhere reasonably nice, so I thought I'd find something a little nicer to wear than my go-to plum dress that you've seen me wear about five times since you met me," I blurt out in one steady stream, suddenly feeling bashful.

"I like it," he says, coming closer.

My shoulders relax slightly, and it's only then that I realized I was tensing them.

"Is it okay for where we're going?"

He smiles softly at me and touches the white lace trim on my shoulder strap.

"It's perfect."

I feel a tiny shiver run through me at the feel of his warm fingers grazing my skin. He must feel it, because his eyes return to mine and stay there, blazing.

My mind goes totally blank. Blank like a check with no amount written on it. Blank like a test question I can't answer. Blank like there is an empty space where my brain should be.

I can't think a single thought. But oh, do I feel everything. I can't speak, but my heart is trying to perform Morse code by ramming itself at my ribcage in a rhythm I'm sure he can hear. Every piece of my body is vibrating with the electricity emanating from his skin onto mine.

Oh, shit, my pupils are dilating. I'm sure of it.

Ronan stays perfectly still as my body suffers the shockwave of his touch, and then he moves his head just a little closer, like he's thinking about kissing me.

Oh, my God, is he going to kiss me?

I bet he's an amazing kisser. Why wouldn't he be? I have a feeling he's good at anything he does. With or without his tongue. The thought of his tongue brushing against mine has my head spinning.

But before he can move any closer to prove my giddy assumption, his phone rings in his pocket. We both visibly startle, and he drops his hand.

"Shit," he mutters and removes his phone from his pocket in great irritation. I finally feel like my brain is back in my head, and I somehow get myself together as he answers.

"Yeah?" he picks up, his eyes fixed on something in the kitchen. "Great, yeah. Send it over." He hangs up without saying goodbye to who I assume was Gina and then looks back at me. "Sorry."

Did he just apologize that we were interrupted? Wow. I...I think he was actually going to kiss me.

I smile. "It's alright." I clear my throat awkwardly, still reeling just slightly. "I'll get my purse."

I do so with the one thought in my head: I must not grin like I'm insane. Don't do it, girl. Play it cool. Keep it together.

I follow him to the elevator, and we ride it down to the main floor. My brain is abuzz with that small interaction we just had and where it was going before we were interrupted. It seems in the span of one night, we're both not interested in hiding what is happening between us.

Because back there? Touching me? You're damn right, there's something happening between us. And my heart has a lot to say about it. Namely, *this man is fine, and he's all mine.*

"It's close, so we can walk," Ronan tells me as we step out onto the street.

"Great. It's a beautiful night for a walk." I fall into step with him as we head down the sidewalk in the direction of dinner. Cabs and cars hum along, some stopping to drop off or pick up someone. I can see why Ronan is interested in real estate here. Chicago is beautiful and urban, the Riverwalk being my favorite part so far. Can't beat the dreamy, romantic vibes of walking along the river.

Thankfully, the city air and hubbub is enough to distract me from whatever just almost happened in our room, and I'm able to think more rationally.

"So, how did it go? Good?"

Ronan stuffs his hands in the pockets of his suit pants and looks down at the sidewalk as a small smile plays at the lips that I'm sure were about to kiss me before.

"Yeah, it was good. Gina is sending the paperwork."

I shake his strong arm in excitement and only half regret it. "That's awesome! I knew you could do it, Wellsley."

He looks at me with that same smile on his face and then looks ahead, seeming much more at ease than I have seen him. Well, when I wasn't comforting him, that is. And then he surprises me. He removes one hand from his pocket and links his thick fingers with mine.

Oooooh, boy. This is so a date. This is the date-i-est date that ever dated. I have never been more thrilled or less connected to the ground.

I'm pretty sure I don't have feet anymore cause I swear I'm floating down the sidewalk right now.

I have zero presence of mind to even look at the name of the restaurant when we come upon it. I just follow my husband like a lost puppy and sit across from him at our table, severely smitten.

There's no getting around it. I like this guy. And he likes me. I'm sure of it.

I can't read even a single word on the menu, despite my desperate attempts to make the words register in my brain. So, when Ronan orders a steak, I tell the waiter that I'll have the same. The dude could bring me a live buffalo, and I wouldn't care. I'm on a date with Ronan.

I'm on a date with Ronan.

And if I had any doubt, it's gone as soon as we start talking. I watch Ronan's expression become more and more relaxed as we talk. And we talk about everything. Ronan's days as swim captain in high school. His tenacity for studying business in college. His pride in being his father's son. My days growing up a lonely only child. The sister I found in Melanie and our high school shenanigans. The car accident and what it was like for me to be there when my parents died. Ronan holds my hand again when I talk about it, and I see his grief for me. He shakes his head slightly.

"How do you do it?"

"Do what?"

He pauses, looking at his hand covering mine. "How do you go through so much shit and still be so happy?"

His question catches me off guard for a moment, but then I understand what he means. He's confused by how "lively" I am despite having lost so much. I take a sip of wine and a slow, steadying breath.

"My parents were taken from me in the blink of an eye. And I could've died, too," I begin thoughtfully, my mind returning to the car accident. "Being that close to death changes you. And even though everything after that moment was stressful and difficult, I really have tried to enjoy my life as much as I can." I swallow hard, looking at the candle flickering between us. "Honestly, that's why I started seeing Spencer. I was trying to live my life and be happy again."

At the mention of his name, Ronan stiffens.

"And even though that obviously turned out really freaking badly, I still feel like I have this responsibility to live a happy, fulfilling life." I raise my eyes to his. "So, I do my best not to let Spencer's demons control how I respond to people. I try not to let my grief over losing my parents consume my life. Because life is so precious. And short. And can be taken from us at any moment. I want to live without holding back." My eyes sting with tears. "I feel like I owe that to my parents, you know?"

Saying all of that out loud just reinforces how much I believe it. I have this *one* life. *One* time here on earth, trying to get it all right. And Ronan is beginning to look more and more right to me. This is just the beginning for us, and I know that. But I'm already feeling more sure that when these two years are up, I'll still want him to be in my life.

Ronan is quiet for a moment, taking in what I said. Finally, he shakes his head slightly.

"You're amazing," he murmurs.

I smile slightly and squeeze his hand. He just blatantly complimented me. Oh, my gosh. I could burst right now.

"You're not so bad yourself, Mr. Wells. In fact, you're a regular catch. I bet every girl in here wishes they were me right now." I don't even have to look to know that's true.

He glances around. "I could say the same about the men here wishing they were me."

I snort. "Okay buddy. Sure. If the dudes here wish they were you, it's just because you're handsome and fit and successful and rich. It's not because you're sitting with me."

His eyebrows flicker defensively. "Bullshit," he says and then huffs. "Apparently, you're surprised to find out that you're a beautiful woman. Your asshole ex made sure of that, I bet."

I look away, wishing we were talking about something else. The last time we talked about Spencer, our dinner took an immediate dive bomb. Despite not wanting tonight to go anything like last night, I can't help myself. I still have questions about Sadie.

"Did Sadie ever make you feel like that? Like no one else would ever want you besides her?"

He removes his hand from mine, and I try not to take offense.

"In a way."

I wait for him to say more, but he doesn't, which doesn't surprise me. I know he isn't an open book like me. But I gather my courage anyway and decide against my better judgment to press him.

"What exactly happened with Sadie?" I ask cautiously. "The only version I've heard is from Bodie, and obviously, that was wildly exaggerated."

"No," comes his deep voice, filled with anger and loathing. "It was a flat out lie."

"Right."

He sighs, and a menacingly dark look drags his eyebrows low over his brooding, downcast eyes.

Abort! Abort! You're about to lose him!

"Ronan, I totally get it if you don't want to talk about what happened," I jump in quickly. "It really sucks to talk about stuff like that. It's just that I only heard Bodie out because I didn't know the real story. I almost believed him because I didn't know the truth."

He raises his blue eyes to mine slowly, looking deeply aggrieved as he takes in my explanation. Ronan chews his bottom lip for a moment and then nods.

"I'll try."

I want to reach over and put my hand back in his, but I decide to stay still and just listen as attentively as I can. I know that whatever he's about to tell me is so deeply personal that he will likely never talk about it again.

He sips his whiskey and then begins with slightly hunched shoulders.

"I met her through my mother. Looking back now, that should've been my first clue that Sadie was no good for me," he says to the tabletop. "She was beautiful and witty and smart. I could talk to her about business or whatever, and she was always interested. We just got along really well, and I fell for her almost immediately."

There's a pain in his voice that is totally gutting me right now. I hate hearing him talk about someone he loved, knowing that their story ended in betrayal.

"We were together about four months by the time she started dropping hints about engagement rings. As crazy as I was about her, I wasn't where I wanted to be professionally and was still dealing with my father's sudden death. So, I held off on proposing." He swirls the whiskey in his glass slowly. "I felt guilty about that, so I guess I didn't mind that she was spending a lot of my money. And then..."

Ronan stops here and painfully hesitates for a long moment. I can barely take it. Not because I need him to go on, but because the tortured look from the night of Bodie's wedding is back on his face. I swallow hard and put my hand on his.

"And then you found out about Bodie," I finish for him gently, as if saying it for him will make it less painful.

His eyes flash to mine, but he says nothing to confirm what I said. I give him an empathetic smile and squeeze his hand.

"I'm sorry, Ronan."

His eyes on me, I watch him struggle with what to say in reply. At last, he swallows hard and looks away again.

"After that, I just buried myself in my work," he finishes quietly.

"I did the same after Spencer. I mean, not that I wasn't working like crazy before that, cause I definitely was. But after what he did, I distracted myself from it as best I could, and I haven't dated anybody or even been willing to take a risk like that again." I smile at him warmly. "Well, I guess until you came along."

I mean that in reference to our little agreement, but I realize after it's out of my mouth that the words sound much more intimate. Even though he doesn't return my smile, I feel good about the risk I took by marrying him. I've gotten a good man and millions of dollars out of the deal. Can't be mad about that.

I finish the last of my wine, and suddenly the waiter is standing at our table.

"Anything else for you two tonight?"

"No, thank you. I'm stuffed," I answer. Ronan just nods in agreement.

"Then, I'll leave this with you," the waiter says, setting down a little black folder with the check inside of it.

"Oh, no need," I say and quickly fetch my credit card. He and Ronan both look stunned. "What?"

"I'll pay," Ronan says, looking slightly confused.

"No, I've got it. Here." I thrust the card into the waiter's hand.

"Uh, okay. I'll be right back then." The waiter retreats, and I look back at Ronan, who still has a funny, confused expression on his handsome face. I squint at him slightly.

"Never had a girl pay for a date before, eh?" I ask with a chuckle.

Finally, Ronan's face relaxes a bit. "No, I haven't."

"Well, it's the least I can do for you inviting me to Chicago with you. It's been amazing, Ronan. Thank you again."

"I thought you didn't keep score," he teases lightly.

I grin at him. "There's a difference between keeping score and making sure you know how much I appreciate you." I wink at him. "So, I think what you meant to say is, *you're welcome*."

His mouth makes a small smile, and he gives an even smaller laugh. More like a puff of air escaping his nose than a real laugh. But I'll take it.

"You're welcome, Dani."

After I happily pay the bill, which is the priciest meal I've ever purchased, Ronan stands and extends his hand to me.

"Shall we?"

"We shall, Husband."

He glances at me with an affectionate expression that nearly knocks me on my ass. Witnessing him opening up to me on this date has done nothing but cause me to hope that this really can be something bigger than either of us imagined when we agreed to get married.

And he didn't want to have a love clause. *Ha.*

Chapter Twenty-One

Ronan

Well, I'm fucked.

Dinner with Dani was going so well. It was surprisingly easy for me to open up once I started talking and I saw how intently she listened to the details I shared about my life. It felt good to open up, despite how infrequently I've done it in recent years. But then she had to ask about Sadie. Not that I should be surprised. She has every reason at this point to want to know what happened. But could I do it? No. Because I'm a fucking coward.

Just last night Dani bared her soul to me and told me about her ex-boyfriend almost fucking killing her, and I couldn't even get myself to tell her Sadie faked a pregnancy so I'd marry her. How the hell can I demand Dani tell me the worst moment of her life when I can't even tell her the whole truth about Sadie? I hate myself.

As we head for the exit of the restaurant, Dani slips her little hand into mine, and it only makes me feel worse. This woman deserves the best, and I can't even find enough courage to be honest with her. Fuck.

And the truth is, I only feel this shitty about it because I like her so damn much. Watching her on the plane was one of the cutest things I've ever seen. Her excitement and her wonder captured me completely. And then to come back to the hotel after getting the deal with Roy to find her waiting for me in a new dress...damn. I wanted to take her right then. Make her mine. Make her forget that asshole who hurt her ever existed.

But now, *I'm* the asshole. She deserves better. I resolve to tell her everything when we get back to the hotel, if only to soothe my guilty conscience.

"Well, long time, no see!" comes a booming voice from my right. I turn to see Roy Stanton at the waitstand, looking happy and possibly a bit drunk. Despite making a deal with him and being damn pleased about it, I'm not happy to see more of him. Roy's boisterous, loud personality is nowhere near my cup of tea. Nevertheless, I reach out my hand to shake his.

"Roy, hello again."

He shakes my hand firmly for a moment and then pauses, doing a double take when he sees Dani next to me.

"Oh, my my my, who is this?" Roy asks, his beady brown eyes zeroing in on my wife.

"This is my wife, Dani," I introduce, my stomach twisting as I recognize the heated look on Roy's face as he blatantly takes her in. "This is Roy Stanton, who I met with earlier."

"Oh, so nice to meet you," Dani greets excitedly and shakes his hand. Roy holds it tight when she tries to let go, and my stomach twists even more.

"Very, very nice to meet you, sweetie." He shoots me a teasing glare. "Since when are you married? I thought you'd never settle down. No wonder you wouldn't come with me to the strip club tonight." A loud laugh booms out of him that disgusts me. "Why pay for something you only get to look at when you have a little slice like this waiting for you at home for free?" He laughs again, and Dani finally succeeds in removing her hand from his clutches.

She moves closer to me, and I hold her hand tighter. I glance down and see that her face is white. I need to get her out of here. I clear my throat.

"Well, I—"

"Hell, I don't know how you even got yourself to leave the hotel room. How are you even hungry after eating that sweet muffin? I know I wouldn't be..." Roy licks his lips as he stares at Dani.

My hands start to shake with anger, and my heart begins to pound wildly in my chest. I want to hurt him. I want to punch those vile words right back into his mouth. I want to render him incapable of speaking another fucking word.

But this isn't just some asshole at the bar. This is a man I just made a very lucrative deal with. I look down at Dani, my heart still pounding. Do I risk losing the deal over standing up for Dani? She looks up at me, and I see the fear and disgust and humiliation in her usually bright, hazel eyes. I swallow hard, knowing what the right thing is.

"Give us a minute, will you?" I ask her gently and nod toward the door. "Wait for me outside. I'll be right there."

She glances at Roy nervously and then back at me. "Are you sure?"

I lift her hand and kiss it. "I'm sure." I'm pleased to see a bit of joy flit back into her expression from such a small act of affection.

"Don't be long." Without another word to Roy, she disappears outside. I catch him unabashedly perusing her backside as she walks away.

I take a deep breath, trying to stay in control of myself, and wait for Roy to look at me. When he does, he seems floored to see the livid look on my face. I take a threatening step closer and try to keep my balled fists at my sides.

"Let me make something clear, Roy," I begin, struggling to keep my voice even. "That woman is the best thing that has ever happened to me. She's isn't just a 'slice.' She's my wife," I say, both surprised by the words coming out of my mouth and also deeply certain of their truth. "What you said was extremely inappropriate and disrespectful. You will apologize to Dani."

Roy blinks a few times as he takes in my threatening words, and then a strange smile comes over his smarmy face.

"I didn't know you had it in you, Ronan. You're really in love with her."

My eyes narrow at his insinuation that I'm incapable of love. "Yes, I am." Something eases slightly in my chest after that admission.

He chuckles and then shakes his head. "You're a sucker, boy. She'll chew you up and spit you out. They all do."

I glance over toward the door, where I can see Dani waiting outside for me anxiously.

Before Dani came along, I would've easily agreed with Roy. Because after Sadie, I was ready to believe love wasn't real or worth pursuing. I was ready to be alone for the rest of my life rather than risk feeling something for anyone again. But I realize that Dani has changed all that. She's changed everything.

I look back at Roy. "You don't know her."

"Listen, I didn't mean to cause issues here. If you don't want to do business with me, then fine. I'll have no trouble finding another buyer."

"I didn't say that," I reply at once, holding his challenging gaze. "I said you need to apologize to Dani."

Roy glowers at me. "I'm not apologizing to a *woman*."

I can feel my body temperature rise, and I fight to keep myself from decking this asshole.

"Then, you're right. I don't want to do business with you."

His shock exposes his bluff. "You're seriously blowing this deal because of *her*? You're more of a sucker than I thought."

I grab the collar of his shirt and bring him closer to my face.

"So be it." I hold his fearful gaze with my glare for a moment longer and then shove him back, releasing him. Then, I turn and stride out of the restaurant without a backward glance.

Fuck.

I'm pissed. But it's his own fault. My dad did whatever he could to do business with decent people, and it's clear to me that Roy Stanton is not a decent person. Despite losing the deal I've been after for years, I feel a strange sense of relief. I know I did the honorable thing. I know my dad would be proud of me for standing up for my wife. It's something he would have done.

"What happened? Is everything okay?" Dani asks me, her face full of concern. Her hands are clasped together anxiously as I approach her on the breezy evening sidewalk.

"It's fine. Let's go." I turn toward the hotel, and she follows me.

"Ronan, it's not fine. I can see it all over your face. Tell me what happened."

I stalk on for a moment, chewing my lip. I know she won't let it go, so I relent with a heavy sigh.

"He wouldn't apologize to you."

"Apol—Wait, what?" She grabs my arm to stop me. "You asked him to apologize?"

"Of course, I did," I answer fiercely, looking down at her. "I'm not going to let anybody talk to you like that, business partner or not."

Dani is so stunned that she says nothing. So, I press on and explain.

"My dad taught me that people who are assholes in life are assholes in business. I don't want to be doing business with someone who says that kind of shit to my wife and won't apologize for it."

She gasps. "You mean—you're not—?"

"No. I'm not buying his property."

She stares at me, the night air catching her light brown hair. "You didn't have to do that."

I study her for a moment, mulling over her words. She's wrong. I can barely live with myself enough as it is for not telling her everything about Sadie. If I hadn't had her back in this fucked-up situation, I know it would have gotten between us. And the last thing I want is something getting between us.

So, I shake my head. "Yes, I did."

"Ronan, I would've understood if you didn't say anything in order to save your deal," she says quietly, and there's no doubt in my mind that she's telling the truth. She would willingly take verbal harassment for me.

"I'd be a damn shitty husband for allowing you to put up with that."

She smiles, but it doesn't eclipse the wonder and residual shock on her face.

"It's for the best, I'm sure. I probably just dodged a huge bullet," I add, trying to ease her enough to somehow get our evening back on track.

Dani shakes her head slightly. "Ronan..." She shakes her head again, and then suddenly, her arms are around my neck, hugging me tightly. "Thank you," she murmurs to my shoulder.

I move my arms around her middle and feel the last of my anger fade. Damn. Being close to Dani is like nothing else in the world.

"I'm in your corner," I murmur back. "You're my girl." I don't recognize the intimacy in my voice, but it feels good to be so vulnerable with her. Somehow, I know she's a safe place to land, no matter what happens.

I know that I just made the right choice. She's so much more fucking important to me than that deal with Roy, which is scary as hell and comforting at the same time.

She pulls back and swipes at her eyes, smiling at me.

"I knew you were a good man, Ronan." She looks up at me warmly. "My gut has always been right about you. And if that wasn't enough, you've proved it by not tolerating shitty people and standing up for me when it really matters and treating your employees so well. Remember on your birthday? Your employees had nothing but amazing things to say about you. Do you know how rare that is?" She beams at me. "It makes me so proud to be your wife, Ronan."

I stare at her, my heart thumping painfully in my chest. The only person to ever say they were proud of me was my dad. I'm struck by the effect her words have on me.

She's proud to be mine.

I swallow hard, overwhelmed by emotions I'm unfamiliar with, and lean down without thinking. I place a quick kiss on her mouth, so quick that she barely has time to kiss me back before I straighten up again. I can hear the blood pounding in my ears as I take her hand and nod down the sidewalk.

"Come on," I say quietly and lead her back to the hotel in silence. I know I've completely stunned her with that kiss. And despite how quick it was, I can still feel the warmth of her soft lips on mine. It felt like a spark of electricity. Like lightning.

I've more than crossed the friendship line. But choosing her over the deal with Roy has put everything in perspective. She *is* my girl. And I want her.

We get on the elevator, still in silence, and I find myself hoping that whatever this is between me and Dani is something that sticks around. Somehow, I want this to work. I want her by my side. I'm going to do everything I can to give her a reason to stay when our contract is over. I don't want her for two years. I want her for the rest of my life.

Inside the hotel room, Dani changes out of her dress in the bathroom, while I change out of my suit by the bed. I don a pair of gym shorts and a t-shirt and sit down on the edge of the bed, eager for Dani to emerge from the bathroom in her pajamas as well. When she does, she tosses her dress toward her bag on the floor and then leans against the door jam with her arms crossed. She has a funny expression on her face.

"What?" I ask, plopping my phone on the bed behind where I'm sitting.

She smiles suspiciously. "Sooooo, is that something we're doing now?"

"What?"

Her lips quirk to the side. "Kissing. You kissed me on the sidewalk, in case you don't remember."

I feel the corners of my mouth curl into a smile. "I remember."

She chuckles softly, smiling at me sweetly.

"Is that alright?" I ask.

She chuckles again, more nervously this time. "Mhm."

"Good."

She bites her lip as she looks at me, and I feel butterflies rise in my stomach. When was the last time I felt fucking butterflies? Damn, this girl.

"You know, I didn't really get a chance to kiss you back..." she hints shyly, her cheeks blushing deeply.

My heart beats a little harder at her meaning. I shouldn't be surprised by her directness. She takes what she wants, and more than anything, do I want that to be me.

"Don't get me wrong," she adds quickly. "I liked it. It was like a sweet little...*smooch*. There's nothing wrong with smooches. I'm actually a huge fan of smooches. But I barely got to smooch you back, you know?"

"Then, maybe we should try it again," I suggest, and she blushes even more.

"Yeah, maybe we should." She clears her throat. "I mean, if you want to. Totally no pressure. It's not a big deal or anything," she rambles and then laughs nervously.

I stand up, ignoring how my knees feel a little wobbly, and turn toward her. "I want to."

My directness seems to catch her off guard for a moment, but who am I kidding? Hell yes, I want to kiss her again. And hell yes, do I want to feel her kiss me back this time.

I move closer and take her hands in mine. Even at a reasonable distance from her, I can feel the heat her excited body is exuding. I swallow hard, look into her bright eyes, and move her hands to my chest. She steps a little closer, smiling nervously, and I place my hands on her waist.

My mind flashes back to when I touched her shoulder before dinner, and something sensual and intimate passed between us. I can feel that same chemistry between us now, pulling me to her like a magnet.

I bow my head toward hers, encouraged by the way she moves in close to me. Her flowery scent washes over me as my eyes move from hers to her lips. I hear her suck in a deep breath, and then she closes the distance between us. I close my eyes.

Her lips gently press to mine, and her hands clutch the front of my shirt when I kiss her back slowly and fully. I feel my body coming alive in a way it never has before. Despite the hammering of my heart, I feel a strange sense of peace come over me. I didn't know I could feel this anymore. Something so deep and so consuming. Something deeper than physical attraction. I can feel her melting into my touch, coming undone in my hands from just one kiss.

When I pull away slightly, she follows and moves her mouth back to mine. Her lips part, and now I'm the one melting. Now, I'm the one leaning into her, holding onto her, so my knees won't give out beneath me. I feel her hands exploring my upper body as she presses herself into me. I stroke my fingers gently through her long hair, reveling in allowing myself to touch her and be touched by her, too.

When her fingers thread soothingly through my hair and then tenderly touch my face, I feel myself giving in to this amazing, beautiful woman, who is kissing me with so much passion that I feel whole for the first time in my entire life.

Shit...I'm such a fucking goner.

I angle my head to the side to deepen our kiss, and Dani gives out a small moan that sends a pounding thrill through my body. Her mouth tastes like the sweet wine she had with dinner. Our surroundings have long disappeared from my notice, but with each kiss and each touch, I lose myself in her even more. It's fucking bliss.

"Ronan," says Dani between kisses.

"Mmm," I reply, loving the way she says my name.

"Ronan," she says again and giggles into my mouth. I pull back, realizing that she's trying to get my attention.

"Hmm?"

I know my eyes have that hazy, out of focus look about them, but so do hers.

"Your phone is ringing."

She nods toward the bed where, sure enough, my phone is vibrating and beeping. I genuinely didn't hear it.

I shrug, not the slightest bit interested in who could be calling at this moment. Whatever it is, it isn't as important as what's happening right here between me and Dani.

"I'm a little busy at the moment," I say, looking down into the hazel eyes of my beautiful wife.

She grins. "Damn right, you are."

I move my mouth back to hers, where I'm certain it belongs, and immediately feel myself succumbing once again to her sweet kisses and needy touches. She kisses with such abandon, holding nothing back. Like all this time, she's been desperate for this.

When I kiss along her jaw to her neck, she gasps, and I pull back instantly.

Damn it, slow down, Ronan.

"Too much?" I ask, only just then realizing how breathless we both are.

"No," she whispers, still clutching me by the shoulders. She places a sweet kiss on my lips and then rests her forehead against mine. "Are we really doing this?" she asks, her voice still at a whisper.

"This?" I don't know if she's referring to sex, but the part of me tenting my gym shorts right now definitely hopes she is. I want all of her.

Dani pulls her head away from mine but stays close to me. "Us. You and me...you know, dating or whatever."

I sigh heavily and tilt my head back towards the ceiling. "God, I hate that word."

It feels so...juvenile. To say that we're dating would cheapen this in my eyes, and I couldn't handle that. Besides, dating sounds open-ended. Like we're just trying this out. This isn't a test run for me. It's the long haul.

I feel her posture deflate in my hands at my cool response. "Oh."

I look back down at her to find an uncertain expression on her face that guts me. I need to explain quickly before she thinks I'm just in this for a booty call because it's pretty clear she wants more than just that. And that pleases the hell out of me.

"What we're doing is not dating," I say, my brain still a bit hazy from kissing her. "Dating is too...temporary."

She blinks, and then a beautiful smile blossoms across her face. She bites her well-kissed bottom lip. "You don't want temporary?"

"No," I answer honestly, my deep voice soft. "Not with you."

With anyone else, it would be a drastically different answer. But with Dani, I want permanent. I'd be a fucking lucky man if she was a permanent part of my life. I can't even imagine what the loss of her would feel like. How I could ever go back to living my life without her in it? Her quirky, bright spirit belongs with my battered, well-meaning spirit.

I want to say those words out loud to her, so that she understands more fully how I feel. But I've never been good at talking about my emotions, even the good ones. At least the four words I said seem to be enough for her, if the way she's beaming up at me is an indication.

"Is that...how you feel, too?" I question gently, though I'm pretty damn sure of her answer.

"Yes," she says, breathless, and just like that, I've never felt more whole.

Chapter Twenty-Two
Dani

I've died and gone to heaven.

Not to sound like an eighth-grade girl, but...I kissed Ronan, and he kissed me back! Eeeek! I have never wanted to talk to Melanie more than I do right now. But I'm pretty sure Ronan would rather I stay where I am. Where is that, you ask? Tucked into his arms in our hotel bed. In the dark. After we made out.

He actually wants me. There's no denying that, not now that we kissed like teenagers and admitted to each other that this thing between us isn't what we said it would be. Temporary. Platonic. Contractual. That should scare me, but instead, I feel...stupidly elated.

Sigh. I don't know how I'm going to be able to sleep tonight. I just keep replaying it all in my mind and feeling like the freaking luckiest girl on the planet. I think Ronan must be doing the same thing. He has yet to relax into that steady rhythm of deep breathing. I'm betting that if I stroked my fingers through his hair though, I could get him to fall asleep.

"Dani?" comes his soft voice from behind my head.

"Mhm?"

"Are you awake?"

"Can't sleep either, huh?"

I roll over in his arms and face him. The room is dark, but I can still plainly see the disturbed and almost guilty expression clinging to his sharp features.

"What's wrong?"

He bites his lip nervously. He hesitates, and I get a sinking feeling in my stomach. How could he have *that* look on his face when I feel so deliriously good? Maybe he's regretting this. God, I hope I'm wrong. I think it would kill me to hear him say it was a mistake to kiss me.

Ronan gently strokes his finger tips down my arm, looking pensive.

Please, I think, *please tell me how you're feeling.*

"I wasn't completely honest with you before," comes his deep voice, much quieter than I expect.

"About what?"

Please don't say us. Please don't say us.

He swallows, watching his fingers moving over my arm. "About Sadie."

Oh, no. What if he still loves her? What if he misses her? What if I don't measure up to her? How could I, really? She's gorgeous. And part of the elite, rich world that Ronan belongs to.

I sit up slightly, leaning on one elbow. "What do you mean?"

Ronan sighs heavily and twists behind him to flip on the bedside lamp. When he turns back to me, I can see the guilt on his face much more clearly. My stomach churns with nerves and dread. He leans on his elbow, too and absently twists my father's ring on his finger. He avoids my eyes as he explains.

"There's more to what happened with her. I'm sorry I didn't say it all earlier…it's just really hard for me to talk about." He shakes his head slightly. "I know that's a shitty excuse. I wish I was more like you, Dani. I wish I wasn't such a fucking coward."

My heart breathes a little sigh of relief. It makes me realize how much I really do care about this man and how much I really want him with me. How much my heart is drowning out my head now that I know we both feel something.

Ronan looks up at me finally, his apologetic words moving me deeply. I've never received a more contrite apology.

"I swear I was going to tell you when we got back to the hotel earlier, but then, well…I got a little…*distracted*."

I grin at him, trying not to blush. "It's okay, Ronan," I tell him sweetly and move my hand into his. "It's never easy to talk about the worst moments of our lives, but no matter what, you can always talk to me, okay? About anything."

He nods and looks only slightly eased. He takes a deep breath, and I try to prepare myself for whatever he's about to tell me. Although I have no idea what could be worse than what I already know about Sadie's despicable actions.

"She wanted me to propose, and I wasn't there yet," he recaps from earlier.

I instantly realize my error in finishing for him before and feel a surge of guilt. That's the last time I try to finish his sentence. I've learned my lesson.

"I came home from work one day and—" He stops abruptly, like the words are causing him physical pain. "She told me she was pregnant."

I gasp. "With Bodie's baby?" I exclaim in horror.

He shakes his head, still avoiding eye contact. "She told me I was going to be a father, and..." A deeply tumultuous expression takes over his face, and it makes my heart pound. "And I was so excited..."

Suddenly, he's on his feet, his hands raking through his dark hair as he paces next to the bed. I sit up and watch him as he fights with himself to not become emotional and loses.

"We made a baby registry. We picked out paint colors for the nursery. We talked about baby names. I baby proofed the house, for fuck's sake."

He paces for a few more moments and wipes angrily at his wet eyes.

"She wanted us to get married before she had the baby, so I proposed, and she started making wedding plans. Even though everything was happening faster than I had planned, I had never been so happy. We had never been so happy."

Ronan stops, his hands on his trim hips, looking down at the carpet. The lamp on the nightstand casts a yellow glow from behind him, throwing most of his wet face into shadow.

"But then..." He finally looks up at me, and then I'm crying, too because of how much pain he's showing me. "I got an earlier flight home from a business trip to surprise her. I found her in bed with Bodie." He swallows hard and looks away again as he shakes his head. "It isn't just that I caught them fucking behind my back. It's what I heard them talking about."

I shift onto my knees, keeping my eyes on him, so he knows I'm listening with every atom of my body.

"He was asking her when she was going to come clean about the baby. When she was going to fake a miscarriage, so I wouldn't find out she had lied about being pregnant to get me to propose."

My mouth drops open as shock ripples through me.

"I have never—" His voice catches, and his face crumples slightly, the lines of his face standing out from the light behind him. "I have never felt so broken," he whispers through his tears. He clears his throat. "I wasn't surprised that Bodie slept with my fiancée. He's always been a deceitful asshole. But Sadie...I trusted her." He sniffs and looks up at me. "I put Bodie in the hospital for what he did. I almost killed him. And I cut her out of my life as quickly as I could, despite how many times she tried to apologize."

His words about what he did to Bodie chill my blood, but I still find myself getting up from the bed to approach him.

"I lost everything I had...my whole future was just...a *lie*."

"I'm so sorry, Ronan," I whisper mournfully through my own tears. I can't even imagine how he got through all of that in one piece, especially without his dad. His past has dark places, just like mine, and in a way, I'm thankful for that because we understand a piece of each other that not everyone would. But I'm sure as hell not saying that out loud right now. I'm pretty sure that's the last thing he needs to hear.

I reach my hands out to pull him close. At first, he doesn't react, but then he curls into my embrace, burying his wet face into the side of my neck.

Everything makes sense to me now. His awful relationship with his brother. Why he was such a nervous wreck when we got married. Why he started shaking when his mother told him to his face that he would make a terrible father. Why he's been so guarded with me and everyone else.

He's endured an unspeakably deep wound. I run my fingers through his hair and clutch him to me tightly. I don't know what to say to comfort him. What even *could* I say to lessen his pain? Nothing. Not a damn thing.

"Thank you for telling me," I whisper to him softly because it really means a lot that he felt like he needed to tell me the whole truth. He definitely could've gotten away with what he said at dinner, and I never would've questioned it. But honesty is important enough to him that he let his walls down, so I could see his hurt.

Gah, this man. I respect him so much.

I turn my face toward his and place a kiss on his stubbly jaw. His fingers press into my back, and then I feel his lips brush my neck in reply.

Immediately, a bolt of hot electricity shoots through me from head to foot.

Ooof. Ronan has an effect on me like no other man has. He makes me aware of my body in a way I've never experienced. It's like fire coursing through every vein, igniting something deep inside me.

He seems to sense the heated response my body is giving and kisses my neck again, this time parting his lips and allowing his tongue to brush my skin. The breath catches in my throat. I involuntarily cling to him as my knees quiver.

Ronan lifts his head and looks down at me, his blue eyes blazing with such an intensity that I feel powerless to do anything but return the hungry kiss he gives me.

Giving in to Ronan feels effortless. Like I can give him myself without *losing* myself. He's just...part of me. That aching hole in my heart is being closed up by him, kiss by kiss. The homelessness I felt after my apartment burned down eases away with every caress of his hand and every stroke of his tongue with mine. That sense of homesickness I had after my parents died dulls as I let myself drown in Ronan, gasping and sighing as my brain completely fritzes out.

Damn, what a delicious bliss it is to belong to him.

In my brainless stupor, I don't realize he's walking me backward toward the bed until my ankle hits the padded bed frame behind me.

A distant alarm echoes in my foggy head. It feels so good to be with him like this, but...

I pull back with way more gusto than I intended and fall backward onto the bed. I roll off onto my feet on the other side and extend shaky arms.

"Wait!" I cry out, my chest heaving and my heart hammering.

It takes a moment for my eyes to focus on Ronan across the bed, and I see that his chest is heaving, too.

"Just wait," I repeat as I try to calm myself. I try to catch my breath. But I can't. I need air. "I—I need a second," I blurt out and wobble my weak legs out to the balcony as quickly as I'm able to.

The night air rushes into my lungs as I grasp the railing and try to calm my raging heart.

He isn't Spencer.

He isn't Spencer.

I repeat it again and again because the last time I turned down sex, I almost died.

"It's okay, girl. Get a grip," I whisper to myself.

It isn't that I don't want Ronan. The lust coursing through me right now is evidence enough of that. It would be easy to give him every last bit of me. It would feel *good* to give myself to him.

Despite our mutual feelings that we don't want something temporary, I'm still scared something could change. There's every possibility that my quirks and bright attitude will eventually start to get on his nerves. So, I don't want to rush. I don't want to give him my body before I feel safe enough to give him my heart. I want to know that he loves me before he becomes one with me.

Maybe that's a little old fashioned. But, given what I've been through, I don't care.

When the cool night air has chilled down my heated and excited body, I go back inside to find Ronan sitting on the edge of the bed with his head in his hands. He looks up at me quickly as I close the patio door. He stands up like he's about to come over to me but then painfully takes in how much distance I've put between us and stays where he is.

"I'm sorry," he says, almost in a panic. "I didn't mean to—"

"No, no, *I'm* sorry," I interrupt. "I don't want you to think I don't want you because obviously, I do. Like, I *really* do. My body is so mad at me right now because being with you like that was…" I fan my face at the memory of it. "I'm sorry I just bailed. But I'm not…I'm not ready because—"

"I know. I got carried away—" he talks over me, but I continue talking as well.

"—the last time I told a guy I didn't want to have sex, he tried to kill me."

Ronan freezes, his wide eyes staring at me from across the room.

My heart pounds. Shit. I really just said that out loud.

"Not that I think you would—I mean, I know you would *never*—"

I feel the panic rising in my chest at how that sounded—at how Spencer reacted when I told him no—and back up against the patio door.

He isn't Spencer.

Ronan raises his hands out to me, palms up, in a placating manner.

"Dani, it's okay," he says gently. "It's okay. You had a knee jerk reaction."

"Yes," I say, gasping slightly. "Yes. That's exactly what it was." I'm so relieved that he understands what just happened to me. He knows I'm not accusing him of being anything like Spencer. He knows I still want him.

"It's okay," he says again, and this time, he moves toward me. My heart continues to race, but when he offers me one of his hands, I take it. "I'm not going to hurt you. Ever."

His words hit me hard, and I instantly tear up. "I know that. I *swear*, I know that."

"If this is too much, I'm okay with taking a step back or doing whatever you need to do, okay?"

Take a step back? Hell no, I don't want to take a step back. The idea of going back to being whatever we were before tonight seems impossible.

"I don't want to take a step back," I assure him and pull him closer to me by the hand. "I guess I just have some things to work through still...so I...I need you to be patient with me."

A loving expression takes over his handsome face that makes my heart melt. He tucks my hair behind my ear affectionately. I close my eyes for a second at the feel of it.

"Of course. I can do that."

"Thank you."

I hesitate for just a second and then hug him tightly. He returns my hug eagerly and just as tightly.

"I'm sorry for ruining our night again," I murmur into his warm chest.

"You didn't ruin anything, Dani. Please stop apologizing."

"Sorry. I've always been an over-apologizer."

He gives me a little squeeze and then releases me. His eyes take in my damp face for a moment, like he's studying me and taking notes.

"Come on," he says and leads me over to the couch. "Let's see if we can find Harry Potter on PayPerView."

I follow Ronan into the house, feeling strangely glad to be home. The plane ride back was just as exciting to me as the ride there, and I honestly can't wait for the next time we fly somewhere again. It seems weird that we were only gone one night and so much changed. I feel a little guilty that he essentially went to Chicago for nothing, but I'm also so glad that I married a respectable man who is so firmly in my corner. I've never had a man choose me like that before.

And then, of course, the kissy times.

Ronan sets down our bags near the interior door to the garage and then opens the fridge to get a bottle of water.

Last night, we both fell asleep to Harry Potter again. It's quickly becoming my favorite thing ever. In the middle of the night, I woke up to him carrying me to the bed, where he immediately pulled me close to his chest.

But he's kept a reasonable distance from me since we got up this morning, and it's putting me off slightly. The last thing I want is for him to think we can't move forward from my knee jerk reaction. The last thing I want is to make him think I want to pull back. But I'm sure he's scared to come on too strong again. And that's frankly really freaking sweet.

We're really doing this. A relationship. A thing where we both care about each other and show it in ways that mean the most to the other person. It already seems too good to be true, even if he's been a little distant this morning.

He closes the fridge and opens his water, his eyes avoiding mine. I lean my hip into the counter across from him, hating the idea that he could slip away from me enough to put that wall back up and treat me like he did in the beginning—with that firm professionalism he's perfected so well over the years.

"Hey," I say, getting his attention. "We're okay, Ronan."

My sudden assurance catches him off guard, but then a look of relief crosses his dark features.

"I don't want things to be weird, okay? We're good. I promise."

Ronan studies me for a moment and then nods. I wait for him to say something, but he doesn't. He just looks at me.

I smile softly and fold my arms across my chest. "So, what's on the agenda today? Going in to work?" I ask, only half teasing him because I would not be even a little surprised if he left right now to go into the office.

He sets down his water and then closes the gap between us. I feel the air shrink in my lungs. His close proximity to me both soothes me and riles me up.

"I might go in for a bit, yeah," he answers, looking down at me. His blue eyes roam over my face, taking in each of my features. When they find my mouth, he bites his bottom lip. My heart thuds hard in my chest, expecting a kiss. But then, he looks up into my eyes seriously. "I want to ask—" He stops and swallows hard. "I want to know if it's okay to...touch you."

"Touch me?"

His hands rest on either side of the countertop behind me, caging me in between his muscular forearms in a way that makes me feel safe and not trapped.

I marvel at that for a split second. He makes me feel *safe*.

"Is it okay to hold your hand? Touch your arm or your hair or your back or your face?" A very vulnerable look passes over his face then that has me swooning. "It's been a long time since I've been with anyone, and I just want to know what's okay. I want to know if it's okay for me to be affectionate with you."

I smile sweetly at this amazing man of mine. "Of course, it's okay," I reply warmly.

Is that what's been bothering him? He isn't sure of how to go about this? I guess I never asked how long ago things with Sadie went down, but judging by his use of "a long time," I'm assuming it's been years since he's been affectionate with someone.

He smiles a little and nods.

"And is it okay for me to touch you, too?" I ask him, knowing the answer. But he paid me the courtesy of asking, so I figure I should do the same. Plus, I want to hear him say it.

"Yes."

"Good cause I plan on doing a lot of touching, hot stuff," I tease and wink.

When I beam up at him, something beautiful happens. He smiles back. Like *really* smiles back. The kind of smile I've only seen in a picture. I can see all of his teeth. And—*gasp*—he has dimples! And his eyes...filled with happiness. It takes my breath away.

I can't stop myself from grabbing that handsome face and kissing the smile right off of it. My heart painfully pounds with joy and excitement. I know that this between us is something good. Something better than I knew could exist. Something that could last a lifetime if we wanted it to. And I'm starting to think that I really do want it to.

Ronan kisses me slowly, his arms around me and mine around him. I can't believe how he makes me feel. How kissing him is like a drug. It's hypnotic. Addictive. Deeply fulfilling. It's dawning on me how starved for him I've been all this time. Being on the receiving end of his blatant affection is something I never thought I would have, but here I am...bathed in it.

I hear a low whistle from my left, and Ronan and I both break our kiss to look. Carla is standing on the other side of the island with a huge, shit-eating grin on her face.

"Am I interrupting something?" she teases.

For some reason, I expect Ronan to step away from me or at least let go of me, but he stays exactly as we are. I blush at the realization that he isn't ashamed of us. He isn't going to try to hide this from anybody. He isn't afraid for people to know how he feels about little old me.

"Or were you just performing mouth to mouth on her standing up?"

"Hey, Carla," he greets simply.

"You *do* realize you guys have a room upstairs at your disposal, right?" Carla continues, grinning.

I giggle and hide my hot face in Ronan's warm chest.

"I mean, I know you own the place, boss, but I should probably be warned of any amorous activity being performed in my kitchen."

Ronan groans slightly but still doesn't release me.

"A sock on the front door knob, maybe?"

"Are you done?" Ronan asks, though he doesn't sound as annoyed as I think he's trying to sound. I think he's too happy to even be grumpy with Carla. Sigh. I love that.

"Remember, leave room for Jesus."

I giggle again, just as embarrassed as I am delighted.

"Inspecting her tonsils with your tongue, were you?"

"Alright, alright," Ronan says warningly, but again, he isn't irritated.

I peek up at him and then rest my chin on his chest. He looks down at me as Carla sets down her bag of groceries and starts to unpack it. His eyes are smiling at me. I've never seen him like this. *Happy.*

"I'll be back for dinner, okay? I'll let you know when I leave," he murmurs to me softly. I smile at him a little more, and then he moves in close again to place a sweet kiss on my lips, without caring in the slightest that Carla is still nearby. If there's anything that convinces me of his happiness and the genuineness of his feelings for me, it's that.

Ronan pulls back and steps away slowly, like he doesn't really want to leave. I smile at him, and then he's out of the door.

The second the door closes, Carla stops what she's doing and fixes me with a knowing look. "About time, you two," she says.

I let out a school girl sigh and sink down to the floor, a puddle of butterflies and blushes.

Carla snorts. "I take it Chicago was good."

I giggle softly.

It was better than good. Things with Ronan are way freaking better than just good. And I can't wait to see where things go from here.

Chapter Twenty-Three

Ronan

I t's been a week since we got back from Chicago, and it's been nothing but heaven. Each night, I came home from work earlier than the night before so I could see more of her. Carla has been teasing us, but I don't give a shit. Dani has me on cloud nine, and I don't think anything can bring me down, especially when she kisses me like she'll die if she doesn't. I've noticed she kisses me like that after she's been sitting at the edge of the lap pool, her little feet in the water as she watches me swim back and forth. I've never had anyone do that. The second I get home, I'm seeking her out and spending the evening making out in the hot tub or on the couch in between conversations about our lives.

It feels so damn good to have her. I'm more sure than ever that this thing between us definitely isn't temporary. This is the kind of thing that ends with us on a porch swing, watching our grandkids playing in the front yard. I never knew how badly I wanted that until Dani. I never knew it could sound so perfect until Dani.

And if I had trouble focusing on work before, that was nothing compared to now. It's been a shitty Monday filled with essentially pointless meetings because I can't think about anything except Dani and what happened last weekend. I feel swallowed up by it, and I can't concentrate on a damn thing.

And I...*like* it. I haven't had anything good in my life for a long ass time. I haven't had anything in my personal life that makes me happy in years. You can't blame a guy for being distracted by it. You can't blame me for wanting to dwell in the memory of being with my girl. Maybe Dani's right about me. I'm a fucking softy. And I don't care if I'm a softy, as long as I'm *her* softy.

"What's wrong with you?" Gina demands sharply, suddenly standing in the doorway of my office.

"Nothing," I answer a little too defensively.

Gina sighs and enters my office. She closes the door behind her and then pins me with a suspicious look.

"Alright, what's going on?"

"What are you talking about?"

"The last week, you've been completely out of it."

I huff out my indignance, but she doesn't buy it. She's known me for too long. And even I know my behavior lately has been strange. I don't think I said two words in the meeting we just had. Usually, I'm asking questions and making suggestions, but I just couldn't stop thinking about how fucking good it felt to kiss Dani goodbye this morning before I left for work.

"Please tell me you aren't in a funk over the Roy Stanton deal because there will be others, Ronan," she encourages, coming closer.

At the mention of his name, I feel my shoulders tense.

"No, but Roy can go to hell," I say gruffly to my desktop. I didn't tell Gina any specifics about why I didn't make a deal with that asshole. I don't want to waste another word on that disgrace of a man.

She plops down on the chair across from my desk and places her tablet on her knees. She's wearing her blonde hair up in a bun today, the kind of bun Dani wears sometimes. Fuck, that's all it takes for me to find an excuse to think about her.

"Maybe you need a vacation," Gina suggests. "God knows you've never taken one. You didn't even go on a honeymoon after you and Dani got married."

I look up at the mention of Dani's name, and something must show on my face because Gina gives me a sly, knowing smile.

"Ohhhh, it's *Dani*, isn't it? You're distracted because you have a good woman in your life."

I press my lips together in reply, not wanting to admit it. Not that I have a problem admitting that she's completely changed my life in a short amount of time, but I'd rather not do that at work with my assistant.

She chuckles at the slight blush that creeps up my neck.

"I've never seen you like this," she says warmly. "Love looks good on you, Ronan."

Love.

That's a big word. A word I've only said to two people in my entire life and one of them was my dad. I'm not in love with Dani. I just can't stop thinking about her, that's all. I'm just...infatuated. Not in love.

Fuck, who am I kidding? I'm crazy about her. Crossing that line into a romantic relationship absolutely has me falling for her. And it's the free-fall kind of falling. I'm helpless to stop it.

I try to scoff though because, again, we're at work here, but Gina just grins at me.

"A good woman in your life is all the more reason for you to take some time off. Take Dani somewhere. Unplug. Be a husband and not a boss for a little while."

I can't deny how much that idea appeals to me. Take her somewhere...just the two of us. No work. No distractions. Just enjoying each other. Damn.

But I don't take vacations. I work. And if there's anything I need to do right now, it's to get my ass in gear so that I can continue to be successful. So that I can continue to make my dad proud. The last thing I want is to lose sight of my career goals just because I'm a little heart sick.

"You know I can't take a vacation right now," I argue, nodding toward her tablet. "There's too much going on."

"Then delegate," Gina fires back. When I say nothing, she sighs. "Ronan, in our last meeting, you stared out the window like a giddy school boy."

"The fuck? I did *not*—" Now my face is red, too, and I'm worried that maybe I really *was* staring out the window like a giddy school boy. Shit.

"It's clear that you want to be somewhere else. So *go*. For once, take some time to actually enjoy your life."

I frown at my assistant for a long moment. Part of me knows she's right. Work has been my entire life since things with Sadie ended. I haven't given myself a second to breathe because I knew if I did, I'd realize how fucking unhappy I am. I knew I'd drown under the weight.

But now...being with Dani is all I can think about. She makes me *happy*. I never thought I'd be happy again. And I never thought it would be because of a woman.

"Just think about it," Gina urges and then stands up to leave. Before she slips out of my office, she looks back at me. "I told you she was good for you."

The door closes, and I heave out a sigh.

Fuck. I need to get my shit together. I should not need a talking-to from my assistant. I'm better than this. What the hell happened to my work ethic? My professionalism?

I turn to my computer, intending to bury my brain in something work-related, but instead, I find myself on Google, researching vacation destinations.

I wonder where Dani would like to go? Somewhere tropical? The thought of seeing her sunbathing on the beach in a bikini sends a rush of heat up my chest.

Easy, Ronan.

I can't let myself get carried away again like I did last Saturday night. I triggered her. And I never want to trigger her again. I need to keep letting her set the pace. She needs me to be patient. And I want her to have whatever she needs. She deserves to be with a man who does that. And I really goddamn want to be that man for her.

Before I get too far down the vacation planning rabbit hole, my phone rings, and I'm dismayed to see my mother's name on the caller ID. I haven't talked to her since Bodie's wedding. I was actually enjoying the way she's been ignoring me lately. My life is so much more peaceful without her.

"Hello?" I answer flatly.

"Ronan, good afternoon."

I wait for her to go on, expecting some kind of insult or the same old bullshit she normally spews at me. No matter what I say, she always does that.

"You decided to answer this time," she comments stiffly. I roll my eyes.

"Against my better judgment."

She sighs. "I've decided to forgive you for your embarrassing behavior at Bodie's wedding."

I grit my teeth and try not to growl.

"How kind of you."

"Yes, kind indeed."

The fucked up thing is that my mother actually does believe she's being kind. She hasn't shown me a shred of kindness since the day I was born. I don't think she knows how to be kind. She could take a lesson or two from Dani.

"So, now that we've reconciled, I want to invite you and Dani to the charity dinner I'm hosting on Wednesday."

"Charity dinner?"

"Yes. I'll have my assistant send you the details. It's a fundraiser for heart disease."

My chest tightens. Despite my life-long issues with my mother, I know she's trying to do something good and something that would honor my father and the way he died. I can't, in good conscience, deny her that.

"We'll be there," I say and hope I don't regret it later.

"Great. I'm giving you a second chance here, Ronan. Don't embarrass me like you did at Bodie's wedding," she warns angrily.

"Then tell Bodie to stay the hell away from my wife," I spit, just as angry.

She chuckles derisively.

"Trust me, I'm sure he wants nothing whatsoever to do with that *waitress*."

It's usually at this point in the conversation that I check the fuck out. I've gotten used to just letting her say whatever shit she thinks she needs to say to me, and I shut my mouth and take it like a man. But Dani doesn't deserve to be talked about like that.

This time, something snaps.

"So, he was just joking when he said he would fuck her like he fucked Sadie?"

"Language!" she screeches.

"Fuck," I mutter and pull on the hairs at the back of my neck. "*That's* the most disturbing thing about what I said? The cursing?" I shake my head, and my hands start to tremble. "Listen, we'll be there, but don't expect things to go well if Bodie causes problems."

"Bodie would *never—*"

I growl out my frustration. I hang up and chuck my phone across my office. If it wasn't for my dad, I wouldn't bother going to her charity dinner. Hell, if it wasn't for my dad, I wouldn't talk to my mom at all. But I know he would hate for his family to be disjointed any more than it was when he was alive. He was a family man who believed strongly in family bonds. If only his wife and firstborn son believed in those things, too.

"*Bodie would never!*"

What a load of fucking bullshit.

I have a bad feeling about Wednesday night already, but I'll be damned if I miss a chance to honor my father. And with Dani by my side, maybe everything will be okay. Maybe I can avoid my family. Maybe it won't be a total train wreck.

...Maybe.

When I get home, I feel like a total sap for hoping that Dani will greet me at the door, especially because she doesn't. My phone buzzes in my pocket, and I take it out to see a text from Carla.

Carla: *Alright, get your pants on. I'm on my way.*

I know if I read that text to Dani, she would blush like crazy and laugh that nervous laugh I've come to like so much.

Funny, I type back and then make my way upstairs.

Dani's door is ajar, and I can't help but investigate. I try to tamp down the anticipation I feel in seeing her sweet face, but it's no use. Goddamn butterflies.

I knock softly on the doorframe.

"Come in," says Dani, and I open the door to find her sitting on the floor next to her bed. Scattered around her are a notebook, some pens, various invoices, and a calculator. Even though I wasn't expecting to open the door to her apparently hard at work on the floor, I don't miss the way her face lights up when she sees me.

Damn.

"Hey, Wellsley," she greets warmly.

"Hey." I nod to her papers. "What are you doing?"

"Oh, just making sure I'm keeping track of the money I've been paying people's bills with," she explains brightly.

I don't mistake the pride on her face. Last Monday, she went to a care center and anonymously paid off a bunch of people's outstanding bills. When I got home from work, she was ecstatic and glowed like the sun itself as she told me about it. I love how passionate she is about helping people. She has no instinct whatsoever to hoard the money she's been given.

"By hand?"

She shrugs.

"In case you haven't noticed in your records there, you have enough money to buy a computer," I tease lightly. She chuckles cutely.

"I know. I'm just stubborn like that."

And apparently, she has no instinct to spend that money on herself either. I don't think I've ever met someone so good. To the bones. Just...*good*. Every day that passes, I'm more and more sure of how fucking lucky I am that she wants me. That she sees something good in me, too.

She smiles at me for a moment, seemingly just happy to be in my presence.

"Can I come in?"

"Oh, yeah. Of course. Come on in. Make yourself at home." She chuckles. "I mean it *is* your home, but you know what I mean."

I step inside, leaving the door open, and take a seat on the edge of her bed.

Her room hasn't changed at all since she moved in. Everything looks exactly the same, but it feels different. This room isn't empty, even when she isn't in it. The house feels like that, too. Every corner of it feels touched by her, even if she's never worked out in the gym downstairs or been in my closet. Her presence in this house has made it feel alive in a way it just wasn't before she came along.

"So, how was work?" she asks me from the floor. Her bright eyes warm me inside. I don't think I'll ever get tired of the sweet way she looks at me, or the raspy breaths she takes between kisses, or the way her fingers thread through my hair.

"Fine," I answer with a shrug.

Dani grins at me and shakes her head, probably knowing I'm full of shit.

"Tell me something; do you even like your job? It obviously keeps you busy as a beaver, but do you *like* it?"

I study her for a moment, caught off guard by her question and the answer that immediately forms in my mind.

"Does anyone *like* their job?"

She raises one eyebrow at me and places her pen behind her ear.

"Did you just answer my question with a question? I wasn't asking about *anyone*; I was asking *you*."

Damn her feistiness.

I clear my throat. "I mean, it isn't the worst. Yeah, I'm busy, but it's because I like being busy." Before Dani came along, anyway. Now, I'd rather be home with her.

"Soooo, that's a no, then?"

"I guess it's a no."

"Then, why do it? Because it brings in the dough?"

I secretly love her terminology, but I don't show it on my face.

"It was my father's legacy," I say, quieter than I intended. "I take pride in doing it." That's really the only reason I started working for him. I wanted him to be proud of me. And when he died, that didn't stop. If anything, it made me want to work harder.

Dani gazes at me for a moment. There's both sadness and warmth to it, which sort of confuses me.

"What?"

"I didn't know your dad," she says gently, "but from what you've told me about him, I have a feeling he would've supported you in whatever your passions are because he loved you."

I swallow hard and look away. I wasn't expecting this conversation, but I realize that I can't argue with what she's saying. My dad would've supported me, even if I didn't want to follow him into the real estate business that he started. I'm not sure I could've disappointed him if he knew I was happy.

I nod, my eyes on the rug.

Dani turns back to her materials on the floor and then frantically gathers them.

"I'm sorry," she blurts out desperately. "This isn't any of my business. I shouldn't have said anything." I watch her get up and place her things on the dresser next to the wedding picture of her parents. "I'm always doing that. Just butting in when—"

"Dani," I say gently.

She turns to me, her hazel eyes full of distress.

"It's okay."

Her slight shoulders ease a little. "I just want you to be happy. And I'm sure that's what he would want, too." She slaps her hand over her mouth. "And that's the last thing I'm going to say about it, I swear." She folds her arms over her chest, like she's trying to make herself smaller. Something sinks in my stomach.

Did that asshole ex-boyfriend make her feel like that? Like she should shrink down to a size he could control and manipulate? My brow furrows at that thought, and I instantly get up and go over to her.

Her shoulders tense again as she sees me coming, and it only makes me feel worse for what she's been through. I walk right up to her and put my arms around her tightly, pulling her into me. The breath catches in her throat, and then she embraces me, too. I bring my lips down close to her ear.

"Dani, I *always* want to hear what you think," I murmur to her. "I don't want you to apologize for speaking about my dad. You're my wife. I feel safe talking to you about anything." Telling her everything about Sadie is proof of that.

She sniffs and nods into my chest. "I do, too," she says, her small voice muffled.

"Good." I kiss her temple and smooth one hand up and down her back.

"Mmm," she says and turns her face to the side to rest her cheek on my chest. My heart beats a little harder, and I'm sure she can hear it. "Who would've thought you were such a good hugger?" she teases softly. "That definitely wasn't in the fine print."

I smile slightly.

"The first time I hugged you in your office, you were stiffer than a stiff."

I chuckle softly. "You caught me off-guard."

She looks up at me sweetly, her chin resting on my chest. My heart melts. Damn. I'd do anything for her when she looks at me like that.

"You caught me off guard, too, Wellsley," she says softly, her happy eyes sparkling.

I smile and lean down to kiss her gently. A rush of butterflies and heat flow through me as she kisses me back, her lips soft and sweet. I pull back and rest my forehead against hers.

I want to tell her how much I've been thinking about her since we got home from Chicago. I want to tell her that I miss her every minute I'm at work. But I'm not good at this shit. This vulnerable shit. Despite being admittedly crazy about this girl, I'm also terrified to feel this much. I didn't expect to feel all this for her so soon. And part of me is insecure, wondering if she's as crazy about me as I am about her.

"Such a softy," she murmurs with a chuckle, and I move back to look at her.

"It's your fault."

She barks out a surprised laugh and squeezes me.

"My fault?" She laughs again and steps back with her hands on her hips. "So, if I hadn't come along, you'd still be the same old crotchety stick in the mud?"

"Yep."

She chuckles cutely. "I guess I'll take that as a compliment."

I smile at her, smitten.

Downstairs, the front door opens and closes.

"I'm heeeere!" Carla calls out. "Unless you want me to see you making out yet again, here's your warning!"

Dani giggles and blushes. She covers her face but peeks at me through her fingers.

I grin at her. That big of a smile on my face feels strange. She drops her hands.

"We better go down before she thinks we're doing something promiscuous," she says, still blushing.

I personally don't see why that would be a bad thing, but I nod and follow her to her door. Then, I remember why I knocked on her door in the first place.

"So, listen, there's a charity dinner on Wednesday night," I tell her. "Can you make it?" She pauses in the doorway and looks at me.

"Oh, sure. Absolutely. I'll be there." She glances behind me, toward her closet. "Is it fancy? Do I need a dress?"

"The dress you bought in Chicago is appropriate," I say, mostly because it's my favorite dress of hers. Because it's a dress she bought for *me* and not an event. Because I know when I see it that I'll be taken back to that intense moment when I almost kissed her in our hotel room.

"Awesome. You know me, I jump at the chance to be your arm candy."

I crack a smile at that, but it fades when I recall the last time she was my "arm candy" at Bodie's wedding. I have no reason to think that this charity dinner will go any better. I take a deep breath and decide to get the rest of the details out there.

"You should know that...my mom is the one funding it. She and Bodie will be there," I inform her begrudgingly. Her eyes widen, her pretty face suddenly full of dread.

"Oh."

"Believe me, the only reason I'm going is because it's something to honor my dad."

Dani's expression softens, and she gives me an empathetic smile that hits me hard in the chest.

"Then, we definitely should be there," she agrees softly.

I swallow, grateful that she understands how important my dad was to me. The fact that she's willing to be in the presence of my family means a lot to me. Between my mother's tirade and Bodie's attempted manipulation, she has every reason to stay far away from them. But she's more than willing to be by my side, even if that takes her within reach of being slighted by them again.

"Thank you," I murmur.

She smiles up at me and then comes close again, bringing her arms around my neck and shoulders. I gladly hug her back and close my eyes. I take in a contented breath and let it out slowly because this is where I've wanted to be all day. Dani feels more like home to me than this house ever has.

I bring my face close to the side of hers and kiss her cheek. Her grip around me tightens a little, and she lifts one hand to sift her fingers soothingly through my hair. I feel every stressful thing leave my body. There's nothing in my mind right now but her. I stroke her back with one hand, relishing in how amazing it feels to touch her and how perfect it feels to be close to her. No wonder I haven't been sleeping well lately. Dani's been sleeping in her own bed.

I pull back enough to see her face. I love how happy she looks. How happy I make her. Despite letting her set the pace, I know what I want.

My heart stutters as she moves her hands to my chest and absently touches my tie. I keep my arms around her middle, my mind returning to the times she's fallen asleep snuggled in close to me.

"Dani?"

"Mhm?"

"I want you to move into my room," I say directly, surprising her. "I sleep so much better with you in the same bed." Despite my directness, I feel unbelievably nervous as I wait for her to reply. I don't want to rush her. But I know she feels as content being close as I do.

She blushes slightly and then gives me a cheeky grin.

"That's a little fast, isn't it?" she teases. "What, do you think we're married or something?"

I smile gently at her. "Or something."

Dani giggles and tugs slightly on my tie.

"I'll think about it," she answers with a sweet smile.

"I'm not trying to rush this," I explain quietly. "It's okay if you want your own space. What you want is important to me, too."

She nods with a more serious expression.

"Thank you." She pops up, places a quick peck on my lips, and then steps back.

I follow her downstairs like a goddamn lovesick puppy, but for the first time in a long time, I'm perfectly okay with that.

Chapter Twenty-Four

Dani

I have never brushed my teeth more nervously in my whole life. My poor gums don't know what hit them. But I can't help it. I'm getting ready for bed, and I've decided that my body likes to sleep next to Ronan's body. And there's nothing wrong with that. I married that guy. And we like each other.

So, despite what he said about not trying to rush this, I'm going to sleep in his bed tonight.

Is it a good idea? The wary side of me says no. But the bossy side says yes. And obviously, bossy side wins.

I spit in the sink and then rinse my mouth out with water. When I straighten up, I try to calm my nerves. It's just sleeping. We've done it before. It's not a huge deal. All in a night's work.

I take a deep breath and make my way out of the bathroom, through my bedroom, and across the hall to Ronan's open bedroom door. He's in his office. He said he had to answer a couple of emails before it got too late.

After dinner, we hung out downstairs in the theater room. By now, we've watched all the Harry Potter movies, so I suggested we watch *Chopped*. Needless to say, the man is hooked. He won't *admit* it. But he totally is. Ask me how I know. Go ahead.

Okay, okay, I'll tell you. If he wasn't totally hooked, he would've been watching *me* instead of the show. Like when he thought I wasn't paying attention. He also would've been attempting to make out with me, and well, we both know I don't need to be talked into that.

I'll admit I was a little surprised that he asked me to move into his room. And my head says it's too soon. But my heart just wants more of Ronan. And I don't want to deny my heart happiness. Not anymore.

I feel like I'm doing the best I've done at living my life to the fullest, like I've tried to do since my parents died. I'm actually...*thriving*. And not just because I have the affection of a good man. I'm not treading water anymore with all that constant working, earning barely enough to keep my head above water. I'm making this money mean something to someone other than me. Paying bills for people who really need a hand up, like I did.

The only thing missing is my best friend.

Ever since we got back from Chicago, I've been wishing I could talk to Melanie about how amazing it is to have someone like Ronan actually want me. I wish I could tell her that she was wrong...that what's between me and Ronan is something really freaking *good*. I want to tell her I didn't make a mistake. And I want to tell her I miss her, too.

I peek my head in and spot him through the doorway to his office. He's sitting at his desk, and even from here, I can tell he's looking at his computer without really seeing it. I come closer and anxiously knock on the doorframe of the office.

Ronan looks up instantly and smiles when he sees me. My heart pounds. That smile.

"Hey."

"Hey."

"I'm heading to bed," I say, fidgeting with my hands. "I just wanted to say good night."

He gets up and comes over to me.

"Do you have plans tomorrow? I was wondering if you want to meet me at the office for lunch?"

"Really? Yeah, I'd love that."

"Great. I'll have everything ready at noon."

I beam up at him. I love that I was so right about him. Even from the start, I had a feeling that his cranky, stern-faced exterior was just a bluff. With every passing interaction I have with him, he's showing me the real

Ronan. And the real Ronan is a far cry from the man I met on the third floor of Wells, Inc. The real Ronan is sweet and thoughtful and invested in me. I'm quickly becoming a fan.

"Well, good night. Are you going to be long?"

He glances behind me into his bedroom for a fraction of a second, seeming to realize what I mean. He clears his throat, and I can see him trying not to grin at me.

"No, I'll be there in a bit."

"Okay." I hold my breath, give him a kiss on his sandpaper cheek, and then head back into the bedroom.

I somehow keep myself from gleefully skipping around the bed to *my* side and pull back the covers. As soon as I lie down, I know there's a fat chance in a food court that I'll be dozing off before Ronan comes to bed. Even if that's two hours from now. I'm too hopped up on whatever the hell this feeling is.

To my surprise, the office light goes out only a few minutes later, and the dark shape of my husband enters the room. My face heats up as he undresses, even though I don't look as he removes his shirt and pants. He slides in beside me and wastes no time in pulling me close to him.

I let out a contented sigh that my conscious brain did *not* approve of and feel the initial nerves and heart palpitations ease. I close my eyes and focus in on the peace I feel being so close to him. It's a peace I didn't think I would ever feel again after what Spencer did. But I know without a doubt that Ronan was worth the risk. This is where I want to be. And I can't wait to see what the future holds for us, even beyond the next two years.

I drift off to sleep, my head swimming slightly in Ronan's masculine scent, and I wake up in the morning feeling just as safe and just as happy as I did when I fell asleep.

Ronan's alarm is beeping, and he growls out his annoyance. He's like a werewolf, growling like that. I should start calling him Wolfy. I bet he'd love that.

"Hit the snooze," I plead sleepily. "Spend five more minutes in bed with your wife."

He reaches over, and the alarm silences. He moves back to me again, and I swoon a little. Okay, a lot. I'm practically drowning in the swoon over here.

He sighs with contentment. "I sleep so much better with you," he murmurs into the hair at the nape of my neck.

I smile and squeeze his hand.

"Me, too, baby."

My heart jumps in my chest. I just called him *baby*.

Oof.

I close my eyes tighter, as if that will delete the intimate term of endearment I just uttered. Baby is so much more embarrassing to me than if I had called him Wolfy instead. I could've passed Wolfy off as a joke, but baby? Nope. There's no talking myself out of that one.

I'm not sure what I expect him to say to that, if anything, but he stays silent. I inwardly start to panic and an apology is already readying itself on my tongue when I feel his thumb smooth over the wedding ring on my hand. I feel his lips press my cheek, and then I melt back into him a little more.

This is so...*good*. Better than I had dared to believe was out there for me.

I make up my mind right then to call Melanie today. Even if she doesn't pick up, I'll leave a voicemail so that I can explain how much I deeply believe that I made the right choice here. I imagine she's been wondering if I'm okay, even if she hasn't contacted me to ask. It might be painful for her and I to work through our little break up, but I still want her to be part of my life. I still need my best friend. And I need her to know that I'm falling head over heels for Ronan.

I ride the elevator up, smiling to myself. I remember the first time I arrived on Ronan's floor. I was a complete mess—about to puke in the corner. Now look at me. I'm filled with nerves this time, too, but it's a different kind. Instead of being a mess of nervous energy, I'm a mess of excited energy. Because I get to see my husband. Because he wants to have lunch with me. We have lunch now. That's a thing we do. Because we like each other.

I step off the elevator and approach the reception desk. The noon day sun is shining brightly through the floor-to-ceiling windows to my left, making me feel even more chipper than I already am.

"Hi, I'm Dani. I'm here to see Ronan," I inform her happily. She smiles genuinely at me.

"Yes, he told me you'd be here soon. You can go right back."

"Oh, thank you."

I take off toward the right down the long hallway and then veer over to Ronan's office on the left. I glance at the worker bees at their desks and a few glance back at me.

"Hey, Dani," greets Gina with a knowing smile. She's seated at a desk across from Ronan's closed office door, looking adorable in a purple blouse. Her blonde hair is curled at the ends with one side pinned back behind her ear.

"Hi! How are you?" I haven't seen her since I came in to set up all of the birthday surprises for Ronan.

"I'm good. Just dealing with a space cadet for a boss," she answers with a good-humored eye roll.

My brow crinkles. "Space cadet?"

Gina stands up from her desk and moves around it so she's standing next to me. She glances at Ronan's door, as if to make sure it's closed.

"The man can't concentrate on anything," she clues me in, grinning. "And I have you to blame for it."

"What? Me? What did I—"

Gina laughs and folds her arms. "I told him just the other day that even though he's been absolutely worthless lately, love looks good on him."

The blood rushes straight to my face and my heart pounds hard in my chest. Did she just say—?

"Anyway, he's ready for you. Go on in." She gives me a little push, seeming oblivious to the dumbfounded expression I'm sporting.

I try to clear my mind as I grip the door handle, but it's no use. Gina just said that he's in love with me. Is that even possible? Could he love *me*? So soon?

I know things have been going super well. I mean, I slept in his bed last night. And all last week, he had dinner with me, not just on Friday. And he invited me here for lunch today because, apparently, he doesn't want to even go a full work day without seeing me.

Sheesh, when I think about it like that...maybe he *does* love me. Oh, God, Ronan might actually love me. My little happy heart does such a joyous back flip that it ripples through my chest cavity to my poor, unsuspecting stomach. I don't know if the buzzy feeling floating through me is pleasant or stressful.

I take a deep breath and open the door to find Ronan fussing with the placement of the plates on his desk. He looks up at me and smiles with his adorable dimples and perfect teeth. So freaking different from when I walked through this door to meet him for the first time, a puddle of nerves for completely different reasons than now. My heart beats harder, and I close the door.

"Right on time," he says happily and comes over to meet me in the middle of his office. He kisses me on the cheek and takes my hand to lead me over to our lunch.

He's set up two chairs on the side of his desk that faces the window and two plates with what looks like fettuccine alfredo and salad. And two glasses of wine.

"Drinking on the job?" I tease, pointing at the alcohol.

"Don't tell Gina." He winks at me—*winks*—and then helps me into my seat, which is something no other man has ever done for me. Ronan sits down, too, and gestures for me to dig in.

I take a few bites and try to get myself together. The rational side of my brain kicks in just enough to try to make sense of what Gina claimed. Just because *she* said the L-word doesn't mean that Ronan said it. Besides, it doesn't count unless he says it to my face. My stomach twists nervously, making it difficult for me to eat.

Knowing what I do about Ronan, I can make an educated guess that even if he does love me, he won't say it to me for a while. Probably not until he's pretty damn sure I feel the same way.

So...*do* I feel the same way? Do I love this man?

Objectively, yes. Terrifyingly, yes. Truthfully...*yes*.

I'm all in here, ladies and gents.

"Everything okay? You're quiet," Ronan says, looking over at me.

"Oh, yeah. Everything is totally fine. Finer than this fine wine, even." I laugh nervously and take a big sip, suddenly afraid he just heard my thoughts. He studies me suspiciously. I shake my head. "Sorry. I'm being weird." I clear my throat. "I was just thinking about how different things are since the first time I walked into this room."

Ronan puts down his fork, a thoughtful expression crossing his handsome features. Heavens to Betsy, I love watching him think. Oh, there was that word again.

"Yeah," he agrees finally. "A lot has changed."

I smile. "Who would've thought I could catch the eye of Mr. Serious Quiet Man?"

His blue eyes smile at me as he bites his lip. "Something only a wifey could do."

I grin at him and laugh softly. His usage of the term "wifey" has me high diving off the smitten diving board, straight down into a pool the same deep color of Ronan's blue eyes.

I go back to my food, feeling a little less nervous and a whole lot enamored, but Ronan doesn't pick up his fork again. When I look over, he has the same thoughtful expression on his face. You know, the one that's irresistibly sexy and makes me forget all about lunch. He could totally take me over to that couch right now, and I would give him *all* the kisses.

"What's wrong?"

His eyes flash to mine, and then he takes my hand in both of his, eclipsing it completely in warmth and gentleness.

"Nothing." He smiles slightly. "I...I just didn't expect you, Dani." His deep voice is vulnerable and sweet, and it makes my throat tighten and my ovaries dance.

"Didn't expect me to sweep you off your feet?" I wiggle my eyebrows, hoping to make him laugh. But he just smiles and squeezes my hand, I think because this is serious to him. I *actually* swept him off his feet. Wow.

I lean over and kiss him with my heart beating like crazy. He kisses me back slowly and then pulls away to look me in the eyes.

"I want you to know that—that I really care about you," he says, almost in a whisper. "You make me so happy."

I feel lightheaded at that admission because I know how hard it is for him to open up. For him to say how he feels out loud is such a stupid big deal. L-word or not. I swallow hard.

"You make me happy, too," I murmur back. I'm glad to have the opportunity to tell him that. And when we're ready, I'll tell him how deep this goes for me.

He touches my chin and brings my mouth back to his. I forget where we are or that time exists at all. His sweet kisses have me wondering if this is what it's like to be loved by Ronan. If it is, sign me up for a lifetime of it.

Later, when I step out of his office to go home, I grin at Gina.

"I don't think I helped your cause." I'm sure having made out with me in his office will do nothing to help his concentration or productivity. Selfishly, I'm cool with that.

She chuckles. "Honestly, that's okay. The man has been so unhappy for such a long time. He deserves to wallow in his new life with you."

I reach over her desk and give her a hug, then head back to the elevator. I feel filled to the brim with happiness. I could die, I'm so freaking happy. And hearing him say that I make him happy...just wow.

I can't contain it anymore, so when I get down to my cab, I call Melanie.

As expected, it rings and goes to voicemail. I try not to let myself be too disappointed by that and wait for the beep.

"Hey, Mel," I begin, both a little awkward and yet also filled with joy because of my husband, "I know we aren't really talking or whatever, but

I just want you to know that I love you, and I miss you. Everything is crazy different since we last talked, so I'd love to catch up."

I pause, unsure of how much to say. I realize that there's a really big chance that she might not call me back, and if so, I won't get to tell her about Ronan. So, I decide to press on.

"I know that marrying Ronan was a totally crazy thing to do, but it's actually turning out really great. He's a good man who treats me well, and we really care about each other. Maybe one day, you guys can meet." I regret saying that bit, but I do feel like if she just met him that she would be convinced of his inherent goodness. "So, anyway, please call me back. Love you."

I hang up, feeling a measurable amount of grief overshadowing my joy. It was bad enough losing my parents but then to lose my best friend, too? That's a low blow, Chef Universe. Mel is basically family to me, and I haven't talked to her in a month. But even if she never calls me back, at least I tried to reconcile. At least I made sure she knows I still love her and want her in my life. That's all that matters, right? I can at least feel good about that.

I do my best to put it out of my mind then and return my brain to my amazing lunch with Ronan. After everything I've been through, I think I deserve to wallow a bit, too.

When I get home, I take a moment to really look around. I've gotten mostly used to living in this huge house. I'm still not used to having someone do my laundry and clean for me, but I'll admit it's pretty nice. It's nice not having to worry about a damn thing. Not money. Not how many shifts I can squeeze in this week. Not chores or grocery shopping. Marrying Ronan has been nothing but a blessing. Even before he kissed me in Chicago.

And after being with Spencer, who was constantly trying to control what I did and what role I served in relation to him, being with Ronan feels like heaven. Being with Ronan makes me feel...*free*. I never thought I could feel that way with a man. If there's anything that makes me sure that I love him, it's that. If I didn't love Ronan, I wouldn't feel so secure and safe and free.

So, I go upstairs and move my toothbrush into Ronan's bathroom. I look through his dresser drawers to see if there are any empty ones and find an entire dresser by the bathroom door that isn't being used.

I smile to myself as I move my things into Ronan's room. The last thing I move is my parents' wedding picture. I place it on the nightstand next to my side of the bed and then sigh.

"You would like him," I say quietly to the photo. "Maybe I have you guys to thank for watching over me. Maybe you guys had a hand in sending him my way." I look down at the wedding band on my finger and then close my eyes.

For better or worse, richer or poorer, in sickness and in health, to love and to cherish till death do us part.

I still mean every word I vowed to Ronan. But now, I mean it as a lover in addition to meaning it as a friend. That's all my parents wanted for me, and now I have it.

Chapter Twenty-Five

Ronan

I fidget restlessly with my suit coat as I look in the closet mirror. It's almost time to leave for the charity event, and I'm anxious as hell. The last time I saw my family was at Bodie's wedding, and that went terribly. Is there even a *chance* that tonight won't be a fucking nightmare?

I head out into my bedroom, my expectations low for this evening. But then, I look to the left, into the bathroom where Dani is getting ready. I fold my arms and lean against the doorframe, feeling more relaxed just from looking at her in that blue dress.

When I came home from work last night and went up to change out of my work clothes, I immediately noticed the picture frame of her parents that she moved into my room. It was then that I realized that this bedroom is no longer *my* bedroom. It's *ours*. And I fucking love it.

I cuddled that woman all night, and it was bliss. She makes my life better in every way. And I can say with certainty that if we weren't going to this charity dinner for my dad, I'd be convincing her to cuddle up with me and watch a movie. Because honestly, I'm realizing that that's all I really need to be happy. Everything else is just details that I'm not that interested in. Not in comparison to her.

Dani catches my adoring gaze in the mirror and beams at me. She's wearing a deep maroon-colored lipstick that is putting some naughty thoughts in my head. The more I taste of her mouth these days, the more I want a taste of the rest of her. I'd love nothing more than to strip that dress off of her and haul her into the shower where I could get lost in her completely.

But I know this isn't a race. I'm going to enjoy every slow second of the growing intimacy between us. I'm savoring every touch and every kiss, whether it leads us somewhere more intense or not.

I leave my perch by the door and step up behind her. I reach my arms around her middle and pull her back against me, where her head fits neatly beneath my chin. When I bend my head to kiss her cheek, she giggles.

"You look beautiful," I say to her softly. Seeing her wearing the blue dress from Chicago has my increasingly malleable heart softening just a bit more. She looks even prettier in it tonight than she did the first time I saw her in it.

"You look pretty nice yourself there, hot stuff."

I kiss her cheek again, thrilled by her pet name for me. Fuck, I used to *hate* nicknames. Before her. So many things were different before her. And the crazy thing is, I wouldn't go back. I wouldn't change a goddamn thing.

"You almost ready?" I ask, stepping back.

"Yep." She runs her fingers through her long hair, which she meticulously curled. The overhead lighting glints off each wave. "Just need my shoes."

Dani follows me out of the bathroom and grabs her shoes from the bedroom on the way. I feel my shoulders tense more and more as we head downstairs. I feel like I'm trudging to my doom with how much foreboding dread is pumping through my body.

I wish I loved my family. I wish I had the same relationship with them that I had with my father. It just feels shitty to leave the house feeling anxious because I know that I'll be seeing them. I'm just hoping that because this event is something my mom is doing in memory of her late husband, that nothing fucked up will go down between us. For one night, maybe it's possible that everything will go as planned.

As I put the key in the ignition, Dani's hand presses my bicep. I look over at her to see a sympathetic expression on her face.

"I know we don't get along with your family," she says gently, her sweet voice sounding much more intimate in the small interior of my car. "But we're in this together, okay? We're going to get through it, no matter what might happen."

Her encouragement eases the writhing ball of nerves in my stomach. I've never been more grateful for her than I am right now. For how she sees my discomfort and tries to make it better. I reach out to softly stroke her cheek. She leans into my hand, a small blush creeping across her beautiful face.

"You're right," I answer. "Even if something happens tonight, I still have you."

She smiles warmly and moves closer to kiss me. Her maroon lips on mine send a thrill of excitement through me, and then a calming sense of peace takes over when I lean my brow against hers.

I hope to God I'll always have this woman. I don't know why she wants to be with my cranky ass, but I'm not about to talk her out of this. I'm going to do my damnedest to keep Dani in my life for as long as possible. The contract has long since faded from my mind. It isn't about that anymore. It's just about...us. And I love us.

As I drive into downtown Minneapolis, I try to focus on that instead of my family. I try to think of my dad, who would've loved Dani. And I try to think of her parents, who I wish I could've met. I try to think about good things. I try to remind myself that the most important thing in my life is sitting in the seat next to me, and nothing can change that.

The event is lavishly decorated with flowers and heart disease signage everywhere I look. Everything is very put together and professional, which I expected being that my mother is a perfectionist with no limit on funds. The large room is populated by round tables set for eight, and there is a small stage set up on one end with a podium and microphone. I roll my eyes, not looking forward to hearing whatever speech my mother prepared. No doubt it'll be sappy and fake and everything she ever said to make my father fall in love with her.

The space is bustling with people in expensive suits and gowns, the women donning their best jewelry as if to make a statement about how wealthy they are and, therefore, how much more generous and charitable they are for attending a fundraiser like this.

This is the crowd I grew up in. Stuffy, vain, conceited people who've perfected a polished and charming exterior. Growing up, I never trusted anyone my parents knew, except Lance, who's proved himself over the years to always have my dad's best interests at heart, regardless of money or business. Everyone else, I was deeply suspicious of.

Dani holds my hand tighter as we make our way from the large entryway and into the crowded event space. I look down at her, and she smiles nervously up at me, like she's trying to be a little braver than she feels while she's being surrounded by all these arrogant, wealthy people. It's the same look she gave me at Bodie's wedding when we stood next to my family for photos.

God, I love her.

She isn't one of these yuppies. She doesn't fit in with these image-obsessed sharks. She isn't like Sadie, who treated any public event we went to like her own personal beauty pageant. Dani's everything I didn't think I would find in my busy world. She's so genuine and so good.

And it feels *good* to love her. It feels as right as breathing.

Her gaze on mine turns curious then, and I realize that she's probably wondering why the hell I'm looking at her with heart eyes. Now isn't the time to say something so important. Hell, I don't even know when the right time is, but it definitely isn't here right now.

"Let's get a drink," I suggest and steer her over toward a counter near the corner where a short line is forming for the lone bartender. I feel strengthened with her standing next to me, however short she is, but I still have that prickly feeling crawling up my spine that somehow, some way, tonight is going to be a disaster.

Part of me wants to look around and get a bead on my brother, but I also don't think I'm ready to know if he's here yet. I'd rather just dwell in this time right here before he shows his face and ruins the evening somehow. I'd rather do what I can to enjoy this with my wife.

When we get to the bartender, we both order wine and then find a place to stand out of the way. Dani is looking around anxiously, no doubt trying to find Bodie or my mom. I see a sign for the silent auction taking place in the next room and suggest we check it out.

She follows me, still clutching my hand, and then we slowly peruse each listing. They're spread out across fifteen or so tables, some with pictures of what's being auctioned. Dani's eyes grow wider with each expensive item.

"Holy money balls, do people really bid on these things?" she whispers up to me.

"Yes."

"But there's an all inclusive trip to Europe on here!" she gasps, pointing. "That's thousands and thousands of dollars!"

"Should we put our names down?"

"What?" She looks up at me again in surprise.

"You're right," I agree and pull her along to the next item. "We can plan our own vacation." Out of the corner of my eye, I catch Dani's bewildered expression. I fight back my grin, already enjoying myself more than I thought I would. "Is there anywhere you've always wanted to go?"

She's quiet for a moment as we move on down the line.

"I've always thought Hawaii would be really cool," she says thoughtfully, and I pause to look at her fully. "The beaches and the volcanoes and everything..."

I smile at her, picturing the tropical island she's vaguely describing, and bring my wine glass to my mouth.

"And of course," she continues as I sip, "you step off the plane and get *leid*, so."

I choke on my wine and succumb to a loud coughing fit. Dani grins like the damn Cheshire Cat and thumps me on the back as the people around us stare.

"Jesus, woman," I croak out as I recover.

"What? I've never been *leid*," she presses cheekily.

I wipe my mouth with the back of my hand and give her my most challenging look.

"Oh, I'll get you laid," I say, my voice deep and quiet.

She giggles loudly, her face bright red.

"We'll see about that." She winks at me and then takes the lead as we look at the other auction items.

But I can't think about a damn thing except the fact that she pretty much just gave me a maybe for having sex. Just the thought of being with Dani has me breaking out into a needy sweat. We've fooled around some since Chicago, but none of it without clothes on. I'd be lying if I said I hadn't imagined it, especially when I'm alone in the shower and wishing she was next to me with nothing between us.

But I know that Spencer did a number on her, and that despite what she just said, I need to keep letting her set the pace. I can't risk pushing her too far, not when it could mean hurting her. She's more than just a warm body I could fit snugly into. She's my wife. She's my forever. And after this night is over, I'm going to figure out a way to make sure she knows that.

When we make it back to the bustling event room, I spot my mother by the stage. She's organizing some papers, most likely her speech, and looks dignified in a red pant suit. I muse that I should probably say hello or at least let her know that Dani and I are here, but I can't bring myself to. I'll wait as long as possible.

"This is nice," Dani comments simply, her bright eyes taking everything in. There's no doubt she hasn't been to one of these before. No wonder she was intimidated when we first walked in. My little coughing fit seems to have loosened her up a bit.

By now, almost everyone is here, and there are caterers milling about with trays of appetizers as the room swells with chatting and false laughter. The whole thing reminds me entirely too much of Bodie's wedding. Drinks, appetizer trays, dinner, and then all hell breaking loose.

"Hopefully, we can just eat and then get out of here before Bodie starts anything," I mutter to her.

She nods and gives me an encouraging smile that I appreciate, and then we wind our way through small groups of entitled rich people, trying to find our table. I'm deeply surprised to find that we've been placed with my family near the front. I realize it's probably for appearances and not at all because my mother is trying to actually treat us like family. I'm already dreading what dinner will be like sharing a table with my mother and Bodie.

I pull out Dani's chair for her to sit, but she's standing there absolutely frozen. Thinking that she must have spotted Bodie, I quickly follow her gaze. But she isn't looking at anyone I recognize.

"Dani?" I ask, and touch her elbow.

She doesn't respond to me. She just stares, wide eyed with fear at a server who just passed us holding a tray of appetizers. He looks completely harmless to me. Just a guy with light brown hair and medium build. An absolutely non-descript individual who, for some reason, has caused my wife's spine to go completely rigid.

I've never seen her like this. So pale and so faint.

"Dani," I say again, louder, and she flinches slightly. "Who is that?"

"That's..." She trails off, barely breathing. "That's...*Spencer*," she answers weakly, in shock, without looking away from him. It takes a second for the name to register, but then, my stomach drops.

Spencer.

My blood boils instantly.

That asshole who almost killed her is *here*. My hands start to shake as the memory of her telling me what he did to her fills my brain. The low murmur of talking voices in the room quiets as my eyes zero in on him.

How many other women has he hurt the way he hurt Dani? Does he lose sleep over almost killing my wife? Is he even sorry? Fuck, I'll make him sorry.

Without another thought, I leave Dani's side and stalk after him as he heads toward the hallway, probably back to the kitchen. I don't hear Dani calling after me. I don't hear the comments made about me as I unapologetically push past people to get to him.

I catch up to him before he reaches the double doors to the kitchen. Away from the main room, everything is quieter, and I can hear the blood pounding in my ears. I grip the back of his white dress shirt and throw him against the wall, just like he did to Dani. His empty metal tray clangs loudly on the linoleum floor.

"What the—?" comes his startled voice.

He raises his fists to fend me off but stops when he sees the irate look on my face and my powerful stance. It pleases me so fucking much to see the fear in his eyes.

"Who the hell are you?"

I narrow my eyes and step closer. He presses back against the wall.

"It doesn't matter who I am. What matters is that you remember my face," I answer him gravely. I grab the front of his shirt and pin him against the wall. He winces slightly. "The next time you beat a woman, I want you to remember my face. The next time you strangle a woman, I want you to see my face. Because believe me, I'm a very powerful man. I have more than enough money to have you followed, traced, and tracked. If you *ever* hurt a woman again, you can be fucking sure I'll know about it."

Spencer's chest is rising and falling quickly as the blood drains from his face.

"And if you ever even *think* about going near Dani, I'll do to you what you did to her." I hold his terrified gaze for a moment and then release him.

My heart hammers in my chest as I stare at him. I want nothing more than to strangle him this very instant, but I force myself to walk away.

When I turn, I see Dani standing at the end of the hallway, looking just as white and faint. I quicken my pace and take her ashen face gently in my hands when I reach her.

"Are you okay?" I ask her, bringing my face close to hers.

She just stares at me like I'm a stranger and not her husband. "What did you say to him?"

"Nevermind what I said, okay? It's done." I kiss her forehead and then bring her close against me, wanting nothing more than to protect her in any way that I can.

But she doesn't hug me back.

"Dani?" I pull back to look at her.

She's nearly expressionless. Gone is the lively woman I married. She's been replaced in mere moments by someone I don't recognize. A woman who's drawn herself so far inward that I fear I can't reach her. It fucking terrifies me.

"I...I think I need a minute," she says weakly. "I need some air."

"Of course, let's go."

"I'll meet you back at the table."

She unsteadily walks away from me then, leaving me alone in the hallway. I watch her disappear into the throng of people, feeling sick to my stomach. The fact that she didn't want me to go with her is a bad fucking sign. Especially in addition to the stark contrast of her behavior.

Fuck.

Maybe I overstepped. Maybe I should've just comforted Dani instead of threatening her ex-boyfriend. But I wasn't thinking straight. All I wanted to do was set things right somehow for Dani. That asshole got away with what he did to her, and I was hell bent on making sure he knew that wasn't at all the truth.

I run my hand through my hair and move back out into the event room. I try to get over toward the entryway so that when Dani comes back in, she can easily find me. I'll give her a minute, like she said, and then I'll try to explain. She needs to know that I was just trying to have her back. I was trying to defend her, like I promised I would do when I married her.

And then, I'll tell her we should just go home. I'd rather die than force her to sit through the rest of this evening with that psycho in the same room. My dad would understand, and he would agree with me on this; I know he would. I need to be there for my wife, whatever that looks like to her.

"Fancy meeting you here," comes a woman's voice from my left.

I turn and see Sadie standing there with a welcoming smile. She's wearing an emerald-colored, floor-length dress with a plunging neckline. I grimace at her in greeting. She's the last fucking thing I need right now. This night is already a disaster, and Bodie hasn't even shown his face yet.

"You look handsome as ever, Ronan," she compliments genuinely.

A shiver runs down my spine. I hate the way she can make anyone believe that she means what she says. There was a time when I readily believed every word out of her mouth. But I know better now. She's a master at lying and betrayal, and I don't intend on rehashing that with her now or ever.

I say nothing to her in reply, and just as I take a step to move away from her, she steps in front of me.

"I was actually hoping you'd be here tonight," she says warmly, smiling up at me like she didn't fuck my brother and break my heart. "I've been thinking about you a lot lately...and, Ronan, I really need to say that...I miss you."

My eyebrows shoot up in surprise. "Are you fucking kidding me, Sadie? You *miss* me?"

"Yes," she says firmly. "I do."

Her expression softens, and my heart beats oddly in my chest. I feel like whatever she's about to say will be something I can't trust. It makes me that much more fond of Dani because I realize in this moment that I've never had to doubt Dani's character. She's proven her trustworthiness.

Sadie swallows hard, looking nervous. "I threw away the best thing I ever had," she says quietly, just above the volume of the room. "I'm sorry for what I did. I'm so sorry, Ronan." Her eyes fill with tears. "I know I don't deserve your forgiveness or your love, but I need you to know that I'm sorry. And I need you to know that I still love you."

I stare at her in utter disbelief. Her apology is appreciated, but it's a little too damn late. And as for her loving me? I don't think she knows what love is. You don't lie and cheat on and manipulate someone you love.

Love is what I feel for the woman standing outside, who's dealing with seeing her ex for the first time since he almost killed her.

Before I can open my mouth to set her straight and get her the fuck out of my sight, she lurches forward and forces a desperate kiss on me. I instantly pull back and push her away by the arms.

"What the hell, Sadie?" I exclaim in repulsion and anger. "I'm married, for fuck's sake! And even if I wasn't, I'd have to be an idiot to give you another chance to fuck me up all over again."

Her face scrunches up at my harsh words, and she quickly breaks down in tears.

"But—but Bodie said..." she trails off, and I glare at her. I should've known Bodie put her up to this. That's just the kind of meddling jerk off he is.

"Go ahead. Tell me what my dear brother told you."

She swallows back her tears as guests mill around behind her. "He told me that you married Dani to make me jealous."

I laugh humorlessly. "I hate to break it to you, but he fucking lied. Big surprise. The truth is, I'm very happily married to Dani, and I plan on staying with her for as long as I possibly can."

Sadie wipes at her mascara-streaked face, looking embarrassed. Frankly, she should be. She should know by now not to trust a damn thing Bodie says. He's only out to benefit himself, even at the detriment of everyone else. Maybe this time, Sadie will learn.

"I recommend never speaking to that jackass again, Sadie. He's only using you to fuck with me."

I escape her presence then and stalk back over to the bar. I'm going to need something much stronger than wine this time, that's for damn sure.

This is going to be a long fucking night.

Chapter Twenty-Six

Dani

The night air chills my clammy skin as I step outside. Cars roll by where I stand shivering, each one briefly illuminated by the streetlight next to me.

What are the freaking chances that Spencer would be here tonight? Chef Universe strikes again, apparently.

I haven't felt like this in a long time. I had hoped I would never feel it again. Weak. Powerless. Ineffectual. Scared. Everything I felt the night that everything faded to black. And it all came back again the second I recognized him.

It seems so unfair that all this time, he's just been walking around in the world, coming in for work and going home to bed, just living his life like he always has, while my whole world self-destructed when I woke up alone on the linoleum floor of his apartment.

Maybe Ronan's right. It *does* matter that I didn't report him. But honestly, I just never wanted to see him again. I wasn't strong enough to face him again, even if it brought about a punishment for him. A punishment that he deserved then and still deserves now.

I sit down heavily on a bench outside the building, still feeling weak. Even out here, I can hear the low hum of fundraiser guests talking. People pass by me on the sidewalk to get to the entrance, but I can't focus on anything going on around me.

My mind is still in that hallway, watching Ronan rough up my ex-boyfriend.

There's no doubt in my mind that Ronan was trying to do something good. He was defending me, somehow, I get that. And maybe I should feel protected or cared for or something, but I just can't shake off the brutal epiphany that Ronan is so much stronger than Spencer.

It wasn't hard for Spencer to almost kill me. He overpowered me like I was nothing. And seeing with my own eyes how easily my husband manhandled Spencer, my abuser, makes me realize just how much damage Ronan could do with almost no effort.

It's terrifying.

Ronan could strangle me with one single hand. With one toss of his knuckles, he could put me in the hospital. He could take whatever the hell he wanted from my body without much of a struggle.

In my heart, I know Ronan would never do any of those things. He's a good man who doesn't hurt women. He's been patient and understanding with me since we decided to go all in. He hasn't given me even an inkling of control issues or aggression. I've been feeling so safe with him.

But the part of me that will never forget the irate way he looked tonight is speaking so much louder than the part of me that's in love with him. All those buried fears of falling into the hands of another abusive man come reaching up to the surface with such strength and tenacity that I can't stop it from pulling me down into the depths of that old, primal fear.

Stupid girl.

What do I do? How can I go back in there? How can I look Ronan in the eye again without being brought back to this night? Back to when his eyes flashed with more hatred and anger than Spencer's did all those years ago?

It's only a matter of time before you accidentally set him off and he turns on you, comes Bodie's voice in my head.

And if Ronan ever did turn on me, I know I would be dead.

"Dani?"

I look up from the pavement to see Lance standing in front of me on the sidewalk. I have literally never been more relieved to see him. His sudden arrival has me even more certain that he actually is my Fairy Godfather.

"Lance!" I launch myself at him, and he catches me in a tight hug. I close my eyes, my heart yearning for my dad because of Lance's fatherly embrace.

"What's wrong?"

"Nothing," I gasp into his suit and then pull back shakily. "Nothing. No big deal. Just ran into my psycho ex, and Ronan threatened his life. Nothing to be upset about," I ramble. I throw in a nervous laugh that quickly fades into the previously stricken expression I was wearing before he addressed me.

"Dani girl," Lance says in surprise. "Here, sit down and tell me what happened."

He leads me back to the bench, and we sit down together. He takes my hand and holds it tightly as I attempt to explain.

"It's nothing. Ronan didn't do anything wrong," I say quickly, which is true. Ronan didn't hurt Spencer. He was trying to be in my corner.

"Okay, then, what's the problem?" Lance presses gently. I look up at him for a moment, hating his question because the answer to it is so much more complicated than just one thing. The light breeze stirs his dark hair and wafts a subtle scent of soap in my direction. For some reason, that clean aroma grounds me a little bit, and I make an attempt at stuffing down the fear long enough to think clearly.

"I—I guess I'm just scared," I say finally. "Ronan could put me in the hospital without even breaking a sweat."

The breath catches in his throat, and his outrage eases me just slightly. He really believes Ronan would never do that. He sees in Ronan what I see—a good man.

"Dani—I thought we talked about this. Ronan didn't hurt Sadie, and he would never hurt you," he reminds me, his dark eyebrows low over his serious eyes. He looks so much like Ronan when he does that.

I shake my head slightly. "I know he wouldn't...but just the fact that he *could* terrifies me." I swipe at my eyes. God, it hurts to say this outloud about the man I love. "I hate feeling scared of him, Lance, but I don't think I can make that go away after what I've been through."

He squeezes my hand. "There's no doubt that you've been through more than your fair share of dark times," Lance says gently, his kind eyes focused on mine. "But how long are you going to let fear control your life, Dani?"

My mind flashes back to Chicago, when Ronan asked me how I can be so happy after everything I've been through. Didn't I tell him that I try to live without holding back because I owe it to my parents? Isn't that what I've finally allowed myself to do lately?

I cover my face with my hands. I know Lance is right.

"There might be a small voice in the back of your head reminding you of Ronan's capability, but that doesn't mean you can't be with him. It doesn't mean you can't trust him."

I peek through my fingers at him, trying to be brave enough to do what Lance believes that I'm strong enough to do. Fiercely trying to fight back the fear clutching my heart. I realize right then that if I don't keep fighting, I'll be living with it like a straight jacket...preventing me from loving anyone or anything at all.

What a waste that would be. My parents would be so let down if that's what my life turns into.

"You might always be scared, but you have a choice here, Dani. When that small voice speaks up, you can make the choice to trust Ronan."

I drop my hands and take a deep breath. "I can make the choice to not let fear control me," I say to myself.

Lance smiles and pats my hand. "Exactly. It doesn't mean you won't feel afraid. It means that you aren't going to let your fear dictate your life."

I look up at his friendly face, feeling strengthened.

I have the power to not let fear dictate my life.

I can choose Ronan instead of my fear. I can love him even if sometimes I feel afraid. I know I'll never be able to totally eradicate the mental scars Spencer gave me, but that doesn't mean I have to let it prevent me from living a good and happy life. What Ronan and I have is something pure and real and genuine. It would be a damn shame for me to throw that away just because the man has stacks of muscles and knows how to use them.

"You're right," I breathe out. "Thank you, Lance." I lean over to give him another hug. He pats my shoulder. "You really are my Fairy Godfather."

Lance chuckles at that and releases me with a smile. "I'm honored." He winks at me and then gets to his feet. "I'm going in. Are you coming?"

I nod at him with a smile. "Yeah, I'll be right there."

He smiles at me, too and then turns to walk inside.

I need a second to absorb everything we talked about. I love how talking to Lance is just like talking to my parents. He really has upheld the promise he made to my folks about looking after me if something ever happened to them.

I look down at my mom's ring and rub my thumb over it.

What would they think about all this? Would they be happy for me that I'm in love with Ronan? Undoubtedly. And I know they would be proud of me for loving him despite my fear.

I take in a deep breath and blow it out slowly. The weakness I felt when I came out here has subsided now. Lance has helped me navigate my complex reaction to the way Ronan dealt with Spencer's appearance.

But then, my stomach twists nervously as I realize I have to go back in there. Not only because this event is for Ronan's dad and he needs my support when his family is around, but also because I need to reconnect with him and work through both of our reactions so that we'll be okay going forward.

And I so desperately want us to be okay.

Maybe if I explain how scary it was for me to see him in that hallway, it'll inspire him to never act that way again. Whether it's warranted or not.

I shake the last of my freak out aside. This isn't a dealbreaker. This is a talk-it-through thing. We can get back on track, I'm sure of it. Especially if I make the choice to trust him and not give fear a soapbox.

Compared to outside, it's much warmer in here, even as I hover near the foyer for a moment and look into the main room for Ronan. People are milling around a little less now and are starting to find their seats. I spot Lance greeting Victoria over by our table and find it weird to see such a cold personality hug someone so warmly.

I don't have to look far to find Ronan, though my heart thuds in my chest when I see that he's talking to Sadie. She looks drop-dead gorgeous, just like she did at Bodie's wedding, and I glance down at my own dress. When we walked in earlier and I saw what everyone else was wearing,

I knew I was underdressed. I think Ronan only wanted me to wear this dress because it reminds him of Chicago. And while that's really freaking sweet, showing up in a fifty dollar dress makes me feel even more out of place.

I gather myself and take a breath, intending to join Ronan and say a polite hello to Sadie, but then I freeze with my heart in my throat.

It happens in slow motion.

Sadie moves forward, pressing into Ronan, and kisses him passionately. My heart stutters to see him with another woman. And not just any woman. His ex, who apparently still has feelings for him. I've never been cheated on before, but I realize in that moment how much it would hurt if Ronan ever did.

If that traitorous visual wasn't enough of a shock, then he pulls away and grabs her upper arms. He roughly shoves her back, and I feel my knees instantly turn to Jello.

The fear is instantly back with a vengeance. It's screaming *Alert! Alert! Red flag warning!* And I, being a domestic abuse survivor, immediately drink in that warning like water. Lance's words about trust evaporate from my mind. My sense of self-preservation overrides everything else.

He shoved her.

He could have just stepped away. He didn't have to put his hands on her like that.

"I tried to tell you," comes a voice from the foyer to my left.

I watch Ronan's venomous face spit a few obviously cutting words at Sadie, and then he stomps off toward the bar, leaving Sadie standing there crying. And even though she just kissed my husband, my heart feels for the callous way he rejected her.

My eyes stay on Sadie as she sadly walks away. Her beauty is marred by brokenness.

"I'm sure he told you I was lying," Bodie continues. "But honestly, did *that* look like something he's never done before?"

Pushing her like that isn't a crime. He was caught off guard and vehemently rejected her sudden advance. Regardless of whether he's done that before, that doesn't make Ronan the wife beater Bodie is making him out to be.

But I sure as hell know that if anyone pushed me like that, even once, I wouldn't risk sticking around long enough to let it happen again. Even if I loved him.

I slowly look over at Bodie, feeling outside of my body.

He stands there with his hands in the pocket of his black suit pants, smiling at me sadly. There's a smug I told you so look in his brown eyes that makes a lick of fiery anger flare up in my ever-tightening chest.

I know he's trying to manipulate me again. He wants to convince me to believe that Ronan really did beat Sadie. I still think he's lying to get between us. It isn't his influence that has my feet pinned to the floor. It's the consistency of Ronan's physical reactions.

He almost killed Bodie when he found out about Sadie.

He was swinging fists with Bodie at the wedding because he was verbally provoked.

He cornered Spencer alone in that hallway, crushing him into the wall as he threatened him.

He forcefully sent Sadie backward without a second thought.

Ronan could've settled any of those situations with words. But he didn't. What makes me think he would do any different with me?

Bodie seems to sense my broken spirit and moves closer to me. The steady din of conversation quiets in my ears as wave after wave of uncertainty crashes over me.

"You deserve better, Dani. You're a nice girl. Trust me, he doesn't know how to hold back when he's mad."

"I don't trust you," I correct him distractedly, still looking at the spot Ronan and Sadie kissed, my heart steadily breaking.

Why did I ever really think I could trust Ronan? Why did I think something as big as violence could be something we could talk through? It's clear to me now that Ronan's immediate default reaction is physical, not verbal.

"You should." He moves closer still. "I'm the only one who's been honest with you. I'm the only one who has your best interests in mind. Get away from him before he hurts you." He steps in front of me, seeming pleased at the fear in my eyes. I feel his hand on my waist. "I can protect you from him, Dani."

His unwanted touch on my body makes my stomach roll unpleasantly. I clutch his hand and move it off of me, anger and disgust burning up my back.

"Like you protected Sadie? By sleeping with her?"

What an asshole.

How dare he try to take advantage of me in my vulnerable state? Try to get between me and Ronan, for God knows what reason? My hands curl into fists at my sides as I glare at him. I'm not Sadie, and I'm not falling for his hero act.

But he isn't put off by me calling him out. Maybe he's not capable of feeling shame. Instead of backing off, he grins at me greedily.

"*Now* you're catching on."

The breath catches in my throat. "Don't touch me," I warn weakly. He laughs at my fear, and then his light-hearted smile morphs into a menacing, predatory grimace that turns my blood cold.

"I'll do whatever I damn well please, whether you like it or not."

His grave voice makes the hairs on the back of my neck stand up. I feel fear and adrenaline surging through me because what he's saying is basically what Spencer said years ago on the night he almost killed me. And I remember what Ronan said—that Bodie would try to touch me. I remember what he said to Ronan at the wedding—that he would fuck me like he fucked Sadie.

"I'll scream," I threaten hoarsely, pressing my back into the wall behind me.

He laughs again, but cruelly this time, and grips my hip painfully tight with one hand. The other reaches down and grazes the outside of my thigh and disappears under the skirt of my dress. I gasp in surprise and fight to push his hands away.

I know I've experienced evil before, but I'm still shocked to see it materialize again in front of me. How could anyone be so heartless? So selfish? So cruel?

"Why are you doing this?" I gasp out desperately. "Why do you hate Ronan so much?"

Bodie keeps his hand on my hip and reinforces his hold on me by putting the other hand on my shoulder. We're far enough from what's going on in the main room that no one notices his predacious behavior. The foyer is empty now, so there's no one nearby to call out to.

His eyes narrow at my questions, and he smiles like he's so glad that I asked. He moves his face closer to mine. Gone is the jaunty, playful Bodie. The man standing in my space is filled with a hatred I don't understand.

"Because my father loved him more than he loved me."

My breathing grows shallow as he explains.

"From the minute Ronan was born, my dad thought he could do no wrong. Every aptitude he had was worth celebrating and supporting." The hand on my shoulder lifts and strokes my hair. I shiver with disgust and nausea. "But there's something Ronan doesn't know. My mom made me swear not to tell anyone. She's ashamed, you see."

His eyes follow the curve of my collarbone, and then his fingers follow. My stomach churns so much, I feel like I might puke. Bodie smiles maliciously when his eyes return to mine.

"Because Ronan is a bastard child, born because she fucked my dad's best friend behind his back."

My heart pounds.

What?

Could he possibly be telling the truth? Historically, Bodie hasn't been known for his honesty, but the vehemence in which he's speaking has my gut telling me that, for once, he's saying something true.

"I hate Ronan because he doesn't belong in our family. Because my father treated him like a prince and me like an afterthought even though I was his real son." There's anger in his tone, but there's hurt, too. And jealousy.

Bodie's hand moves to the strap of my dress, and his fingers move underneath it. I can feel my skin trying to crawl off my body away from him. His touch feels vile and filthy.

"So, I will ruin everything he cares about. I will take away everything he has. Because everything my father gave him belongs to me."

"Ronan doesn't know?" I whisper, glancing over his shoulder into the busy room beyond. Still, no one looks our way.

"No," he answers, smirking. "But if you have sex with me, I won't tell him."

"Oh, so now you're giving me a choice?" I say through clenched teeth.

He chuckles. "Not if your answer is no."

I try to shove him off of me, but he doesn't move. He isn't as strong as Ronan, but he's still stronger than me. My heart jackhammers sharply through my upper body.

"You and I both know it would crush him to find out that Lance is his real father."

I gasp and stop struggling, in shock at his words.

He grins at me, deeply satisfied by my reaction. For a second, I forget about Bodie's evil attempts at blackmail and his reasons for hating Ronan. Everything disappears as I try to make sense of the secret Bodie just revealed.

"Lance *Bertram*?" I ask incredulously. "No. No, he would never—"

"Haven't you ever wondered why they're so close? Lance is just a family friend and his lawyer. And yet, Lance has been present for every major milestone in Ronan's life, including his wedding."

My breathing picks up. This can't be true. There's no way this can be true. *Lance*? My*Lance*?

"So, we can agree that this news would be devastating to poor Rone. I have no doubt this information would send him into a downward spiral so fast, he'd be taking it out on your pretty face by morning."

He strokes my cheek, and I jerk my head away.

I don't want to agree with him, but he's right. This would kill Ronan. He loved his father, and for him to find out that he wasn't his father after all...he would absolutely lose his shit. It would destroy him.

"My brother has taken everything from me. So now, I'm going to take everything from him."

Revulsion consumes me as Bodie's hand smoothes down my neck, over my breast and waist, back to the hem of my dress. His fingers move under the skirt of my dress once more. My body shakes in panic, and it only seems to excite Bodie more.

I try to shove him, but he blocks me. I try to stomp on his foot, but he throws his weight into me and pins me against the wall. His breath is already ragged with lust, hot on my cheek.

"There's no use in fighting back, sweetheart," he growls into my ear. "It'll be over soon." Then, his strong arms are tightly wrapped around me, and he drags me into the empty foyer, toward a door to an office that stands open.

"No!" I exclaim as I struggle against him. I manage to wiggle out of the grasp of one of his arms, but he expertly pins me back against the wall with his body, so he can use his free hand to undo his belt.

Despite the absolute terror, I can't help but feel like he's done this before.

My heart thrashes in agony, and I try to cry out so someone in the next room might hear me, but he's pushing into me so hard I can barely breathe.

I can't believe this is really happening. In broad daylight.

I look around desperately for anything near me that I could use to defend myself, but the only object nearby is a wooden console table.

I feel his hand under my dress again, pressing upward toward my underwear. I feel the panic set in tenfold and try again to fight him, to scream, to kick him where it counts, but nothing stops him. He licks up the side of my neck, his breath plastering my skin with sickening heat.

It hits me like a punch to the gut. He's going to rape me. This is happening. No one is coming to save me. The panic dissipates as I realize that being afraid isn't going to help me.

"You asshole," I gasp as he fights with my dress. "It's *my* body, not Ronan's. I don't belong to him. I belong to myself."

He moves back to look me in the face, his body releasing me just enough that I can breathe easier. I boldly hold his amused gaze.

"It's my heart that belongs to Ronan, and that's something you can *never* take from him."

Bodie narrows his eyes at me. "That may be true, Dani. But I know without a doubt that taking your body will unravel my brother. He loves you. More than he loved Sadie. And he'll have to deal with the fact that I will always have a piece of you."

He loves me.

Before I can say or do anything else, he throws himself at me. His mouth and hands roam unwelcome over my body. I can feel the aggressive hardness of him rubbing against me, and he yanks one strap down, trying to expose my breast to his mercy.

No, no, no.

Ronan loves me, and I love him. I will *not* let Bodie ruin it. I try again to scream. I manage to get out just a tiny squeak that seems to snap him back to the original plan—get me into that office where no one will hear me. Which is his mistake because as soon as he grips me around the middle to attempt to carry me, I'm finally able to draw in a deep breath.

With all of my hope standing on its tiptoes, I let out the loudest, most ear-piercing scream I can manage.

Bodie curses at the sound, cocks his fist, and powerfully rams it into my mouth.

Everything spins. I can't see straight. My ears ring. My face throbs.

I shake my head slightly to get my eyes to focus and manage to grasp that Bodie is attempting to pick me up off the floor. I place a well aimed kick to his stomach, and he falls back with a shout. He gets up quickly, rage disfiguring his face. Before I can get away, he tackles me. I land on my back, my head smacking against the floor as Bodie's body comes down hard on top of mine.

"You fucking bitch," he growls into my face.

It takes me only a split second for it to register that this is the worst possible position for me to be in. I can't overpower him like this. Tears cloud my eyes, and I let out a helpless sob as he presses his forearm down into my chest. His other hand successfully undoes his belt, button, and zipper.

"No," I rasp out breathlessly, still trying to fight him off somehow. "No, no, stop..."

And then, I hear people running into the foyer to find out what's going on. Someone heard me scream. A small bit of relief hits me, but then I look over Bodie's shoulder.

Ronan is standing there at the front of a small crowd of people, all of them gawking and shocked. I see the comprehension cross his panicked face as he realizes what Bodie's trying to do. His eyes connect with mine for a fraction of a second before he lunges forward and drags Bodie off of me by his hair and suit coat.

I get to my feet with difficulty and try to get out of the way as Ronan and Bodie immediately attack each other. I back up unsteadily into the console table as I see the full force of Ronan's unbridled fury. He straddles Bodie and mercilessly delivers blow after blow with his fists. I watch in horror as Bodie stops fighting back.

"Ronan!" I shout, but he continues, deaf to my voice. "Ronan, that's enough!"

The crowd next to me has gotten bigger, and I hear a few women shout out in fear and distress as Ronan beats his brother unrelentingly.

There's no doubt in my mind that Bodie deserves a good whooping, but what Ronan is doing goes far beyond that. I've never seen him snap so violently before. It feeds every fear I've ever had about him.

Despite what Bodie tried to do to me, I can't let Ronan kill him. Because I'm terrified that if someone doesn't intervene, he won't stop until Bodie is dead.

So, I stumble forward and grab at Ronan's shoulder, his elbow, anything to get him to hear me. Anything to stop him from committing murder. Ronan's fist is now covered in Bodie's blood, and his face has been reduced to an even bloodier pulp.

"You're going to kill him! Stop!" I shout and pull on his strong arm as hard as I can.

Instead of preventing him from delivering any more punches or getting his attention, it seems to only irritate him. Ronan tries to shake my grip off his arm, but when I don't let go, he pushes me hard enough to throw me off balance.

The small crowd gasps, and one woman even shrieks as I stagger back and fall hard into the console table. I bounce off of it and land in a terrified heap on the floor. The side of my arm burns with pain from where I hit the edge of the table.

I look up at Ronan, petrified. He returns my gaze, realizing what he just did. He quickly gets off of Bodie and reaches for me, but I instinctively scramble back away from him with a pounding, bleeding heart.

I could've gotten past what happened in the hallway with Spencer. We could've talked it out. But this...?

My heart shatters.

This is a dealbreaker.

In an instant, the little flame of love I felt for him goes out. I can't love a man who makes me feel like this. I can't love a man who only knows how to use his fists.

And he sees it in my eyes. He must because the rage on his face is gone. All I see now is pain. Regret. Sorrow.

And then security bursts through the crowd of people and lays their hands on my husband. He struggles to get free, to get to me.

"Dani—" he exclaims desperately. "Dani, please!"

But I can't respond.

I can't feel anything when the police arrive and arrest Ronan because his mother demanded he be charged for assaulting Bodie. I can't feel anything as Bodie is loaded into the ambulance. I can't feel anything when the police take my statement and confiscate the security camera footage to back up my attempted rape allegation.

I don't feel anything until I get home and start packing a bag.

Chapter Twenty-Seven

Ronan

I burst through the county jail doors with only one thought on my mind: get home to Dani.

I was only incarcerated for a few hours, but it was hell. Not because of other inmates or the limited accommodations. It was hell because all I could think about was the terrified look on Dani's face and the way she moved away from me when I reached for her.

Like I was a monster. Like I was Spencer.

I can't believe I pushed her like that. All my brain was focusing on at that moment was inflicting as much pain upon my brother as I possibly could. Because seeing him on top of her...it had me seeing red in seconds. All rational thought vanished. It was like tunnel vision. Just me, Bodie's smug face, and my fists.

I was so consumed with hatred that her little hands on my arm did nothing to break that tunnel vision. Nothing was going to stop me from exacting justice.

Because of that, I did what I swore I would never do.

As soon as she hit the table, her cry of pain snapped me out of it, but it was too late. There she was...on the floor, holding her arm and looking terrified of me.

The woman I love heaped on the floor. Because of me.

I tear into the bag the jail used to put my personal belongings in and clutch my phone. I have to call her. I have to fix this. It's been agony to be imprisoned and unable to talk to her or do anything that could help this fucked up situation that I created.

Thankfully, Lance showed up and posted bail, otherwise I would've been there till morning or longer. I stop, peering down at my phone. Not a single damn missed call or text from Dani. This is bad.

"Fuck," I mutter and quickly find her contact so I can call her.

"Ronan—" Lance calls as he follows me outside. The darkness of the night, even in the city, descends on me like a blanket. It just reminds me how much time has passed since I caught my asshole brother trying to rape my wife.

I should've followed her. I shouldn't have let Sadie distract me. If I had just stayed by her side, Bodie never would have gotten the chance to overpower her. This is all my fucking fault.

Lance catches up to me, huffing and puffing. "After you were arrested, I took Dani home."

Thank God for that. At least I know where she is. At least I can go home and talk this out with her. If she'll let me.

"Give me a ride back to my car," I say and press the call button. It rings and then goes to voicemail as Lance and I head for the parking lot. I hang up and immediately call again.

Lance unlocks his car with a beep, and we get inside. I feel uneasy as soon as the doors close, like everything is pressing in on me. The call goes to voicemail again, and I start to panic more than ever.

"Dani, call me back. Please," I plead into my phone and then hang up. "Shit, shit, shit." I run my hand through my hair in distress. Is she not answering because she doesn't want to talk to me? That seems glaringly obvious. If she isn't taking my calls, will she even let me in the house when I get there?

I would deserve it.

"Ronan, she might need some space after what happened tonight," Lance warns me gently.

"No, no, I need to explain," I argue desperately. "She needs to know I didn't mean to hurt her."

I dial her number again, but it goes to voicemail just like the times before.

Lance tenses next to me as he takes a right turn toward downtown, like he understands how bad it is that she isn't answering.

"Did you see her face, Lance? I have to make this right. I can't lose her."

He says nothing, and I feel fear sink down on my shoulders because he doesn't console me or tell me everything will be alright. He doesn't assure me that she's just asleep and not ignoring my calls. He doesn't tell me that I won't lose her over this, which makes me so fucking scared that I already have.

When we get back to the now deserted charity event, I hop out of the car before Lance can put it in park. My bruised hands are trembling as I get my keys out.

"Ronan!" Lance calls out the open window. "Give her some time—"

I get in my car and slam the door shut. He doesn't understand. I need to get to her. I need to fix this before I lose the best thing that's ever happened to me.

But when I turn up the long driveway and race toward the house, my stomach sinks. Every window is dark.

No, no, no. She *has* to be in there. Lance dropped her off.

I park on the driveway and sprint for the front door. My hands are trembling so badly now that I can barely get my key in the lock.

I swing the door open and flip on the foyer light.

"Dani!" I call out and start up the stairs. I get no response, but I still keep screaming her name as I barrel down the hallway.

I check her room first, whipping the door open and throwing on the light without knocking. Because I know in my gut that she isn't inside. And my gut is right. Her bed is perfectly made and everything untouched, like she's never set foot in this room before.

"Fuck," I gasp, my chest heaving with panic, and turn to go into *our* room. I switch on the light and find the room empty. No Dani.

I glance around, trying to pick up on anything that says she's been in here, hoping for a note or *something* telling me where she is. But there's nothing.

I scramble to be positive. Maybe after Lance dropped her off, she went for a walk and took a cab back into the city. Maybe it isn't as bad as—

My eyes land on the nightstand as I realize what's missing. The picture of her parents is gone.

My whole body tenses. The blood pounds in my head.

There's only one reason that picture is MIA.

She's gone.

"No!" I shout and tear open the dresser she just moved her things into. Two of the drawers are completely empty.

No.

I sink to my knees and put my face in my hands.

She left. Not just for the night. She left for good.

But where is she? Where else does she have to go? Is she safe? Is she okay? Why isn't she answering her goddamn phone?

I dig my phone out of my pocket and call Lance. My lungs work overdrive as I start to hyperventilate. He picks up quickly.

"Is she still there?" he asks without saying hello.

"No. No, Lance, she's gone. Fuck, she left..." My eyes blur as the tears come.

"I'm sure she's fine," Lance says, though not very convincingly. "She probably just—"

"No, she packed up her stuff," I interrupt brokenly. "She left me, Lance."

She left me. God, it hurts to say out loud. She left, and I don't know where she is or if she's safe or in her right mind or even how hurt she is after what Bodie did. Fuck, she must feel so overwhelmed and scared. Sexually assaulted and then betrayed by her husband within just minutes.

The image of her pale face swims in my mind's eye. A swollen and bloody mouth. The same mouth I kissed with such fervor and meaning. I see her wide, shocked eyes filled with tears and pain. The same eyes that looked at me with such brightness and life.

Of course, she disappeared without a trace. She had every reason to.

There's harsh silence on the other end of the phone as I feel myself overcome by the magnitude of what I've done.

"What do I do?" I whisper. "Please, there has to be something I can do..."

"I think the only thing you can do is wait until she comes home," he answers softly. "I'm sorry, Ronan."

I hang up and collapse into sobs.

I knew tonight was likely to end in some kind of disaster because that's just what Bodie does, but I didn't expect to lose the love of my life. I didn't expect to lose her so quickly. God, if I could take back that one moment, I would still have her.

Because now, I realize that I have nothing if I don't have Dani.

I call Dani every hour all night. I don't know what else to do. I can't sleep. I can't sit still. I can't think about anything else.

Eventually, my calls go directly to voicemail. Even though she wasn't picking up, the act of calling her made me feel like there was *maybe* some hope.

But now, I just keep replaying that moment over and over in my mind, studying it, examining how I acted. Every time, I come to the same conclusion.

I made the biggest fucking mistake of my life.

I betrayed her in the worst way possible. I promised her I would never lay a hand on her. In that moment, I chose to hurt my brother instead of listening to my wife. I chose to let my hatred and my ire drown out the woman I love.

I've never hated myself more than I do now.

Morning dawns without hearing a word back from Dani, not even a text to tell me that she's somewhere safe. Not even a "fuck off," which I rightly deserve. I call Lance at six to see if Dani has contacted him, but he says he hasn't heard from her either.

At eight, I get in my car and drive to her old neighborhood. It's a last ditch effort to find her, because I don't have any other ideas where she could have gone. I know she has that friend she had a falling out with, but I don't know how to track her down.

I feel the last of my hope fade. Dani wouldn't do this just to make me suffer. She wouldn't give me the cold shoulder just to hurt me or get back at me.

No, she's gone. And I don't know how to get her back. I don't know *if* I can get her back.

I call Gina as I drive back to the house and let her know I won't be in the rest of the week. I can't. Work doesn't matter right now. I don't give a shit if we lose an opportunity or miss a deadline. It's just not important. Not as important as Dani.

Gina is horrified to hear that Dani left, but she assures me that if she hears from Dani, she will let me know. I also call Carla because I know she and Dani have gotten close lately. Maybe Dani will reach out to her.

I go home then and pace obsessively through the empty house all day. I try calling her a few more times, but it's no use. She doesn't want to hear from me. She may never want to see my face ever again, and I would deserve it. I would so much rather her come home and berate me endlessly for what happened instead of endure this radio silence.

I have no other choice but to hope that she'll come home when she's ready. I hate feeling like the fate of our relationship is out of my control, but I can't blame her for leaving. Fuck, I knew I wasn't good enough for her. I knew all along that she deserved better than me. It was inevitable that I would lose her somehow. I just didn't think it would be like this.

Chapter Twenty-Eight

Dani

I pay the cab driver and get out with my duffel bag. I stand there in that spot long after the taxi drives away, the warm night air swirling around me. My mouth is swollen and painful from Bodie's fist, and I probably have a mild concussion.

The last thing I wanted was to show up at Mel's door with tears and snot pouring down my face, much less sporting a fat lip. But I don't know where else to go. I can't seek out Lance, not now. There's no way he wouldn't tell Ronan. And I'm pretty sure if I stayed at a hotel, Ronan would be able to track me down just by asking the front desk if his wife had checked in yet.

God, it's been a long time since I've wanted to disappear like this.

So, here I am. Standing in front of Mel and Max's apartment building, feeling so sick to my stomach with nerves that it makes me all the more sure that I have a concussion. But I'm not going to the hospital. Ronan would find me there, too.

As I tentatively make my way up the stifling stairwell to their floor, I remember how just yesterday, I called Mel and told her how happy I was and how great everything was going. Boy, how things can change in twenty-four hours. Or just thirty minutes.

I feel so stupid. I feel like I'm crawling back on my hands and knees, begging for Mel to take me in like the poor, lost soul I am. There's no doubt in my mind that she'll tell me how right she was. I think that's what hurts the most. Mel *was* right.

The house felt different when Lance dropped me off. It was like everything was a slightly different color or maybe a few inches to the left than it was before Ronan and I left for the event. Again, maybe it's the possible concussion, but I'm certain it all felt so strange to me because the faith I had in Ronan snapped cleanly in two tonight. Suddenly, there's a very clear before tonight and after tonight, and the after hurts like hell.

I pause in front of 2B, sorrowful and broken, realizing that this is my reality now. There's no going back to before tonight.

I raise my shaky fist, close my eyes tightly, and knock. I wait, tears still falling from my eyes, and then the door opens with a loud creak.

Max stands before me, looking surprised to see me.

"Dani? What happened?" he asks quietly, like he's in shock. He's definitely seen me look better.

"Is Mel here?" I choke out. I don't even care that he's naked with all his wedding tackle on display. In this desperate moment, it even seems endearing to me instead of annoying and weird.

"Uh, yeah, she's here," he answers and then steps back into the apartment. His eyes fall on my duffel bag and then back on my teary face. "Babe!" he calls over his shoulder.

"What?" comes Mel's voice from inside. Just the sound of my best friend's voice makes me cry harder.

"C'mere, someone's here to see you."

I hear footsteps approaching, and my heart pounds.

"Who the hell—" she's muttering as she appears in the doorway, then stops and stares at me with her mouth hanging open.

I want to explain what I'm doing here. I want to properly ask her if I could please come in. But all I manage is a sob.

"Dani..." Mel says faintly. "What the fuck happened to you...?"

"C-can I st-stay here tonight?" I sob pathetically. I can't even look her in the eyes, I'm so broken up.

"Dani, for fuck's sake, get in here," she orders and pulls me inside. "What the hell happened?" she demands as she takes my bag and pushes me down onto the couch. "Max, get her some water," she barks, and he quickly walks into the kitchen, full mooning me as he passes. She hands me a tissue, and I blow my nose loudly before trying to answer.

But where do I even start? How do I explain that things really *were* going well up until tonight? My heart beats oddly in my chest as I try to figure out what to say first.

"What happened to your face?" Mel asks, grasping my chin so she can get a good look at my swollen lip. She gasps. "Did he hit you?"

"No," I croak and swat her hand away lightly. "No, that was his brother."

She's dumbfounded to hear that answer, and I realize that I'm going to have to start from the very beginning. Because if I start with tonight, nothing will make sense.

So, I take a deep breath, and I start talking. I tell her everything. Every detail. Our wedding ceremony. Our Friday night dinners. Meeting his mother. Telling him about Spencer. Bodie's wedding. Chicago. Everything.

Mel listens raptly, and with each word that leaves my sore mouth, I feel eased. I've missed her so much. I've been dying to tell her about Ronan all this time, and it feels so good to tell her about him opening up to me and kissing me in Chicago. For just a minute, I forget about tonight, and I remember how amazing it feels to be Ronan's wife.

Mel seems to sense this, or it must show in my face because she reaches over and squeezes my hand.

But then, I remember the next part. The part where I saw Spencer again. The part where Bodie assaulted me. The part where Ronan broke his promise to never lay a hand on me in anger.

My face crumples slightly, and I take a deep breath.

"I saw Spencer tonight," I murmur to my knees.

Mel gasps and grips my hand painfully. "Shut the fuck up."

I nod. "He didn't do anything. But Ronan did. He threatened him." I sniff and reach for the fifteenth tissue. "It scares me how much stronger Ronan is, Mel. Spencer tried to kill me and failed, but Ronan...he could do it with one hand tied behind his back."

"Dani, just because he *could* doesn't mean—"

"I know." I look up at her. "But what if Bodie was right? What if it's just a matter of time before he snaps?"

Mel frowns at me.

"Speaking of Bodie..." I whisper, and with difficulty, I recall what he did as well.

"That *fucker!*" Mel exclaims, her eyes wide and her strawberry blonde hair flying as she hops to her feet.

"And Ronan came to stop him and then started beating the shit out of him," I continue quietly.

"Damn right, he did!"

Mel's defense of Ronan reminds me that he really was doing the right thing...Bodie deserved that.

"But then..." My tears bubble back to the surface again. "I tried to pull him off Bodie because he was going to kill him. Bodie wasn't fighting back anymore, and I was so scared that—" I stop abruptly and cover my face.

Mel sits down next to me again. I drop my hands.

"Ronan shoved me away from him. I hit a table and—" I rub my bruised arm, surprised it isn't broken. I shake my head slightly. "I know it sounds like I have it backward," I murmur. "What Bodie did was so much worse than Ronan pushing me. I should be more traumatized by being sexually assaulted...but all I can think about is how it felt for him to just swat me away."

She reaches for my hand again and waits for me to go on.

"He was arrested for beating up Bodie, and I went home. I packed up what I needed and came here." I look up at her with a sniff. "Thank you for not turning me away. I know I have a lot of nerve showing up like this when we—"

"Shut up, Dani," she dismisses vehemently. "I would never turn you away, you know that. Even if there's shit between us."

I nod, feeling slightly better. "I guess I should've listened to you, huh? If I did, none of this would've happened."

Mel's blonde eyebrows scrunch up. "First of all, I shouldn't have just ghosted you like that, Dani. What I did was really shitty, and believe me, I've been feeling shitty about it ever since."

I squeeze her hand and then throw myself at her in a bear hug.

"And hey," she says, pulling away, "if you had listened to me, you never would've been able to pay off people's medical bills. And you would've never let a man close to you again."

I shake my head slightly. "I should've just listened to Ronan and agreed we only be roommates. Love is just an unnecessary complication."

"Fuck that," Mel spits. "Take it back."

"Mel, I can't be with Ronan. Not now...I'll always be afraid of what he's capable of."

She gives me a sympathetic look. "I'm here for whatever you need, okay?"

"I'll stay here for a couple days and then I'll...I'll find somewhere to stay," I tell her. "This time, I can't call Lance, so I guess I'll have to stay in a motel or something until I can get into an apartment." My stomach sinks at that thought. Here I am, back to being homeless again.

"Why can't you call Lance?"

"He'll tell Ronan."

Mel sighs heavily. "I'll talk to my landlord. Maybe he knows somewhere that has openings. Until then, the couch is all yours."

"Thanks." I give her a small smile that hurts like hell. "Even if your couch sucks," I tease, and she smiles. "I missed you so much, Mel."

She hugs me again. "Missed you, too, girl."

Mel and Max fill me in on what they've been up to lately, which isn't much. But it's such a relief to be with them. It's a relief to feel like I have a safe place again. They ply me with food and beverages, but I mostly just watch Max stuff his face. I'm beginning to feel just slightly better about things, but then my phone rings.

I see Mr. Serious Quiet Man on the caller ID and feel my heart shrivel up in my chest. I can't talk to him right now. I haven't made up my mind whether I should talk to him ever again. All I know is that I'm scared, and I need space.

So, I don't pick up. He calls again. I ignore it. He calls all evening until I finally turn my phone off. I'm too hurt...it's all still too raw for me.

In the morning, I listen to his many voicemails against my better judgment. He sounds panicked and worried. It breaks my heart to hear him like that, and I'm glad I didn't pick up last night. I know if I did, he would've convinced me to come back. And right now, I don't want to come back.

Mel comes into the kitchen, where I'm leaning against the counter with a cup of coffee.

"Sleep okay?"

I give her a *get real* look, and she chuckles. She emerges from the fridge with a carton of orange juice and then parks herself against it.

"He called all night," I tell her quietly, looking at my mug.

"He's probably worried sick wondering where you are. You should've left a note," Mel says. I nod. "Maybe you should just text him so he knows you're not in a ditch somewhere."

I look up at her and shake my head slowly. "I know if I communicate with him at all, it will be hard to stop. He'll just call me more. He'll want to talk."

Mel nods sadly. "I could text him."

"What? No," I answer quickly. "Then, he'll just badger you for information."

She shrugs. "Alright. Let the man suffer, then."

I stare at Mel as she drinks directly from the orange juice carton.

"Mel...I can't..." My eyes fill with tears again, and I realize how freaking sick I am of crying. I'm basically a sad fire hydrant at this point. "He hurt me...I don't want anything to do with him."

She returns my tearful gaze thoughtfully.

"You wouldn't be so hurt if you didn't love him, Dani."

My heart thuds painfully in my chest.

No, I can't love Ronan. Not now.

"Whose side are you on, Mel? I'm not in love with him, and I'm not texting him," I exclaim stubbornly.

"Okay. Whatever you say, girl. But when you wake up in six months, still broken up about this, I'll be the first to tell you it's because you're madly in love with that man."

She puts the orange juice back in the fridge and leaves the room without another word or glance back at me.

"I'm *not*," I whisper to myself.

But it's no use. I do love Ronan. A part of me will probably always love him. But that doesn't mean anything now. I can love him from a distance. I can get to a point where I can wish him well and do what I can to move on.

Move on?

My lower lip trembles at that thought. Why does the idea of a future without Ronan in it feel so...*wrong*? It feels like an alternate universe.

Mel is so right. Damn it, why is Mel always so right? In six months, I will absolutely still be wishing things hadn't gotten so messed up. Who in the hell will I ever find to move on with that's better than Ronan?

I'll never get over him, will I?

But how I feel changes nothing. I'll have to just learn to live with missing him for the rest of my life because I can't risk being hurt by him again.

I lay low with Max and Mel for a couple days and then check myself into the nearby Super 8. It's dingy and has a funky smell to it that I can't place, but at least the front desk agreed to plead the fifth if anyone calls or comes by asking about me.

I could definitely afford to stay somewhere nicer, but I almost feel like this is where I belong. In this weird-smelling room with a lumpy bed and a TV that only gets half the cable channels. In a strange way, it feels familiar. Like my old apartment's ghost took up residence here, making me feel both slightly comforted and also slightly stupid for taking a chance on Ronan. Because even though I went with my gut, I still ended up back where I started...homeless and homesick for somewhere that doesn't exist anymore. Alone, again.

What have we learned, Dani?

You can never trust your gut. Your gut's a damn liar.

Ronan doesn't stop calling. My bruised arm has changed colors several times by now, but my lip isn't swollen anymore. I'm wracked with nightmares, either to do with Bodie succeeding in raping me because I try to scream and nothing comes out or with Ronan getting off of a bloodied Bodie and then coming for me next.

For days, my brain continually relives what happened that night, but then something comes back to my memory that didn't before. I remember what Bodie said about Lance. Despite how I feel about Ronan, I can't help myself from wondering about it. I have to know for a fact whether it's true.

There's only one way to find out. I call Lance. And damn, am I nervous when he picks up on the second ring.

"Dani girl," he says, sounding both relieved and worried.

"Is Ronan with you?" I ask instantly, walking slowly down the sidewalk to the street and then turning around to walk back to the front step of the motel. The late morning sun is baking off last night's rain, making the air feel sweltering and stuffy.

"Uh, no, he's not. Why? Have you talked to him?"

"No, but he's only called me twice today so far. Listen, Lance—"

"We've been worried sick about you," Lance interrupts. "Where are you?"

"I'm somewhere safe; that's all you need to know, and that's *all* you're going to tell Ronan, got it?" I demand sternly and mindlessly turn back to go down the sidewalk again.

Lance sighs heavily. "Got it."

"Good. You and I need to talk about something. Can you meet me for coffee?"

"Me? Not Ronan?"

"No, I don't want to see him." My voice breaks slightly, and I clear my throat. "But I need to ask you something important, and it isn't the kind of thing you ask over the phone, so. Are you free tomorrow?"

"I'm free right now," he offers.

I reach the end of the sidewalk and turn around with a sigh.

"Alright. Meet me at the Second Street Coffee Shop."

"I'll on my way."

I shouldn't have picked this coffee shop. It's the same one where I met with him to discuss how my life was royally screwed. This is where everything started, and sitting here brings to mind all the things that happened in the beginning.

The desperation. The indebtedness. The hope.

It's almost one in the afternoon, and this time, the cafe is less crowded, but there's still enough chatting people to cause a drone of sound that is slowly turning my mind to mush. These days, my mind is mostly mush though, to be fair.

Lance enters, wearing a black suit and gray tie and looking every bit his normal self except for how wide his blue eyes become when he spots me. I don't get up, and I don't offer him a hug, even though I regret it when I see him realize my cold greeting. That's not like me; I know it isn't. But I haven't felt like me since Ronan broke his promise.

He sits down across from me, looking very serious and even a little nervous.

"It's good to see you," he says genuinely, and I notice him taking in the scabbed-over cut on my lip. "How are you?"

I smile grimly. "I've been better."

"I could say the same for Ronan."

I nod jerkily. "I'm sure." I'm not comfortable knowing about how Ronan is doing.

"He's losing his mind without you, Dani. He just wants a chance to apologize."

I swallow hard and shake my head. "I didn't come here to talk about that."

Lance's pleading expression deflates just slightly, revealing that he had every intention of trying to get me and Ronan back on speaking terms. And why wouldn't he? He's Ronan's father. I'm sure all he wants in the whole world is to fix this for his son. But it isn't that easy, and I'm not going to let Lance believe otherwise.

"What is it you want to talk about, then?"

I look down at my hands, fidgeting slightly on the table. My mind flits back to that night when Bodie threatened me. I wouldn't normally believe anything he says, but I can't deny that Lance has been a much bigger part of Ronan's life than just his lawyer.

I clear my throat and look up at him. Why did I never realize how much he and Ronan look alike? I definitely noticed that Ronan looks nothing like his mother and brother. But now, I see it when I look at Lance. Ronan's blue eyes and broad shoulders. Ronan's strong jaw and dark hair. My heart beats in my ears as the question forms on my tongue.

"Are you Ronan's real father?"

Lance stares at me in shock. The blood drains from his face. With that reaction, I have no doubt that what Bodie said was true. My stomach turns, and I feel like throwing up.

"Bodie told me," I say before he can ask how I found out. I shake my head slightly. "How could you do that, Lance?"

He leans toward me and tries to touch my hand. I move it away.

"You have to understand that I didn't mean for it to happen," he explains, and it hurts me to see the pain in his eyes. "I was drunk, and she seduced me."

I look away, over the heads of the people sitting two tables away, hating how much that sounds like an excuse and not an explanation.

"Believe me, when she told me she was pregnant and the baby was mine—I—" Lance sighs, becoming more agitated than I've ever seen him before. "I thought she was just trying to get me to pay child support or some other God forsaken reason, but I took a paternity test..." He shakes his head, looking like he's about to cry. "She made me promise not to tell Scott. We both knew it would've hurt him too much."

I say nothing, mostly because I don't know what to say, and wait for him to continue. No matter his intentions to not hurt his best friend, he still did the unthinkable. And I'm not going to comfort him for that.

At length, he goes on.

"I've watched my son grow into a respectable, successful man," he whispers to the table. "Scott took so much pride in him," he adds with a sad smile. "And it was my pride, too."

I can't believe Lance would do something like this, and I hate it, but I can't stop the bit of compassion I feel for him from sneaking in. It's obvious he cares about Ronan, and I'm sure it was torture to see his little boy being brought up by his best friend instead of by him.

"I can't imagine how it felt to watch someone else raise your son," I say gently.

He nods sadly, tears forming in his blue eyes, so much like Ronan's. I clear my throat and say what I know is the last thing Lance wants to hear.

"Ronan deserves to know."

Lance stares at me like I just shot him in the chest.

"He has a right to know the truth, Lance."

"Even if it hurts him? You know how much he loved his dad," he answers painfully. I lean forward and put my hand on his.

"Tell him. He should know. The truth doesn't change the fact that Scott loved him. It just means that he has you, too."

Lance wipes at his eyes. "What if he doesn't want me?" he whispers, his lower lip trembling.

My eyes moisten as well, and I squeeze his hand. "He deserves the right to make that choice."

He nods and covers his face with one hand. His bulky shoulders shake slightly. I've only seen Lance cry once, and that was at my parents' funeral. Despite the horrible thing he did all those years ago, I know Lance is a good man. It was a mistake, one he made while under the influence of both alcohol and Victoria. So, I give him a moment to collect himself, trying to figure out how to be supportive without him thinking I condone what he did.

After a long moment, he looks up at me with red eyes.

"I'll tell him," he agrees with a sniff, "but only if you're there, too."

"No," I answer firmly, my anger already rising at him trying to use this to get me in the same room as Ronan. "Don't bring me into this. This is between you and Ronan."

"He needs you, Dani."

I shake my head and get up from my chair. "Tell him, or I'm never speaking to you again."

"Dani—"

"Everyone is making threats, I might as well join in," I mutter to myself as I grab my purse.

I leave Lance in the coffee shop and walk back to my lonely motel room, feeling grief for them. I know the truth will change everything and will be difficult for them to navigate, but I don't want to be the one to walk Ronan through it. He's a grown man. It's *his* life.

I have my own life to figure out.

Chapter Twenty-Nine

Ronan

It's been a week since I've seen Dani.

It hurts every second. It doesn't matter how many laps I swim downstairs or how much I drink or how many times I call her. I'm learning that I have no say in what happens going forward. This is all up to her.

I wish she would just let me apologize because I have never been more sorry. I wish she would let me tell her that it was the biggest mistake of my life. I wish she would let me tell her that I'll do anything to get her back.

But the days press on painfully in this quiet house. I don't know how I lived here alone all these years. It's awful. I dismissed Carla this weekend. I couldn't handle her showing up each day with that slightly hopeful look on her face, like maybe *today*, I would have something good to tell her. Laurie has more work than ever, even though Dani isn't here. I can't get myself to care about the state of the house. I can't even get myself to care about work, even though I know things are piling up without me there.

I just want Dani.

The doorbell rings downstairs, and my heart lurches. I charge down the hallway and then the stairs to the front door. I wrench it open and am disappointed to find Lance standing there.

He sees it on my face and gives me an apologetic smile.

I run my hand through my disheveled hair, feeling foolish. Why did I think Dani would fucking ring the doorbell? Just goes to show how desperate I am.

"Hey, Ronan. Can I come in?"

I leave the door open and turn to go into the living room. Lance's footsteps track behind me, echoing slightly on the marble floor. I plop down on the couch, and he sits opposite me. I stare up at the ceiling blankly, completely unconcerned with how shitty of a host I'm being.

"How are you holding up?"

I lower my eyes to his, and it's the first time I realize that Lance looks terribly nervous. His eyebrows are drawn in, and there are dark circles beneath his eyes. I squint at him slightly.

"What's wrong?"

"Hmm? Nothing, nothing." He waves one hand at my question. "I just want to tell you that..." He shifts slightly and clears his throat. "I saw Dani."

I sit bolt upright, my heart pounding. "What? You did? When?" I demand quickly, my eyes wide.

Lance fidgets with his hands. "A few days ago."

"What the hell, Lance? Why didn't you tell me?" I exclaim angrily.

"Because she—she didn't really have anything she wanted me to tell you, other than that she's somewhere safe."

My heart is hammering in my chest like it does after I swim. I cover my face with my hands and take a few breaths.

She's safe.

"I tried to tell her to call you, but she wouldn't hear it."

I drop my hands and nod. "How was she? Is she okay?"

Lance swallows and leans forward slightly. "I think she's okay. Just trying to work through what happened."

"Right."

Even though she still doesn't want anything to do with me, the fact that Lance saw her warms me inside. I was starting to think she had never existed at all. Without her in this house, I was starting to feel like I imagined it all.

"Did she ask about me at all?" As the words come out, I know what the answer will be, but it still hurts to hear it.

"No," Lance answers softly.

I nod. "Do you think...do you think there's a chance I can get her back?"

He looks at me sadly. "I really don't know, Ronan."

I sniff, tears stinging my eyes.

Fuck.

She's really done with me. It's really over. At least for her. It'll never be over for me. My life will never be right again until she's back in it. Without her, I'm a lifeless man.

We sit in silence for a moment, each distracted by our own thoughts, and then he clears his throat.

"Listen, I came here to talk about something else, too," Lance says anxiously. His voice has a pinched quality to it that I've never heard from him before.

I study him curiously. It's deeply strange to see him nervous. My stomach sinks as I realize that he has something to tell me that I may not like to hear. My mind races with possibilities. Did Bodie pay his way out of his charges? Is my mother suing me?

"What is it?"

Lance closes his eyes and takes a deep breath.

"When I tell you, please, please try to understand," he murmurs mournfully.

I give him a confused look, and before I can ask what the hell that means, he begins.

"Decades ago, I was at a party your parents were hosting. Bodie was just a toddler then," he says, avoiding my eyes. "Obviously there was a lot of drinking, and I imbibed more than I should have."

He pauses here and lifts a shaky hand to rake through his dark hair. I've noticed in the last year how he's starting to grey around his temples.

"I wasn't in my right mind," he explains, glancing at me. "I didn't really understand what I had done until it was over. Then, it dawned on me...I had just slept with my best friend's wife." He raises his regretful eyes to mine. "She seduced me, Ronan."

"Shit," I whisper in shock as I understand who he's talking about. I knew my mother was evil, but this is beyond evil. To betray my dad like that... I fucking hate her.

"We both knew it would kill your father if he found out, so we kept it a secret. And besides the burning guilt I felt, it was going fine until a few months later when Victoria told me she was pregnant."

Lance's eyes flood with tears as I start to feel the room spin and move like a carousel. I forget about hating my mother. I even forget about Dani. A deep sense of dread fills me at what Lance is insinuating.

Don't say it. Please don't fucking say it.

"I thought she was just trying to blackmail me or pin child support on me or something, but—" His voice catches in his throat. "I took a paternity test. And six months later...you were born."

I hear a funny buzzing in my ears as I stare at him in utter disbelief.

No. No, no, no.

"I watched your father raise you, love you, support you in all the ways I couldn't." Lance smiles through his tears. "He was so proud of you, Ronan."

Tears form in my eyes, too as anger and denial sinks in. I stand up and pace in front of the coffee table.

"No," I blurt out. "This is—this can't be true."

"I'm sorry," he says, and he truly looks it. "This doesn't change the fact that your dad loved you. He was still your dad—"

"Did he know?" I stop and look Lance straight in the eyes. He looks older, suddenly. Like telling me this horrible truth has drained a few years off his life. Despite the anger I feel, I'm sure it was torture to keep this secret for so long.

"I don't believe so. If he did, or even if he had suspicions, he never voiced them."

Suddenly, my mother's shitty treatment of me makes sense. I was a constant reminder of her unfaithfulness. I was a walking mistake. I was a walking secret she was desperate to keep from her husband.

I swallow hard as a wave of pain hits me like a brick wall.

He wasn't my real father...

I've prided myself on being his son my entire life, and now? I share no blood with him whatsoever. I never have.

"Ronan, I know this is a lot to take in. I know this is huge," Lance says kindly.

I shake my head slightly, feeling overwhelmed.

If I'm not a Wells, who the hell am I?

"But I think you deserve to know the truth. I understand if you need some time..."

I look at him. My real father. A man who has always been there when I needed him, business or otherwise. Now, I know why.

"I just want you to know that I'm sorry for what I did to your dad. He didn't deserve that...I betrayed him in the worst way, and I've had to live with that every day." He stands up. "But I have never, not even for a second, wished I could take it back. Because if I did, you wouldn't have been born."

We share a teary look, and then he takes a step back.

"Take as long as you need. I'll be here when you're ready to talk through what things will look like for us going forward..."

My heart skips a beat. He means a relationship with me. A proper father-son relationship.

Lance gives me a sad smile and then sees himself out. The door closing softly behind him and the silence that follows bring a flood of emotions that I don't know how to sort through.

Disbelief. Hurt. Disgust. Anger. Emptiness. Betrayal.

I pick up my phone and dial Dani for probably the fiftieth time. It goes to voicemail, as I was expecting. But even just hearing her cheerful voice asking me to leave my name and number soothes something in me.

"Dani," I say after the beep, "I really wish I could talk to you right now." I sniff. "I just found out—" My voice cuts out, and I clear my throat. "I just found out that I'm not who I thought I was... My dad wasn't—" I stop again, my face crumpling as the tears come more forcefully. "I'm not my father's son," I whisper. "How could they do that, Dani? How could they betray him like that? Hell, now what am I supposed to do?" I wipe my hand down my wet face. "I wish you were here. I know you would have something sweet to say. Lance told me you're somewhere safe though, and I'm so glad to hear that. I miss you. Please call me."

I hang up, feeling slightly eased by just saying those things aloud, even if Dani doesn't call back. At this point, I know she won't.

Fuck, what do I have left of my life? Everything is different. Lance is my real father. My wife won't speak to me. I hate living here. I don't want to go back to work. What do I do? I've never felt so lost or so alone.

I can't be here. I need to get out of this damn house, where I'm just reminded that Dani is gone and my dad isn't my dad.

So, I get in the car and drive. I hit the highway and speed around Minneapolis with no destination in mind. But then, almost like I can't help it, I pull into the small cemetery parking lot. I hate that the last time I was here, it was with Dani. I glance in the direction of her parents' graves as I automatically make my way to my dad's.

Each step hurts. I'm suddenly glad he's dead. Because maybe he died blissfully unaware of what his wife and best friend did.

It's a blustery day that dries my wet face as I plant my feet on the grass in front of his ornate headstone. New tears fall, and I reach out to touch the stone, like I'm resting my hand on his shoulder.

"Did you know?" I whisper. The wind takes the words and blows them away. A whisper comes back to me, but it's from inside.

It doesn't matter if I knew, son. I still loved you.

It takes me a couple days to process everything. I sat at the bottom of my lap pool two different times, my mind screaming at me to just breathe in, so the pain would end. But each time, Dani's voice told me to swim back to surface, back to her.

I haven't spoken to Lance or anyone. The silence has become like a companion to me now, albeit a shitty one. It just reminds me that I'm alone and have no one I can talk to about my life being so severely upended. I'm not a Wells, and I feel like I have no right to my dad's real estate legacy. In a way, that's almost a relief. Dani helped me realize that I don't like what I do. I only ever did it because my dad did it first, and I wanted to make him proud.

But he wasn't my real dad. And he isn't here. Besides, I have enough money in my bank account that I could retire right now and never have to work again. Gina was right when she said I needed a vacation. She just didn't mean a permanent one.

Another week passes. The quiet becomes familiar, and I use it to my advantage. I think. I evaluate. I scream at nothing. I swim twice a day to keep my sanity, even if it doesn't numb my mind like it used to.

But with each lap, something starts to happen to me. Things start making sense again. My priorities align themselves in my mind. The people I care about the most start to crowd out the people I don't care about. I feel myself starting to form boundaries with my family, and what I want for my future starts to become clear.

In the middle of the night, I find myself at my desk, and each goal flows out of my fountain pen onto a sheet of paper.

Get Dani back.

I'm going to do whatever Dani needs me to do to make things right. Undoubtedly, I want Dani. I'll always want Dani. She's the woman I love. I'm going to give her the time she needs, but I can't give up.

Cut them off.

I'm disowning my mother and brother. Our relationship has never been anything other than toxic. And now that I know the truth, I have no intention of speaking to her ever again. That goes for Bodie as well. If I have to file a restraining order to keep him from contacting me, I will.

Find a new job.

I'm quitting my job. It doesn't make me happy. It's just robbed me from doing anything else with my life. I'm going to find something that I enjoy doing. Maybe something that does some good for someone else.

Figure it out with Lance.

I'm going to give Lance the opportunity to be something more to me than just my lawyer. Despite how he betrayed my dad, I think he deserves the chance to be a real father to me. For some reason, I feel like my dad would approve of that.

So, I set about to make those things happen. I acquire a restraining order against Bodie. I make my mother aware that she's no longer my mother, and I'm no longer her son. I have dinner with Lance, and we work through the complicated feelings we have about my parents. I back off and resort to texting Dani twice a week to let her know that I miss her and am thinking about her. I tell Gina I'm not returning to work. I decide to sell my shares in the company, which pads my bank account even more.

Despite the steps forward I'm making, being in the house alone is still close to unbearable. Each room feels like a cavernous void without Dani's sweet laughter filling it up. So, I decide to put it on the market and move out. Deep down, I know that Dani isn't going to walk through that door anytime soon. I take the last of her things with me and move into an apartment downtown. It doesn't feel remotely like home but neither did my house. Not since Dani left. It's nice to have something smaller, actually. Something that's more manageable by myself now that I let Laurie and Carla go. They cried when I told them, but I promised to pay them the rest of this year's salary because of how short notice it was.

When the house sells two days after it hits the market, it feels deeply bittersweet. It hurts to leave it, because that's where Dani and I lived together, but I have hope that one day, maybe she and I can find a place together. It's a small hope, but it's there. And I'm clinging to that small hope with everything I have.

A month after the charity dinner disaster, I get a call from an unknown number as I'm walking home from the Y. I pick up, assuming it's a prospective client who hasn't gotten the memo that I'm no longer working for Wells, Inc.

"Ronan Wells," I answer.

"Uh, hi," comes a woman's voice on the other end. "My name is Mel. You don't know me, but I'm a friend of Dani's."

"Is she okay? What's going on?" I demand worriedly, my heart instantly hammering in my chest.

"She's fine; everything's fine," Mel assures me. "I just wanted to talk."

"About Dani?"

"Yeah." She clears her throat. "Listen, I really wasn't on board with you two from the get-go, but hearing her talk about you has changed my mind. Despite what happened, she isn't over you."

She isn't over me.

That knowledge feels like my first true lungful of breath in weeks. I've been hoping there was still a chance to get her back, somehow, and Mel may be that chance.

"How is she?"

"She's fine. I mean, she isn't great. But. I think she's just stuck. And she wouldn't be stuck if she wasn't hung up on you."

I reach the steps to my apartment building and sit down on the top one. The sounds of downtown Minneapolis fill the evening air. Car honks. Loud music blaring out of passing vehicles. People talking as they walk by. All of it echoing off the buildings stretching upward. It's vastly different from where I lived before with Dani, and it's been helpful to have so much noise. It distracts me enough to not feel like I'm constantly walking around with my heart dragging on the ground behind me.

"She still won't talk to me."

"I know," says Mel with a sigh. "I keep telling her to. She's way too fucking stubborn for her own good, so I decided it was time for me to get involved."

"Okay...so, what do I do? How do I get her back?" I ask instantly, feeling a deep sense of relief that Mel is willing to help me.

"Well, I have a plan."

Chapter Thirty

Dani

I turn over with a groan and try to get comfortable. I hate to say it, but I really miss Ronan's bed. And not just because I could usually find Ronan in it.

I need to figure out where I'm going to go. I can't stay in this motel room forever. I need to get back on my feet.

There's still millions of dollars in my bank account. Frankly, I'm surprised no one has showed up with papers that nullify the contract I signed and take all the money back. I remember it said that I have to be living with Ronan for it to be valid, and well, I'm definitely not living with him. Part of me wonders if Ronan has thought about the contract at all. Being the businessman he is, it wouldn't surprise me. I know how much he didn't want his mother to get the money in that trust fund, but...I don't know if I can go back to the way things were before.

And I don't think I can use more of the money in my account anyway...it just doesn't feel right.

So, that means I need to get a job. I need to support myself like I did before, even if I barely scrape by. I had a break from all the overworking I was doing, and now it's time to get back to it. Maybe if I get a job, it'll distract me from what happened. Maybe if I move on, the hurt will fade. At least this time, I'm debt free.

In the morning, I take the city bus over to Mel's, so I can borrow her laptop to look for some employment options while she's at work. I call on several waitressing ads that tell me the position has already been filled. But finally, I get a nibble that the Second Street Coffee Shop needs a barista. It's part time, but it'll have to do for now.

I nail the interview the next day and come back to the motel feeling good for the first time in a month. I forgot what it feels like to be excited about anything. But that excitement also has a strange aftertaste of bitterness that I don't want to think about.

"That's great, Dani," Mel congratulates with a smile that night at her place.

"It's part time, but honestly, I'll take whatever I can get, you know?" I say and snag a slice of pizza from the box sitting on the coffee table in front of us.

Their little apartment has become my second home in the last month. I mostly just sleep at the motel. I'll always be grateful to them for how kind they've been for letting me crowd their space and their lives while I figure out what the heck to do with mine.

"Right," says Max.

"No, she's *not* right," Mel argues, "I think she's going about it totally fucking wrong." She narrows her eyes at me, and I stare back at her, surprised.

"Sorry? What?"

She takes a sip of her beer and then sets it down, taking her sweet time.

"Don't get me wrong, girl. I'm happy for you that you got this job. But you shouldn't be focusing on that right now."

I look away, feeling an angry blush creep up my neck. I know where she's going with this. She's been a little more than vocal lately about me trying to work things out with Ronan.

"I know you don't want to talk to him, but you need to."

"No, I really don't," I answer, my voice louder than I meant. I swallow and try to calm myself. "I don't want to be with someone who hurts me like Spencer did."

Mel gapes at me, her mouth so far open that I can see her tongue ring winking at me.

"Are you fucking kidding me, Dani? What Ronan did was *nothing* like what that asshole did to you."

I feel the anger and the hurt bubbling up inside me again. I don't want her to defend Ronan. She wasn't there.

"It boils down to the same thing, doesn't it?" I say wearily, keeping my anger tamped down. "They both used violence against me."

Mel gives me a deep scowl, her blonde eyebrows like little caterpillars over her eyes. "Bull fucking shit, Dani. It's not the same. What Spencer did was malicious and intentional, and you never heard from him again. Ronan didn't mean to hurt you, and you know that man is dying to apologize to you properly."

I avoid her eyes, inwardly squirming. Maybe she's right. Even if she is, it doesn't change the fact that Ronan broke my trust. Because that's why it hurts so much. I truly believed he would never hurt me. I trusted that he would always be my safe place. But then, he turned around and shoved me like I was nothing.

I've replayed it in my mind at least a hundred times by now, and it always looks the same. Ronan using his colossal arm to send me flying when he should've comforted me with it. I was the one who was hurting—Bodie was so close to accomplishing his evil goal... But that didn't matter to Ronan. It was more important that he make Bodie suffer for what he did at that exact moment, with fists that have struck his brother countless times before. Not just at Bodie's wedding, but when he caught him and Sadie in bed as well, and God knows how many other times before that. My pain and my fear were just an afterthought to him.

What he did to Bodie went beyond protecting me. Beyond defending me, even. And what he did to me went beyond the boundaries I set for myself after things went south with Spencer. I promised myself that I would never be with someone who hurt me like that ever again. And it kills me that now Ronan falls into the same category in my mind that Spencer does.

"Dani," Mel presses quietly, sensing that I'm getting emotional.

I look back at her to see a soft expression on her face that I haven't seen very often.

"You know that Ronan has tried to apologize to you countless times, but you won't let him. Why not? Why not just hear him out?"

"I don't owe him anything," I murmur painfully. "Not a chance to apologize and not a second chance either."

"But you love him, Dani."

My heart pounds at that word. That stupid, stupid word. Ronan was right all along. Love is just an unnecessary complication. Because loving him didn't save me. Loving him has only brought me unspeakable pain.

I sniff and swipe at my eyes. "I never said I loved him."

"Just because you haven't said it, doesn't mean you don't," argues Mel stubbornly. "And it's pretty fucking clear that he loves you, given that he still hasn't stopped contacting you."

I shake my head. It doesn't matter if I love him. And if Ronan loved me, he wouldn't have pushed me.

"He's just a man, Dani," Max says gently. I look up at him, grateful that his plate is covering his manhood. I'm surprised to hear him say anything about this. He's steered pretty clear of me and Mel when we get talking about my pathetic life.

"What's that supposed to mean?

He sighs. "It means that he's...*fallible*. He's a human being. He made a *mistake*. That's what humans do, no matter how hard we try."

I don't want to hear that Ronan is human. I don't want Mel to talk me into trying to work things out. I know if I let myself admit that I miss him like crazy, all of my resolve will vanish into thin air. I know if I call him back or text him, I won't be able to keep myself from letting him back in. Because despite what he did and how hurt I am, I can't seem to shake the memory of what it was like being with him before. How good it was.

I swallow hard and look back down at my untouched pizza.

"It was a pretty big mistake to make," I whisper.

I know I made it sound like this part time barista job was no big deal, but damn. There's a lot more to learn than I realized. It isn't like waitressing where I just deliver food to patrons with a smile and a good attitude. I actually have to make things, and make things *right*, and do it quickly.

While the customer stands there in full view. I've only been here a week, but I feel just as clumsy and out of place as I did the day I started.

At least my boss, Carrie, is cool. She's one of those girls with a full sleeve of tattoos and fun-colored hair. When I met her at the interview, I may have fangirled just a bit. Maybe that's what got me the job.

It's three-thirty, and I'm in the home stretch now. Only a half-hour left and then I can go collapse on Mel's couch and look through the paper for an apartment to rent while Max plays World of Warcraft naked at his desk. Just what a girl needs after four hours on her feet.

The bell on the front door jingles, and I glance up from where I'm wiping down the counter. I do a double take, thinking that I must be imagining Ronan standing there. It must be someone who looks just like him. After all, he isn't wearing a suit. Just dark jeans and a gray t-shirt. Oh, but his face...and that apologetic, scared expression... No, that's definitely Ronan.

Shitskies.

My stomach rolls with nerves so strong, I actually bend over slightly. God, it hurts to see him. Really? Of all the coffee shops in the city, he had to pick this one? I think my heart is about to break all over again as he hesitantly approaches the counter.

He swallows hard, his blue eyes feasting on me like he may never see me again. I notice he doesn't look surprised to see me.

"What can I get you?" I manage to squeak out.

Ronan clears his throat and looks behind me at the menu unseeingly, then back at me again.

My fingertips start to shake. I try to put on the most unaffected expression I can and wait for him to answer me. He says nothing, so I frown slightly and get him a black coffee. It hurts that I remember how he likes his coffee. I pass it over to him on the counter.

"What do I owe you?" His deep voice shakes my knees together.

"It's on the house."

He reaches for his coffee with a quaking hand.

I'm surprised that I don't feel scared. I thought if I ever saw him again, that would be the first thing I felt. I thought seeing him would take me right back to the last time I saw him. But that's not what comes to mind. The only thing I can think about is how exhausted and beat up he looks. Like he's lived a thousand lives since we last saw each other.

I feel my guard already slipping, which I don't want, so I go on the defensive.

"How did you know I worked here?" I ask him quietly. "Did you hire a private investigator? Are you having me followed?"

"No, no, nothing like that," he assures me. "But I do have a source. He or she wishes to stay anonymous."

I narrow my eyes at him.

Damn it, Mel.

"It's good to see you," he says gently.

I glance away, feeling tears forming in my eyes from the sweet way he said that. I remember when I first met him and how assertive he was when he spoke. Hearing the softness of his deep voice makes my heart shudder with the desire to dive right into the sound of it.

Damn him.

He clears his throat. "Well, I'll let you get back to work."

I watch dumbfounded as he turns away. That's it? I was expecting him to ask when I get off and if I want to talk. But there he goes. I unabashedly stare at him as he exits the shop, and then Carrie is suddenly at my side.

"Oh, my God, who was *that*? Do you know that Adonis?"

I swallow, keeping my eyes on Ronan as he passes by the window outside.

"That's my husband," I answer sadly.

Carrie turns her head so quickly to look at me that her neck cracks.

"Shut. Up. I didn't know you were married!"

I look down at my left hand, to my bare ring finger. It was deeply painful to take it off, but it kept reminding me of the vows I made, and I didn't want to be reminded of those. I've been wearing it on a chain around my neck instead.

"We're kind of separated," I explain, and before I can stop it, a tear tracks down my face. I swipe at it quickly and turn to my boss. "Sorry. Um, what else can I do before—"

"Uh, absolutely nothing. You're done. Go on," she shoos me toward the back room so I can grab my purse. I don't argue. I know I'm worthless to focus on anything now that I've seen him again.

I text Mel as I walk to her apartment, giving her a piece of my mind for telling Ronan where I work. She assures me she has no idea what I'm talking about and maintains her innocence all evening.

Ronan comes back a few days later. He says hello and orders a black coffee, while looking at me with longing eyes. It hurts even more to see him this time because I know without a doubt that he isn't here for the damn coffee. He's here to catch a glimpse of me. He's here to put himself back in my orbit.

But he doesn't make much conversation with me. He doesn't apologize or beg me to hear him out. He doesn't linger too long. He doesn't sit down at a table. He does the same thing two days later, and I start to catch on to what he's doing. He's trying to wear me down. He's trying to get me to cave. He's trying to get me to make the first move toward reconciliation. He's trying to remind me of how much I miss him.

The fourth time he comes in, he sits down by the window.

Carrie demands I go wipe down tables, despite the fact that I just wiped them down ten minutes ago. But she's my boss, and I sort of have to do what she says.

Each time I've seen him, he hasn't been wearing a suit. I'm still not used to it, though he looks damn good in a t-shirt. What am I saying? He would look delicious in a potato sack. But the lack of business attire makes me wonder if he's not working right now. Maybe he's on a staycation or whatever. Good for him, I guess.

When I get to the tables near him, he looks up and gives me a little smile, but that's all. He doesn't initiate conversation with me or ask anything of me. It's starting to freaking drive me crazy. Why does he keep coming here if he isn't going to say anything to me?

I glance over at the counter and see Carrie gesturing for me to talk to him. She's been less than subtle. Every time Ronan walks through the door, she finds a reason for me to be the one who serves him. I swear, she and Mel are in cahoots.

I wipe down the last table and then retreat back behind the counter. Carrie looks less than impressed.

"You know, it's slowing down. Why don't you just take off early?" she suggests.

I frown at her but do as she says. I grab my purse from the back and then go out to the front. I pause by the door, glaring at the back of Ronan's head.

This has to stop. I don't need him to keep coming in here and making my heart lurch with both joy and pain at the same time. I'm over everyone canoodling behind my back about how to get me to give him another shot.

I march right up to Ronan and cross my arms.

"So, is this just how it's going to be now? You just showing up at my work all the time? How is that working for you, buddy?"

He blankly takes in my annoyed face for a moment and then swallows, his Adam's apple bobbing.

Before he can say anything I ramble on. "Look, if you need me to, I'll write you a check right now, so your mom's lawyer doesn't have to seize the money when they find out the terms of your dad's trust were—"

"Dani," he interrupts, aghast at what I just said, "I'm not here because of the fucking contract."

I feel a reverberating pang of guilt. Of course, he's not. My face reddens.

"I'm here because I just...I want to know that you're okay."

My shoulders drop slightly. That's not what I was expecting him to say.

"And if you don't want me to come around anymore, I won't," he adds quietly. "But...if you want to catch up, I'd like that."

My irritation comes back at full force. Really? That's all he's here to do? I laugh humorlessly.

"Catch up? You want to catch up? Ha! Right. Let's catch up," I say sarcastically and sit down across from him. "You want to know what's been going on in Dani World? I'll tell you. My husband scared the shit out of me, and broke my trust, and won't stop calling me. I've been staying at a motel, and the bed is lumpy and kind of smells like feet. I got a part time job as a barista to try and get back on my feet, but it's totally kicking my ass, and my estranged husband keeps showing up during my shifts," I list off angrily.

Despite my rant, he takes in every word I say with deep interest.

"Dani," he says gently, consolingly. Damn it, I've missed hearing him say my name. "I'd say you should come home, but I can't because...I sold the house."

My anger dissipates and is immediately replaced by surprise.

"What? You sold your house?" I blurt out, utterly baffled.

He nods somberly and looks down at his coffee.

"And I quit my job."

I gasp, and he looks up at me again. "Why?"

"I don't want to do it anymore," he answers simply. "The apartment I moved into doesn't have a lap pool, so I've been swimming at the YMCA. They had a posting for a swim coach position at the high school, so I'm doing that now. I started last week."

I stare at him. I'm overcome with how freaking perfect of a job that is for him.

"Ronan," I murmur, taken aback by how much his life has changed while we've been apart. "I'm so glad to hear that."

He holds my gaze for a moment, and I see the apology forming on his lips. Feel it coming in the space between us like a gathering storm. I look away, not sure if I'm ready to hear it. He clears his throat.

"Lance and I are working things out," Ronan says, surprising me again. "He told me that you knew about it before I did."

"Yeah, I did." I wonder if Lance told him that Bodie was the one to spill the beans.

"It's been hard to accept, but I don't really have any other choice."

My guard slips a little more. I know how hard it was for him to find out Lance is his real father. I almost can't believe he's on speaking terms with Lance, much less trying to figure it out with him. I'm impressed. I'm happy for him. For both of them.

He nods and looks back at his coffee again.

It hurts me to see him so subdued. It's like he's back in his shell, but I can see through it now because I know him.

That thought hits me hard. *I know him.* No.

I *thought* I knew him. I *thought* he would never hurt me. I *thought* he was where I wanted to be. Now, I don't know any of those things for sure. I can't trust my gut anymore.

But I can't deny how it all dwindles in my mind when he's sitting in front of me. His angular face, so stoic when I met him, now full of pain and turmoil. I can almost feel it radiating off of him, and it makes me hurt for him. Despite what happened, I still hurt for what he's going through.

"I also got a restraining order against Bodie. I'm not giving him another chance to fuck with me. I'm done with him and my mom." His blue eyes stay on his coffee. "It's for the best."

I nod and struggle for something to say. My head is spinning with how much things have changed. He was a creature of habit who was addicted to work when I met him. He was a son who took every blatant insult his mother hurled at him without so much of a word back in retort. I almost don't recognize the man sitting in front of me. There's so much less anger in him than when I saw him last.

"I won't lie, Dani," he goes on softly "It's been pretty damn rough. Everything fell apart all at once. I feel like my life is a house that caught fire, and everything inside is burning. But...there's only one thing I would go back in to save." Ronan looks up at me finally, his vulnerability slicing through me. "You."

I look out the window, tears coming and heart pounding. I knew he was going to say it, but hearing just that one word, *you*... I'm dangerously close to losing grip on my guard. The fact that of everything he lost, I'm the one thing he cares about...well, I'd have to be made of stone to not be affected by it.

"I lost everything I knew...everything I had, but you're the only thing I want back. You're the only part of my old life that I miss. The only thing that means anything to me." His voice shakes slightly as he speaks, and I know that if I look at him, I'll see tears in his eyes, too. "I know I fucked up, Dani. And I'm so, so sorry."

I can't help it. I turn my face back to him and see his brown head bowed, tears rolling down his sorrowful face. When he looks up at me, I see the contrition in his wet eyes. It pierces me like a sword through my chest. And my untrustworthy gut whispers to me that he's telling the truth. That he's genuinely sorry for what he did to me.

"I shouldn't have pushed you," he continues quietly. "I broke us. With just that one action, I broke us." He sniffs. "And there's nothing I want more than to fix us."

I put my face in my hands for a moment, willing myself to choose protecting my heart over letting this man try again. Because ultimately, love isn't enough to make this right. If he busted out the L-word right now, it wouldn't change what he did. When I find the right words, I drop my hands and look up at him.

"You can't fix this, Ronan," I say brokenly. "What are you going to do? Promise you'll never do it again? It doesn't matter; you already did it. Are you going to just bank on the fact that getting a restraining order against Bodie will keep you from being violent ever again? That's bullshit. You can't blame your actions on him or anyone else."

Ronan's handsome face blanches at my words. It hurts to say them, but those are the only words I can anchor onto in order to keep my heart safe.

I watch as a panicked look crosses his features. "Then, what do I do?" His voice is so quiet, I almost don't hear it.

God, he's being so vulnerable and open with me. When has a man ever thrown himself at my mercy like this? I can't help but believe him and his apology.

But it doesn't change what happened, a scared voice whispers in my ear. I take a deep breath and try to keep my resolve.

"I won't deny that you've made positive changes in your life, Ronan. I'm proud of you for that; I really am. But your overwhelming tendency to solve conflict with violence is something I can't get past because that isn't something I can help you with. That's shrink level shit, and I'm not qualified for that."

Ronan thinks about what I said for a long, silent moment. I can almost hear his mind racing.

"Then...that's what I'll do," he says finally. "I'll see a counselor. I'll work through my issues. I'll be a better man for you. A man you can feel safe with."

Gah, my heart. It would be so easy to give in to him. It would be easy for me to let him better himself for me. But that wouldn't be right. That's the kind of shit that causes resentment later.

So, I give him a sympathetic smile and put my hand on his. I regret it instantly because it feels inexplicably good to feel my skin on his. When he glances down and notices my ringless finger, I can visibly see the pain ripple through him. I feel it ripple through me, too.

"I don't want you to do it for me," I say gently. "You need to do it for you."

He nods thoughtfully and looks back down at my hand resting on his.

"You're right," he murmurs.

"I know," I say with a small smile and a chuckle. He looks up at me and takes my small teasing as comfort.

"Will you go with me?" he asks tentatively. "I know I'll be able to open up better if you're there. And everything I say is going to be something I want you to know."

I bite my lip. I absolutely want to know everything he says in therapy, too. I want to know what makes this man tick. I want to know how to understand him and how to love him better.

Uh oh. Did I just—was that the L-word slipped in there? Damn it and a half. But I'm not ready to throw that out there. It would be unfair to say something like that to him without promising to go back to him. But I can support him, right? As a friend? Like in the beginning?

"I'll think about it," is what I ultimately decide to say.

"Thank you."

I slowly pull my hand away, hating it.

"Dani...I really am sorry," he adds genuinely.

I swallow hard.

"I know."

Chapter Thirty-One

Dani

Ronan walks me out. His car is parked a few spaces down from the entrance.

"Are you far? I can give you a ride," he offers. I look at him suspiciously.

"Ohhh, no. I'm on to you, buddy."

His blue eyes smile at me as we stop at his car.

"I'm going to keep walking, and you're not going to follow me," I stipulate lightly. "You're just going to get in your car and take your sweet cheeks home."

His eyebrows flicker with amusement, and I blush slightly. My heart pounds, and I take a step back, as if that will keep me from dwelling on how good it would feel to put everything behind us and move forward...so that I could say weird shit like that to him and he could smile back at me like I'm the cutest thing he's ever seen. I've missed that so much. I've missed how good we are together.

I clear my throat. "Well, see you around, I guess." Because I have no doubt that I'll see him back at the coffee shop in a couple days.

Ronan smiles at me softly. "See you around."

He gets in his car, and I walk away. When I turn the corner, I glance back and see that he's gone, and he isn't following me.

I take a deep breath as I tread on, feeling like I might burst with an avalanche of emotions.

I just talked to Ronan.

He apologized.

He wants me back.

These are the facts, which is what I tell myself and what I try to keep my mind on as I walk, but my stupid heart keeps interrupting. The mushy part of me that misses Ronan can't help but dwell on how I forgot just how deeply blue his eyes are, and how warm his hand was when I touched it, and how deep his voice is, and how much I wish he hadn't messed everything up. I miss being his girl.

By the time I get to Max and Mel's, I'm a mixture of sorrow and smitten. I walk into 2B, and Max looks up from his video game.

"Sup," he says in greeting and goes back to it without asking about the turmoil on my face. I don't even have to look to know he's not wearing shorts in that chair.

I plop down on the couch and mindlessly watch Max play his first-person shooter game. If I wasn't so distracted by talking to Ronan, I would be hypnotized by it. Part of me wishes I was still talking to him. I can't believe how much his life has changed, and yet he still can't move forward without me. Me. I'm the missing piece in his life, even in his *new* life, and if I'm honest with myself, he's the missing piece for me, too. Maybe he always has been; I just didn't know it until I met him.

I glance at the clock. Mel should be home from work in an hour, and then I can talk this through with her. Although, I already know what she's going to say.

Give him a chance, Dani.

You love him, Dani.

He apologized, Dani.

I sigh heavily and go downstairs to sit outside on the doorstep. I watch the cars go by for a while as I try to cling to my resolve. Even though I love Ronan, he still terrified me that night. Even with his apology, I will always be scared of him.

But then, I hear Lance's words come back to me.

You can't let fear dictate your life.

I close my eyes tightly. My heart beats wildly as I hear Lance's voice in my head. But then, I hear my mom saying the same words. And then my dad, too.

After the car accident and losing my parents, I knew that the best way to honor their memory was to live as fully as I could. I don't want to shrink back from my life like this. What a waste of a life it would be if I let fear control me.

I open my eyes again to see Mel coming up the sidewalk, looking worried.

"What happened?" she demands as she books it toward me. She sits down and puts her arm around me.

"I talked to Ronan today," I tell her with a sniff.

"Oh, shit," she says nervously. "How did it go?"

"How do you *think*, Mel? He wants to fix us."

"Annnnd...?" she urges, removing her arm and turning toward me a little more.

"And...I don't know," I answer softly. I sniff again and put my face in my hands.

"What's holding you back? Do you really think he would ever hurt you like that again?"

No, I think to myself, but the problem is that I don't know that for sure. I *can't* know that for sure. But maybe that's the whole point. It's trusting him again that I'm struggling with. And I hear Lance in my head again:

You can make the choice to trust Ronan.

But is it a smart choice? Is it really a choice at all if the consequence is losing Ronan forever? If the result will be my own broken heart?

My phone buzzes in my back pocket, and I grab it to find a text message from Ronan.

"Is it from him?"

I nod and open it.

Ronan: *Hey Dani, just wanted to let you know that I got a counseling session set up for next Tuesday. Let me know if you can make it.*

I read it aloud to Mel, and her jaw drops.

"Are you fucking with me? He's willing to go to counseling? You talked about *counseling* today?"

I nod, teary-eyed. I can't believe he already has something scheduled. He must have gone straight home and made the call. The man means business, as usual.

"Do you know how fucking hard it is to get guys to go to counseling? If you weren't sure whether he loved you, there's your proof, girl."

Damn it, she's right. Ronan is more than on board with doing whatever I need him to do in order for us to move forward together. He's doing everything he can to fix us, even if that means he needs to fix himself. Even if fixing himself is going to hurt like hell.

"Ronan's willing to do the work here, Dani, but...are *you*?"

I look over at her. "What do you mean?"

She takes a breath and lets it out slowly like she knows what she wants to say will be hard for me to hear. I brace myself.

"Dani, you know I love you. But Spencer has made you so afraid of love. I think maybe you're ready to throw in the towel with Ronan like this because of what Spencer did, not what Ronan did."

I stare at her, my heart beating hard.

"You need to work through that, just like Ronan has things to work through, too."

I look away, towards the street unseeingly. Oh, God, is that what I'm doing? Punishing Ronan for something Spencer did? Is disappearing after the charity dinner just an even bigger knee jerk reaction than the one I had in Chicago?

That isn't freaking fair to Ronan.

"I hate it when you're right," I mutter.

Mel chuckles and bumps my shoulder with hers. "That's what I'm here for."

I sigh heavily. "Lance told me I shouldn't let fear control my life," I add quietly and wipe my eyes. "He's right, too."

"Hell yes, he is."

We sit in silence for a few moments as I come to terms with what the truth really is. Ronan made a mistake, but I'm not perfect either. And I *don't* want to keep living my life afraid of love. I know that Ronan makes me happy, and that with some work on both our parts, maybe I can feel safe with him again.

"You gonna text him back?"

I look down at my phone and then slowly nod.

Mel squeals out her excitement.

"Yes! Okay, I'll go in and give you some privacy. You're doing the right thing, Dani." She gives me a squeeze around my shoulders and then disappears inside.

I stare at my phone for a moment, but I don't text him.

I go back in my mind and try to think about what I could've done better that fateful night. What do I wish I had done differently? Because Mel's right. Ronan isn't the only one who messed up.

The last six weeks, Ronan's entire life has been upended, and he's had to do it alone. I put him through six weeks of just hoping that I was okay and somewhere safe. That was cruel of me. That was unloving of me.

I take a deep breath, and instead of texting him, I call. It rings only twice, and then he picks up.

"Hello?" I hear the hope in his voice, and it makes my heart pound because I know he's been waiting all this time for me to finally call him back.

"Hey, it's me," I say unnecessarily. "I—I got your text, and Tuesday works for me. I'm assuming Mel—I mean, your anonymous source—told you that's my day off."

"My anonymous source may have told me that."

I crack a smile and then chuckle.

A beat of silence passes in which I want to say something but don't know exactly what. I sigh nervously and realize that what I actually want is to look him in the eyes.

I want to look my husband in the eyes and apologize because that's what he deserves. And I want to accept his apology, too.

"Are you busy? Do you want to meet up?"

There's dead silence on the other end, which I'm guessing is because he wasn't expecting me to say that.

"Hell," he says in surprise. "Yes. Absolutely. I'd love to."

"I'll text you the address. See you soon."

"Great. I'll be there."

I hang up and text him Mel's address. And then, I wait.

It takes Ronan twenty minutes to roll up and park on the street in front of Mel's apartment building. I'm still on the doorstep, feeling everything from nerves, to doubt, to anticipation.

Counting the streetlights distracted me enough to not dissolve into a pile of tears, but when I see him get out of his Rolls Royce and round the hood, my eyes are already prickling.

I shakily stand up when he reaches the sidewalk. He pauses at the end of it when he sees me, and I understand why. He needs me to close the gap. He needs to know that he isn't forcing himself back into my life. He's still letting me have control. He's respecting whatever my choice will be.

And what are you choosing, Dani?

I take a deep cleansing breath and let it out slowly.

Him. I choose him. In all his moody, professional, sometimes aggressive glory. He isn't perfect, and he's more than admitted that. Despite how he pushed me, I still want him. If that isn't love, I don't know what is. If I'm preparing myself to willingly forgive him for doing the unthinkable, I must love him. There's no other explanation. And I hope to God, this is the right thing. Just seeing his face again feels deeply *right*, but this time, I need to remind myself that just because Ronan is right for me, that doesn't mean he won't mess up. And just because I love him doesn't mean that I'll get it right either.

We're human. Imperfect. Trying and trying to just get it right. And I want to get it right *together*.

I swallow hard, my heart pumping in my ears, and then I move toward him. As I do, I feel something snap in me. It hurts, but it's a good hurt. I think it must be the last of my pride or the last of my stubbornness in keeping myself away from him.

Ronan moves toward me, too, but my feet eat up the sidewalk much quicker. He stops when I get near enough that he assumes I'll stop, too, but I don't. I keep going. I move right up to him and throw my arms around his wide shoulders.

The breath catches in his throat, and he tenses up, almost like he did when I hugged him in his office after I paid off my bills. But this time, he gathers me up in his strong arms and holds me to him closely.

The tears come quickly because I've missed my husband so freaking much. I realize that I haven't felt like myself without him, and that giving him a second chance is as much for me as it is for him. I clutch him tightly and deeply breathe in his familiar scent. I feel that same feeling I felt every single time we've been close. The feeling that this is where I need to be.

"Fuck," he whispers, one hand sifting sweetly through my long hair. "I'm so sorry for hurting you, baby."

His words are the last thing to break the dam. I pull away just enough to land my lips on his.

He pulls back in surprise and looks at me in the eyes, absolutely stunned.

"I'm sorry, too," I say softly, which intensifies his astonishment. "I should've let you know I was somewhere safe. You were worried sick about me, and I just disappeared. I'm sorry."

Ronan stares at me, taken back by my apology.

"I deserved it," he says finally.

"Maybe for a couple days, not for six weeks."

"I never want to be away from you for that long ever again," he whispers.

His eyes take in every inch of my teary face like he's never seen me clearly before and then gives me a passionate, longing look before he leans down and kisses me.

It's a messy, sloppy, desperate kiss. The kind of kiss that says something deeper than words can. The kind of kiss you remember for the rest of your life. The kind of kiss that makes me feel like I'm home again.

When we pull away, we're both breathless and dizzy. He rests his forehead against mine, and I feel a deep sense of peace ripple through me. The truth about us is clear to me then, that we're just two imperfect people trying to love each other despite the shit we've been through. And it isn't easy, but it's worth it. And I want to do it all with him.

I slowly pull back enough to look up into those blue eyes I love so much and give him a shy smile.

"So, you said you moved into an apartment. Any chance you need a roommate?"

His dark eyebrows raise in surprise, then lower thoughtfully.

"Not a roommate, no," he answers, then smiles slightly. "A wifey though? Hell yes, I do."

I smile and giggle at him. I release him as I step back.

"Well, then, I think we're going to need this."

I pull the chain from around my neck and remove my mother's wedding ring. I hold it out to him with a sweet smile. He keeps my gaze for a moment, and I see the tears filling his eyes. Ronan takes the ring from me and looks down at it lovingly. I hold out my left hand, so he can slip it back on my finger where it belongs, but instead, he gets down on one knee in front of me.

"Danielle Marie," he says with emotion clogging his voice, "will you be my wife?"

I beam down at him through tears of my own because I realize he never did officially propose. We got married as brand new friends, neither of us really expecting what would happen between us. Even though it hasn't been perfect, I can confidently say that I still want to be this man's wife. I want to make the choice to trust him.

"Yes." A grin splits his face, and my heart pounds. "For better or worse, richer or poorer, in sickness and in health, to love and to cherish till death do us part. I'm your wifey for lifey."

He laughs, like really laughs, which I've never heard him do before. Then, he puts the ring back on my finger and stands up. He kisses me, like we really just got married all over again, and then I pull back, feeling truly happy for the first time in weeks.

Ronan's arms stay around my waist as he gazes down at me with so much love in his expression that I feel wrapped up in it. Safe. Whole. New.

I grin up at him and stroke my hand over his scratchy cheek, over the dimple that appears when he smiles.

"I missed you," I murmur.

"I missed you, too," he whispers back, leaning his forehead against mine. "So fucking much."

"I promise I'll never leave like that again," I vow, my eyes closing.

"I promise I'll never give you a reason to." He dips his head to the side to meet his lips with mine.

I kiss him back slowly, believing him. And then, the words slip out before I can stop them.

"I love you," I whisper between drugging, emotional kisses.

Ronan's entire body goes taut as he pulls back, looking at me with an absolutely stunned expression on his face.

My insides shake as a silent moment passes, in which he digests my words. I'm about to open my mouth and say he doesn't have to say those words back, but then his face breaks into a dazzling grin.

"You...you love me?" he whispers, and I see how his blue eyes cloud with moisture.

"Yes."

He steps back, his hands releasing me so that he can put them over his face for a moment. The insecure part of me thinks I shouldn't have said that. But the sure part of me...the part of me that knows it's the truth, wants to laugh at him. I think I just broke his brain.

When his hands finally drop, he looks at me with wonder and disbelief, but also with pure joy. He moves close again, taking my face gently in his hands.

"I love you, too, Dani," he whispers, and the broken way he says it has me surer than ever that this is real. He loves me. I love him. And everything will be okay as long as we're together.

After another breathless kiss in which I lose myself completely, I bear hug his big body for a moment and then step back.

"So," I say, clearing my throat, "you want to go up? You'll probably see Max's twigs and berries, but I'll get to officially introduce you to my best friend."

"Uh, yeah, sure," he says with a smile. I have a feeling he would spend an entire awkward evening with Max and Mel if it meant he could be with me.

I tug on his hand, and we walk up the sidewalk to the apartment entry door. I see Mel standing in the second floor window, and she's jumping up and down like a lunatic. I just grin at her and bring my husband inside.

Epilogue

Ronan

I head out of the locker room with my gym bag, excited to head home and see my wife when she gets home. I send off a quick text to let her know I'm taking off, and that's all it takes to put a smile on my face.

Tomorrow is our first anniversary. They say that the first year is the hardest, and that turned out to be incredibly true for us. We did six months of counseling together and came out so much stronger because of it.

Not that it wasn't painful because it really fucking was. I sifted through years of inner turmoil and family bullshit that I never let myself properly deal with. I talked about the emptiness I felt in finding out that I wasn't really my father's son. I received tools to deal with my anger and ways to understand what I'm really feeling instead of just the overwhelming anger.

Dani spoke about what it was like to lose her parents so suddenly and, of course, being hurt by Spencer and by me. She explained how at odds she felt—how torn she was between not wanting to let fear control her life and protecting herself. It was fucking painful to hear her talk through all of that, knowing that I had contributed to her fear.

It wasn't easy to work through everything, but it was worth it. And frankly, it was needed. Dani was right—it took a shrink to solve my issues.

After our counseling concluded, I surprised her with a trip to Hawaii. She didn't know where we were until we stepped off the plane and got *leid*. She giggled and beamed up at me like the most adorable wifey I've ever seen.

It was on that trip, which we call our unofficial honeymoon, that I discovered what it's really like to be loved by Dani. Being with her is like nothing I've ever experienced. Dani doesn't fuck. She makes love. Every single time. She uses her body as so much more than just a tool to make me feel good. She presses into me like she can't get close enough to me and kisses me like she might never kiss me again, and I feel how deeply she loves me, loves us. She gives me everything she has, not just her body. All of her.

I'm one lucky man.

I hop into my car and drive home full of anticipation. I want to make tomorrow a special day. I have some plans, but it may be a little tricky to pull it all off before Dani gets home from work.

After working at the coffee shop for a couple months, I suggested that she find something else. She isn't meant to be doing something meaningless. She has too big of a heart for that. We talked about starting a foundation or a scholarship, but then I found out that the battered women's shelter needed volunteers and funding. Dani cried when I told her about it. She went down the next day and has been there ever since. Some days, she comes home feeling fulfilled and ecstatic, and other days, she comes home weary and heartbroken from what these women are going through. On those days, I do my best to spoil the shit out of her and hold her a little tighter when we go to bed.

As for me, the boy's swim team went to state and kicked some ass. I couldn't be more proud of my boys. There's a few that take it a little more seriously than the rest, and one in particular who I'm sure could make it to the Olympics if he wanted to. But they all put in the work. Dani shows up for every swim meet with snacks that she makes with Carla and obnoxious signs. She screams the loudest of all the fans, and it makes me so fucking happy.

I don't miss my old job. I thought maybe I would eventually. But coaching is something that brings me so much more joy than I expected. Pouring into these kids just makes me more excited to have children with Dani one day.

When I get home, I head into the house and tidy up a bit before Dani gets home. She always stays to serve dinner at the shelter, so we tend to eat later. We picked out this house together shortly before we finished counseling, and it's perfect for us. Four bedrooms, three baths, three levels, and a big fenced in yard on the outskirts of town. It's big enough for us to grow into, but it isn't so huge and lavish like my house was. I've fucking loved making this house a home with Dani. And I love hearing her singing to herself in this room or that. She's even gotten me to participate in a few impromptu dance parties.

My phone beeps, and I pause my sweeping to see a text from Lance.

Lance: *Let me know if you need me to set stuff up tomorrow. I have a couple hours open at the end of the day.*

I type back a quick thank you and finish sweeping.

We spent the holidays with Lance and his family. I was beyond nervous, but Dani stayed close to me as I met a handful of relatives that I never knew I had. I met my two uncles and their wives, as well as a couple cousins. I met my grandmother, who teased me over my good looks and cute wife. It was so odd to sit there in the presence of strangers and feel...*welcome.* I laughed and smiled and had a good time with these people who I had never met but who all had the same blood in their veins.

Lance and I get together for breakfast every week, and it's been good. In a way, I almost feel like I got my dad back, but just in a different body. We've worked through what we both want, and ultimately, we're on the same page. I don't feel right calling him Dad. But when Dani and I become parents one day, our kids will call him Grandpa, because that's who he is.

As for the rest of my family, who I disowned, my mother has left me completely alone. I think she's glad to be rid of me. Bodie was formally charged for the attempted rape of my wife. The security camera footage and Dani's testimony were enough to convict him. He'll be in prison for the next two years, though I wouldn't be surprised if he gets out on good behavior. Even so, Dani and I both have restraining orders against him.

It feels good to be free of them. It feels good to have a new family. It feels good to have a job that fulfills me. It feels good to be so fucking in love with my wife.

When Dani walks in the front door, I know right away that something is different. She usually greets me with a smile and a kiss, but today, she sprints into the kitchen and leaps up into my arms. I laugh as her legs wrap around my waist, and she kisses me.

"Wait a minute, isn't *tomorrow* our anniversary?" I tease her between kisses.

"I know," she says and hops down with eyes full of pure joy. "But I have something to tell you, and it's going to blow your freaking mind, Wellsley." She squeals and reaches into her purse. When she looks up at me again though, she has a thoughtful expression on her face. "Oh, unless you're a fainter. Maybe you should sit down."

She grabs my hand, drags me into the living room, and pushes me down on the couch.

"What the hell is going on?" I ask, but she holds up one finger.

"Close your eyes," she instructs.

"Fuck," I mutter and do as she says. She knows I don't like surprises, but that doesn't stop her from surprising me. For Christmas, she got me a pair of swim trunks with her face printed all over them. I laughed my ass off and then laughed some more when she brought out a matching bikini with my face on it.

"Hold out your hands."

I open my hands in front of me and feel something long and smooth placed onto my palm.

"Okay, open," says Dani and I can hear from her voice that she's about to burst with excitement.

I brace myself because I genuinely have no idea what all of this is about and open my eyes.

In my hand sits a pregnancy test.

I freeze and stare at it. "Holy shit," I whisper.

"Look at it, Ronan," she urges me, turning it around so it's right side up.

I swallow hard as I see two little pink lines. My heart hammers in my chest.

"Oh, my gosh, you're totally going to pass out," Dani says, laughing from faraway. "Keep breathing, buddy!"

I look up at her in shock and then back at the test. I smooth my thumb over the pink lines. They don't rub off.

"Holy shit," I say hoarsely.

Dani moves close and sits on my lap, straddling me. She takes my face in her little hands, and I look into her bright, happy eyes.

"You're going to be a daddy, Ronan," she murmurs and then kisses me.

It's my undoing. I feel myself getting choked up as it dawns on me. She's pregnant. We're having a baby.

"I love you so much," I whisper, pulling back to look at her. Dani wipes at my eyes.

"I love you, too."

I kiss her again and then look down at her stomach. I put my shaky hand there, and she covers it with her own.

"There's really a baby in there?"

Dani lifts my chin. "Yes. This is real. It's happening."

I close my eyes and feel the joy come. Fuck, I'm going to be a dad. For real this time.

"I made an appointment tomorrow morning for an ultrasound," she says, and I open my eyes to find her expression is tentative and sympathetic. "I want you to see our little jelly bean as soon as possible. I thought maybe it would help you...you know, believe it's real."

My brow furrows with emotion at how much she understands me. I sniff.

"Thank you."

She runs her fingers through my hair, and I hug her tightly.

Damn.

Just when I thought life with Dani couldn't get any better, it does.

That night, I can't sleep. All I can do is try to make it sink in. I turn over, and Dani stirs slightly. I move my fingers lightly through her hair, and her sleepy face relaxes a little more. When I'm sure she's deeply asleep again, I move my hand to her stomach and close my eyes.

Everything changed the minute Dani walked into my life. Some of it hurt like hell, but I don't regret a single minute of it. Without her, I would've never gotten to this place. I would've never become a better man, and I never would've dreamed I could be a father. But here I am...deeply in love with my best friend, and so fucking happy for what the future is bringing us.

For better or for worse.

Acknowledgments

This is my first published work. It has taken me decades to finally believe I could possibly have what it takes to become more than a daydreaming, private writer. I didn't think I would ever have the courage to let someone read anything I wrote. So I have to give a huge shout out to Lyndsey Eckhardt, who was the first person to read this book in its entirety. To say I was terrified is an understatement. But then, I sent it to Emily Ciochetto. And then to Marti Galbraith. And then Darla Anderson. It's because of you beautiful ladies, my amazing beta readers, that I gained confidence and managed to make this story the best it could be. Your feedback was invaluable to me. Thank you for letting me pick your brain, for answering my questions, and for giving me your honest thoughts. Without each of you, I never would've dared to follow this lifelong dream.

But this lifelong dream could not exist without you, dear reader. It is such a deep honor for this book to be in your hands. From the bottom of my heart, thank you for deciding to give it a try. I hope you laughed and felt for the characters, because they haven't left me alone for the last four years.

And of course, I couldn't have finally gone for it without the support and encouragement of my husband, Jon. The first thing you said to me when I told you I had written the ending was "alright, now you get it published." You hadn't read it or even really known what it was about, but your first thought was that *of course* it was good enough to publish. Your blind faith in me is my favorite example of how much you love me. Thank you for encouraging me and for all the times you kept our kiddos distracted enough that I could write uninterrupted. I love you, buddy.

About The Author

Katie Stearns is a contemporary romance author from southwestern MN. She lives in a 125 year old farmhouse with her husband, two amazing little girls, and their German Shorthair Pointer, Porkchop. In what little spare time she has, she enjoys baking, photography, reading and rereading romance novels by her favorite authors, traveling with her husband, and watching *The Office*. She's always daydreaming about the next story.